Date: 1/7/15

LP MYS MAXWELL
Maxwell, Alyssa,
Murder at Marble House : a Gilded
Newport mystery /

MURDER
AT
MARBLE HOUSE

Center Point
Large Print

Also by Alyssa Maxwell and available from Center Point Large Print:

A Gilded Newport Mystery
Murder at the Breakers

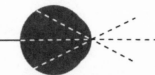

**This Large Print Book carries the
Seal of Approval of N.A.V.H.**

MURDER
AT
MARBLE HOUSE

A Gilded Newport Mystery

ALYSSA MAXWELL

CENTER POINT LARGE PRINT
THORNDIKE, MAINE

This Center Point Large Print edition
is published in the year 2015 by arrangement with
Kensington Publishing Corp.

The text of this Large Print edition is unabridged.
In other aspects, this book may vary
from the original edition.
Printed in the United States of America
on permanent paper.
Set in 16-point Times New Roman type.

ISBN: 978-1-62899-421-6

Library of Congress Cataloging-in-Publication Data

Maxwell, Alyssa.
  Murder at Marble House : a gilded Newport mystery / Alyssa Maxwell.
— Center Point Large Print edition.
  pages ; cm
  Summary: "With the dawn of the twentieth century on the horizon, the
fortunes of the venerable Vanderbilt family still shine brightly in the
glittering high society of Newport, Rhode Island. But when a potential
scandal strikes, the Vanderbilts turn to cousin and society page reporter
Emma Cross to solve a murder and a disappearance"—Provided by
publisher.
  ISBN 978-1-62899-421-6 (library binding : alk. paper)
  1. Balsan, Consuelo Vanderbilt—Fiction.
    2. Vanderbilt family—Fiction. 3. Newport (R.I.)—Fiction.
    4. Murder—Investigation—Fiction. 5. Large type books. I. Title.
PS3613.A8983M866 2015
813´.6—dc23

                                                              2014037685

In loving memory of
Mary O'Neill, my husband's grandmother,
who inspired the character of Emma's "Nanny,"
and Sara Allen, the real-life Aunt Sadie,
who wore pants when few women did

MURDER
AT
MARBLE HOUSE

CHAPTER 1

August 1895

The tide splashed against the boulders at the tip of my property, the spray pattering my face to mingle with the single tear I could not prevent from rolling down my cheek. I stared out over the ocean in an attempt to channel all that great strength and make it my own. The waves, however forceful, didn't quite drown out the footsteps receding through the grass behind me, and I wrapped my arms tightly around my middle to keep from calling out, from turning and running and speaking the truth that crashed like a thunderous sea inside me.

I stood immobile, buffeted by the briny winds while Derrick Anderson—no, I now knew he was Derrick *Andrews*—strode away. He had lied to me about his identity for days on end, and the sting of his deceit had left me feeling like a naïve fool. But that wasn't the only reason I'd sent him away, or why, however much I yearned to recall my cold words, I could not. Not if I wished to remain true to myself, to continue to be the woman I had struggled, and would continue to struggle, to be.

Finally, when I deemed him far enough away

that I would be safe from temptation, I turned and glimpsed his retreating back—his dark hair and tall figure and the sturdy shoulders I'd come to depend on so much in the previous days. Shoulders with the power to make me lose all sense of myself, and that even at this distance proved an enticement I very nearly could not resist.

And wasn't that but one more reason to deny his suit? How long had we known each other? Days? A couple of weeks? In that time, we'd lived through more than most people experienced in a lifetime. Our emotions, sensibilities, indeed our very lives had been thrust into turmoil as fierce as any ocean storm. We had survived. We had triumphed. Is it any wonder, then, that we might have become caught up in an attachment to each other? But one that might not last once the final currents of upheaval had settled.

Despite the blustery winds, the sun shone sharp and bright that morning, the glitter on the water dazzling, while glaringly white clouds scuttled gaily across a brisk blue sky. How dare a morning be so happy. Tears fell like frigid rain on my cheeks as Derrick disappeared around the corner of my rambling, shingle-style house.

I stood for an indeterminate length of time, staring at that space beside the hawthorn hedges where he had disappeared. I wondered which would finally win out—regret or resolve. I allowed myself that much self-indulgence before straightening my spine, dropping my arms to my sides, and giving myself a hard shake. Did I love Derrick Andrews? If this sinking, ill sensation inside me could be interpreted as love, then perhaps. Or then again perhaps what I felt had more to do with being thrown together into a maelstrom of events over which we had little control, other than to form an alliance and pool our resources.

Either way, I'd made my choice. I would not be the wife of a wealthy, influential man and have my life mapped out in a series of festivities that would accomplish nothing of substance in this world. Yes, Vanderbilt blood ran through my veins, but I wanted no part of the gilded prison in which my aunt Alice and all the other society matrons resided.

I glanced back out at the tossing ocean and realized the brine of Newport, of rocky, resolute Aquidneck Island, also ran through my veins to mingle with the blood of the Commodore, that first stubborn Vanderbilt who had set out to build an empire. So yes, I was a Vanderbilt, but I was also a Newporter born and raised—salty, sturdy, and fiercely independent.

Thus assured, I picked my way over my shaggy lawn—I really needed to purchase a new goat since poor Gerty had died last spring—toward Gull Manor, the house my equally independent aunt Sadie had left to me in her will. She would be proud of me today. She would approve.

Yes. There. I wished Derrick Andrews well, always, but I'd made the right decision. For me, and in all likelihood for him as well.

The jangling of the telephone startled me as I neared the open windows. Knowing there were others at home, I didn't run to answer the device, installed months earlier at my uncle Cornelius's generous insistence. I sighed. As independent as I liked to be, sometimes it was easier to accept my relatives' largess rather than argue a case I'd likely lose in the end anyway. If my illustrious extended family was happy to provide little luxuries I couldn't afford, who was I to deprive them of that satisfaction?

As I said, I didn't run to answer the ringing summons. It had been reverberating all morning, not for me but for my half brother, who was temporarily staying with me. Friends and acquaintances—some of them barely known to us—had been calling almost nonstop to congratulate Brady on being released from jail the day before. He'd been accused of murdering Uncle Cornelius's financial secretary on the night of our cousin Gertrude's coming-out ball at The Breakers, but Derrick and I had discovered the true culprit even as the police had been preparing to ship Brady off to Providence for trial. That is what had brought Derrick and me together. But that, friends, is not a story I care to revisit.

I was surprised, therefore, when Brady held the ear trumpet out to me the moment I entered the house. He raised a hand to cover the ebony mouthpiece protruding from the oaken call box.

"There you are, Em. Thought you'd run off to elope with Derrick." He waggled his pale eyebrows at me. Less than twenty-four hours out of his prison cell and the color had already returned to his cheeks, the mischievous sparkle to his eye. His sandy blond hair fell in rakish disarray across his brow, and he wore neither suit coat nor collar, his shirtsleeves rolled up to his elbows. Somehow Brady managed to wear his dishabille with a relaxed, thoughtless style that men often envied and women found delightful. It seemed no matter what happened to Brady—the good, the bad, and the drunkenly disastrous—he somehow emerged unscathed and unjaded; unchanged from the boy I'd grown up adoring.

But on this particular day, I was in no mood for his teasing. "I don't wish to talk to anyone," I answered wearily. "Whoever it is, tell them I'll return their call later." I dragged myself toward the parlor, where Nanny O'Neal, my housekeeper and surrogate grandmother, would embrace me briefly in her pudgy arms and pour me a cup of tea.

He extended the earpiece as far as the wire would allow. "It's Cousin Consuelo. And she sounds a bit frantic."

I frowned but didn't question him. Instead, I moved to switch places with him in the alcove beneath the stairs, waited for Brady to make his way back into the parlor, and spoke into the mouthpiece. "Consuelo? It's lovely to hear from you, dearest. We missed you at Gertrude's ball—"

"Emmaline. I don't have much time. I need you. Can you come over right away?"

"What is it? Is something wrong?" I cringed at my stupid question. Consuelo's parents, William and Alva Vanderbilt, were recently divorced—quite the scandal of the moment. They'd been bickering for years, and there were rumors of lovers on both their parts. The two younger sons had been at boarding school and were now with relatives on Long Island, so they missed the worst of it. But poor Consuelo had been caught in the middle like a doll fought over by two recalcitrant children, each tugging on an arm until the seams threatened to split.

"No time to explain," she said in a breathless rush. "You're my only hope, Emma. Please, can you come? Now?"

"I . . ." Frankly, after some very close scrapes in the past several days and now this morning's emotional trial, I very badly needed one of Nanny's strong cups of tea. But Consuelo's sense of urgency all but made the ear trumpet tremble against my palm. Besides, she had deepened her appeal by calling me Emma. My Vanderbilt relatives almost always insisted on Emmaline, as if that could somehow raise me up to the status of the rest of them. Only Consuelo, and my young cousin Reggie, seemed able to take me as I was.

I glanced with longing through the parlor doorway, where I could just see the rather thread-bare edges of Nanny's velveteen house slippers propped on a footstool. Brady's and her quiet voices called to me like a soothing aria. With a sigh I spoke into the mouthpiece again. "Yes, all right. I just need time to hitch Barney to the buggy. . . ."

Consuelo gasped. "I have to go!"

The line went dead.

Some twenty minutes later Barney and I rumbled up Bellevue Avenue. Our pace didn't exactly match the urgency of my cousin's summons, but I didn't dare push my aging hack any faster than a sedate walk. And even if I had pushed, it's doubtful he'd have deigned to oblige.

Gravel sputtered beneath the carriage wheels as we turned through a pair of broad marble columns onto a raised circular drive bordered with stone railings that framed the manicured front lawn in gleaming ivory arcs. Marble House, with its Corinthian-columned entry flanked by two massively solid wings, represented, both to me and the world at large, the fierce competition between the William K. Vanderbilts and the

Cornelius Vanderbilts, who lived nearby at The Breakers. Or, perhaps more accurately, the two houses embodied the intense rivalry between my aunts Alva and Alice, who each vied to stand supreme as the queen of all society.

From some unseen door off to one side, a liveried footman ran out to help me down and relieve me of my rig. He blushed to the roots of his slicked-back hair as I bid him good morning, thanked him, and asked after his grandmother, who was a longtime friend of Nanny's. I always made a point of greeting servants as though they were human beings. Some appreciated the gesture; others, like this young man, were left flustered by my familiarity.

Morning sunlight glittered on the house's pristine façade. I paused before approaching the front entrance, blinking in the glare and remembering how, after nearly four years of construction behind high, concealing walls, it had been the unveiling of Marble House that had spurred Aunt Alice to have The Breakers rebuilt on such a dizzying scale. Alice Vanderbilt simply could not live in a house smaller and humbler than Alva's. If Aunt Alice's one-upmanship had infuriated her sister-in-law, however, Alva never once allowed Alice the satisfaction of seeing her haughty smile slip, not even a notch.

I wondered what role Alva had played in Consuelo's frantic call this morning. I'd heard rumors—we all had that summer—but I would save judgment until I had the facts from my cousin.

"A good morning to you, Miss Cross," a youthful voice hailed from the corner of the eastern wing. A young man wearing a tweed cap tugged low over a riot of golden red curls sauntered closer, gazing up at me from the lawn beyond the raised driveway. Swinging a rake in one hand, he nodded in that deferential way servants had, yet in his case the gesture brought a genuine sparkle to those bright blue eyes of his.

"Good morning, Jamie. How are things going? Are you liking it here at Marble House?" This I inquired in an undertone, for if Aunt Alva caught us conversing I'd receive an admonishing tsk, while her newest gardener could very well find himself sacked. It was one thing to trade a quick pleasantry with a footman, but a gardener? Had I been an expected guest, he would not have been permitted anywhere near the front drive until everyone had arrived and been brought safely into the house, lest the sight of a workman offend their sensibilities. In houses such as Marble House, servants learned to perform their duties at both the whim and convenience of their employers.

"Why, 'tis going splendid, and I've got you to thank for that, miss." His earnest reply, with its lovely Irish cadence, acknowledged my role in securing his present employment. Jamie was a friend of my Irish housemaid, Katie, and I'd intervened at her hearty request.

I waved his thanks away. "I'm glad it worked out for you."

With that I proceeded between two massive, Corinthian-topped marble columns, which always made me feel impossibly small. The double front doors presented an equally intimidating prospect with their grillwork of elaborately wrought bronze. Lifting the knocker that was several sizes larger and a good deal heavier than my hand, I let it fall once, cringing at the echoes resounding on the other side of that forbidding door.

As if I'd been expected, indeed looked for, one of those doors opened immediately. Instead of the porter, however, Grafton, Marble House's head butler, greeted me with a frown. "Miss Cross, good morning. Are you come to see Mrs. Vanderbilt?"

Did I imagine wariness in those sharply aquiline features? "Good morning, Grafton, and no, I'm here to see Miss Consuelo."

"I'm afraid she is not at home, miss. Would you care to leave your card?"

"My card?" I narrowed my eyes at the man, at his intimidating six-foot frame, his thick but silvered hair, the arced nose with its resolutely flaring nostrils. He eased backward from the doorway as if about to shut me out. What was going on here? "I don't typically carry cards when I visit my relatives, Grafton, especially when I'm arriving at the request of my cousin, who called me not a half hour ago."

"Perhaps she called you from the country club, miss."

"She most certainly did not. Miss Consuelo was quite clear when I spoke to her. Now, may I please come in, Mr. Grafton?"

His peppered eyebrows went up in an unspoken admonishment: Was I calling him a liar? Good heavens, I might be able to make a footman blush with no more than a gentle good morning, but it seemed Grafton would not be budged by my persistence.

Well, I wasn't about to turn tail and run either. "Is my aunt at home, then?"

The lines above his nose deepened. "She is . . . however, she is not quite at liberty at the moment—"

Clattering footsteps echoed in the entry hall. "Grafton, who is at the door?"

I recognized the voice. Not giving the servant the chance to block me from view, claim I was a vagrant, and shut the door in my face, I quickly ducked my head around his shoulder. "It's me, Aunt Alva."

"Emmaline! Oh, Grafton, don't be a goose and let my darling niece inside."

Like Cornelius and Alice Vanderbilt, William and Alva were not my aunt and uncle, but rather cousins several times removed. But with a generation separating me from them, I fell naturally into the role of niece. In all honesty, I'd never been Alva's "darling" anything until recently, when she'd realized how much of a favorite I was of Aunt Alice's. From then on Alva became determined to flood me with affection and bestow little favors on me, especially if word of it might reach Alice's ears.

Still, I smiled and greeted her warmly, letting her enfold me in her sturdy arms and returning her kiss.

"I'm so glad you're here, Emmaline," she sang out gaily, her voice bouncing on the cold Sienna marble of the floor and walls. I'd been told the house had been fashioned after the great palace of Versailles, on a smaller but no less grand scale. "I have special company this weekend," she said, "and I'd love for them to meet you."

She would? She'd never been that eager to introduce me to her society cronies before. "That would be lovely, Aunt Alva. Is, er . . ." I assumed my most innocent, nonchalant expression. "Is Consuelo here, too?"

"Well, of course she is. Where else would Consuelo be? Surely not with her father out on that ostentatious yacht of his."

Funny, Alva hadn't considered the yacht

ostentatious when she'd taken Consuelo on an exhausting European tour all last summer and autumn. Her sudden scowl drew me from the memory, and my stomach clenched in anticipation of one of her quick, wildfire tirades outlining the many sins of her newly ex-husband. She surprised me, however, when her smile returned and her voice dipped lower on a conspiratorial note. "Did Grafton tell you she wasn't at home?"

I cast a glance over my shoulder to discover the man had shuffled quietly away, probably through the grand dining hall and to the servants' domains. "He did. Why would he lie?"

"Consuelo . . . hasn't been feeling at all well lately."

A surge of alarm went through me. "She's been ill?"

"Oh, not ill exactly. . . . Come with me." She grasped my wrist and whisked me through a doorway into the Gold Room, a sumptuously gilded, Louis XIV–style ballroom whose ornate décor rivaled that of The Breakers' Great Hall. The Gold Room was situated at the front of the house. Her guests couldn't glimpse us through the windows here, which essentially belied her reason for overstepping Grafton and admitting me to the house. Here, amid rich carvings and chiseled marble, French silks, Italian brocades, and vibrant porcelain from ancient

Chinese dynasties—riches enough to feed several orphanages for several years—she told me of a plan that raised bile to my throat and urged me to rush to Consuelo's side.

"He should be here in about a week, Emmaline, so you see the urgency."

I nodded absently, not truly hearing her question as my mind spun with a dozen contrary thoughts. The "he" she spoke of was Charles Richard John Spencer-Churchill, recently dubbed ninth Duke of Marlborough—or Sunny, as his friends apparently called him. Even now his transatlantic steamer headed toward New York, where he would turn north for Newport and officially become engaged to the eighteen-year-old Consuelo.

Aunt Alva hadn't counted on one small problem: Consuelo was having none of it.

"If anyone can convince her, Emmaline," Alva said, "it's you."

I stepped back as though she'd struck me. "Me? I'm sorry, Aunt Alva, but you cannot imagine I'd approve of a forced marriage. Or that I'd ever step into the middle of a family matter. You know me better than that."

She took an ominous stride closer, forcing me back another step, and then another. Alva followed my backward course until my calves struck a thronelike side chair. She loomed mere inches away. Her features hardened; her eyes turned icy. A lethal finger rose to point squarely at my heart. "Make no mistake, Emmaline. Consuelo *will* marry the Duke of Marlborough. There *is* no other choice in the matter. The only question that remains is will she do so willingly, or will I have to drag her by her hair to the church?"

The breath froze in my lungs and chills traveled my spine. Yet this was nothing new. Alva wasn't acting out of character with her threats or her sudden vehemence, or with her desire to live vicariously through her daughter. Alva had *always* intended for Consuelo to marry into minor European nobility, landed gentry at the very least; hence last year's European cruise. But a duke! I could already hear her, announcing to all of society: *Oh, yes, my daughter the duchess . . .* What a triumph: every society mother's fondest ambition. Here was a prize this bull terrier of a woman had sunk her teeth into and would never, ever, *ever* let go of.

With Alva standing so close, all but threatening to sink her teeth into me as well, I became very afraid, not for myself, but for Consuelo. Because I knew that no matter what I or anyone else did, in the end her mother would prevail. She always had; she always would.

With or without a handful of her daughter's hair.

In a perverse way, then, Alva was right. The

best thing I could do for my cousin was comfort her and help her face her impending marriage bravely. But to do it I would have to disavow everything I believed in, such as a woman's right to choose her own fate, as I had chosen to do only that morning. To help Consuelo, I'd have to lie to her and do so with a smile.

How I dreaded the role I must play.

"Is she upstairs?" I asked in quiet resignation.

With a victorious spark in her eye, Alva nodded. Her smile returned, but her chin lifted and her nostrils flared in a way no doubt intended to remind me of my place—my lowly place—in the family. "She respects you, Emmaline. Even has a silly notion that you're better off than any of the rest of us Vanderbilt women. That's why if you, of all people, tell her this marriage is in her best interests, she'll believe you."

As she spoke those last words she took in my carriage dress, the dark blue one formerly belonging to my aunt Sadie, but which Nanny had freshened with new velvet trim and shiny jet buttons. Her assessing gaze didn't stop until it reached my hemline, where Nanny had done a splendid job of concealing the slight fraying of the fabric where it skimmed the floor.

"Remember, Emmaline, as a duchess, Consuelo will never want for anything. And if it is a bit of independence she's after, between her new title and her inheritance, no doors will be closed

24

to her. Good grief, think of the good she'll be able to do, if that is what she wants. She'll have the means to fund charities, form scholarships—whatever strikes her fancy, so long as the cause is a suitable one and her husband is agreeable."

Yes, independence. Aunt Alva's definition of the word dripped its bitter irony on my already sagging spirits.

She reached out and gave my shoulder a little nudge. "Go on. She'll be delighted to see you." Her eyes narrowed. "Don't think I'm not aware that she called you earlier. The little sneak. Why, I should have—Oh, but we'll work it to our advantage, won't we?"

"*Our* advantage?"

She nudged me again. "Just talk to her. She adores you. And make her come downstairs. Tell her I have a surprise for her."

"What is it?"

Alva rolled her eyes. "A surprise. Now go."

I turned and began walking, wondering how much Consuelo would adore me—or respect me—once she discerned my part in this debacle. Somehow the task ahead seemed even more difficult than tracking down a murderer, nearly being murdered myself, and clearing my brother of false charges. Gripping the cold, wrought-iron banister until my knuckles whitened, I started up the staircase.

Alva's parting words drifted from the doorway of the Gold Room. "I'm counting on you, Emmaline. Do not let me down."

The *or else* hovered in the air between us.

CHAPTER 2

Upstairs, I was met by one of the maids coming down the hallway. She held an oval silver tray, and cutlery and china clinked with each step she took, while the domed covers sat half off their platters. The aromas of hotcakes and eggs tickled my nose. Upon spotting me, the young woman, a slender, curly-haired blonde about my own age, jerked toward a doorway as if to duck into it and become as invisible as possible, tray and all. It was one of Aunt Alva's rules that maids should never be seen, or, if they must, to make themselves as much a part of the background as possible.

But then Clara Parker recognized me. Although we had grown up in different parts of Newport, we had attended the same church growing up, and still did. She kept on toward me and offered a deferential smile, the kind that reminded me that, while she might not feel the need to hide, my Vanderbilt background sometimes made it difficult to meet my own neighbors on an equal footing. Such deference never failed to make me slightly uncomfortable, but I did my best not to show it.

"Good morning, Miss Cross," she said, curtsying despite the burden she carried. "Nice to see you again."

"Good morning, Clara. Was that Miss Consuelo's room you just came from?"

Clara frowned down at the tray, then once more lifted her elfin face to me. "It was, miss. She's hardly eaten a thing today. Poor dear."

"She's terribly upset, then?"

"She's . . . well . . ." Clara's large-eyed gaze held a trace of wariness as it skittered toward the staircase. She continued in a whisper. "Maybe you can cheer her up, miss."

I nodded and allowed Clara to resume her duties. I moved on to Consuelo's door, where my knock was answered with a tremulous "Come in," and a sniffle I could hear through the paneled wood.

The room was a masterpiece of rose-colored silks and velvets framed in gold leaf, every piece of furniture and every priceless knickknack arranged just so. French provincial shelves held dolls from around the world, and Alva claimed the daintily carved chaise lounge in the corner had once graced a room in Versailles. A canopied bed draped in rich satin and ivory lace dominated the space, and I found my cousin lying carelessly across its rumpled surface, her chin propped on an elbow while with the other hand she grasped a gold-plated pen. An open book lay on the counterpane in front of her, and a gray Angora cat was curled against the curve of her waist, its chin resting on the bit of moiré silk sash that trailed from the back of Consuelo's gown. The animal's contented purrs traveled across the room. My cousin stole a teary-eyed glance at me and dropped her pen. She scrambled to her feet, swept across the room, and propelled herself into my arms.

"Emma, Emma, thank God you're here!"

Simultaneously, the cat raised an indignant yowl, jumped down from the bed, and disappeared beneath the tiered lace spread. From over Consuelo's muslin-clad shoulder I could see the bottle-brush tail swish once and thump against the Persian rug before vanishing along with the rest of its owner under the bed.

"She's holding me prisoner, Emma. A virtual prisoner. She's even sent my darling governess, my Miss Harper, back to the New York house. Mama means to deprive me of everything comfortable and cheerful. All because I refuse to marry that dry toast of a man. He's horrid, just horrid, all stiff and proper and superior, but there are things going through his mind, Emma, especially when he looks at me. Like he's tallying up his future stock earnings or pricing out a new racehorse. I hate him. And I don't care if I have to scrub floors for the rest of my life—"

"Shh," I said somewhat forcefully, before she made any further assertions we both knew she didn't mean. I held her close and patted her back.

"No one is scrubbing floors, Consuelo. It's not as bad as all that."

"Isn't it?" She pulled slightly away to look at me. Tears magnified her dark eyes, and I could see now by the puffiness around them this wasn't the first time she'd cried today. Angry red blotches mottled her cheeks, and the tip of her nose glowed pink. Her mouth was nearly colorless in comparison, except for a raw patch where her teeth had obviously been worrying her bottom lip. She gave another sniffle and shoved a dark, bedraggled curl away from her face.

"Of course not," I tried to assure her, and drew her back into my embrace. It tugged my heartstrings to see her reduced to such a state; Consuelo, the young beauty of the Vanderbilt family. Yet to me, she remained my little cousin, three years younger than I, an introspective girl who feared the dark, hated to be sent up to bed before the rest of us, and who always hugged me longer than any of my other cousins each summer when we were reunited.

I had once believed it was simply in her nature to be affectionate. Only as I grew older did I realize that from the earliest age, Consuelo had felt deprived of the affection most of us took for granted in our lives.

No, not *felt* deprived. *Was* deprived.

"Did you see *her* when you arrived?" she asked me, her voice harsh with bitterness.

"Your mother? Yes."

"Did you meet her guests? Did she parade you before them like you were the latest altruistic project to her credit?"

"Uh, no, not yet."

"She will."

"Yes, I know. But I'm not concerned with that right now. I'm concerned about you, dearest. Tell me what has been happening, but calmly, so I can understand you."

I took her hand and led her back to the bed. As we settled ourselves, she gathered up the pen and the book she'd been writing in and set them on the bedside table. Before she'd closed the scarlet velvet cover, however, I'd glimpsed the watery ink splotches staining the page in several places.

She turned back to me, her eyes narrowing. Even in her distress, she held her back perfectly straight, and I remembered about the rod she was once forced to wear as a child during her lessons—a length of steel that ran along her spine, held in place by a strap at her waist and another around her forehead. I'd been horrified to learn of it years ago; now I was struck by the symbolism of it, of the complete control her mother wielded over Consuelo's very existence.

"They're all plotting, you know," she said, breaking into my thoughts. "To get the vote."

The abruptness of the statement confused me, and I blinked. "To what? Who's plotting?"

"Mother and her houseguests. They want women to have the vote and they plan to start petitioning Congress. How can they, Emma? How can they do that while I am up here . . . trapped up here—" Her head went down and a tear splashed the flowered pattern of her skirt.

Still baffled, I shook my head, though she couldn't see it, and reached out to stroke her hair. "Consuelo, I'm sorry, but I don't follow. What has that to do with your engagement?"

Her head swung up, her moist eyes blazing with anger. "Don't you understand? Mother is down there with her cronies planning ways to gain independence and political power for women, while at the same time she's holding me prisoner and planning my life for me. Taking away all my choices. Telling me I'd better hold my tongue and do as she says . . ."

Or else. She didn't say it. She didn't have to. The same phrase still rang in my mind from downstairs, though Alva hadn't come out and said it then either.

"She treats me as though I'm one of those dolls." She jerked her chin at the shelves of bisque faces staring lifelessly back at us. "Those wretched, insensible, staring dolls. They're horrible and I hate them. Mother's horrible and I hate *her.*"

Part of me wished to agree, at least about the injustice of the situation. Instead, I seized her hands in my own. "You don't mean that, Consuelo. I know you don't. Your mother . . ." I drew a breath and tried not to loathe myself. "Your mother wants the best for you. The very best. She may be a bit . . ." I bit back the words *vainglorious* and *misguided,* and replaced them with something more diplomatic. ". . . A bit overbearing at times, I'll agree, but I believe her heart is in the right place."

Good Lord. So much for not loathing myself. So much for Consuelo respecting and adoring me.

She snatched her hands out of mine. "You're with her on this," she said flatly. Bitterly.

"No. Yes. No." I shook my head and swallowed the growing lump in my throat. "Consuelo—"

Before I could get out another word, she said, "How can you be? You, who have all the independence in the world. Who may decide each and every day what to do and where to go. Whom you'll see. Whom you'll someday marry." This last came out as a choked whisper that nearly wrenched my heart in two.

"You're wrong," I said, not altogether dishonestly. Hadn't what occurred that morning between Derrick and me proved my options were limited, that I couldn't simply do as I pleased whenever I pleased; that so-called independence came with a price, with often painful sacrifices?

"My life might look appealing to you, but not a day goes by that I don't sit down with our household account book and decide whether we'll eat meat for the next week, or eggs and toast in order to pay our bills. When something in my house needs repairing, that's another several items crossed off our grocery list. Barney should have been put to pasture a year or two ago, but I can't afford a new horse. And I need a goat because I can't afford a gardener."

She had set her head on my shoulder as I spoke and now I heard a watery chuckle against my neck.

"And when was the last time you saw me in a frock as new and fashionable as this one?" I stroked the folds of her dress where they spilled across my own.

She fingered the edge of her coral silk sash. "You don't care about new dresses, Emma. You never did."

"You're right," I said with such fervor she flinched and sat up straight. "It's not dresses I care about, it's helping people. People like Katie, my housemaid, and Jamie, your new gardener. I made a difference in both their lives, I truly did. Just consider, Consuelo, how many people I could help if I had the resources . . . and the connections. Just think . . ."

I trailed off to let that much sink in. Her brows converged, not in anger or sorrow this time, but in contemplation. I could all but see her mind working it over. Her bottom lip eased between her teeth. I leaned closer to her. "Just think how many people you'll be able to help once you take your place in society. Not your mother's place, Consuelo. But when you're no longer under her thumb and you can step out as your own person. A woman of influence in your own right."

"I . . . I hadn't thought of it that way. . . ."

"Well, no. You've been too upset."

"I've been selfish, worrying only about myself." The ridges between her brows deepened. She wasn't quite there yet, not completely convinced. Doubt continued to niggle at her, yet when I should have moved in for "the kill," when I should have gathered every persuasive ploy at my disposal to seal the bargain, guilt reared up to stop me cold. Guilt . . . and my own doubts.

If I truly believed my own words, then why hadn't I accepted Derrick's proposal of marriage this morning? He was a good man. And what about all the people I could help with the Andrewses' fortune at my disposal?

But I'd seen all too well what fortune does to people, how it changes them. Especially women. Yes, society matrons like Aunt Alva and Aunt Alice could support any number of causes—as long as those causes were approved by society, and by their husbands. Take on a "wrong" cause and society would close ranks in opposition. Be seen as too forward or assertive or unconventional, and a woman would find herself ostracized by friends and family, her connections severed, her influence to do good works stripped away. It was a harsh reality . . . and all too often it produced hardened women, forced to subdue their own true natures behind a gilded façade of gentility that very often bore no resemblance to the person within.

No. I had the means to be myself, to be independent—poor perhaps, but self-sufficient and unrestrained. I could envision no other way of life for me. But for Consuelo, raised so differently than I had been . . .

"Little cousin," I said gently, "you must make this decision yourself. In the end, no one can truly force you to marry the Duke of Marlborough. All we can do is help you to see all of your options and then stand back and allow you to decide."

"It doesn't always feel that way. In fact, it rarely does."

"No, you're right. We're all bound by our circumstances. It's just that some circumstances come with greater possibilities than others. You need to bear that in mind."

She let go a long, heavy sigh. The lacy ruffles hanging over the bed fluttered and a warm, fuzzy body arched itself against my ankle. Bits of fur penetrated my stocking to tickle my leg.

Consuelo looked down and opened her arms. "Here, Muffy."

The cat bounded up into her lap, its sweetly flat

face tilted lovingly up at its mistress. Consuelo bent over the creature and rubbed her nose in the fur between its tufted ears. I reached out and stroked the bushy, snaking tail.

"I thought I would marry Winty," Consuelo said without looking up. "I believed it with all my heart until Mother blatantly informed me otherwise. Winty believed it, too." She glanced up. "He'd have been a good catch, I think. Not much money, relatively speaking, but a good man from a good family."

I nodded. She was speaking of Winthrop Rutherfurd, an older gentleman past thirty, whom she had known most of her life as his New York family belonged to the same circles as the Vanderbilts. In many ways the Rutherfurds boasted an even more sterling pedigree that could be traced back to Peter Stuyvesant, the last Dutch director-general of New Amsterdam before the city was sold to the British and renamed New York. Many families like the Rutherfurds considered the Vanderbilts to be upstarts—new money gotten through trade. But poor Winty didn't have a title and the family coffers had been a bit depleted through the years, which in Aunt Alva's book made him a most unsuitable suitor.

"I could have accomplished just as much as Winty's wife as the Duke's," Consuelo went on stubbornly. "After all, the Duke's hardly got any money either. It'll all be mine. Why couldn't I take that same money and settle in New York with a man I . . . I . . ."

I stroked my palm up and down her back, my fingers tripping over the tiny buttons securing her frock. I was searching for something consoling to say when she spoke again. "Winty wasn't good enough for Mother, and now, apparently, I'm not good enough for Winty."

My hand went still. "What do you mean?"

"Oh, Emma, he's dropped me completely. Just stopped trying to see me."

"How can you know that? Maybe he's been here and turned away. For all you know, he might come calling every day."

Consuelo was shaking her head. "It's true, Mother wouldn't have let him in. She's been sending away all of my friends ever since we arrived in Newport. B-but Gertrude came by a few days before her coming-out ball. Mother didn't dare turn *her* away for fear of what Father and Uncle Cornelius would do. Gertrude wanted to apologize for the fact that I couldn't be invited to the ball, not with Mother and Father's divorce and all." She paused for a shaky breath and dabbed tears from her eyes with the back of her hand. The fingers of her other hand combed through Muffy's lush fur. The cat closed her eyes, then opened one and winked up at me. For an instant I was reminded of Alva, gratifying her own ambitions while selfishly ignoring her daughter's pain.

"Did Gertrude say something about Winty?" I prodded gently.

"She said . . . he'd b-been seen at the Casino and the Yacht Club and all a-around town—laughing and indulging and h-having a splendid t-time. While I've been here, trapped in this room I loathe with every fiber of my being."

At that she broke into a fit of tears and choking sobs. She slumped onto my shoulder again and reached her arms around me, holding on for all she was worth.

"Oh, Consuelo, darling, I'm sure Winty isn't having a splendid time." I stroked her back as I tried to reassure her. "It's just that men behave differently than we do. They throw themselves into their daily activities when they're unhappy. It's their way of keeping their minds off their distress. And I'm sure he's very distressed right now."

She poked her head up from my shoulder, turning her tear-streaked face to mine. "You really think so?"

I nodded.

"Oh, but still. It's impossible for us to ever be together. Mother will never allow it. She'd rather see me dead than give in."

"No, darling, that isn't true."

She was inconsolable, so I held her and let her cry herself out while Muffy, who had become squished between us, crawled off her mistress's lap with a grumbling meow and headed for the beribboned pillows propped against the headboard.

Some ten minutes later Consuelo's tears showed signs of slowing, so I slid my hands to her shoulders and set her at arm's length. "Listen to me, Consuelo. You are a beautiful, strong, intelligent young woman, and whatever happens, you will prevail."

"I don't know . . ."

"I'm positive of it. Now, you can go into this marriage with tears and regrets, or you can stride into it with your head held high and your shoulders squared. Do you know what my aunt Sadie would say to you?"

Consuelo shook her head and sniffed, but her chin inched higher than it had been.

"She'd say marry the damned duke if you have to," I improvised, wondering if Aunt Sadie would have said anything of the sort. The twitching of my cousin's lips when I swore encouraged me to continue. "She'd say marry him and be every inch a duchess. Let him and everyone else know you're a force to be reckoned with. Map your battleground and determine a way to be happy in the life you must lead. Soldier on. That's what Aunt Sadie would say."

"I always liked your aunt Sadie," Consuelo murmured with a weak chuckle, "no matter what Mother said about her."

"I can only imagine what that was." I grinned at her. "Come now. Let's freshen you up and go downstairs. Let's show everyone you're not going to hide away in your room anymore. Let's show them Consuelo Vanderbilt isn't afraid of anything."

She gave a decisive nod. "Let's. Help me fix my hair, Emma. I'm going down."

"As a duchess," I said.

"As a duchess," she repeated, then looked uncertainly into my eyes. "Is it all right if I'm still a little afraid?"

"I won't tell if you won't."

Some forty minutes later my cousin and I descended Marble House's Grand Staircase. When my help fell short we'd called in her maid to work her magic on Consuelo's hair, choose a new frock, and pinch some color back into her cheeks. She'd emerged from her bedroom sanctuary in a silk sapphire-blue tea gown that made her eyes sparkle, indeed looking every inch the young duchess. Even I felt some awe of her, this beauty of the Vanderbilt family and the belle of every ball she'd attended since her coming-out a year ago.

It wasn't that Consuelo took on airs. It was that, along with her lovely features and dark, lustrous hair, she'd been blessed with a natural grace that never seemed to fail her, that made her appear self-assured and elegant, at least to those who didn't know her well. I, however, perceived the tension in her slender neck and the repeated balling of her hands into fists.

"Stop that," I admonished gently. "Never let them see you doubt yourself."

"Never let them see the whites of your eyes," she countered.

"Exactly."

"Soldier on," she repeated from earlier.

"Always."

Voices from the rear veranda echoed lightly in the main hall. We made our way outside, whereupon Aunt Alva hurried over to us issuing a delighted exclamation, as though we had just returned from an extended journey away.

"Consuelo, Emmaline—oh, how delightful that you've both decided to join us. Emmaline, I have guests I'm longing to introduce you to. And, Consuelo dear, I have a special surprise for you. Oh, how very lovely you look, my dear." She ran her hands lightly over the billowing, elbow-length sleeves her daughter wore. She spared a cursory glance at me, then looked away, but not before I caught the "Well, what can one do?" assessment as for a second time that day she took in my simple coiled braid and Aunt Sadie's hand-me-down carriage dress.

"Ladies, I'd like to introduce you to . . ."

As Consuelo and I approached the wrought-iron

garden table where the guests sat, she whispered out of the corner of her mouth to me, "A surprise? Do you know anything about this?"

I had all but forgotten about Aunt Alva's surprise to coax Consuelo from her room. But we'd reached earshot of the four ladies sitting round the table, so I only shrugged and pasted on a smile.

They were quite varied, those houseguests. Two of them looked to be about Aunt Alva's age and from similar circumstances, as each sported the latest summer fashions of leg-of-mutton sleeves, knife-pleated underskirts peeking out from lace-edged overdresses, and curving, wide-brimmed hats trimmed with a colorful array of silk flowers. Like Aunt Alva, these women were on the stout side, the kind of figure that comes from child-bearing and an unlimited supply of rich food, and their hair, though meticulously dressed, bore a faded sheen where gray had encroached on the natural brown. Their names were Miss Edwina Spooner and Miss Roberta Spooner, sisters, as it turned out. Which explained how immediately after learning their names, I couldn't have said which was which. I found them pleasant but rather interchangeable.

No, it was the other two women who held my attention. Lady Amelia Beaumont spoke with an uptown New York accent despite the European roots suggested by her title. My estimate put her somewhere in her mid-thirties. Where the Spooner sisters wore their pleats and flounces and tufts of lace, Lady Amelia was sleek and tailored with a minimum of fuss, but in fabrics even I could see were of the very finest quality to be had. Burnished green silk hugged her figure in the very latest, almost scandalous fashion, outlining her bosom, hips, and thighs before spilling away in voluminous folds to a trailing hemline; gold embroidery embellished the cuffs and collar, echoing the brightness of the golden curls piled high on her head. A tiny chapeau sporting a glittering emerald and a shiny green feather completed the outfit.

I noticed Consuelo eyeing this woman with a gleam of envy; we both knew her mother would see Consuelo dead before she'd allow her to wear such a daring ensemble.

Our attention was next drawn to the elderly woman sitting at the far side of the linen-covered table. "And this is Mrs. Calvin Stanford," Aunt Alva said. "Or Mrs. *Hope* Stanford, I should say, shouldn't I, Hope, dear?"

"Indeed," the woman shot back in a no-nonsense sort of way. "I might be married, but I am still my own person."

There was little to envy about Hope Stanford's person. I guessed her age to be somewhere around seventy. She wore her white, wispy hair pulled back in a simple bun beneath a straw boater-style hat that might have been sat upon a time or two; her eyes looked sunken above her prominent cheeks, her nose was long and her mouth thin, and her serviceable cotton day dress displayed nothing of the latest fashions, might have been a year or a decade old; the garment hung limply on a frame one might almost call gaunt. And yet, upon hearing her name, both Consuelo and I gasped.

"*The* Mrs. Hope Stanford?" I whispered reverently.

"In the flesh, missy," the woman replied with a force that belied her frail appearance. "I take it you've heard of me? Are you a supporter of women's suffrage?"

"I-I . . ." I nodded rapidly several times. "My aunt Sadie was a huge admirer of yours, Mrs. Stanford. Huge," I repeated stupidly. I was aware of Consuelo staring at me, her mouth open. "She even wrote to you right after you went before the Rhode Island legislature. You might not remember her letter, but—"

"Does she support the temperance movement?" Mrs. Stanford brusquely asked.

"Oh, well, Aunt Sadie passed away a year ago, but ah . . ." Now that I thought about it, this had been a point of contention between Aunt Sadie and many of her friends who supported the suffrage movement.

"A woman's right to vote is surely not an end in

45

and of itself, young lady." Mrs. Stanford sent an angry glare around the table, as if any of the small group had dared to argue with her. "We have a moral obligation to see that alcoholic spirits are prohibited in these United States before they rip our society apart at the seams."

"Yes, I . . . I see." Aunt Sadie had never been averse to a glass of wine or sherry in the evening. And then there was dear Nanny, who claimed those wee splashes of whiskey in her tea—and occasionally in mine—were for medicinal purposes only.

I mentioned neither to Mrs. Stanford.

"Well, well," Aunt Alva interrupted. "Isn't this lovely. Emmaline, Consuelo, sit and have some tea, dears. The surprise should be here any moment."

I realized, too, that under normal circumstances Aunt Alva might have served tiny glasses of chocolate or cherry cordial to her afternoon guests, but today there were no crystal decanters in sight. Did that mean Aunt Alva favored prohibition? I doubted it. And I wondered if her sudden interest in women's suffrage was simply a way to mortify her ex-husband and the rest of the Vanderbilt family.

As Consuelo and I took our places, the other ladies continued conversing. The sudden rise of Mrs. Stanford's voice drew my attention. "And so I walked into that tavern last night," she was saying, "the one near the corner of Long Wharf and Thames Street, and I pounded away at the bar top with my sledgehammer."

Lady Amelia plucked a fan off the table and snapped it open. "You walked in with a sledgehammer and no one stopped you?"

"I don't believe they quite knew what to make of it," the older woman replied with a chuckle, "until I started hammering."

"Didn't a shout go up for the police?" This came from one of the Spooner sisters. Roberta, I think, the more square-jawed of the two.

"Yes, and where was your husband at the time?" the other sister asked. She looked scandalized, and as if she could use a flutter or two of Lady Amelia's fan. "Didn't he go to town with you? Surely he can't have been in favor of you—"

"Calvin is entirely in favor of me driving the demon spirits out of American society. He was standing right behind me, making sure none of those drunken heathens dared accost me as I did the Lord's work."

"But I don't understand what purpose it served to—"

Mrs. Stanford cut off Lady Amelia's words by striking the table with her fist. My gaze flew to her hand, crisscrossed by blue veins and raw at the knuckles. "My action served notice that the time for sobriety has arrived. It also sent a good number of those men running for cover. If nothing else, their drinking for the night ended early."

"They probably crossed the street and slipped into the next closest tavern," Lady Amelia said under her breath. I appeared to be the only one who heard her, and I stifled a laugh.

"What an inspiring story," Alva exclaimed. "Such a good, loyal man, your husband. Why, I wish . . ." She trailed off with a sideways glance at Consuelo, whose cheeks reddened. Yet Consuelo met her mother's gaze with a lift of her eyebrow, as if daring Alva to say one unkind thing about her father. For once, Alva seemed disinclined to meet the challenge.

As the conversation drifted, my cousin raised her teacup to hide her lips and whispered to me, "So Aunt Sadie was a suffragette?"

"In a way, yes," I whispered back. "But not in favor of temperance. And in her view it was hardly worth voting anyway until women were able to run for office."

Consuelo had taken a sip of tea and at my words she sputtered. "Good heavens, Emma. No wonder you're the way you are."

I opened my mouth to demand what she meant by that, when Grafton stepped through the terrace doorway, a figure swathed in varying shades of plum half-hidden behind him.

"Madame Eleanora Devereaux," he droned

with the slightest curl of his lip, and then stepped aside.

A woman came forward, her jeweled turban, beaded necklaces, and countless bangles glittering in the sunlight. Clattering as she moved, she bobbed a little curtsy, holding both arms out with a theatrical flourish. She wore a shapeless frock with arm slits rather than sleeves, and the sides of the garment caught the breeze like violet sails. Her eyes were lined with kohl, her skin powdered, her lips and cheeks rouged—almost shockingly so. She reminded me of a tropical bird, from her flashy attire to the penetrating look in her eye as she surveyed us without blinking.

From across the table came a breathless murmur, almost too low to be heard. "Ellen Deere."

I peered over at Mrs. Stanford, but her face was a blank, her lips the same thin line as usual. I swung back toward the newly arrived guest to find her staring daggers across the table, straight at Hope Stanford. But only for the briefest moment. Then her expression cleared, became serene and cordial.

Aunt Alva came to her feet. "Consuelo, darling. This is your surprise!"

CHAPTER 3

"Come, Consuelo!" Aunt Alva held out a hand as she urged her daughter to stand. "Come meet Madame Devereaux. She is here to read your fortune. Isn't that exciting?" She turned her attention to the rest of us. "Madame Devereaux will read all of our fortunes in the garden pavilion just as soon as she has set up for us." She gestured to the bit of curving roof just visible above the tall hedges lining the garden path. "Her instruments for divining the future were delivered earlier, and in a little while we'll all head across the garden to hear what life holds in store for us. Remember, ladies, choose your questions wisely!" She ended on a note of laughter, but the women around the table traded wary looks, myself and Consuelo included.

My better sense proclaimed the medium a charlatan. Such individuals typically preyed upon the elderly, the bereaved, and the desperate. But even if the woman could genuinely divine the future, did I really want to glimpse what lay in store for me? An uneasy sensation told me I didn't, that such things were best allowed to unfold as they would. Consuelo's troubled expression mirrored my sentiments.

But her mother wasn't about to let her daughter

demur. "Come *here,* dear," she said with barely suppressed impatience.

Consuelo stood and approached the medium. Though Madame Devereaux had seemed tall standing beside Grafton, I realized now that was merely an illusion conjured by the height of her turban. Her dress consisted of layers of draped fabric in shades of amethyst, violet, lavender, and lilac, flowing unbelted from her shoulders to the floor, essentially hiding her figure and making it impossible to determine if she were slim or stout.

Her numerous bracelets jangled as she held out her hand to Consuelo. "Miss Vanderbilt, a great pleasure." Her voice was deep, throaty, and held a hint of an accent that wanted to be French, but wasn't quite. At least, not the French accent I'd learned at school.

My cousin hesitated. The tension had returned to her neck and shoulders, and I guessed Consuelo wanted no part of the afternoon's entertainments. Yet after a pause, she grasped the medium's hand and gave it a single, cordial shake. "How do you do?"

Madame Devereaux gasped. Snatching her hand back as if Consuelo had placed an ember in her palm, she staggered backward. Her eyes shot wide open, then glazed over as she stared at Consuelo. Her mouth gaped like that of a beached fish.

"You'll never be happy. Never be happy with

him," she intoned in a strained voice. "Oh, child . . . you poor child . . . stay away from him. Never, never trust him. Consuelo Vanderbilt . . . hear me. You'll never know happiness with a scoundrel such as he. . . ."

"Whatever do you mean?" Consuelo demanded when the woman trailed off, her voice fading like the lingering note of a plucked harp.

Her mother hurried forward and sandwiched herself between Consuelo and the medium. "There, there, now, Consuelo, dear—"

Before Alva could say another word, Consuelo snapped, "Let her speak, Mother. What does she mean?"

"Don't be ridiculous." Alva whirled about to face the medium. "You didn't mean anything, did you? Just a little joke, although not a particularly funny one, to be sure."

Madame Devereaux blinked several times and gave her head a little shake. "I . . . I'm sorry, Mrs. Vanderbilt. Yes, just a joke to . . . to break the ice. I'm sorry if . . ."

"That was no joke." Consuelo's voice trembled. "And I insist—"

"Consuelo," her mother said through gritted teeth, "we have guests."

"I don't care. I—"

"Emmaline," my aunt called to me, "please take my daughter into the house. Up to her room, in fact, until she calms herself."

"I *am* calm, Mother."

Alva's voice plunged to a whisper. "Do as I say, Consuelo. Madame Devereaux didn't mean anything, so do stop making a scene. Go upstairs. Now."

Side by side, Consuelo and I climbed the stairs with a good deal less spirit than when we'd descended them.

"She makes me want to run away."

I slung an arm about her waist but said nothing as we followed the graceful curve up to the second floor. I wasn't about to speak in my aunt's defense, not when she'd essentially humiliated Consuelo in front of the others, treating her like a naughty child when all Consuelo had wanted was some kind of reassurance after the medium's odd, ominous prediction.

When we reached her bedroom, she opened the door. In a streak of gray, Muffy darted out past our ankles and barreled away down the hall.

"Oh!" Consuelo cried. "Stop her! Mother hates it when she gets downstairs."

It was too late. Muffy had reached the staircase and galloped down. "I'll go get her," I said, fearing if Consuelo went her mother would think she was disobeying and scold her yet again.

Downstairs in the entry hall I glimpsed Muffy's swishing tail darting toward the library, and when I entered the room she scampered beneath the desk. I bent down to coax her out, but she crept past my groping hand, shot out from under the desk chair, and leaped onto a glass-fronted cabinet. As soon as I came to my feet, Muffy dived onto a satin brocade sofa, sending a hiss through the down-filled cushions. That was her mistake, for there I had her, trapped between my open arms and the sofa's high back.

"Got you, you imp. And not a moment too soon. Do you have any idea what Alva Vanderbilt would do to you if she caught you pawing her precious Italian brocade?" I scooped the furry being into my arms, and when I expected her to struggle against me, she instead went limp and rested her head against my shoulder. Her whiskers tickled my neck. "Oh, you just wanted to play, didn't you, you naughty thing? Don't like being cooped up in a bedroom all the time, do you?" Just like Consuelo, I thought sadly.

Before I could set out to return Muffy to her mistress, voices drifted through the open library windows—the ones that overlooked the terrace.

"You'll do as I say." My aunt's hissing voice raised the hairs at my nape.

Curious, I moved to the window, standing where the curtain would hide me. The four houseguests were strolling in the gardens, and snippets of their conversation and laughter bounced on the breeze. Closer, Aunt Alva and Madame Devereaux stood together near the garden table. Those same breezes fluttered the edges of the medium's frock and prompted Aunt Alva to grasp the brim of her silk-covered hat. Both were red-faced and gesturing angrily.

"I do not lie." The medium's lips curved disdainfully downward. "I am an ethical woman."

"Whom do you think you're dealing with? A fool? You're a fortune-teller." Aunt Alva's eyes narrowed dangerously. She thrust a finger squarely at the woman's chest, just as she had with me earlier. "That makes you a fraud, a con artist. And believe me when I say I can make your life exceedingly difficult. So difficult you'll never practice your hokum anywhere again, except perhaps in a Providence prison cell."

The medium blanched. "I am no fraud," she said, but a good portion of her conviction had drained away, along with her almost-French accent.

"Here is what you are going to do." Aunt Alva stepped toe-to-toe with the woman, and I pressed closer to the window so as not to miss a word. "You are going to go down to the pavilion and prepare to tell our fortunes. When it's my daughter's turn, you are going to spread your cards across the table, gaze into your crystal ball, and with every shred of false enthusiasm you can muster, you will convince her of the glorious, loving, successful future she'll enjoy as the Duchess of Marlborough."

Or else.

I heard the warning as clear as day, though the words once again went unspoken.

Or so I thought. After a pause during which the tension shivered palpably in the air between the two women, Aunt Alva eased closer and brought her lips beside the medium's ear. Madame Devereaux turned a shade of scarlet that sent my pulse leaping with alarm. Muffy twitched her tail as I squeezed her too hard, pressing forward as I was with my head nearly out the window in my attempt to hear what my aunt was saying.

My efforts proved unfruitful. But when Aunt Alva leaned away with a cunning smile, the medium's features froze in dismay. "You will tell her the man you meant, the man who would only make her miserable, is Winthrop Rutherfurd," Aunt Alva said, "or you will be very, very sorry."

Madame Devereaux gave a wobbly nod.

"Have you all thought of what you wish to ask Madame Devereaux?" Aunt Alva led her guests along the garden path toward the pavilion. Her smiles and the carefree swinging of her arms belied the conversation I'd overheard no less than twenty minutes earlier. Now she seemed as cheerful as the summer sunlight glittering on the ocean beyond the cliffs at the rear of the property. The Spooner sisters trailed immediately behind her, the tiny blossoms on their wide hats rivaling Alva's meticulously tended flowerbeds.

"I'd like to ask Madame Devereaux if dear Roberta will ever find a husband," the sister who must be Edwina said, tittering into her hand.

"Me? What about you, sister? At forty-eight you remain as unmarried as I."

"Quite true, Roberta, but I remain single by choice. Whereas we all know you have been pining over that Mr. Armandale for years now."

"Mr. Armandale doesn't appear to be the marrying kind," Roberta replied wistfully.

Behind them, Hope Stanford and Lady Amelia seemed locked in a heated debate.

"You must take a stand, my dear. The property is yours by rights. Your grandfather left it to you in his will. Do not allow yourself to be swindled."

"He may have done, Mrs. Stanhope, but the law in England supersedes a man's last will and testament. I may have been Grandpapa's favorite, but the title will go to my younger brother, and with it all the property. There is simply no way around it."

"Bah!" Hope Stanford swatted her fingertips at a bush beside the path as if the branches had somehow offended her. "Such laws, that leave women destitute or dependent on the charity of their menfolk, need to be changed."

"I agree wholeheartedly, ma'am. But that's not likely to happen until women can vote."

"Then we must be tireless in our efforts, on both

sides of the ocean," Mrs. Stanhope concluded in her no-nonsense way.

"Lady Amelia," I said, gathering my hems and trotting a few steps to catch up to them, "are you from England, then?"

The emerald in her hat caught a sunbeam and momentarily blinded me as she turned toward me. Blinking, I saw that her smile held approval. "You're very observant, Miss Cross. You noticed that I don't sound particularly English, didn't you?"

"If you'll pardon my saying so, you sound more as though you're from New York's Fifth Avenue than London's Mayfair. Am I wrong?"

"No, indeed. You see, my parents separated when I was sixteen. My mother is an American, a Wentworth as a matter of fact, and she brought me to New York to continue raising me among her family."

"And your brother?" Mrs. Stanford asked, though the angle of her chin suggested she knew the answer.

"Father wouldn't allow Mother to take him out of England. He stayed there and attended Eton, and then Oxford. We barely know each other."

"How very sad." This came from Consuelo, who had been in the rear but now moved up beside me.

"Sad my eye," Mrs. Stanford all but spat. "It's a travesty. He'll inherit every bit of the English fortune while Lady Amelia gets nothing. Nothing at all."

"I wouldn't say nothing," Lady Amelia corrected her. "I've gotten heaps from Mother's side."

"Still and all, it isn't right."

As the others strode on in Aunt Alva's wake, Consuelo came to a halt beside a rosebush. I stopped beside her and waited for her to speak. She remained silent, however, staring at the scarlet blossoms but not seeming to see them; her eyes held a faraway, pensive look.

"Is something wrong?" I asked her gently.

"It's what Lady Amelia just said about her parents separating, and her being taken far from home, from her brother and her father. It's so sad, Emma. It's . . . it's exactly what's happening to me. If I marry the Duke, I'll leave this country. I won't see you or my friends or my brothers anymore. Soon, we won't even really know each other. We'll be strangers."

I slipped an arm around her waist. "You and I will never be strangers. I can promise you that."

I reached out and plucked a rosebud, careful not to prick my thumb, and handed it to my cousin. She bowed her head to it, dabbed at a tear with her free hand, and inhaled deeply. Her lips parted as if she were about to say something more, words that never came.

In that instant, a scream ripped across the garden.

• • •

Gripping each other's hands, Consuelo and I set off running down the path. Another scream filled the air and echoed off the rear of the house behind us. Up ahead, Mrs. Stanford and Lady Amelia came to sudden halts in front of the pavilion. Just inside the wide archway, the Misses Spooner stood clutching each other's hands. Aunt Alva was lost in the shadows under the pavilion roof.

"Oh, good gracious, Emma, what can it be?" Consuelo squeezed my hand as we ran, her fingernails cutting into my flesh. Then we, too, reached the pavilion. My hand flew up to press my bosom. Consuelo cried out.

"Is she . . . is she . . ." Roberta Spooner—or was it Edwina?—craned her neck to see around Aunt Alva.

Aunt Alva didn't utter a word. I pried Consuelo's fingers from my hand and then pressed forward, placing a hand on Lady Amelia's shoulder so I could squeeze between her and Mrs. Stanford and continue up the two steps into the pavilion. The aroma of some pungent incense tickled my nose and stung my eyes. I stepped around the Spooner sisters and came to Aunt Alva's side. My breath froze in my throat.

I saw Clara first—Clara Parker, the young maid I'd spoken to outside Consuelo's room that morning, who had fretted over how little Consuelo had eaten and who had hoped I might be able to cheer my cousin up. Clara, her severe black frock contrasting sharply with the white pinafore and starched cap she wore, stood facing us, the whites of her eyes gleaming in the shadows, her head moving side to side in a continual gesture of denial. The already-petite girl seemed further diminished by the fear magnifying her eyes, and by the incongruously cheerful yellows of the sunflowers, daisies, and black-eyed Susans that bedecked the pavilion.

To mirror the happy destinies about to be foretold?

Or to sit in garish contrast to the gruesome image that greeted me as I lowered my gaze.

A figure swathed from head to toe in varying shades of violet sat slumped over a cloth-covered card table, her head angled awkwardly to one side. The jeweled turban had fallen off her head and rolled to the edge of the table, and short, thin wisps of graying brown hair stuck out in all directions from her scalp. I moved farther into the pavilion until I could see her face; her eyes protruded from their sockets, staring unblinkingly at the crystal ball inches away. A colorful deck of cards fanned out from beneath her cheek, several of them scattered on the floor beside the table amid a sprinkling of coins. Her lips were a sickly shade of blue and . . .

A crimson gash scored her throat. My stomach

roiled—but no. I looked again and realized there was no blood anywhere. Instead, around her throat a scarf of deep red silk was twined so tightly her neck bulged from around the fabric.

"Dear God." I circled the table and shoved a stupefied Clara aside. From behind Madame Devereaux's chair, I grabbed the woman by the shoulders. I hauled her upright, then leaned her limp body against the back of the chair.

In a frenzied blur I dug my fingers around the silk scarf to loosen its grip. Even as the ends slipped free I knew it was too late. Madame Devereaux had breathed her last, and no amount of hoping would coax her lungs to fill again. A trickle of blood spilled from the corner of her mouth. Her lips gaped and her tongue lolled, showing where she had bitten clean through. A bruise was already forming on her temple, where her head had struck the table in front of her. Or . . . perhaps she'd been struck, before being strangled.

A whimper came from one of the ladies grouped in the entrance of the pavilion. I looked up to see them gaping, dumbfounded. Then, as one, they lifted their gazes to the person whose presence I'd all but forgotten.

"I didn't . . . I didn't . . ." Clara stammered. She stood with her small back plastered to one of the structure's carved columns, looking like a child called to the headmistress's office and babbling incoherently.

Aunt Alva's arm came up, her forefinger aimed at the maid. "Your hands were around her neck. I saw you."

"I swear . . . I didn't . . . I swear . . . she was like that . . . I only tried to help . . ."

"Shut up," Aunt Alva ordered. "Just shut up."

Her command may have silenced Clara, who clamped her lips tight, but it also released a flurry of cries and exclamations from the other women. Alva whirled about to shush them. Her gaze must have landed on her daughter, because she immediately said, "Go back to the house. Tell Grafton to call for the police. Go, Consuelo, now."

I don't know how much my cousin saw. I wanted to go to her, to comfort her, but when I looked up from the sight that held me so horribly entranced, she had gone.

CHAPTER 4

"We caught you red-handed, girl. What other reason could you have had for being out here?"

Aunt Alva had Clara backed up against that support column so tightly I could have sworn the wood creaked in protest. Clara sobbed hysterically, continuing to shake her head in denial.

"Why did you murder Madame Devereaux?" Aunt Alva pressed her flushed face close to Clara's, spittle flying from her lips. "You'd better start talking, girl . . ."

It was that imminent *or else* that propelled me across the pavilion to them. I'd wanted to stay with Madame Devereaux until the police came, just stand at her side to watch over her. It seemed heartless to simply leave the poor woman half slumped so grotesquely in her chair, where she could easily tip to one side and slither to the floor. She deserved more dignity than that, didn't she?

Yet the living also deserved their dignity, and Aunt Alva was doing a blasted good job of stripping Clara of hers. I stepped up beside them and placed a hand on each of their shoulders— Clara's thin, shaking one and Aunt Alva's much sturdier one. Aunt Alva veered toward me as if to swing a punch. I winced, but the blow never came.

"Aunt Alva, we don't know that Clara did anything wrong. Please, we should wait for the police."

"What other reason could a housemaid have for being in the gardens?" Alva never took her eyes off of the blubbering Clara. "Well? Why were you out here?"

Clara clutched at the railing on either side of the column behind her until her fingernails scraped the wood. "I . . . I . . . came to see if anyone needed anything. If Madame wanted—"

"Liar!" Alva's shout squeezed a sob from Clara, who shut her eyes and turned her face away. "It's not your job to see if my guests need anything. Grafton wouldn't have sent you out here." The emphasis Aunt Alva put on *you* reduced Clara to the status of the lowliest street urchin.

"I only w-wanted to . . . to help, ma'am."

"Then why did we catch you standing behind her, as if you'd just wrapped the scarf around her neck and squeezed the life out of her?"

"I didn't . . . I didn't." Releasing the column behind her, Clara buried her face in her hands and broke down into unintelligible sobs.

"Mrs. Vanderbilt, your niece is right." Mrs. Stanford's stern face appeared beside me. "Badgering the girl will accomplish nothing. Leave it to the police. They should be here soon enough."

I noticed now that the other women had

retreated back down the pavilion steps and stood gathered on the walkway. The Spooner sisters had their arms around each other. Their faces were mottled, their eyes watery. Lady Amelia stood off to one side hugging her middle, a pained look on her face.

Hope Stanford, on the other hand, seemed her usual self: stoic, sensible, single-minded. In fact, she moved away now to extinguish the incense and the candles Madame Devereaux had apparently lit in preparation of telling our futures. Was Mrs. Stanford always so unshakable, so calm in the midst of a crisis? Or was her composure due to some other reason? I moved back to Madame Devereaux's lifeless body, but I studied Hope Stanford until the police arrived.

Three of the ladies made their way back to the house while Aunt Alva and Mrs. Stanford and I waited in the pavilion until the police arrived. At Mrs. Stanford's insistence, Aunt Alva stopped pressing Clara for answers, though she never unpinned her gaze from the girl, not even for an instant. Not that she had much to worry about. Clara barely moved, but instead continued in an almost catatonic trance with her back jammed against the column.

I maintained my vigil beside Madame Devereaux and on one occasion even had to nudge her upright or she might have tumbled over at my feet. That slight movement of her body had seemed so lifelike, bolts of alarm shot through me, and only a firm inner admonishment could resettle my nerves. I'd closed Madame's eyes, but that didn't make it any easier to gaze down at that lifeless face or place my hand on that frigid, stiffening shoulder.

Once I felt assured of having her well balanced in the chair, I used the opportunity to study my surroundings. The tarot cards, fanned across the table, meant little to me at first—merely tools of the woman's trade—until I connected them to the coins littering the tiles beside the desk. Then it struck me. The medium hadn't simply been awaiting the arrival of Aunt Alva and her guests; she had been engaged in reading someone's fortune.

Whose, Clara's? Would a maid have money for such a frivolity? I considered questioning Clara right then, but another glance at the glazed vacancy in her eyes assured me of the unlikelihood of receiving a lucid answer. I resumed my inspection of the pavilion, until something sent me hurrying from Madame Devereaux's side.

"Look at this," I said to no one in particular. I bent low, examining bits of muddy grass and tiny pebbles tracked across the floor. I traced the untidy path from Madame Devereaux's chair to a few feet from the pavilion's entrance, where the concentration of plant matter suddenly thinned, no doubt due to the arrival of the ladies and me.

Apparently we had scattered the evidence with our own footsteps.

Still, I searched for telltale contours that might with some accuracy be called footprints, yet I could make out nothing substantial enough to identify a type or size of shoe. My only educated guess was that the shoes had been damp in order to have tracked in the mess.

Odd. It hadn't rained in days.

"Finally. The police are here." The sounds of tramping feet rendered Aunt Alva's announcement unnecessary.

I couldn't have said which emotion reigned supreme inside me, relief or chagrin. Yes, I was thankful the authorities had arrived, but the expression on Detective Jesse Whyte's face made my stomach sink. But perhaps I should clarify. The moment our gazes met, his ironic expression proclaimed he'd not only realized I was once again caught up in a murder investigation, but that he wasn't the least bit happy about it. I suddenly wished I'd returned to the house when Consuelo had.

Jesse's first words to me dismissed any doubts I might have had about his sentiments. "Really, Emma? So soon after last time? Is this something you particularly enjoy?"

"There were footsteps. I heard them, sir. Running across the grass."

"She's lying!"

Once again I hastened to intervene between my aunt and Clara Parker. "Please, Aunt Alva, let her answer Detective Whyte's questions. How else will we learn the truth?"

"We won't learn the truth if the chit insists on lying."

While the uniformed men proceeded to question Marble House's battalion of servants, the rest of us had moved into the house and upstairs to the room that had once served as Uncle William's study during the short time he'd lived here before the divorce. Of all the rooms in Marble House, this was the least ornate and the most practical, with clean, masculine lines rendered in leather and hardwood furnishings. Here, one needn't hesitate to sit for fear of ruining priceless embroidered silks or smudging a gilded finish.

Clara was seated in a stiff-backed side chair in the middle of the room, her body so rigid she might have been held with ropes. One by one, Roberta and Edwina Spooner gave their statements to Jesse and his partner, Detective Dobbs. Next, the officers questioned Lady Amelia, and finally, Hope Stanford. Each gave a nearly identical version of the story. Had they seen anyone other than their little group enter or leave the pavilion? No. Had they seen anyone else in the vicinity of the pavilion? No. In the gardens?

No. Were they together during the estimated time of the murder? Yes. And what did they see upon entering the pavilion?

Again, the answers were all the same: Madame Devereaux slumped over the card table and Clara Parker standing directly behind her, her hands on the dead woman's neck.

Clara protested with a loud whimper at each mention of that last detail. "I was trying to take the scarf off her!"

"There were the tracks of grass on the pavilion floor," I reminded Jesse. "That does seem to indicate that someone had been in the pavilion before the rest of us arrived."

"Yes—her!" Aunt Alva's finger jabbed in Clara's direction.

I swung to face her. She and I sat together on the camelback sofa beneath the mounted sabers Uncle William had brought home from the family's trip to India last year. I couldn't help feeling those crossed swords symbolized Aunt Alva's and my currently opposing views. I only hoped they were mounted securely. "Are you so eager to see your own maid accused of murder?"

Clara let out another whimper as Aunt Alva replied, "Of course not. But neither am I eager to see a murderess go free."

"The grass could have been tracked in by Madame Devereaux herself." This came from Jesse's partner, Detective Anthony Dobbs. The man sat at Uncle William's sturdy desk, a pencil in hand, a writing tablet open before him. I scowled at the sarcasm that dripped from the medium's name. Whether or not the woman had been swindling her customers, she didn't deserve anyone's mockery now. Especially this man's. I narrowed my eyes at him, but he took no notice.

I'd known both police officers most of my life. Jesse lived near my childhood home on the Point section of Newport, beside the harbor on the other side of town. Though he was quite a bit younger than my father, they'd been friends and Jesse had joined us for supper on many a night. Now he was my half brother Brady's friend, and as often as not kept Brady out of trouble—and jail—whenever my boisterous brother over-imbibed or became tangled in any number of ill-advised activities.

Jesse and his partner couldn't have been more different, neither in looks nor temperament. Where Jesse's features bore the youthful, almost delicate look of a boy and his frame tended toward the lean and wiry, Anthony Dobbs sported the face of a bulldog and the body of a prizefighter, and it seemed he derived no shortage of pleasure from bullying my brother at every opportunity.

Would he enjoy doing the same to Clara?

"Clara could have tracked in the grass," Aunt Alva pointed out.

"I didn't, ma'am. I stayed on the path."

"So you say," Aunt Alva countered.

No one commented, but Detective Dobbs scribbled in his tablet.

One by one Jesse dismissed the ladies until only Aunt Alva and I remained. Aunt Alva I understood; she owned Marble House and was Clara's employer. As for me . . . I couldn't help a twinge of pride that perhaps Jesse thought I could help, as I had in Newport's last, and still quite recent, murder investigation.

Jesse went to look over Dobbs's shoulder at the notes scrawled in the tablet. He glanced up with a frown. "Mrs. Vanderbilt, isn't your daughter in residence?"

My aunt stiffened. "She is."

"We'll need to question her, too, then."

"Oh, no, you will not." Aunt Alva compressed her lips and glowered.

"Was she with you all when Madame Devereaux's body was discovered?"

Aunt Alva started to shake her head, but a quick glance at me seemed to change her mind. "She was, but she didn't see anything. I sent her back up to the house before she ever entered the pavilion. It was she who instructed my butler to call the police."

"And where is she now?" Jesse asked.

"In her room. Where else would she be?"

Jesse scrubbed a hand across his eyes. "Will

you please send for her, ma'am." It wasn't a question. "It's possible she might have seen or heard something from her room. On a day like this I'm sure her windows must be open."

"Her room faces the south garden. She couldn't have witnessed a thing."

Jesse met my gaze and I gave a tiny shrug. When Aunt Alva dug in, nothing could persuade her to change her position. If Jesse wanted to question Consuelo, nothing short of a warrant would grant him access to her.

"I can attest to the fact that Consuelo was in her room immediately before we all went out to the pavilion," I said calmly. "And I'm equally sure she returned there after asking Mr. Grafton to call the police."

"What makes you so certain?" Dobbs's voice held a belligerent note.

"I know my cousin."

"All right, we'll let it drop," Jesse conceded. "For now." He perched at the edge of Uncle William's desk and crossed his arms over his chest. "Miss Parker, tell me about these footsteps you heard."

"Allegedly heard," Aunt Alva murmured. She seemed about to continue. I placed a hand over hers and shot her a warning look, which had the desired effect of silencing any further protests. Instead, she rolled her eyes at me.

Clara fidgeted with the edges of her pinafore,

ripping tiny threads from the hem. "I heard them as I came down the path. I looked around, but I didn't see anyone. Hardly surprising what with all the trees and hedges around the pavilion. Honestly I didn't think anything of it at the time. There's so many of us working here, it could have been anyone, or it could have been one of Mrs. Vanderbilt's guests."

"According to each of them," Officer Dobbs mumbled as if to himself, "they were together during the time of the crime. They're each other's alibis."

"Think, Clara." Jesse bent at the waist to peer into her face. Dobbs scratched away on his pad. "Were they heavy steps, like a man's? Or lighter, like a woman's?"

The maid scrunched up her forehead as she considered. She sniffed loudly and wiped the back of her hand across her nose. "I suppose . . . they were heavy. Could have been a man's. Except . . ."

"Except what, Clara?"

Officer Dobbs's rapid scratching paused and the room grew silent. Clara's head turned, her red-rimmed gaze landing on the sofa where Aunt Alva and I sat watching. Clara's arm came up and she pointed a shaking finger in our direction.

"Except it could have been a woman, if the woman were as stout as Mrs. Vanderbilt."

"Why, you!" Aunt Alva sprang to her feet. "How *dare* you, you little guttersnipe!"

Alarm sent me to my own feet, but Aunt Alva was too quick for me. Before I could speak up or reach for her, she was across the room, lifting Clara by the front of her dress, swinging one hand high in the air. . . .

I braced for the slap even as I scrambled after her. Jesse had better reflexes than I; a lengthy stride brought him to Aunt Alva, and he grasped her raised wrist at the same time he commanded, "Mrs. Vanderbilt, release Miss Parker this instant or I'll be forced to restrain you in a more permanent way."

The shock of being spoken to in such a manner proved more efficient than any physical force could have. Aunt Alva released her hold on Clara and swung about. "Restrain me? Restrain *me?*"

"Yes, Mrs. Vanderbilt, that is what I said," he replied mildly, his reserves of patience endless. He released her wrist.

On the other side of the desk, Anthony Dobbs held his pencil aloft and forgotten as he took in the scene. His heavy features filled with pure glee.

"There's your criminal." Aunt Alva gestured to Clara. "That's whom you need to restrain. Do you not know who I am? Do you not understand what I am capable of, young man? Do you wish to continue in your employment as a police officer, or would you prefer to sweep chimneys or muck stables?"

"Aunt Alva, please, Detective Whyte is simply doing his job. He can't allow you to attack Clara, or anyone else for that matter. And besides, Clara wasn't accusing you of anything. She was merely pointing out that . . ." Oh dear, how to put this delicately, especially with Aunt Alva's fuming wrath now aimed at me.

I swallowed audibly. I'd never seen her quite like this before. Oh, I'd seen her angry. I'd seen her railing at Uncle William, Consuelo, her younger brothers, the servants. . . . But just then, with the fury emanating from her like summer heat off a cobbled road, she did indeed seem capable of anything. Anything at all. Even, perhaps, with the right provocation, wrapping her hands around my neck.

I stepped back. Her last words to Madame Devereaux echoed inside me, sapping my body of warmth.

You will tell her the man you meant, the man who would only make her miserable, is Winthrop Rutherfurd, or you will be very, very sorry.

Some twenty minutes later, two uniformed policemen stepped into the room to report that all of the servants had been questioned, their statements taken, and each seemed to have been where he or she ought to have been at the time of the murder. In other words, they all had proper alibis.

"As well they should," Aunt Alva mumbled.

Again I reminded myself that each of her guests had attested to the same thing: They had been together in the gardens immediately before our sojourn to the pavilion. I'd heard Aunt Alva threatening, or seeming to threaten, Madame Devereaux through the open library windows, but could she have had time to follow the medium to the pavilion, strangle her, and take her place among her guests quickly enough that they hadn't noticed her absence?

It didn't seem likely, and the Vanderbilt part of me breathed a sigh of relief. Aunt Alva had her faults, but she was, after all, family.

The officers led a weeping Clara out of the house. No sooner had they left than another officer entered the room with Lady Amelia close behind him. "The coroner's finished for now, sir, and the body's being loaded into the wagon for transport into town," he told Jesse. He only then seemed to notice Aunt Alva and me in the room, and he cast us a sheepish look. "Beg pardon, ladies." He held out a hand from which dangled a red silk scarf. "Here's the murder weapon. This lady here says it belongs to her."

Lady Amelia stood with one hand pressing her bosom, the other dabbing a lace-edged handkerchief at her eyes. Yet when the delicate confection came away from her face, her cheeks were not mottled, nor were her eyes reddened. "This is most horrible." Her accent had become subtly more English since I'd seen her last. "I didn't recognize it when we first found the poor woman . . . well, I was distraught, of course. To think, that dreadful girl stole my scarf right out of my room and used it to . . . to . . ."

"We don't know that for certain yet," I told her. "Clara is innocent until proven guilty. Isn't that right, Jesse?"

"Bah!" Aunt Alva exclaimed at the same time Detective Dobbs snorted.

Jesse crossed the room to take the scarf from the policeman. He held it up, allowing it to unfurl to its full length, a good four feet. "Do you know when it went missing, Lady Amelia?"

Lifting her hems, she moved elegantly into the room, almost slinking, with the way her body swayed within the trim, tailored lines of her emerald gown.

Why hadn't I noticed it before? If Madame Devereaux had conducted herself with the practiced finesse of a stage performer, this woman did so to no less of an extent, though her mannerisms were of a different sort. Refined rather than theatrical, but no less affected.

I stored the impression away for later and concentrated on her reply.

"I couldn't tell you when it was taken," she said, reaching out to finger the end of the scarf trailing from Jesse's hand. "I hadn't had occasion to wear it since arriving at Marble House."

"Where had you kept it?" Jesse asked.

"In the clothespress in my dressing room. Where else would I keep it?"

"Did you put it there, or did your maid when she unpacked your belongings?"

Beneath a layer of powder, Lady Amelia's cheeks turned pink. She hesitated, her gaze flickering over my aunt and me in turn. Her chin came up. "I put it there myself."

Why so defensive? Before I could wonder, Jesse turned to Aunt Alva. "Was Clara serving as Lady Amelia's maid?"

Aunt Alva sounded almost surprised, as if something about those circumstances had only just struck her as strange. "She was, when I could spare her from her other duties."

"Then Clara had access to Lady Amelia's things." Jesse blew out a breath, and I realized that, like me, he very much hoped to find Clara innocent. He turned back to Lady Amelia. "I take it your own maid has been delayed in coming?"

"She is ill," the woman replied without missing a beat, then added, "poor dear."

"People get ill," Anthony Dobbs commented to no one in particular, as if summing up a conundrum. He shrugged his shoulders, closed his tablet, and got to his feet. "I think we've heard enough."

"You go ahead back to the station and write up the report," Jesse said to him. "I want to take another look at the pavilion."

Dobbs frowned. "We been through it already. So have the bluecoats. What else you expect to find?"

"Whatever we might have missed."

"Suit yourself." Dobbs headed for the door.

Jesse handed the murder weapon back to the policeman who had brought it in. "Bring this back to the station. I'll be along later."

"How you gonna get back, sir?"

Jesse glanced at me, and I nodded. "I'll get back," he told the officer. Then he nodded at Lady Amelia, bid Aunt Alva good day, glanced at me and gestured toward the door. "Emma, would you mind?"

We walked back out to the pavilion together.

"What *do* you hope to find?" I asked once we'd cleared the terrace steps. I felt eyes on our backs. Aunt Alva's, no doubt, but I judged that we had gone beyond her hearing.

"I'm not sure. Maybe nothing. But I want you there all the same."

I couldn't help smiling and uttering a quiet, "Thank you."

"This doesn't mean I want you getting involved. Not in any active way. But . . ." He sighed. "I can't deny that you've got the instincts of a real detective, Emma."

"Not to mention the brains?" I couldn't resist adding.

He nodded. "Yes, the brains, too. Absolutely."

The pavilion came into view through the hedges and my steps began to drag. Jesse stopped a few feet ahead of me and looked back. He studied me a moment before saying, "I'm sorry, Emma. What was I thinking? You shouldn't be out here."

"No . . . no, it's all right." I drew a deep breath and strode to where he waited for me. "I want to help. I have to, Jesse."

He smiled grimly. "Aunt Sadie?"

"In a way. She taught me to care about them. About everyone who has no voice. Girls like Clara. Like Katie, who used to work for my uncle Cornelius and lives with me now."

"You really think Clara's innocent?" We'd resumed walking again, side by side. Jesse offered me his arm, and I slipped my hand into the crook of his elbow. We continued in companionable silence until we reached the pavilion steps.

At the top, I answered his question. "I don't know for sure. It's just a feeling I have. When I look at her, with that delicate frame and those huge eyes of hers, I just don't see a murderer. Do you?"

"Oh, Emma, murderers look like all kinds of

people. If recent events have taught you anything, it should be that."

He referred to the case I'd helped solve, the murder my own brother had been accused of committing. In the end, the guilty party had been someone I'd never have suspected if I'd lived a thousand years. And yet, looking back, there *had* been signs. . . .

I turned away from him to glance around the pavilion. The card table still occupied the space at the center of the floor, and the crystal ball caught the rays of sunlight slanting beneath the roof and sent them dancing on the ceiling, floor, and columns. The coins had been scooped up, the cards removed. A light scent of incense, though long extinguished, still permeated the air. Better that than the scent of death, I thought morbidly.

I walked farther in, then stopped and turned. "So, what are we looking for that we haven't already noted?"

Jesse strode past me, circled the card table, and went to the far railing. He turned and stared at the pavilion entrance, then shifted his gaze closer, to the table. "Madame Devereaux sat there, waiting for Mrs. Vanderbilt and her guests. Tell me exactly what you saw, and what you think might have happened, Emma."

"Well . . ." I studied the table for a moment, picturing the scene as it had been earlier. "Actually, Madame Devereaux might not have been sitting and waiting. It makes more sense that she was busy preparing. Lighting the candles, the incense, placing everything just so. The scene was set when we arrived."

Jesse nodded. "Go on."

"If she sat, my guess is it was because someone had come asking about their future."

"Why do you say that?"

"Because of the cards and the coins. It looked as if she'd been in the middle of reading a fortune. And because . . ." I fell silent, trying to put my finger on why Madame Devereaux hadn't been surprised by her killer. Finally, it hit me. "The tablecloth. It wasn't askew or rumpled. It was just as it is now, except that Madame Devereaux had fallen over facedown on it. As if someone had placed her gently down."

"Someone who'd been standing behind her, perhaps?"

"Exactly."

"As you found Clara." This was not a question, but a statement of fact.

My shoulders slumped. "Yes, but . . ."

"Let's think this through." Jesse moved to stand behind the chair, just where Clara had. "Now, supposing you've just strangled the woman, and you hear someone coming. What would you do?"

His expression held knowledge of the answer, yet he waited for my hypothesis. I studied the artfully winding path leading from the gardens to the pavilion. I realized with a start that although the shadowy interior of the pavilion wouldn't be visible from the upper gardens because of the foliage, it was possible from this raised vantage point to catch flashes of anyone on their way down the path. If Clara had come from the house, her white pinafore and cap would have stood out against the greenery, visible to the killer in a succession of glimpses at each break in the hedges.

"He saw her coming," I murmured. Then, louder, I said, "He—or she—saw Clara coming down the path and made his escape."

Jesse was nodding. "My guess is our culprit went over the railing directly behind Madame Devereaux's chair, and then ran between the azalea hedges and through those trees." He pointed to a stand of dogwoods and graceful willows. He beckoned me beside him. "My colleagues have already noted the broken branches in the hedge. See?"

I went to the railing and peered out over the shady vista. The growth Jesse indicated stood twisted to awkward angles among the perfectly trimmed hedge, as if forcefully shoved aside and then allowed to fall haphazardly and brokenly back into place. "Did they find any torn fabric, or even threads, in the branches?"

"Unfortunately not," he replied. "Which in itself provides a clue. It tells us the person was wearing sturdy clothing."

"Not delicate silk or muslin," I said. "The footsteps Clara heard . . . By the time she reached the pavilion, he was well away, and Clara was too distraught over what she found to give those footsteps another thought."

I turned back to Jesse, reaching back to clutch the railing behind me. "The question is why?"

"Why was Madame Devereaux murdered?" Jesse sent me a warning glance. "Mind you, Emma, this is all speculation. We could be dead wrong, and Clara is guilty as sin."

"I doubt that very much. What reason could Clara Parker have to murder anyone? What would her motive be?"

"Fortune-tellers make enemies all the time. Clara might simply have managed to make it to the front of a long line of people waiting to wring Ellen Deere's neck."

"Ellen Deere! I heard that name spoken once before today. Mrs. Stanford said it when Madame Devereaux first arrived." The earlier incident flashed in my mind. "For an instant she looked furious . . . and so did Madame Devereaux, for that matter. But it was quick, and at the time I thought maybe I'd imagined it. Now, however . . . well. It certainly makes one think."

"Mrs. Stanford, you say?" When I nodded, Jesse raised his eyebrows. "Looks like I'll have to question Hope Stanford again, won't I?"

"Jesse . . ." I pushed away from the railing. "Did you know her?"

"The medium?" He looked down at his feet, smiling slightly. "Yes, I knew her. All of us on the force did, like we know *all* of Newport's more *interesting* entrepreneurs. She came down from Providence about two years ago—"

"Mrs. Stanford is from Providence," I said quickly.

"Yes, I know, Emma. That doesn't make her a murderer."

"Maybe not. But someone committed a murder here today, and I'd bet my best hatpin it wasn't Clara Parker."

CHAPTER 5

Jesse and I returned to the house, where he instructed Aunt Alva's guests not to leave Newport until further notice.

"Good heavens, are we suspects?" Roberta Spooner reached for her sister's hand and the two women drew together as though against a common enemy. Even Jesse's reassurances didn't smooth the alarm from their brows.

"No, no, it's merely a precaution, ladies. I might have more questions for you. But if you wish, the two of you may return to your own home."

"But you said not to leave Newport," the shorter, frailer-looking Edwina said. "And Sister and I live in Portsmouth. Though I must admit, it would be ever so comfortable to be amongst our own things. Not that it hasn't been splendid staying at Marble House, mind you," she added hastily with a startled glance at Aunt Alva. "Then again, perhaps *splendid* isn't quite the proper term under the circumstances."

"Oh, Edwina." Roberta slipped an arm around her sister's waist. "I'm sure Detective Whyte meant we're not to leave the island. Since Portsmouth is *on* the island, our going home shouldn't pose a problem. Isn't that correct, Mr. Whyte?"

Jesse seemed to be fighting a grin. "Quite right,

ladies. We'll know where to find you if we have further questions for you."

Hope Stanford brushed off the sisters' concerns. "I for one have no intentions of running off. I've got important business in Newport and I'm not about to let a little thing like a murder deter me one bit."

A *little* thing like a murder? I bit my tongue to keep from retorting. Instead, I said, "I'll drive you back to town now, if you like, Jesse."

Downstairs in the main hall, he drew me aside, out of the hearing of the footman attending the front door. The ladies had all retired to their guest rooms. I assumed Aunt Alva had likewise gone to her room, or perhaps she was with Consuelo. The house had grown quiet, and Jesse spoke just above a whisper. "Would you mind if I borrowed your carriage to get back to town? I can have it returned to you in an hour or two."

"Well, yes, but why go to the trouble of having someone return it when I can take you?"

"Because I want you to stay here, Emma." His voice dropped lower. The clinking of someone putting away china in the serving pantry drifted from across the large expanse of the dining room. The footman standing by the door looked straight ahead. We might have been invisible for all he registered our presence, but for a slight pricking of his ears.

Jesse ran a hand through his bright auburn hair

and flicked a glance to the top of the staircase. "I'd like you to talk to your cousin and ask her the questions I can't. Would you do that, Emma?"

I couldn't help chuckling. "Do you really think I have more authority over my aunt than you do? After all, you have the law on your side."

"Challenging Alva Vanderbilt is not worth the trouble that would inevitably follow. But you're Miss Vanderbilt's friend as well as her cousin. Will you please talk to her for me, and let me know what she says?"

The word *friend* pricked my conscience, but I said, "Of course I will. I'll go up and see her now, and I'll call you later from home if there's anything you need to know." I grinned. "That's if I'm allowed to go home. I'm not under house arrest here, am I?"

"As if you would stay put if you were." He smiled ruefully, then took my hand. "Thank you, Emma."

"You're welcome. I'll talk to you later."

He nodded and continued holding my hand a moment too long, long enough to become more than a friendly gesture. This wasn't the first time he'd made such an overture, albeit a subtle one, and now, as then, a sense of awkwardness flooded me. Gently I slid my hand free, careful to keep a smile on my face as if nothing out of the ordinary had occurred. As if I hadn't just glimpsed a bit of Jesse Whyte's heart.

Despite an age difference of some dozen years, he and I would surely have made sense—so much more sense than Derrick Andrews and I ever could. Not only were we both Newporters born and bred, we hailed from the same Point community, whose inhabitants were probably the saltiest and most straightforward of all Newporters. He and I understood each other. . . .

Jesse was my father's friend as well as Brady's, and to me he'd always been like an older brother. Could there be more between us? Suddenly his image faded in my mind's eye while another formed, Jesse's straight auburn hair darkening to wavy brown, his boyish features strengthening to a square jaw and chiseled profile.

Derrick. Had it been only that morning I'd sent him packing, as they say? After all that had happened in the hours since, it seemed like years ago. Yet it was too soon—far too soon to even consider another. Jesse was my friend, and I was grateful for that friendship, but for now, at least, there could not be more.

As if he read my thoughts, his smile turned wistful, then sad. He left and the footman closed the door behind him. The servant was new to the household and I didn't know his name; but even if I had, my throat had closed and my tongue ran too dry to allow speech. I wandered into the Gold Room, where the events of this dreadful day had begun, and where I stood leaning with my back against the wall to regain my equilibrium.

Good grief, that made two men in one day I'd sent away disappointed—on top of everything else. Feeling wretched and drained, I pushed away from the wall and made my way up the stairs.

Outside Consuelo's room I tapped my knuckles lightly on the door. No answer came, so I tried again. Finally, I turned the knob and poked my head inside. Consuelo's bed lay empty, as did the bedside chaise. A quick glance around the room failed to reveal my cousin. Was she in the dressing room?

"Consuelo? Are you here?" I ventured a few feet inside. "Darling, it's me . . . Emma."

Silence.

"Consuelo?" Unease churned inside me. Something felt utterly, entirely wrong about this empty room.

Hurrying down the corridor, I pressed my ear to her mother's door. The silence within sent me on to the next bedroom, this one draped in rich greens and burgundies—my uncle William's former suite. Somehow I could picture my cousin seeking solace among her father's things. The door was open and I came to an abrupt halt on the threshold. "Consuelo, are you in here?"

When no answer came I strode through into the dressing room, but it, too, stood empty. I doubled back, following the zigzagging hallway past the large front bedroom currently occupied by Lady

Amelia, reserved for her due to her rank as an aristocrat. Here the hall turned and led to a small sewing room. I barged in, panting, but found no one inside. My concerns spiraled, though I couldn't quite say why. This was a large house and while my cousin might have been under house arrest of sorts, she was certainly allowed to wander where she wished. The library? But Jesse and I had been standing in the main hall and we never saw her come down the stairs.

It was then I realized that in all the uproar of finding Madame Devereaux, of Clara appearing to be the guilty party, and the police arriving and questioning the rest of us, no one had spared a thought about Consuelo's welfare. No one had questioned how badly the day's events might have upset her. No one thought to check on her after we all returned to the house. We had simply assumed she'd seen little or nothing at the pavilion and had returned to find comfort in her dolls and books and the many luxuries to be found in her bedroom.

But I, better than most, knew how little comfort Consuelo gleaned from that room, from this house, and how terribly sensitive she was, though she struggled always to conceal it.

So then, if her room brought her neither cheer nor reassurance, where would she go?

"Consuelo?" I called out, the inexplicable panic now rising in my throat.

A door opened and Lady Amelia swept into the hallway. "Is something wrong, Miss Cross?"

She looked annoyed; I had apparently disturbed her rest. I also noticed her accent had diminished once again. "Have you seen my cousin?"

"Miss Consuelo?"

"Yes," I almost snapped in my impatience. "Since her brothers are away, there is only one person in this house I'd refer to as my cousin."

She smoothed a hand down one side of her beautiful emerald gown, from ribs to hip. "I haven't seen her since . . . you know."

I released a breath and rushed past her. As I reached the staircase landing, Aunt Alva came out of her room. "What is going on? Is that you I hear caterwauling through the house? Really, Emmaline, a lady—"

"Where is Consuelo?" I asked over her admonishment.

That cut her off short. She blinked. "In her room. Where else?"

"No, she isn't."

For a full moment Aunt Alva stared back at me, looking nonplussed. Then her face cleared. "Downstairs, then. She probably wanted a book."

"I think we had better see." I hefted my hems and hurried down, hoping, yet doubting, we'd find Consuelo in the library. Aunt Alva's footsteps followed heavily in my wake, making me remember what Clara had said earlier.

It could have been a woman, if the woman were as stout as Mrs. Vanderbilt.

I wiped the thought from my mind and concentrated on finding Consuelo. My own thudding footsteps echoed off the glass-fronted bookshelves in the library; there was no sign of Consuelo. Then Aunt Alva brushed past me on her way to the rear-facing windows; she braced her hands on the sill and peered out. "She's not on the terrace either."

With a look of determination that bordered on anger, she fisted her hand around the bellpull in the corner and gave an aggressive tug, leaving the tasseled length of embroidered brocade to swing vigorously as she rounded on me.

"How long has my daughter been missing, and when were you planning to inform me?"

I raised my eyebrows in a show of wounded dignity. "I didn't know she was missing—I still don't. But I am concerned about her. I think we should search—"

Grafton walked sedately into the room and tipped a bow. "Ma'am?"

"Were you below stairs just now?"

"I was, ma'am."

"Did you see my daughter down there?"

I expected him to look mystified; instead, he appeared to try to hide a guilty look that admitted Consuelo did occasionally seek out the servants' domains in order to escape the oppression of living in this echoing, shadowy house, always under her mother's thumb. "No, ma'am. I haven't seen Miss Consuelo since tea on the terrace."

Aunt Alva tapped her forefinger against her chin. Then she said, "I want the house searched, Grafton." With a brisk nod he started to turn away. "Grafton!"

He turned back.

"I want the house searched by you alone. Tell no one what you're doing. Go through each room, including the attic, until you find my daughter. Then bring her here to me."

His expression never changed. "Yes, ma'am."

"When I get my hands on that girl . . ."

"Aunt Alva!"

As if she'd forgotten my presence, she jumped at the sound of my voice, then scowled. I pushed on anyway.

"Don't you think perhaps a lighter touch with Consuelo might be in order? It's been a horrendous day and she was already upset before it even began."

"Do not presume to tell me how to raise my daughter." She seemed to bring me into focus as if through the crosshairs on a rifle. "Did you manage to convince her to marry the Duke?"

I stared down at my feet. "I believe I did, though I'm not proud of it."

"Good." Her smile held relief but little warmth. "Now if we can just clean up this mess before

95

he arrives. If we're lucky, he'll never hear of it."

My mouth dropped open. "Is that what you're worried about? Need I remind you a woman is dead? Another is in grave danger of spending the rest of her life in prison. And at the moment your daughter is nowhere to be found."

"Oh, Emmaline." She waved a hand in the air, a dismissive gesture that so infuriated me my pulse pounded and spots danced before my eyes. "Consuelo is playing a little game for attention. All right, I'll give her some attention. I suppose you're right in that I should look upon her antics with a bit of tolerance and show her that Mama is not the ogre she likes to believe I am." Here the light in her eyes became fierce, searing in its intensity. "But as for what happened here today, it has nothing to do with me, and nothing to do with my daughter."

"It happened on your property."

"An unhappy coincidence. I'm sorry a woman died, Emmaline, truly I am, but it's simply not my business. Nor yours, if you're wise."

"I'm sorry, ma'am," Grafton said an hour later, "but Miss Consuelo does not appear to be anywhere in the house."

"Nor in the stables or the gardens or anywhere else I can think of," I added as I strode into Aunt Alva's private sitting room on the second floor. "I even checked the Cliff Walk."

"She'd never go there," Aunt Alva said absently, as if other thoughts held her attention. "She's terrified of heights." She stood up from her writing desk, where she'd been writing some sort of list, and went to gaze out the window at the rear of the property. The tops of meticulously pruned trees swayed beyond the open casement, and a raucous squawking of seagulls carried on the breeze. "What is that child up to?"

"Aunt Alva," I said to her back, "I think it's time to resummon the police."

She whirled. "Are you mad?" Her gaze flicked to the butler, still hovering a few feet from the escritoire. "That will be all, thank you, Grafton. Say nothing to anyone and should you discover my daughter . . ."

"I'll escort her to you, madam."

Aunt Alva followed him as far as the door, which she shut firmly behind him before turning back to me. "You are not to speak of calling the police, Emmaline."

"But if Consuelo is missing—"

"Oh, she is not *missing*. The very idea. If she's gone, it's because she stole the opportunity of today's distraction to slip out without my noticing."

"I hardly think Consuelo would be so scheming. It's not like her—"

"She's gone to one of her friends' homes, I'm sure of it. Why, she's probably sipping tea this very moment with May Goelet or Carrie Astor or . . . let's see . . . are the Oelrichses in town this summer?"

"And if she's not with May or Carrie or Blanche," I persisted. "What then?"

Aunt Alva's dark eyes went wide. "Good grief, you don't think she's . . . she's . . ."

"She's what?"

"With Winthrop Rutherfurd? What if . . . what if they've eloped? Oh, dear gracious heavens, Emmaline, we've got to find them. We've got to stop them!"

She started for the door, but I stepped in front of her and gripped her shoulders. "Don't you think you're jumping to conclusions? We have no reason to believe . . ." I trailed off, releasing my hold on my aunt.

"What are you thinking?" she demanded. Suspicion narrowed her eyes. "Do you know something?"

"No, but I might."

Hurrying down the corridor, I returned to Consuelo's bedroom. Nothing seemed disturbed since I'd been there earlier, no signs of sudden flight. I went into the dressing room. Again, nothing seemed rummaged through, no drawers gaped half open, and upon opening the wardrobe, I saw that all looked as neat as a pin. There were no signs that Consuelo had run upstairs during the chaos of the murder and packed a bag.

I went back out to the main room and yes, even

her diary sat where she had left it that morning, when I'd interrupted her writing. Why would she have left it behind? Two possibilities presented themselves to me. Either someone had snatched her from the property against her will, or she had left on her own but impulsively, perhaps even blindly. Had she been desperate enough to do so?

I snatched the tome from the bedside table, but then I hesitated. Did I have the right, under *any* circumstances, to read my cousin's private thoughts? Was I once again betraying her confidence? Oh, but if I could forestall her making a grievous mistake . . .

Knowing I might be partially responsible if Consuelo had done anything drastic, I flipped the book open to the last place she had penned her innermost thoughts, the page marked with a satin ribbon, and read:

> Mama refuses to take me seriously. This horrible house is more important to her than I am. I won't be sad to leave it, or her, but despite what I told Emma earlier, I tremble at the thought of how Mama has planned out my life for me. I feel so alone, so desperate. I feel as though I'm screaming and no one hears me—

Here a blotchy stain blurred the words. My own eyes stung. Had I believed my meddling had helped earlier today? Had I thought I'd helped my cousin face her future with a bit more courage? I'd only fooled myself into thinking so because I couldn't bear the truth—the truth Consuelo felt she could impart to no one but the cool, white pages of her journal. Apparently, I'd placed a sorry second when it came to confidantes. But there was more, and I read on.

My cousin Emma tells me I am strong and intelligent, and that I shall prevail. I'm not quite sure how, but she tells me also that I must let people know that I am a force to be reckoned with. That I must soldier on, map my battleground and discover a way to be happy. I think what that all means is I must now take matters into my own hands. Go where I want. Take what I want. Live how I want. I believe she is right. I—

"Well, Emmaline?"

Startled, I snapped the diary closed and looked up to see Aunt Alva poised in the doorway. "What?" I said stupidly, trying to blink away the guilt I was sure blazed in my eyes. Good heavens, not only had I *not* made things better with my interference, I'd made them much, much worse. If Consuelo had run off somewhere, it was only because of what I'd said to her and my foolish notions of courage.

Could she have run off to elope with Winthrop Rutherfurd?

"Did she leave us any hints in that ridiculous book of hers?"

"I . . . ah . . . no." It wasn't a lie. Consuelo hadn't left so much as an inkling of where she might have gone, or with whom. But as the seconds ticked past, I became more and more convinced that she had, indeed, gone.

And then I realized why her bedroom felt so completely empty.

Muffy was gone. Perhaps Consuelo had been in too much of a rush to grab her diary, but she would never abandon her cat. . . .

"You have to find her, Emmaline. That's all there is to it."

"Aunt Alva, surely this is a matter for the police—"

"If you say that one more time, Emmaline, I swear I'll scream. The police cannot be involved. Can you imagine the scandal? And with the Duke due to arrive within the next two weeks?" Her fist flew to press her chest just below her collarbone. Her breath rasped in and panted out in such rapid succession I became alarmed and went to her.

"You'll faint if you don't calm down."

She grasped my wrist and squeezed like an iron vise, until I began to fear the bones would snap. "She is with one of her friends, Emmaline. She must be. And you must find her. Don't go telling me you can't. You were the one who discovered who murdered my brother-in-law's financial secretary. Surely you can discover the whereabouts of one silly girl."

Her intensity frightened me. And she was hurting me. "Yes, all right. I'll find her, Aunt Alva. Just let me go before you break my wrist, please."

"Oh." She looked down, saw how her fingers were trembling because of how tightly she held me, and immediately let go. "Sorry. I think you should try Ochre Court first; she's very probably with May Goelet. Or . . . Let's see, where else would she go?"

Her eyes closed and a little groan escaped her. With one arm clamped around her middle, she made her way back to the chaise and sank onto the cushions. For a moment I feared she'd be ill.

"Aunt Alva?" I knelt beside her and reached up to put an arm around her shoulders.

"Oh, Emmaline, if she's eloped with Winthrop Rutherfurd it'll be the end of the world."

"That's a rather extreme outlook, don't you think?"

"After all the care I took in raising her," she lamented as if I hadn't spoken. "All the planning I've done. She's meant for better things than being the wife of some obscure New York fop."

"The Rutherfurds are hardly obscure."

Her eyes opened and she treated me to one of her quelling glares. "That's not the point."

"No, I suppose not." I stood. "I'll call on the Astors and the Goelets on my way home. I'll check with cousin Gertrude, too."

"Home? Emmaline, there isn't time to go home. You must find her immediately and—"

"If I've learned anything, it's never to underestimate the power of the servants' rumor mill. I would never have discovered who killed Alvin Goddard if it hadn't been for Nanny's help. She has ways of sweeping hidden little details out into the open. We need her in this, Aunt Alva."

"She'll be discreet?"

I wanted to shake sense into the woman. What was more important, her daughter's life or some silly reputation?

But I knew the answer. In Alva Vanderbilt's world, a woman's reputation was everything, every bit a commodity as the empires their men controlled. Oh, there were limits for every woman from every rung of society, but for most of us it was nearly impossible to imagine how much harm even a breath of scandal could do to a young woman like Consuelo. In my aunt's eyes, her daughter would be better off dead than with a tarnished reputation.

That made me immeasurably sad.

It was on the ride home that a thought struck me. That last conversation with Aunt Alva kept

103

playing over in my mind, until I suddenly stopped my aging hack short.

"Barney," I said out loud for no other reason than that sometimes voicing a thought helped me judge its validity, "you don't suppose . . . No, never mind." I shook my head and was about to cluck my tongue to the horse. His ears twitched in my direction for the signal to resume our trek home. But I hesitated, my mouth slightly open.

"Would Aunt Alva stoop so low?" I whispered to the gathering afternoon shadows.

Was it possible she knew exactly where Consuelo was, and Aunt Alva's distress was nothing more than a ruse to distract . . . me? Beneath the trees in the quiet of Bellevue Avenue, near the bend where that grand street turned onto Ocean Avenue, I began ticking off the facts one by one, to the rhythm of the ocean waves at nearby Bailey's Beach.

Four suffragettes currently inhabited Marble House; five if you counted Aunt Alva.

Consuelo faced an unwanted marriage and virtually choked on the irony that her mother's bullheaded independence would never extend to her daughter.

Aunt Alva had orchestrated today's so-called entertainment with Madame Devereaux in an effort to persuade Consuelo to cooperate. But in this instance, it was the medium herself who balked at cooperating. Who had outright told

Consuelo she'd never be happy if she married *him.*

Madame Devereaux was dead, and Consuelo was missing. The two incidents couldn't be a coincidence, and the sudden, sickening question was, would Aunt Alva resort to murder and then kidnap her own daughter to avoid letting Consuelo's future slip through her fingers? And setting me on Consuelo's trail? Well, wouldn't that distract me from discovering the truth?

"Oh, Barney, tell me this can't be true. Tell me I'm jumping to conclusions."

But that loyal old soul simply gave his head an impatient shake to let me know he was tired, hungry, and wanted a brisk brushing down. I clucked to set him back in motion. I needed Nanny and Brady to help me sort out my suspicions and approach the matter with a clear perspective. Furthermore, I needed Nanny to work her magic among her well-placed connections in Newport. If so much as a breath of a hint existed as to where Consuelo might be hiding—or was hidden against her will—Nanny would get wind of it, eventually.

CHAPTER 6

"What do you think?" I asked my little family back at home once I'd filled them in on the details of that harrowing morning.

Saying nothing, Nanny pursed her lips and reached for the teapot. When I arrived some half hour ago, feeling and probably looking battered after my day at Marble House, she, Brady, and I had gathered around the morning-room table for sandwiches and a pot of strong Irish tea that Katie had brewed for us. And dare I confess each time Nanny poured a cup she also trickled in a tiny bit of the spirits, just to shore up the constitution.

Brady cradled his cup in his palms and leaned back in his chair. "Alva Vanderbilt is no murderer. The old girl doesn't have it in her, Em. If I'm certain of anything, it's that."

"But that temper of hers," I reminded him. "We've all seen it. Goodness, just about *everyone* has seen it at one time or another."

"All bluster," he replied with a quirk of his lips.

"I think so, too," Nanny said. "As far as murder goes. But as for her possibly using that poor woman's death to hide her daughter away . . . well. Can't say as I'd put it past her."

"Then again . . ." I watched the thin stream of whiskey make its way into my tea before Nanny handed me the refilled cup. "Alva was with the rest of us the entire time. It was Consuelo who slipped away, supposedly to her room."

"Alva might have had a servant do her dirty work," Brady said, "to steal Consuelo away."

I shook my head. "I doubt she'd trust any of them enough."

Nanny's eyebrows went up. "How about the butler?"

"Grafton? Alva had him search the house for Consuelo—" I broke off, and the other two studied me with burgeoning "aha" expressions.

Brady nodded. "Bet he didn't find a thing, did he?"

"No, he didn't," I conceded. "Or at least he said he didn't."

"Mm-hmm." It was Nanny's turn to nod knowingly. "But if Consuelo was there, my guess is she's gone now to who only knows where." She reached for the whiskey again. I shot her a glance. She returned it with an unapologetic narrowing of her eyes. "Are you going to play mother with me now, Emma?"

"I wouldn't dream of it." And really, it wasn't Nanny fogging her mind I worried about. I'd never in my entire life seen her tipsy, except, of course, each Christmas Eve, but that was a mellow, contented form of tipsy where she sat in her favorite overstuffed chair and smilingly contemplated the Yule log. No, Nanny often suffered from dyspepsia and I feared the strong liquor might exacerbate her condition. She wasn't a young woman. I didn't want her doing anything that might shorten the time we had together. "Whether Alva is behind it or not," I said, "you're probably right that Consuelo is no longer at Marble House. But where would a girl like Consuelo Vanderbilt hide?"

"She's much too beautiful to simply 'blend in' anywhere," said Brady. "Or for that matter, to travel anywhere unless someone put a bag over her head. Even if she managed to cross the harbor without being noticed, somewhere along the line someone would recognize her. And then we'd hear about it."

"So she's most likely somewhere on the island." The thought raised my hopes. If Consuelo was somewhere on Aquidneck Island, chances were I'd find her eventually. I leveled my gaze on Nanny. "Can you alert the network?"

She gave me one of her shrewd little grins.

"But . . ." I placed my hand over hers where it lay on the tablecloth. "We need the utmost discretion. You can only share this with friends you trust absolutely."

"That does narrow down the field quite a bit," she said with a sigh. "But I believe I might be able to tap into a few prudent, well-placed sources of information."

"Good. Thank you, Nanny. Brady, if you think

of anything that might help, or hear anything, you'll let me know, yes?"

"Of course. And exactly what are you going to do, little sister?"

"I've got several important social calls to make. But first I've got an article to write and deliver. I'll be hanged if I let Ed Billings steal a byline from me again."

Oh, yes, I'd written up a brilliant article only two weeks ago after a body had literally fallen at my feet during my cousin Gertrude's coming-out ball at The Breakers. Eagerly I'd brought my article to my employer at the Newport *Observer*, confident in having reported the facts exactly as they happened, without the taint of sensationalism. What did Mr. Millford do? He literally patted me on the head and advised me to stick with the society page. Then he proceeded to publish Ed Billings's ridiculous ramblings about events he hadn't witnessed.

The injustice rankled.

The unfairness continued to fester the next day when, upon seizing the morning's *Observer* from my front stoop, I saw that no headline peered up at me from the front page. I scanned the main articles again before running to the morning room, where I spread the paper out on the table and began flipping through the pages.

Nothing. Not even another byline stolen by Ed.

There was simply no article relating to Madame Devereaux's murder.

Well, I'd see about that. But first, of course, there were obligations to be met. Despite Aunt Alva's impatience, I didn't begin actively searching for Consuelo until later that morning. Midmorning, to be exact, when I knew I'd catch everyone on my list at home and unawares. The wealthy never stirred from the comforts of their "summer cottages" before noon, nor did they expect to be disturbed before that hour. Yet the ocean air would surely prod them from their beds much earlier than they typically rose, and I'd likely find Consuelo's friends wrapped in silken dressing gowns enjoying tea and scones from the comfort of cushioned lounge chairs placed just so on their wide verandas facing the sea.

Putting my frustrations about my missing article on a backburner, I knocked first on the door of Winthrop Rutherfurd. From Consuelo I already knew he was spending the summer in one of the older, shingle-style homes on a shady side street off the west side of Bellevue Avenue—not a mansion, no ocean view, but fashionable enough for a single man. For propriety's sake, Katie stood beside me, so his neighbors wouldn't gossip about how that poor Vanderbilt relation visited Mr. Rutherfurd alone. I was about to tap the knocker again when Winty, as Consuelo called him, surprised me by opening the door himself.

He squinted out at me, recognition slowly dawning. Winthrop was not a young man; in fact, he was at least a decade older than I. He was, however, a trim man, tall and athletic-looking, his hair dark and full, though typically worn slicked tightly back. Invested in his family's New York real-estate concerns, Winty had money of his own, though not in the sort of heaping abundance Aunt Alva deemed necessary in a suitor.

With the morning sunlight slanting across his features, he looked even older than usual, or perhaps a late night had deepened the creases across his brow and beside his eyes. I wondered what—or who—might have kept him up.

"Miss . . . Cross, I believe? To what do I owe the pleasure?" His expression didn't register pleasure, only perplexity.

I wasted no time with niceties. "May I come in, Mr. Rutherfurd?"

"I . . . uh . . . I suppose . . ." He gave his lightweight morning coat a dignified tug as he stepped back from the threshold. Katie and I stepped into a dim foyer, made all the darker by the brown and beige pattern of the wallpaper.

"Is there somewhere we can talk privately?" I asked, my bluntness obviously taking him aback once more.

He glanced around at the various doorways opening into the foyer, then seemed to settle on a direction. "Follow me."

Katie moved to trail me, but I gestured for her to wait by the door. I trusted my maid, in my employ since the spring, to a point, and I felt not only protectiveness, but a sincere fondness for her. But I had to admit the young Irishwoman possessed a nervous constitution and could be something of a chatterbox. I couldn't take the chance of her blurting private information to the greengrocer, the butcher's wife—or whomever else.

I followed Winty across a parlor furnished in rich leather and through another doorway that led down a narrow passage. A wary tingle grazed my back—where was he taking me? But finally we entered a morning room much like my own, with sturdy oak furniture and a homey, informal air. We were no longer alone; a footman busily gathered plates from a sideboard and voices drifted from an open door through which I glimpsed a service pantry.

Good. Though my fears were certainly unfounded, a woman had been murdered yesterday, and until the murderer was apprehended I shouldn't fully trust anyone.

"Please have a seat, Miss Cross." Winty pulled out a chair for me at the table. "I'd just finished my breakfast when you knocked, but may I offer you some coffee or tea?"

The footman stopped midway to the pantry, the stack of plates balanced precariously in his hands.

When I shook my head and said no thank you, the young man nodded and continued on his way. Winty sat at his own place, where the morning issue of the Newport *Daily News* blazed a headline up at me.

MURDER AT MARBLE HOUSE!

A part of me selfishly wished Winty subscribed to the Newport *Observer* instead, and that it was my article splashed across the page. I still didn't understand it. I'd rushed into town yesterday evening to deliver my account of the murder before the presses stopped for the night. For once I'd beaten Ed Billings at his own game, and Mr. Millford, the owner and editor-in-chief of the *Observer*, had assured me my article would run in the morning's edition.

"Nasty business, that," Winty said, pointing at the paper. The comment roused me from my ambitions. "Poor Consuelo—uh, Miss Vanderbilt. Tell me, how is she taking it? Is she very distraught?"

He sounded sincerely worried about my cousin, although who knew how accomplished an actor he might be? "Have you spoken with my cousin recently?" I asked.

He blinked and then raised his eyebrows. "No, how could I?"

I ignored his question and asked another.

"You're quite sure you had no word from her yesterday?"

"I wish I had, Miss Cross. Maybe I could have comforted her. I've been trying to speak with Consuelo ever since she arrived in Newport, but that wooly mammoth of a mother of hers won't let me anywhere near her. Not in person and not by telephone."

I'd never heard Aunt Alva described in quite those words and, despite the seriousness of my visit, I stifled a snort of laughter. "So you've had no communication with Consuelo all summer?"

"Well, I wouldn't exactly say that. There was the Astors' ball last month. We were both there, and when her mama wasn't looking we managed to exchange a few words. Someone obviously saw us, though, and reported back to Mrs. Vanderbilt."

"So that's why my aunt had Consuelo virtually under lock and key in recent weeks."

His gaze swept over me before connecting with my own. "What is this all about, Miss Cross? I understand Consuelo must be terribly upset over what happened in her gardens yesterday, but why are you *here?*" His eyes sparked with alarm. "Has something happened to Consuelo?"

"That's what I'm trying to find out."

"Miss Cross, I wish you'd stop speaking in riddles."

"But that's precisely what this is, Mr. Rutherfurd.

A riddle." I paused to choose my words carefully. "You see, Consuelo isn't . . . presently at home. I don't know where she is—"

"And neither does her mother, does she?" I expected an ironic smile; instead, lines of concern aged his face beyond his thirty-odd years. "This isn't like Consuelo, not like her at all. She doesn't do things like this, doesn't rebel or run off in fits of temper. Or fits of anxiety. Dear heavens . . ." A waxy pallor suddenly replaced his outdoorsy complexion. "Do you think whoever murdered that woman . . . but no, the maid did it, didn't she? And she was caught red-handed. Surely the woman couldn't have had time to strike twice. . . ."

I cut his outburst short. "Is she here?"

"I—what? Who?"

"Consuelo, Mr. Rutherfurd. Is she here?" I ground out each impatient word from between my clenched teeth.

Winty's palm slapped the table in a way that had me wishing for the reappearance of his footman or a maid or anyone else. "How *dare* you imply such a thing, Miss Cross?"

His anger all but shuddered in the air between us. I drew back in my seat, but I forced myself not to look away. "I am not implying anything, Mr. Rutherfurd. I'm merely asking a direct question. You did ask me to stop speaking in riddles."

His nostrils flared. "That was no simple

question, Miss Cross. You're practically accusing me of . . . of stealing Consuelo away from her home and hiding her here."

My hands balled into fists around the purse strings in my lap. "Did you?"

Winty sprang to his feet. "I most assuredly did not. Do you honestly believe I'd play with her reputation in such a dastardly way? The woman I lo—"

He broke off, but I heard his unspoken sentiment. The woman he loved. "All the more reason to steal her away from her impending marriage. An *unwanted* marriage."

"I'm afraid it's time for you to leave, Miss Cross."

I came to my feet but refused to budge any further. How I managed such audacity I couldn't say. Instinct forced from me words and actions I'd never have been capable of under normal circumstances. But just as when Brady had been accused of murder and my faith in his innocence compelled me to hazard any risk to clear his name, so did my concerns for my cousin's life prompt me to defy a man in his own home.

"If Consuelo truly isn't here," I said calmly, "then you shouldn't mind if I take a look about."

"You may not, Miss Cross," he said in a tone that brooked no debate. He worked his jaw from side to side. His gaze swept to the servants' doorway, then back to me. When he spoke again, his voice was less stern, but adamant. "You'll have to take my word for it that your cousin isn't here, nor have I seen her since the Astors' ball last month, except now and again from a distance as we happened to pass each other in town. As for searching my house"—he drew in an audible breath and smiled grimly—"how dare you insult me, Miss Cross. You have all but called me a liar."

"I'm sorry, but my cousin's life is at stake," I began, but before the words were fully out of my mouth, the servants' door swung inward, as if the footman who appeared on the threshold had answered Winty's silent call of a moment ago.

He bobbed a deferential greeting to his employer. "Will you be wanting the lamps in your study lit now, sir?"

"Yes, Davis, thank you. On your way, please see Miss Cross out." With that, Winty sank back into his chair and lifted his newspaper, giving it a brisk snap before hiding his face behind it. "Good day, Miss Cross."

I briefly considered trying to question the footman once we were out of Winty's hearing, but I conceded to the unlikelihood of his answering at all, much less telling me anything I wanted to know. Was Winty hiding Consuelo, or had his refusal to allow me the run of his house stemmed from some other matter of which he preferred I remained ignorant? Consuelo's erstwhile beau might very well have something to hide, but the question persisted as to what.

But if young Davis, the footman, possessed any knowledge of my cousin, it was far more likely I'd hear about it in the roundabout way, once the information traveled through Newport's network of servants and reached Nanny's ear. With little other recourse, then, I trailed the young man through the house until he summarily deposited both me and a bemused-looking Katie on the front stoop, bid us a terse good day, and shut the door behind us.

My next stop brought me to The Breakers. Halfway up the sweeping drive, I brought my rig to a halt and sat staring up at the palatial mansion, newly rebuilt to withstand fire and any other catastrophe nature might conjure. I fully believed those solid stone walls could withstand even the power of the nearby ocean. Yet a sense of irony filled me. With all their vast stores of wealth, my Vanderbilt relations could protect themselves from only so much, could keep the ugliness of the outside world at bay for only so long.

My own brother, Brady, had been accused of committing a murder in this very house only a few short weeks ago. As those awful memories filtered through my mind, my gaze drifted to the balcony where a man had been pushed to his death—to land at my feet. And now here I was, so soon after one horrific experience, entangled in yet another murder involving my Vanderbilt relatives. A dreadful coincidence?

Sitting on the seat beside me, Katie shifted and adjusted the brim of her squat straw hat. "Is something wrong, miss?"

I blinked, not having realized how long I'd sat staring. "Oh, Katie. Is there some kind of curse hanging over the Vanderbilt family? How can this be happening all over again?"

She patted my wrist. "If it means anything, miss, I don't believe in curses, though my granny Norah back in Killarney would call me daft. The Vanderbilts are havin' a bad run o' luck is all."

"To say the least." An unsavory thought struck me. "I was in the vicinity of both murders. I hope I'm not some kind of jinx."

"You, miss? Never have I heard such nonsense. Why, you saved me last spring when I was in the family way, sacked from my job, and had nowhere to turn. And you saved your brother when he might have been hanged for a murderer. I just know you're goin' to find Miss Consuelo and you're goin' to save her, too, in whatever way she needs savin'." Katie gripped my hand and squeezed; her eyes shone bright against her fair, freckled complexion. "Because that's the kind of person you are. You don't let others suffer an injustice if you can do aught about it. So no more talk of jinxes, miss. I won't be hearin' another word about it."

I regarded her in astonishment. Though a case of nerves might bring on a slew of chatter, my otherwise shy housemaid had never strung together so many eloquent words at one time in all the weeks she had been working for me. And because of that—and because the words had come out calmly and deliberately—I knew she meant every one and hadn't merely said them in an attempt to placate her employer.

In short, she'd spoken as a friend. And as a friend, I slipped my hand free of hers and reached my arms around her. After a moment's hesitation she hugged me equally tight, and we rocked gently side to side like two sisters, or how I imagined sisters could sometimes be.

"Thank you, Katie," I whispered through the curling tendrils of her fiery red hair. "That was quite the nicest thing anyone has said to me in the longest while."

"It's all true, miss."

With a cluck I set Barney walking again. We drew up beside the front portico and immediately the main door opened. Beside me Katie stiffened, but I was quick to reassure her. "You can wait for me here. I'll tell the footman he needn't bother with the carriage."

She wilted slightly in relief. It had been here at The Breakers last spring, when a visiting youth, a friend of my cousin Reggie's, had first seduced and then forced himself on Katie, resulting in her pregnancy and dismissal from her job. With no references, no family in this country, and no prospects of any sort, she had shown up on my doorstep, because when my aunt Sadie had been alive, Gull Manor had become known as a haven for young women in trouble.

I did what I could to keep Aunt Sadie's legacy alive.

Katie had lost her baby one awful night, but she had never quite lost her fear of this house or the people in it, who had shown her so little compassion when she needed it most. I wasn't always proud of my relatives.

So while she waited huddled against the squabs of the carriage, I hurried inside and searched for my cousin Gertrude. There was no one else here who might have heard from Consuelo, and though her having contacted Gertrude was unlikely, I couldn't yet rule out the possibility.

"Good morning, Parker," I said to the young footman who had admitted me. I let him take my light linen wrap from my shoulders. "Is Miss Gertrude at home?"

"She is, Miss Cross. She was outside with the family last I saw her. Would you like me to inquire after her for you?"

"No, thank you. I'll just go on out and see for myself." Thanks to my being a relative and a frequent visitor, I had the privilege of being allowed to walk in unannounced and roam the house as I pleased, something no ordinary visitor would have dared do.

As I passed through the entry hall into the open expanse of the Italian palazzo–inspired Great Hall, I blinked just as surely as if I'd stepped into a garden bathed in dazzling sunlight. No matter how many times I entered this room, the grandeur of marble and gilt and priceless art never failed to stun me, to leave me both breathless and speechless.

I stopped just at the top of the few steps leading down to the main floor of the room. Two under footmen passed into view from the dining room, where they appeared to be gathering up the silver, probably to be taken below stairs and polished. Above me along the open gallery that looked down upon the Great Hall, a maid exited one of the bedrooms with an armful of linens. I let my gaze slide past her, higher and higher, until it came to rest on the ceiling, painted to resemble a clear, sunny afternoon sky.

I pulled my gaze earthward as voices drifted in from the terrace that spanned the rear of the building. Listening, I could make out Uncle Cornelius's and Aunt Alice's voices . . . and the higher, eager tones of my youngest cousin, Gladys. They were discussing an upcoming yachting excursion. I listened for Gertrude's voice but didn't hear her, and as the downstairs seemed quiet but for the soft murmurs of working servants, I crossed to the staircase and hurried up. I found Gertrude in her room, still in her dressing gown, though a pile of dresses littered her bed and she seemed to be studying them with a critical eye.

"Oh, good morning, Emmaline," she said when I stepped through the open doorway.

I smiled. It always both amused and annoyed me that most of my Vanderbilt relatives, with the exception of Reggie and Consuelo, called me by my full name rather than the shorter version I preferred. The men could be nicknamed; hence there were Reggie, Neily, Willy K., etc. Ah, but nothing so sporting or casual would do for the females of the family; thus, we remained Emmaline, Gertrude, Consuelo, and the rest. I had long since given up trying to persuade them otherwise.

"This is a lovely surprise," she continued brightly, "especially since I was just thinking of you."

"Were you?" We embraced and kissed each other's cheeks in the European fashion Gertrude had learned during her travels last summer.

She leaned over her bed and selected a sleek frock with a matching jacket, both the color of spring leaves. She held them up for my perusal. "Do you want this? The color simply doesn't

123

work with my complexion. I'd told Mama that when she chose this fabric, but she wouldn't hear it. Now that she's actually seen me in the outfit, however, she can't help but agree."

Even I had to admit neither the color nor the tailoring suited my tall, substantially framed cousin.

"Oh . . . I . . ." I reached out a finger and stroked the brushed sheen of the silk bodice. I couldn't begin to estimate how much the walking ensemble had cost—more than I could ever afford, that much was certain. That she could simply give it away with hardly a thought . . .

"Do take it, Emmaline. I know Nanny O'Neal can take it in a bit and shorten the hem, and make it just perfect for you. And with your dark hair and hazel eyes, I do believe the color will do quite well for you."

"Thank you, Gertrude."

She waved away my gratitude. "I'm assuming you're in your little rig, so I'll have it sent over later. Now, was there something you wanted to see me about?"

From her expression I judged she hadn't heard yet about Madame Devereaux's murder. I needed to be careful. Although I believed I could trust Gertrude with a confidence, tensions existed between her mother and Consuelo's, and if Aunt Alice gleaned so much as a hint of Consuelo's disappearance, she'd no doubt find a means to use

124

it against Aunt Alva, socially if in no other way. The two women were forever trying to discredit one another, each being intent on rising to the top of the social register as *The Mrs. Vanderbilt.* I was not about to let Consuelo become ammunition in their genteel warfare.

So, pretending to be preoccupied with the piles of satin, silk, and lace covering Gertrude's canopied bed, I casually asked, "Have you heard from Consuelo lately?"

"No, and I feel just awful about it," she said without hesitation. "Poor Consuelo. I know she's not happy about this engagement to the Duke. I'm not sure I understand, not completely, but she is young still and I can see how marriage in general might seem a rather frightening prospect." She absently reached for a white linen tennis dress with a big, square collar and navy blue piping at the cuffs and hem. She held it up in front of her. "I've been wanting to call on her, but Mama's refusal to invite either Aunt Alva or Consuelo to my coming-out ball made for such an awkward situation between us." She held out the tennis dress. "Do you want this, too?" She didn't wait for my answer but tossed it beside the bright green walking outfit.

Although I had rarely in my life played tennis, I nodded my thanks and said, "So you haven't spoken to her in a while, then?"

"No." Her gaze sharpened. "Why? Has something happened? Is Consuelo ill? Or have she and Aunt Alva been arguing again?"

I saw no harm in disclosing what had happened at Marble House yesterday, minus Consuelo's disappearance. Gertrude paled as I told her about the murder. Then she dragged herself to her dressing table chair and sank down into it.

"Good heavens . . . *again?*"

I left Gertrude to resume sorting through the contents of her dressing room. Satisfied that Consuelo hadn't contacted her, I went out to the terrace to bid good day to the family. Leaving it to Gertrude or the local newspapers to reveal the details of the murder, I said fairly quick hellos and good-byes and let myself out the front door. I met my eldest cousin, Neily—short for Cornelius—out on the drive. He had just ridden up on horseback.

To his credit, he acknowledged Katie with a short wave, to which she gave a polite nod. There had been a time when I'd held Neily responsible for Katie's troubles last spring, but that's all another story. He and I had always been good friends, possibly my closest out of all my Vanderbilt cousins, though lately his interests had been diverted elsewhere.

With a grin he dismounted, grabbed me up in a hug, and swung me about. I slapped at him to put me down; after all, we weren't children anymore, but I secretly relished his playfulness. Being Uncle Cornelius's primary heir, twenty-one-year-old Neily ran the risk of becoming too serious, not to mention too grand for his britches. But somehow, so far, he remained immune to the burdens he'd one day assume.

"Are you leaving?" he asked with a bit of a pout.

"I am. Are you living here again?"

He'd recently moved out after arguing with his parents over a young woman he'd begun courting. They didn't approve of her; Neily didn't give a hoot.

"I'm back home for the moment," he said, then lowered his voice. "But Grace and I are planning, Emma."

"Do be careful. There could be serious repercussions."

"I am. But eventually Mother and Father will have to accept my choice."

"Oh, Neily." I looked up into his handsome face and pressed my palm to his cheek. "No, they don't, and you could end up disinherited."

"Then I'll have to find a way to earn a living, won't I?"

Would Grace want him then, I wondered. With all my heart I hoped so.

"I have to be going," I said, "but come by Gull Manor for supper some night. Bring Grace, if you like. You know Nanny would love to cook for you."

"Nanny loves to cook for everyone." His expression darkened. "Is Brady still staying with you?"

Neily had reason to resent my half brother. Brady had attempted to steal business secrets from Uncle Cornelius, though in the end his conscience won out and he hadn't been able to carry out his subterfuge.

"Can't you try to forgive him, Neily?"

He shrugged and kissed me good-bye.

Katie and I spent the next hour or so coaxing Barney up and down Bellevue Avenue and its surrounding area. The streets bustled with activity, there being quite a well-heeled crowd riding up and down the fashionable avenue to see and be seen, waving hello to acquaintances and stopping to talk to friends. More than once the genial traffic brought my rig to a complete halt, not to mention the several times I was obliged to stop and exchange greetings and news with those who recognized me as a Vanderbilt relation. I might not have been a desirable acquaintance in my own right, but my connections kept me in fairly high social demand during the Season. That I wrote a society column that extolled the grandeur of their houses and their glittering summer activities didn't hurt either.

One of the interruptions in my travels did bring an unexpected benefit, for as I climbed down from my carriage to trade pleasantries with Mary

Hazard and her mother, who should happen by but Carrie Astor—really Carrie Wilson now, but most people still referred to her as an Astor. Her younger cousin, Waldorf, who was about Consuelo's age, strolled at her side.

The Beechwood estate had been my next intended stop. Earlier, calling on the Goelets and their nearby neighbors, the Oelrichses, had produced little in the way of results. I'd forgone the direct approach I'd taken with Winty and instead steered the conversation in ways that encouraged Consuelo's friends to divulge whether they'd seen or heard from her in recent days. May Goelet hadn't encountered my cousin since the same ball where Consuelo had managed to speak with Winty, and Blanche Oelrichs hadn't glimpsed Consuelo at all since they'd met in Paris in the spring. Both expressed concern for her, and nothing in their attitudes or bearing led me to believe either had reason to lie.

I hoped for better results with Carrie and Waldorf. Yet when I casually brought up her name, they stared back at me with blank expressions. "Heard from Consuelo?" Carrie parroted. Her mouth formed a rigid line as she raised a hand to adjust the netting around her beribboned chapeau. "No, I have not, and I am beginning to take it rather personally. I had believed she and I to be friends."

"As did I," her cousin agreed. "But it seems

she's been too busy for old acquaintances this summer." He gave a shrug, and his voice lost a bit of its resentment. "Planning her wedding, I suppose. Clever Consuelo, to land herself a duke."

Consuelo and Waldorf had never been sweethearts, but like many friends who'd essentially grown up together, they shared a sibling-like closeness and kept few secrets from each other. It didn't surprise me that her apparent abandonment of her friends had been taken to heart. But no matter where Consuelo's future took her, she would need these old friends. I couldn't let them slip away because of her mother's actions.

"Consuelo hasn't been ignoring you," I said earnestly. "She's been longing to see you, to see all her friends."

"Then why have we been turned away each time we've called at Marble House?" Carrie demanded to know. Waldorf nodded his consensus.

"It's . . . she's . . ." If Aunt Alva got wind of my interference, I'd never hear the end of it. But concern for my cousin took precedence. "It's her mother. She's been refusing to let Consuelo's friends see her all summer. It's because of the engagement." Having said too much, I closed my mouth. They didn't need to know the ugly truth about Consuelo's impending nuptials. They were as aware of Aunt Alva's penchants as everyone else in their social circle. Her temper was legendary, her tendencies familiar if inexplicable.

But I'd obviously given too much away. "Consuelo isn't happy about the engagement," Waldorf said rather than asked. His youthful gaze sharpened. "She's being forced."

I wanted to backtrack, to lie and say Aunt Alva simply wanted Consuelo to focus and prepare for her new role as a duchess, for an American, however much an heiress, had much to learn when it came to mingling with European royalty, as she surely would once she married. But the Astors had been lied to enough when it came to my cousin.

"She's not happy, I'm afraid. To be honest, she's rather afraid of the prospect, but she's determined to make the best of it."

Carrie studied me, her blue eyes shrewd. "Then why are you looking for her?"

"Oh, I'm not," I replied, probably too quickly. I looked out over the phaetons, victorias, and curricles, as well as single riders passing by. "I only wanted to know if you'd heard from her. I thought . . . well . . . perhaps my aunt relented and allowed her to at least speak with you."

Neither Carrie nor Waldorf replied for a long moment, their expressions burning with speculation. Then a soft-gloved touch descended on my forearm.

"If there is anything we can do . . ." Carrie murmured.

"Yes, please let us know," Waldorf finished for her.

I nodded my thanks and moved to climb back into my carriage. Waldorf offered a hand to help me up, and when I'd settled in the seat he smiled at me. "How's Brady doing, by the way?"

"Much better and vastly relieved," I said. "As you can imagine."

"Never did believe he was guilty. I just wanted you to know that, Emma."

Carrie moved beside Waldorf, a head taller than she despite being so much younger, and slipped her hand into the crook of his elbow. "Me neither. We're glad it turned out well for him. And things will turn out just fine for Consuelo, too. You'll see."

"Thank you. Both of you." I hoped Carrie was right. If nothing else, her optimism bolstered me on my way into town after I dropped Katie off at home. There was one more person I was eager to question, but first I had a stop to make.

Ed Billings's voice boomed from Mr. Millford's office as I stepped into the tiny lobby of the Newport *Observer* on Lower Thames Street. I shot a glance at Donald Larimer, Mr. Millford's secretary, half buried behind the stack of paperwork on his desk.

"What's going on?" I asked him as the voices from the inner office crescendoed a second time. I tried to make out the words, but only the name

Anthony Dobbs penetrated the walls and the mostly closed office door.

"Big scandal," whispered Donald with a sidelong glance into the narrow corridor off the lobby. Sunlight from the large front window glinted on his oval spectacles. "Ed just got the scoop."

I tightened my grip on the doorknob I hadn't noticed I was still clutching from when I'd closed the street door behind me. "Please don't tell me Mr. Millford decided to scrub my article on the Marble House murder and run some rot Ed tossed together. Is that why my article wasn't on the front page this morning?" What *had* been on the front page? In my eagerness to find my own article, and then my disappointment at not seeing it, I'd ignored the actual headlines.

Oh, but it wouldn't be the first time Ed Billings stole a byline from me with a hastily scrawled, uninformed report. And merely because he was a man, while I, a woman, should focus my attentions on fashions and parties and other such rubbish. Or so Mr. Millford often told me.

Donald wrinkled his nose, a flash of his glasses recapturing my attention. "I wouldn't know anything about that, Emma. But at this point no one is going to care about the murder of some charlatan with no real Newport roots. Not now."

I released the doorknob and strode to the desk, only just stopping myself from leaning over its littered surface to grab Donald's shoulders and shake him. How dare he imply my article was unimportant? "What *are* you talking about?"

"Anthony Dobbs. He's been suspended from the police force under suspicion of extortion."

My mouth dropped open; I backed away from the desk. Yet I can't claim to have been completely shocked. I'd never liked the man, never fully trusted him, and I had ample cause to resent the way he'd treated my brother through the years. Had the bully Dobbs finally gotten his comeuppance? It had been Dobbs who had most wanted to see Brady hang for a crime he didn't commit, who had been ready to seal Brady's fate before all the evidence was in.

I frowned. "Whom was he extorting money from?"

"Oh, you know . . . the town bookies, that so-called doctor who likes to prescribe mint oil for all manner of ailments, and apparently a real-estate broker who was selling land that didn't exist off the mainland coast. And then there were the usual run of townies—barkeepers watering down the liquor, restaurants serving horse instead of beef . . . and the like. You see, they were all paying him to turn a blind eye. And a blind eye he turned, for quite a profit from what I understand."

I started to wonder how I'd had no inkling of any of this, when a notion dawned. "Fortune-tellers?" I whispered, my mind turning the information over.

Donald shrugged. "I suppose so. Newport has a fair amount of those."

One fortune-teller in particular, who would never gaze into her crystal ball again? I searched Donald's bland features for affirmation of my unspoken theory, but he'd already turned his attention back to the documents under his nose. I headed down the corridor to Mr. Millford's office to see what I could learn.

From the *Observer* office I made my way across town and wound a circuitous path through the bustling activity of Long Wharf. Here commercial hulks vied with elegant sailboats and steamers for docking space and waterfront access, while trains snaked slowly along the wide arcs of the adjoining tracks. Amid billowing clouds of steam, shouts, horns, and bells clamored in the air around me, and I felt Barney's discomfiture in the pull of the reins wrapped around my hands. I maneuvered through the throng carefully yet almost absently as new revelations filtered through my mind.

Mr. Millford had had to step out when I arrived in his office, so I'd questioned Ed Billings about the Anthony Dobbs case. His answers had been measured and evasive. It didn't surprise me; Ed typically guarded his information jealously, apparently suspecting in others the unfair tactics he himself employed. I had no intention of stealing his story from him. But I wondered . . .

If the charges were true and Anthony Dobbs had been extorting not only con artists but local businesses attempting to cut corners to maximize the profits that would plummet when the summer season ended, who had reported him? Ed either couldn't or wouldn't answer that question; my guess was the latter.

A new and unexpected motive for murder had arisen, widening the pool of possible culprits. Aunt Alva had spoken harshly to Madame Devereaux, demanding the woman lie to soothe Consuelo's fears concerning her impending marriage; and the medium and Aunt Alva's guest, Mrs. Stanford, had certainly seemed to share a mutual abhorrence. Motives . . . perhaps. But flimsy ones when compared to the end of a police detective's career, the ruination of his good name, and the very real possibility of his spending the next several years in prison.

A familiar face roused me from my speculations and reminded me I hadn't come to the wharf to solve a murder, but to continue the search for my cousin. Near the far end of the wharf, all but lost between a freight barge and a proud, three-mast schooner, an ancient-looking skiff bobbed up and down with the gentle tide. A man with shoulder-length red hair pulled back in a queue, a fair, freckled complexion, and a weathered countenance that belied his youth sat hunched in the bow of the boat. His gaze found me as I steered Barney to a stop beside the boat slip.

"Hello, Angus. Are you free for the next hour or so?"

His grin revealed a broken front tooth and a missing incisor. "Are you hiring me, Emma?"

One of seven children, Angus MacPhearson had grown up two blocks away from our house on the Point. He and Brady had gotten up to no end of mischief during their early years, but upon finishing their schooling Angus had joined the navy and gone off island with boastful promises of someday commanding a frigate. Six months later Angus had returned to Newport a civilian and refused to talk about his naval experience. He somehow managed to win his skiff during a night of gambling and had operated his transport service from this same boat slip ever since.

"I most certainly am," I said in answer to his question as I wrapped Barney's reins around the dock railing. Angus's rough calluses scraped my palm as I grasped his offered hand and stepped down into his skiff. His were boatman's hands, gotten from rowing his passengers through all manner of weather and tides.

"Let me guess . . ." Angus turned away as I settled on the middle seat, facing him. His pale blue eyes searched the harbor, and then his grin returned. "You almost never leave the island, so we're not rowing to Jamestown."

"No," I confirmed, and his relief was palpable in his loud exhalation.

"Good. This swelling in my thumb wouldn't like a row that far." He held up the offending appendage, an angry red blister encompassing the skin from the pad of his finger to the knuckle.

"Have you had that looked at?"

He shrugged and placed an oar in its rowlock before bending to lift the other from the deck of the small craft. "What doesn't kill you makes you stronger."

I vowed to tip him well for his services and urge him to see a doctor.

"*The Valiant*, then?" he asked with his gap-toothed grin.

"How did you know?"

"There's no other ship a decent young lady like yourself would visit but her uncle's." Something in his expression warned that if I'd had other ideas, I'd better be able to justify them or he wouldn't take me. An old loyalty to Brady? I believed so. And somehow the notion warmed me. Poor Angus might not have fulfilled his dream of becoming a naval officer, but despite his unkempt appearance, something of a gentleman lived inside him.

"To *The Valiant*," I said with a flourish, and we set off, easing away from the pier. "I don't suppose you rowed my cousin Consuelo out yesterday or today," I asked, as if spurred by mere idle curiosity.

His back to *The Valiant*, his shoulders bent to his task, Angus replied with a grunt that sounded like a *no*. I didn't attempt to press his memory. Though few town locals had actually met her, nearly all of Newport recognized my cousin from catching glimpses of her riding in her parents' carriages. If Angus had encountered her he'd have known it, and what's more, he had no reason to lie to me.

Unless, of course, he'd been well-paid for that lie. I shook my head and sighed. I was becoming paranoid, suspecting guilt at every turn.

Soon the lively noises faded to a low hum behind us, and for me at least, the tranquility of the harbor and the salt-tinged breezes filled my lungs and eased my troubled mind.

My respite was short-lived. Upon arriving at *The Valiant*, a 300-foot steam brigantine that dwarfed all other craft anchored nearby, my nerves began to buzz. What excuse would I give Consuelo's father, my uncle William Vanderbilt, for intruding upon his afternoon?

I didn't have long to contemplate my options, for as soon as the skiff gently thumped against the yacht's hull, the call of my name poured down from the top deck.

"Emmaline, is that you?"

I glanced upward, squinting against the bright sky to make out my uncle's face peering down at me. He held a pair of binoculars in one hand.

He'd obviously been observing the sights and had spotted me on my way here. "Good afternoon, Uncle William. Am I disturbing you?"

I hoped he didn't have guests, for that would make my task so much more difficult.

"No," he called down. "Come on up. Do you need help?"

A flight of spindly wooden steps with a rope railing spanned the side of the ship from the waterline upward to the promenade deck, just below the deck upon which my uncle stood. "No, thanks," I shouted up at him. "I can make it just fine."

Angus rowed the boat closer to the steps. Reaching out, he grasped the hemp railing and held us steady as I stood and carefully picked my way to the side of the skiff. I slipped a foot onto the lowest step, wrapped a hand around the rope, and swung myself up and over. For a moment the world seemed to spin out from under me. Though I'd grown up on an island and small craft like Angus's were second nature, boarding a yachting vessel always taxed my equilibrium. My knuckles whitened around the thick twine railing and I stood a moment, feet braced on the step and my legs rigid, until steadiness returned.

"Not much of a sailor, are you," Angus remarked.

I shook my head. "You'll wait here for me?"

"Are you hiring me to wait here, Emma?"

"I am, Angus." I did a mental calculation of the coins presently weighing the purse that dangled from my wrist. Well, if I didn't have enough I'd send Brady down later with more. "Please don't leave me stranded here."

Angus let go a snort. "As if King William up there wouldn't see you safely back to land."

I let his derision of my relative pass without comment and started up. Uncle William met me at the top, swung me off the steps, and deposited me firmly on the solid deck.

William Vanderbilt was a younger, trimmer, more handsome version of his older brother, Cornelius. Though the resemblance was plain to see, where Uncle Cornelius was blunt featured and heavy-jawed, on Uncle William those same features took on longer lines and smoother planes that lent an aristocratic elegance his brother was missing. Uncle William smiled more easily, and those smiles reached his blue eyes without the secretive, calculating look his brother often bore whether he willed or no. And where Uncle Cornelius was solid and stocky, Uncle William's frame was much more athletic, his step more energetic.

"Emmaline, dear, what brings you here? Are you all right? It's awful what happened at Marble House yesterday. I've tried calling, but your aunt Alva won't come to the telephone."

Then he couldn't know about Consuelo, at least not yet.

When it came to a sharp intellect, Uncle William was no less astute than his older brother. On my way here I'd realized I couldn't very well announce that Consuelo had vanished without a trace, or her disappearance would become a national emergency within minutes. Aunt Alva wanted Consuelo found without sparking rumors, and while I entertained doubts about the wisdom of that course, I'd respect her wishes for the time being.

Thinking quickly, I apologized again for intruding upon my uncle's afternoon and smiled brightly. "I'm fine, thank you, Uncle William. Consuelo and I had plans to meet in town, but since she said she'd be stopping by to see you I thought I'd row out and meet her here."

"Consuelo has no plans to come here today that I know of." His expression became skeptical and I realized my mistake, confirmed by his next words. "You mean to say that after what happened yesterday, her mother allowed her out of the house?"

"Oh, well . . . Aunt Alva thought a change of scenery might be best. Besides . . ." Within the folds of my skirts I crossed my fingers. "Consuelo is meeting with a dressmaker in town. She's ordering some things for her wedding trousseau."

"Alone?" Uncle William's doubts seemed to grow with each word I uttered. I found myself wishing I'd never come, much less opened my mouth.

"Surely not alone." I tried a bit of lighthearted laughter, but it came out harsh and jarring. "I'm sure one of the maids accompanied her. And me, once I meet up with her."

"Ah." He didn't sound convinced. "Emmaline, is there something going on I should know about? Is Consuelo all right? Has my ex-wife done something unconscionable again?"

The question sent my pulse spiking, for it was one I myself pondered. Did Alva have anything to do with Madame Devereaux's murder or Consuelo's disappearance?

Before I could answer, Uncle William drew my arm through his own and escorted me through the nearest doorway, into a parlor fitted out with velvet furnishings and dark-wood tabletops. He sat me down on a small sofa and settled beside me. "Well?"

"Consuelo is fine. Well, not fine exactly. Who could be fine after nearly witnessing a murder? Which she didn't actually, so you can set your mind at ease on that count. She saw very little at all, really, because the other ladies and I were blocking her view." I was babbling, but I couldn't seem to stop. Our close proximity magnified the concern in Uncle William's face and made it blasted difficult to continue lying. Which might explain the snippet of truth that fell next from my ingenuous lips. "But you should know she isn't at all happy about marrying the Duke of Marlborough."

As soon as the statement was out of my mouth I wanted to smack myself. What was I thinking? That it would help Consuelo's case if her father knew the truth? That he would step gallantly in and undermine Aunt Alva's plans, save his daughter from her unhappy fate, and then what? Allow her the freedom to choose her own future?

He wouldn't. I knew that even before he looked down at his hands, breathed a deep sigh, and looked back up at me with a regretful frown. "Emmaline, you have altogether too much time on your hands. I don't mean to criticize and Lord knows, I find you to be a steady, resourceful young woman—most of the time." He patted my wrist. "But don't you think it's time you found a nice young man and settled down? Or better yet, let your aunt Alice make a good match for you. She's just dying to see you married into a good family."

He referred to his brother Cornelius's wife, who was always on the lookout for a suitable bridegroom for me. No one too lofty, considering my less-than-stellar origins, but as Uncle William implied, someone from good stock, maybe one of the old New England families of modest fortune.

It was my turn to sigh. "I didn't come here to discuss my prospects, Uncle William. I take it Consuelo isn't here, then?"

"I haven't seen her." I watched his face carefully and detected no guile, but then again why would he lie? "Would you like to search the boat?"

I chuckled despite my disappointment. "I'll take your word for it."

Sudden ire claimed his expression, taking me aback. "Believe me, Emmaline, even if Consuelo wanted to visit me, she wouldn't dare because she knows how her mother would react. Alva would make her pay—pay dearly. The woman is doing her confounded best to turn my own children against me. It hasn't worked so far with the boys—"

"It hasn't worked with Consuelo either," I hastily assured him.

"No? Give Alva time, she'll work her devil's magic. Let me tell you, it doesn't surprise me a murder took place on the Marble House property. Everything that woman touches turns evil. . . . Good grief, it wouldn't surprise me if she herself . . ." Scowling, he trailed off, unaware he'd echoed my own thoughts.

"She deserves to be toppled from her self-made throne," he continued. "Wouldn't it serve her right if the murder creates a scandal she'll never recover from, that makes her a world-renowned social pariah. . . ." His smile, more a sneer, sent a foreboding shiver through me.

I sprang to my feet and stared down at him, awful possibilities gripping me like claws at my nape. Could kindly Uncle William have had reason to see Madame Devereaux dead? Reasons that had nothing to do with the woman herself, but with the wife who had so recently divorced him? Though unwelcome at Marble House, he did still have access to both the house and the grounds; the staff would never question his presence there. It begged the question, how far would a bitter man go to satisfy his need for retribution?

Then again, Alva had divorced William because she had discovered he'd been unfaithful. How *did* she discover his infidelity? Fortune-tellers, however deceptive, had their ways of uncovering the secret truth about people. And come to think of it, while fortune-tellers and mediums were all the rage among fashionable society, Aunt Alva had never struck me as fanciful enough to put stock in the supernatural. Yet she knew Madame Devereaux well enough to invite her into her home. . . . I wondered how, and under what circumstances, they had met before.

Oblivious to my speculations, Uncle William stood up beside me. "Would you like some lunch before you go?"

"No, uh . . . no, thank you." The thought of food made me queasy. Did I believe Uncle William— or Aunt Alva—capable of murder, not to mention framing an innocent woman for the crime? No, not in my heart. But my believing it or not had little bearing on whether it was true. "I think

I'll . . . uh . . . head back into town . . . and wait for Consuelo at the dressmaker's."

"When you do see her, tell her to come visit me. Just to stick a blade between her mother's ribs and give it a little twist." It was his turn to chuckle, a cold sound that left me trembling. With a hollow smile I left him and began the climb back down to Angus's skiff.

CHAPTER 7

"Where to now?" Angus asked me as he shoved off from *The Valiant.*

"Where to, indeed." I sighed. Thus far all I'd achieved today was to widen my circle of suspects to include Winthrop Rutherfurd and my own Uncle William. Add Aunt Alva to that list, and it seemed everywhere I turned a suspect appeared out of the air. The queasiness of minutes ago seemed to settle in permanently. And yet my common sense ordered me to let it go, to acknowledge that events had sent my imagination and my suspicions barreling out of control. Uncle William? Aunt Alva? It was ludicrous. I'd promised Jesse I'd let the police solve Madame Devereaux's murder. It was time I focused on what I had promised to do: find my cousin.

"Back to town," I said half-heartedly, with no particular plan in mind. Where else could I search?

I set my sights toward where Long Wharf stretched into the harbor, but something closer caught my eye. A skipjack bounced across the waves twenty yards or so away. Some thirty feet in length, its two sails flashing silvery in the afternoon sun, the vessel maneuvered easily between the other pleasure craft, fishing boats, and freighters navigating Narragansett Bay. But that's not what held my attention. No, it was the man at the helm, whose stance and figure might not have attracted my notice if I hadn't just seen him that morning.

"Angus, may I borrow your binoculars?"

He reached to hand me the pair occupying a corner of the bench beside him. "Suit yourself. Bird-watching?"

I nodded and discreetly wiped the lenses on my skirt before raising the device to my eyes. It took only seconds to confirm the identity of the man guiding the skipjack. There were two other men with him, neither of whom was familiar to me. They headed in the direction of Rose Island, twenty acres of sand and rocks about a mile out on the harbor. The island held only one structure, the Rose Light with its attached living quarters, inhabited by the lighthouse keeper and his wife. What on earth could Winty want there? And why would he be manning a boat typically used for oyster dredging? Hardly what one would call a gentleman's sport craft.

As the sailboat rounded the west side of the island, which faced away from Newport, Winty's reason for using the shallow-bottomed skipjack became apparent, for the shoals on that side of the island would scrape a deeper V-shaped hull. With a frown I shifted my gaze toward the island's landward side. The Curtises' dock and boat slip lay vacant, their own small sailboat nowhere in sight. Clear blue skies and the bay's light chop left little reason why the couple wouldn't have taken the opportunity for a trip into town. In all probability, their clapboard house and the attached tower were deserted.

"Angus, any idea when the Curtises are due back today?"

"They're not coming back today."

Surprised, I lowered the binoculars. "Where are they?"

"Took a little vacation south."

"Then who's operating the light?"

He shrugged. "City hired someone for the time being. Don't know his name."

"Angus, would you take us out farther, please?"

"Are you hiring me to—"

"Yes, I'm hiring you to take me farther out on the bay." My purse felt decidedly light for the occasion, but again, I could send Brady with more money later to make up the difference. In my impatience I wished I could have rowed myself out, but wouldn't that have set tongues wagging about that poor Vanderbilt relation who not only drove her own rig, but rowed her own boat. I'd never have heard the end of it from Aunt Alice.

Angus shrugged and turned us about. He didn't appear to pay me any attention as I brought the binoculars back up to my eyes. If he found

150

anything strange in my request, he showed no sign of it.

I didn't worry about Winty glimpsing me in return, for there was enough boating traffic today to conceal me, if one didn't know where to look. And if Winty hadn't noticed me on his way out to the island, there was no reason for him to be looking for me now. Within minutes, Angus had rowed us far enough out that I could once again see the skipjack, only now instead of cutting a path through the water, it drifted gently, moored a mere few yards out from the island's rocky ledge.

What happened next made me feel foolish. Abandoning the helm, Winty bent down to retrieve something I couldn't see from the deck, and when he straightened it was to toss a baited line into the water. He sat on the bench seat spanning the width of the deck at the rear of the craft and adjusted the fishing pole in his hands.

Here I was, my suspicious mind leading me to imagine I was spying on a guilty moment, to discover a man who wanted only a private place to fish. I opened my mouth to tell Angus to start back to shore, but in the next instant I snapped it shut.

Working quickly, Winty's two companions, men dressed not as he was in a stylish linen suit, but in the coarser jersey and corduroy of work-men, hoisted some dark-colored object over the side of the boat. I blinked as the water sent up a splash, and thought I saw something catch the sunlight at the water's surface. Not the heavy thing that had caused the splash, but something buoyant and lighter in color. Something that might blend with the waves and the frothy white-caps, at least by day. By night . . . I wondered. Might that floating object stand out against the darkened waters?

Leaning, the rough-clad men peered down into the water until, seeming satisfied, they straightened, moved to the other side of the boat, and hauled up the little anchor that had kept them moored as they completed their peculiar errand. Winty reeled in his line and returned to the helm. He turned them about until the sails caught the wind, and the craft once more skipped its way around the island and then across the harbor toward the wharf.

"What was that all about?" I murmured. Winty's fishing—a diversion to distract from whatever those two men had tossed in the water?

I thought of asking Angus if he'd ever noticed Winty skulking about Rose Island before, but then I became aware of a sound I'd been hearing all along, that of my old neighbor whistling a gay tune as he sat staring into the water beside him. No, it was my guess that by design Angus noticed little during his jaunts on the harbor. He finally glanced up at me. "Ready to go home?"

I nodded and showed him a crooked, sheepish smile. "I'd appreciate it if you wouldn't mention this to anyone."

"Mention what?" He appeared genuinely puzzled.

"Nothing. Thank you, Angus."

He merely gripped the oars and set both shoulders to the task of turning us about and heading landward. Need I say I nearly had to bite my tongue to keep from asking him to head over to Rose Island instead, so I could see what Winty's companions had tossed in the water.

A small voice inside me asked why it mattered, what business was it of mine what Winthrop Rutherfurd did? But his connection to my cousin made it my business.

Might Winthrop have been marking a spot for a later rendezvous to secrete Consuelo off Aquidneck Island, perhaps a signal for where a boat should put in? Her mother dreaded the idea of their eloping, but that would certainly save her daughter from her unwanted marriage to the Duke. Good heavens, it made sense. Why, even now she might be holed up in the lighthouse, awaiting her chance to escape. And Mr. and Mrs. Curtis were conveniently away.

I had to return to Rose Island, but now wasn't the time, not in full sunlight when someone might see me. Later then, once darkness fell, I'd go alone. At night the Rose Light would shine its beams out across the water, deepening the shadows directly below it, shadows that would safely conceal me.

If Aunt Alice, or anyone in society for that matter, could have seen me later that night, the shock waves would have been felt from one end of New England to the other. Yet I thanked my deceased aunt Sadie once again as I pulled on her old work trousers, button-down shirt, boots, and corduroy workman's coat. Aunt Sadie had always said a single woman—as she had been by choice—had work to do, and she'd be damned if she went about sowing her garden or mending the house shingles in petticoats and lace.

A tweed cap stuffed with my hair and pulled low over my brow completed my look for the evening. I even smeared a bit of coal dust across my chin to give the illusion of beard stubble should anyone peer too closely as I drove beneath a streetlamp. Satisfied, I turned away from my mirror.

"Well?"

From her perch at the foot of my bed, Nanny surveyed me with a pout. "It's not a good idea, you know."

"Yes, well, it's been more than twenty-four hours and I still haven't found Consuelo. If my suspicions are correct, I can't let this opportunity slip away. Or *she* might slip away."

"Then let Jesse handle it."

"I can't, Nanny. I promised Aunt Alva complete secrecy. Calling in the police is a last resort." My promise, however, weighed heavily on me. What if Consuelo hadn't run off voluntarily? What if . . . but I refused to entertain the notion that she'd come to harm.

"Send Brady," Nanny suggested next.

"Have you lost your wits? Brady? Oh, he's the soul of discretion, all right. No, Nanny, I have to go, and don't you dare breathe a word to him about this. I promise I'll be careful. One hint of danger and I'll turn right around and row back to the harbor."

"Someone might recognize you."

I glanced again in the mirror. "I doubt that."

"Someone might recognize Barney and the carriage."

This made me pause and sent my bottom lip between my teeth. I'd been so engaged in making sure I'd be unidentifiable that I hadn't given a thought to my means of transportation. I glanced at the clock; it read nine forty-five. "Well, it's late. Most locals are either getting ready for bed or they're sitting in a tavern already beginning to see double. It's the social set that will be traveling the streets now and they aren't likely to spare me a glance. Besides, at night Barney could be any brown horse and the rig any black carriage. It's not as if there's a shiny gold crest on the side panel proclaiming my identity."

"And what if the McPaddens' rowboat isn't where you're expecting it to be? For all we know, the thing rotted away years ago," Nanny persisted. "What then? Are you going to swim out to Rose Island?"

I snapped my hands to my hips. "You're making me regret ever telling you my plans. You know that, don't you? If the McPaddens' rowboat isn't docked behind their house, I'll find another. This *is* the *Point* we're talking about. Every house on the water has a boat."

"Why is this your obligation, Emma?" Nanny asked so quietly I had to prick my ears to hear her.

"I just told you. I promised Aunt Alva—"

"No, Emma. The question I'm asking isn't *what* you promised, but *why* you made the promise. Why do you think it's your responsibility to put yourself at risk to find Consuelo?"

"I . . ." I turned back to the mirror, gazing at the reflection of the young man I'd become. But that young man could barely bring himself to meet my gaze. He glanced away and found Nanny's unwavering questions staring at him through the glass.

"Look at me, Emma." She waited until I turned back around before continuing. "If you can't tell *me* the answer, at least tell yourself."

The tops of my leather work boots suddenly

became fascinating, and I fell to studying them. I knew the answer to Nanny's question, but in rushing around today to try to find some trace of Consuelo, I'd managed to avoid the truth.

I felt responsible—wholly responsible. I couldn't help thinking that if I hadn't betrayed her yesterday, if I hadn't taken her mother's side in trying to persuade her to see the sense in marrying the Duke of Marlborough, she might now be safely tucked away in her bedroom. I'd tried to believe my encouragement had been for the best, to help her face the unavoidable future bravely, but, oh, how my words must have singed Consuelo's heart. That I, her older cousin, should take her mother's side . . . should do anything other than fight for what *she* wanted . . . She'd trusted me, confided in me, and I had let her down completely. How devastated she must have been. How utterly bereft and alone.

"I have to do this, Nanny," I whispered. "If anything happens to Consuelo, it'll be my fault."

Nanny shook her head, her expression as serious as I'd ever seen it. "No, Emma. It won't be your fault. It might be her mother's fault, or her father's, or the fault of this man who wants to marry her for her money, or . . . and don't turn away again . . . but Consuelo isn't necessarily blameless in all of this either."

"That's ridiculous."

"Is it? If she did run off, shouldn't she take responsibility for her own actions?"

"She's a frightened girl, practically a child . . ."

Nanny's eyebrow rose. "If you believe that, aren't you treating her just like her mother does? Like a beautiful but empty-headed doll?"

Was I? An answer prodded, but it wasn't one I liked to acknowledge. "Either way, I can't simply forget all about what happened. I can't go on with my everyday life with my cousin out there somewhere, missing and possibly traumatized."

"No." Nanny sighed and perused me with an assessing look. "I don't suppose you can."

She knew me far too well to continue arguing with me. I went to her and leaned down to deposit a kiss on her cheek. Her soft skin smelled of lavender and I breathed in the fragrance, the sense of comfort I'd known since my earliest days bolstering my determination. Unfortunately, being the source of my stubborn courage probably wasn't what she'd had in mind.

"Don't worry, Nanny dear. I'll be careful, and I'll be home before you know it. Promise."

That only brought a frown. "And if you're not?"

"Then send the cavalry." Standing straight, I touched two fingers to my cap brim and headed for the door.

"I'll do that," she mumbled to my back.

Some twenty minutes later, I brought my rig to

a stop at the end of Walnut Street, near the train tracks that separated the street from the cemetery beyond it. My old home sat a few dozen yards away. We rented out the first two floors and Brady, when not staying with me or working in New York with our relatives, occupied the garret apartment. Tonight the windows were dark but for a glow on the ground floor overlooking the back garden. I set the brake and slipped the straps of Barney's feedbag over his head. That would keep him contented until my return. I didn't worry for his safety or about the prospect of someone stealing the carriage. Such crimes occurred rarely on the island, for any thief would be caught long before he could make his getaway on the morning ferry.

With the unaccustomed sensation of trousers encasing my legs and producing a disconcerting *woof-woof* sound as I walked, I proceeded toward the harbor. There I discovered Nanny's cautions were unfounded; the McPaddens' rowboat appeared sound enough, drifting to the length of its twine from the short dock behind their house. All appeared quiet in the house. Noiselessly I made my way across the weathered planks, went down on one knee, and reached to tug the boat closer through the blackened water. Out in the bay the Rose Light burned brightly, a beacon to warn incoming ships away from the dangerous shoals near the shoreline.

A thwack of boots hitting the timbers behind me nearly sent me tumbling head over heels into the water. I'd barely caught my balance—and caught a splinter in my middle finger—when a stern voice sent my heartbeat careening.

"Emma Cross, you are incorrigible."

For a brief moment eyes darker than the surrounding night held me immobile. My heart continued to thump, but no longer from fear; from a multitude of other emotions, however, desire and exasperation not the least among them.

"Derrick." I released the boat line and pressed to my feet. "What in the devil's name are you doing here?" I demanded, making a monumental effort not to allow my voice to rise above a whisper lest the McPaddens come to investigate. "You're supposed to be back in Providence by now."

"Am I, Emma?" He strode closer, taking care to muffle his footsteps now that his dramatic appearance had effectively captured my full attention. "And leave you to your own devices?"

"My de—" My chin hefted in the air of its own accord. "You've been spying on me, haven't you?"

The scoundrel had the audacity to smile, the fog-tinged moonlight caressing his lips with a silver glint. At the sight of that now-familiar gesture a slight tremor went through me, and I pressed my own lips together. "My plans changed the moment I got wind of what happened at Marble House yesterday." His gaze swept me up and down, and a chuckle blended with the light slap of the water against the seawall. "Oh, Emma, how predictable you are. Did you think I'd let you investigate another murder on your own?"

Predictable? Why—I opened my mouth to protest but quickly realized the futility of arguing the point, at least there on that little dock, with my errand waiting to be accomplished. However . . . "That shows how much you know, then. Because it so happens I am not investigating a murder."

"Ah, then you're dressed like a boy and stealing a boat . . . because you're off to a costume ball on your uncle William's yacht?" He reached out to graze my chin with his fingertips, then held them up so we could both see the coal dust smudging them.

"Borrowing, not stealing," I said with a huff. "And it so happens I'm looking for someone, and I can assure you that someone is *not* a murderer."

I expected a return quip; I did not expect Derrick to grip my shoulders and pull me closer. "Stop playing games with me, Emma. Yes, the moment I heard about the murder at Marble House I began following you. You mean to tell me you never sensed it?"

In a whirl of confusion fueled as much by the scent of his shaving soap as by his anger, I could only stare wide-eyed up at him and shake my head.

"Then maybe you're not as good at this as you think you are. Didn't getting mixed up in one murder and nearly getting yourself killed teach you anything?"

That time I did intend to answer him, but before I could gather the words his face dipped, bringing with it the scent of his skin, the heat of his breath, and the press of his lips against mine. His evening stubble was rough against my cheek; his mouth was hard, punishing. All at once I felt myself spinning as if the dock had broken loose from its pilings, leaving us at the mercy of the tide.

But then he released me, his face tight, pained, his own chin now shadowed by traces of that dratted coal dust. Slowly he pulled back from me, though his fingers continued their vise grip on my shoulders. "I'm sorry." He looked away. "That was uncalled for."

"Derrick . . . I . . ."

"No, leave it, Emma. You don't need to repeat the things you said the other morning. There is no need for either of us to be redundant." He released me, his arms swinging to his sides. As the cool air claimed my neck, I couldn't remember the things I'd said to him that morning, or why on earth I *would* have said them. I only wanted him to hold me again.

Kiss me again.

He shoved his hands into his coat pockets and eyed me levelly, all hint of turmoil gone from his gaze. "So . . . who is this mystery person we're off to find?"

"It's my . . ." Aunt Alva's admonitions stilled my tongue, but then Derrick's choice of words struck me. "We? Who said anything about you and I . . . ?"

His cool amusement returned. "Come, Emma. It's you and I or nothing. I'm not letting you row off across the bay or wherever you're going alone. So start talking. Now. Or I take you home."

It was all I could do to keep from stomping my foot. "Impossible man."

"Yes, now, as we say in the newspaper business, who, what, where, and why?"

I heaved a sigh. "My cousin Consuelo. She's missing—been missing since right after the murder."

"And no one saw fit to call the police?"

I explained the reasons why not. "And before you decided to take ten years off my life moments ago, I was on my way to Rose Island. I think she might be there, or might be going there tonight, possibly to meet up with another boat to take her off the island."

"Sounds rather cloak-and-dagger, don't you think?"

"It's just a hunch, but one backed up by a strange coincidence." I told him about seeing

Winthrop Rutherfurd out by the island today, how his companions had dropped some sort of marker into the water. And how, with the light glaring its beams out across the water, anything happening directly below the lighthouse would be draped in shadow.

As I fell silent he regarded me for such a long moment I nearly squirmed. Then he shrugged out of his coat and tossed it to the deck of the boat, his shirtsleeves glowing white in the darkness. "All right, then, let's go."

Moments later we shoved off, Derrick manning the oars.

CHAPTER 8

We put in on the east side of Rose Island. Derrick let our small craft drift the last few yards before hopping out—ruining his half boots and trousers in the process—and almost noiselessly pulling the dinghy up onto a spit of sand. Taking his offered hand, I crept out and we set off across the island, heading thirty or so yards down from the lighthouse.

I'd been right. Beyond the lighthouse proper and wan light spilling from the windows of the keeper's cottage, the island lay in inky darkness. We stopped at intervals, listening but hearing nothing but the waves rippling against the island's banks.

Finally, a low murmur brought us to an abrupt halt. We were nearing the westward shore, and here Derrick immediately tugged me down behind a rocky outcropping. I pricked my ears, again hearing nothing, until the breeze carried a throaty whisper that could not have originated from nature. Derrick held up a hand to me, signaling me to stay while he proceeded, but I snatched his wrist and shook my head no. He hesitated, his annoyance felt rather than seen, but then he nodded and we crawled forward together, bellies close to the ground.

We came to the low wall that surrounded the cottage grounds, extending some fifty yards out from the house itself. The property encompassed a neat kitchen garden, several sheds, and pens for small livestock. Just beyond the wall a steep, rocky shoreline tumbled into the bay. There a single-masted catamaran sat anchored, exactly where Winty's skipjack had lingered earlier. Like Winty's boat, this vessel had a flat bottom that wouldn't scrape the rocks hidden beneath the waves. Now, as then, men stood at the railing—I counted four of them—but instead of dropping anything into the water, they were carefully lowering, by means of ropes and pulleys, what appeared to be barrels that were caught by two more men standing on the rocks at the water's edge.

I attempted to creep over the wall, but Derrick grabbed the back of my coat and held me fast.

"I want to be able to hear them," I whispered.

His only answer was to press a finger to his lips.

Soon the lines were hoisted and the men onshore climbed back into the boat via a rope ladder. The anchor was raised and the boat turned about. Once again I started to rise, my intent to slip down to the water's edge to see if I could discern what type of barrels and how many now sat waiting on the shore. Once again Derrick tugged me back.

"It's none of our business, Emma. Whatever's

going on here obviously has nothing to do with your cousin."

"Aren't you the least bit curious?"

"No, and you shouldn't be either. You know what they say about curiosity and the cat, don't you?"

"But the men have gone. There's no one to see . . ."

I trailed off at the putter of a steam engine. The sound became progressively louder and soon a small freighter, no larger than twenty-five feet in length, rounded the north end of the island, the farthest point from the lighthouse. About halfway between there and Derrick's and my position, they cut the engine and drifted the rest of the way, dropping anchor exactly where the catamaran had been.

"What the . . ." Derrick seemed to have forgotten his eagerness to leave the scene, for now he craned his neck. I didn't prod him; I was just as interested in this new development as he.

Would Consuelo make an appearance now?

Another rope ladder was dropped over the side of the boat and a pair of rough-looking men clambered partway down and leaped onto the rocky shore. Ropes were tossed over from the deck. Working together, the two men coiled the rope around the first of the barrels, which was then hoisted up the side of the boat. Another pair of men reached over the rail and hauled it the rest of the way, carefully unwinding the rope from around the stout cask and lowering it to the deck. Then they leaned over to await the next piece of cargo.

"What do you suppose is in those barrels?" I whispered to Derrick.

He glanced at me, then stared back at the activity on the water. I made a decision and before Derrick could react, I scrambled over our stone wall.

"Emma!" His frantic whisper grazed my back, but I kept going. I had to learn as much as I could about these goings-on. That they were somehow connected to Winthrop Rutherfurd meant they could also be connected to Consuelo. Quickly, stooping low to keep myself small, I made my way closer to the waterline.

"Hurry it up, dammit. Stanford's waiting. Said he'd dock our pay for every minute we delay."

I stopped in the shadow of a clump of scrub pine and crouched. Stanford. I knew that name. Hope Stanford . . . Oh, but that was ridiculous. What would the temperance leader be doing consorting with midnight brigands? Stanford was a common enough name—

A presence at my back nearly forced a gasp from my lips, but I swallowed it down. Derrick had followed me and now he slipped a hand around my forearm and squeezed. He didn't have to speak to convey his meaning. He wanted us gone from there. I turned back to the steamer, hoping to catch a glimpse of something that made sense before Derrick dragged me away.

"D'ya see that?"

"What? Where?"

"Up there! I think someone's there."

"Shit!"

More expletives followed, but Derrick and I didn't wait around to hear them. Our feet were in motion taking us back the way we'd come, heedless now of how much racket we raised. Footsteps pounded behind us. Derrick's hand clamped around my own and he pulled me along over the wall, then over rocks, dips, and hillocks. My feet protested inside Aunt Sadie's boots, which pinched my toes. My cap flew off and bits of my hair came loose and flopped in my face. I gasped for breath and ran blindly, until Derrick's arm went around me, scooped me off my feet, and I was tossed to the deck of our little boat.

The dinghy rocked with Derrick's weight as he jumped in after me. Our pursuers reached the narrow beach, their strides sending pebbles skittering across the sand to ping against our oaken hull. Fear clawed at my throat and clouded my thinking. Just as groping hands reached out to catch hold of the boat, we shoved away from the shore.

Derrick rowed madly, grunting with the effort. And I . . . I could only sit and watch the island recede, with those men standing on the sand, their fists raised in our direction.

My breath of relief was drowned out by the chugging of a steam engine.

Like some hulking sea monster angry to be awakened from its slumber, the freighter rounded the island and headed straight for us. It cut through the water, gaining momentum, and within seconds Derrick and I both knew he could not out-paddle the larger craft. We knew, too, that it would not swerve away at the last minute.

I thought to lean out over the water and paddle with my hands, anything to help Derrick bring us to land faster. But each instant brought the freighter closer, the water it displaced sending a bulging wave beneath us that hindered our progress even more. Soon, the freighter was nearly upon us, and, heart surging to my throat, I glimpsed one of those men standing at the center of the prow, grinning fiendlike as he anticipated our demise.

"Emma, jump!"

Derrick's shout filled me with terror. He dropped the oars, one hitting the deck, the other sliding ineffectually through its rowlock and into the water. Jump? I shook my head. But at the same time I realized there was no other way, no other hope.

"To your right! Go deep!" As if he didn't trust me to understand, Derrick lunged to his feet, locked a hand around my shoulder, and shoved me even as he sprang over the side of the dinghy himself. Together we went in headfirst, and in the last instant before we hit the water I sucked in a breath.

Instinct took over; I kicked my feet and flapped my arms. I searched frantically for the surface, but Derrick tugged me lower and lower still. Boulders struck my sides and scraped my legs through my trousers. For a moment I fought him, but then I remembered his command and realized the sense in allowing him to tow me as deep as we dared for as long as our breath held out.

A sound like distant thunder boomed in my ears, eerily muffled but no less violent. A shock wave followed, pitching us sideways into the currents. Through the darkness, with my eyes shut tight against the brine, I rolled, spiraled, then thudded side-first into Derrick. His arms went around me briefly before falling away. In that instant I panicked. But his hand found mine and he held on as never to let me go.

My lungs shrieked for air, but I resisted the urge to surface. When cruel talons tore at my lungs and I thought I could stand it no longer, Derrick kicked away from the rocks we clung to and began our ascent—too slowly for my comfort, but I trusted him. We didn't know what we'd find when we broke the surface. Would those awful men be waiting?

But it was the quiet night, disturbed only by the wistful tolling of a buoy bell, that greeted us. My mouth surged open and I dragged in precious oxygen, filling my lungs painfully but gratefully. The freighter was nowhere in sight, and any sound from its engine now merged with the tide, the breeze, and the other ordinary sounds carrying across the water. Perhaps they'd circled back around the island, or perhaps they'd sailed farther along the coastline to blend in with the other vessels moored in the harbor. Would Uncle William gaze out from *The Valiant*, glimpse the men who had almost killed us, and, with an aristocrat's indifference to the commonplace, think nothing of them?

At that moment I couldn't summon the strength to care. I realized the only thing holding me above the waterline was Derrick; I'd collapsed against him, my cheek sunk against his shoulder. He kept tight hold of me, his own panting breaths heaving me up and down. I searched the water for the dinghy. Splintered boards littered the gentle tide, no more useful to us now than driftwood.

"Grab hold of a board," he whispered, "it'll help us float." With one arm around me, Derrick dragged his other through the water to pull us in the direction of the shore. "We've got to swim for it."

I lifted my head and nodded, still too exhausted to speak. Together, both of us kicking and using the broken board as a floatation device, we struggled toward land. Thank goodness I'd worn trousers; with skirts and petticoats holding us back—well, I wouldn't like to contemplate what might have happened.

We reached the shore some half mile from where we'd started, no longer at the McPaddens' dock but farther north, near where the Point gave way to the shipyards.

"Dear God, Emma," Derrick managed between panting breaths, "we need to double back south."

We'd reached the seawall, which soared some twenty feet above our heads, creating a slick, vertical barricade between us and land. "It's all right." I had barely enough strength left to croak the words. "Just a little farther north. Trust me."

Derrick apparently did trust me, because without another word we felt our way along that slippery barrier until my outstretched hand found what I was searching for—steps built into the wall, rising up and out of the water.

With our remaining strength we yanked our ankles free of tangling seaweed and pulled ourselves up. I went first, crab-walking on all fours to avoid slipping off the steps. Derrick followed close behind me, his hands never fully releasing their hold on the back of my waist. Finally, we pulled ourselves up and over, and fell facedown onto a weed-choked mound of earth beside the road that ran along the seawall.

My eyes fell closed, and when I opened them again I was no longer sprawled on the ground with the sandy grit between my teeth, but lying with my cheek on Derrick's chest, his hard body like a shield beneath mine protecting me from the elements. His arms once more encircled me tightly, I might even say forcefully. I let out a sigh deeper and longer than I believe I'd ever sighed before, a trembling breath of relief and gratitude and, yes, tremendous affection for the man who was somehow always there when I most needed him. And then I promptly passed out.

When I awoke sometime later, the stars were gone and the sky had turned a tarnished silver color. Dawn couldn't be far off. I stirred, disoriented and half-disbelieving the memories that rose up like a sudden squall. But I held no illusions as to where I was: on a sandy, narrow bank beside the harbor, cradled by the man who had saved my life.

I still lay on top of him; his arms still held me, though looser now, as though he slept. Yet when I slid one hand to the ground and pushed up to peer into his patrician features, his dark eyes were open and staring into my own. His lips curved into a smile. Good heavens, that he found both the energy and the frame of mind to reassure me with that small gesture . . . I can't say how much that meant to me, how it warmed me despite the predawn chill.

Our clothes had dried, leaving them stiff and caked with salt and bits of seaweed. My skin itched everywhere, and my hair clung to my cheeks, neck, and the underside of my chin. With one hand I swept back the encrusted strands. Then I summoned a smile for Derrick.

"Thank you."

His hands moved gently up and down my back, warming me further. "How do you feel? Does anything hurt? No, don't try to move too much yet." He gently cupped my head and lowered it back to his chest; and when he spoke again the rumble of his voice traveled through me with the steadying strength of brandy. "I wanted to carry you to safety," he said, "but I was afraid to move you. There were those rocks we hit and if anything is broken . . ."

I shook my head against him. "I don't think so." I stretched slightly, wiggled my feet, and moved my legs. "I ache all over, but it's a dull ache. Nothing sharp."

He released a breath. "That's good."

"What about you?"

"The exercise did me good."

I chuckled, then started to sit up. "We should go."

"In a minute. Just give me another moment to . . ." With one hand he gathered up my hair, lifting it off my back. He rolled us until we lay side by side, and then his face was close, his lips closer. And yet he didn't kiss me; not quite. He merely touched his lips to mine, our foreheads pressing, his nose grazing my cheek. We stayed like that for some moments before he slowly eased away, sat up, and helped me to my feet as he rose to his.

"You'll be the death of me yet, Emma Cross."

The words were anything but flattering, but the tone in which he spoke them lit a flame in my heart.

The sky had lightened, the eastern horizon tinged with pink. The place where we lay was adjacent to a row of houses whose yards faced the harbor. People would be stirring soon and we needed to make haste back to my carriage—and he to his, I supposed. "How on earth did you follow me without my knowing?"

"Oh, Emma . . . dear Emma." He chuckled softly. "Once I saw the direction you were headed in, and in those clothes . . ." He tugged on the sleeve of the man's coat I somehow still wore. "It wasn't hard to figure out where you were going. I stayed well behind, and when you turned your carriage onto Walnut Street I continued on foot."

"But at what point did you *start* following me?"

He smiled that same smile he'd shown me when I'd first accused him of spying on me. I should have been furious. Only, I couldn't deny the simple fact that if he hadn't trailed me, I'd be dead.

"We'll collect your carriage and mine," he said briskly. "I left it at the end of Third Street. And then I'll follow you home. If you think you can drive, that is."

"You don't have to do that—"

"Are you going to waste your breath arguing with me?"

I couldn't help a quick roll of my eyes. "No, I suppose not."

As we proceeded down the street the distance between us grew—not by any conscious agreement, but instinctively. We walked as a pair of men would, close enough to speak without being *too* close. Yet I continued to feel the echo of his arms around me, and I found it difficult to concentrate on what he was saying until he cast me a dubious frown.

"Do you think you have the strength to handle your rig?"

"We're talking about Barney here, hardly a challenge. I'll be fine. But speaking of conveyances . . . I'll need to replace the McPaddens' dinghy." I blew between my lips. How would I scrape up enough cash for a boat, even a small one? And how would I ever explain it to them?

As if he read my thoughts, Derrick said, "I'll take care of it."

"No, I couldn't let you do that."

We turned onto Walnut Street. I continued protesting about how the night's debacle was entirely my fault and I would take proper responsibility for the damages I'd caused. Derrick brought us to a halt. With his hands on my shoulders, he turned me to face him.

"Shut up, Emma. For once, please just shut up."

I had nothing to say to that.

When we arrived home we unhitched both rigs—mine, and Derrick's hired curricle—and settled Barney and his guest in the barn with oats and water and piles of fresh hay. The chores helped settle my nerves. We worked in companionable silence, and once the task had been accomplished, Derrick and I strolled to the house, the invitation for him to join me unspoken . . . not needing to be spoken. I wasn't ready to relinquish his company yet, and he seemed equally intent on remaining. When we reached the kitchen door he opened it for me, and I was overcome by a rush of how it might be to share a home with this man, to share those casual daily acts such as having breakfast, planning our days, settling in together each night. . . .

A cheerful fire in the kitchen hearth greeted us as we stepped inside. A pot of coffee simmered on the stove, and the aroma of baking bread made my stomach rumble.

"I was just about to send out the cavalry." Nanny stood in the doorway of the corridor that led to the morning room, her tight-lipped expression one of mingled censure and relief. She wore her dressing gown wrapped tightly around her faded cotton nightdress; a kerchief secured the coil of her salt and pepper curls.

I embraced her and kissed her cheek. "Oh, Nanny, have you been up all night?"

"Of course not," she retorted as she hugged me back. Despite her denial, the shadows beneath her eyes told a different story. "I can see *you* haven't slept a wink," she concluded after assessing me from head to toe.

"Actually, we did get a bit of sleep," I said, then regretted it when her eyebrows shot up. Before I could explain, Derrick spoke.

"I assure you Emma's virtue is safe, Mrs. O'Neal. Which is more than I can say for the rest of her, with the way she insists on chasing danger."

I swung about and struck him on the biceps, hard. Not that it fazed him in the least. Nanny clucked her tongue and, grabbing two towels off the counter, wrapped them around her hands and went to the stove.

"You both look like something the tide dragged up. Smell like it, too. You should both go and get changed. Emma, I'm sure you can find something of Brady's for Mr. Andrews." The oven door hinges whined. The toasty scents of breakfast bread—stuffed with raisins and walnuts, and dusted with cinnamon—enveloped me and I knew, in a way I hadn't up until then, at least not wholly, that I was home. That I was safe. Once again relief poured through me, this time sapping the remaining strength from my legs. I sagged, and before I knew it Derrick's arm was around me. He pulled out a chair from the kitchen table and lowered me into it.

"I need something to eat first or I'll faint," I said. A nod from Derrick indicated he'd gladly put the needs of his stomach over clean clothing.

Nanny sliced her savory-sweet bread and handed it round while Derrick poured the coffee. The hearth fire snapped and hissed. I was glad we'd stayed here in the kitchen rather than moving to the morning room. This felt homier, cozier, like when I was a child and padded downstairs before any of the rest of my family to steal some private time with Nanny. Gradually my remaining anxiety eased away. I chewed slowly and, with a finally clear head, began to contemplate the events of last night.

"One thing is certain," I said, breaking the pensive silence, "if Consuelo *was* on Rose Island, it wasn't by choice."

"What makes you so sure?" Derrick asked.

"She would never have anything to do with men like that. Never."

Nanny plucked a walnut from her slice of bread and popped it into her mouth. "What if she was there against her will?"

I shook my head. "I don't think she was there

at all. Whatever those men were doing, I don't think it had anything to do with her. They were criminals . . . some kind of smugglers is my guess."

I looked to Derrick for consensus. He nodded faintly. I waited for him to elaborate, and when he didn't I prompted, "Well? What do you think they were up to?"

He shrugged a shoulder, cradling his cup in both hands. "Judging by the barrels we saw, molasses, possibly."

"Why on earth would anyone smuggle molasses?" Nanny laughed as if this were the most ridiculous notion in the world. "You can buy it anywhere. Not as if it's illegal or anything. I've got plenty right in the pantry."

I had to admit, I couldn't fathom an answer. Once more I looked to Derrick, who reluctantly met my gaze.

"Molasses is used in rum making. It would seem someone is going into business for himself, distilling black market rum to avoid paying the liquor tax. Could be trying to corner the market, create a monopoly by running legitimate distillers out of business." His gaze sharpened, practically pinning me to the back of my chair. "Whatever their intentions, it had nothing to do with your cousin and therefore nothing to do with you."

"Hear, hear," Nanny murmured.

I scrunched up my nose. "Maybe not, but

what's Winthrop Rutherfurd's part in all this? I can't see him putting in with rum smugglers."

"A coincidence?" Nanny suggested.

"I doubt it. Just as I doubt it's any coincidence the Curtises are away."

"Who are they?" Derrick asked.

"The couple who run the Rose Light. When I spotted Winty heading out to the island yesterday, Angus told me they were away for a few days."

Derrick made an impatient gesture. "Winty? Angus?"

"Angus was the boatman who rowed me out to *The Valiant* yesterday afternoon. Winty is Consuelo's pet name for Winthrop Rutherfurd." I blew out an equally impatient breath. "Do keep up."

Nanny chuckled and Derrick sent me a glower. "Could *Winty* be having money troubles?" he asked.

I glanced at Nanny. "Have you heard anything to that effect?"

She sipped her coffee. "He wanted to marry Consuelo, didn't he?"

"Because he cares for her," I shot back.

"The Rutherfurds are an old family, Emma," she said mildly. "And none of the old families is as wealthy as they used to be."

"That's right," Derrick said. "It's the so-called nouveau riche who control the bulk of the wealth in this country now. People in industry like your

Vanderbilt relatives and yes, my family. The Vanderbilts' hands are sooty from the railroads. The Andrewses' hands are ink-stained from the newspaper business." He held up his hands as if to prove his point, though there were no stains that I could make out, nothing to indicate he'd ever worked a hard day in his life. "People like the Rutherfurds didn't believe in soiling their hands in business, and as a result their fortunes have been dwindling away for generations."

"I suppose it would be naïve of me to insist he wanted Consuelo only for herself." I sighed. Consuelo had certainly believed it, at least until Winty had stepped all too willingly out of the picture once Alva made it clear she'd never allow them to marry. Yes, elopement remained a possibility, but Consuelo would be disinherited, virtually penniless. Would Winty want her then? "Poor Consuelo . . ."

"Emma . . ." Derrick placed a hand over mine where it lay beside my plate. "Don't you think it's time the police were notified of Consuelo's disappearance? How long has it been?"

"Two days." Across the table from me, Nanny nodded her agreement. "I know you're right," I said, "but Aunt Alva . . ."

"What are you most afraid of?" Nanny asked. "Your aunt Alva's temper or your cousin coming to harm?"

Her words put matters into perspective and I

realized the decision was already made. "I'll go to Jesse tomorrow. Surely he'll be able to keep things quiet and out of the newspapers." I couldn't help eyeing Derrick. We were newspaper people, he and I; we both knew the lure of a good story. "Consuelo's disappearance would make national headlines, Derrick. You'll keep my confidence, won't you? Please promise me."

A glimmer of hurt entered his eyes. "Do you honestly think I'd betray your trust for a headline?"

"No, of course not," I said quickly. But hadn't I? Or was I just exhausted and not thinking straight? "Derrick, I'm sorry. I needed to be sure."

He came to his feet. "You know, Emma, perhaps you've been spending too much time with your Vanderbilt relatives."

"What does that mean? Derrick—"

"It means you need to learn to take people at their word and trust them. Good day, ladies." With that he crossed to the kitchen door and was gone.

I stared after him, then looked to Nanny in hopes of gleaning some sort of comfort. There was none to be found, just a look of disappointment and a sad shake of her head.

After Nanny's warm breakfast and a hot bath, I slept for several hours. One might think nightmares would have awakened me at every turn, but the truth is I slept like the dead and dreamed of nothing. Not of my missing cousin, not of those murderous men on Rose Island, not of the chilling, rocky depths of Narragansett Bay . . . and not even of Derrick, whom I'd wronged inexcusably that morning. Exhaustion claimed me completely, and I might have slumbered in that dreamless state until the next day if the telephone downstairs hadn't jangled me awake sometime in the mid-afternoon.

I bolted upright, disoriented at first, confused by the angle of the sunlight hitting the backs of the window curtains. What was I doing in bed in the middle of the day? It took only a glint off the ocean through a gap in the curtains, and another jingle of the telephone bell, to bring the memories flooding back. Could the caller have news of Consuelo?

Katie's Irish tones drifted up the staircase as I hurried down, securing my dressing gown around me. "Miss Cross isn't available just now—"

"I'm here, Katie." My slippered feet slid on the floorboards as I circled to the alcove beneath the stairs and glided to a stop in front of her. "Who is it?"

"Mr. Millford from the paper, miss."

I practically snatched the earpiece from her hand. We sidestepped each other and Katie made her way down the corridor to the rear of the house. "Mr. Millford? What happened to my article yesterday morning? The one about the murder at Marble House? Why wasn't it—"

"Emma, glad I caught you at home," he said, neither acknowledging my question nor pausing for pleasantries. "How quickly can you get into town?"

I glanced down at my dishabille, thought about my aching side, and winced. "Oh, uh, not long. Has something happened? Is this anything to do with the murder?"

"In a way, yes. You'll be here soon, then?"

Within the hour I brought my carriage to a stop outside the *Observer*'s offices. Whatever Mr. Millford wished to talk to me about, I resolved not to give him the chance until I'd learned why my story about Madame Devereaux's murder hadn't been run.

The question never left my mouth. I strode into Mr. Millford's private office to find Ed Billings there as well, and looking as pleased as a popinjay in full plumage.

"Emma, you'll never guess what." My fellow reporter practically danced a jig in front of me while Mr. Millford looked on from the other side of his desk with the air of a proud parent.

I blew out a breath, knowing whatever had happened, I'd been beaten once again. "I give up, Ed. What?"

"Anthony Dobbs has been implicated in the murder at your aunt's house. Implicated by *me*, Emma."

I staggered to Mr. Millford's old, scarred desk and clutched the edges of it for support. Ed's words pounded through me. Anthony Dobbs . . . a murderer? The man who not two weeks ago had accused my own brother of a similar crime? Black spots danced before my eyes and a rushing like ocean waves filled my ears.

After what might have been only seconds, or as much as several minutes, I found myself able to gain control of my breathing and face Ed. "How do you know this?"

"I've been asking questions all over town ever since he was charged with extortion." Can a peacock flash a self-satisfied grin? This one did. "Seems our detective is quite the braggart, especially when he's been drinking. More than one source told me Tony's been, ah, having *relations* with that little maid, the one who actually did the dirty deed."

CHAPTER 9

"Anthony Dobbs and . . . Clara?" The notion clashed like cymbals inside me, because here might be the elusive motive—the reason Clara might have had to kill Madame Devereaux.

"You bet," Ed returned almost joyfully. "I've just been to the police with my evidence, and Tony's already been arrested. He'd tried extorting that medium just like he did the other shady characters in town. She threatened to expose him, so he put Clara Parker up to it. Probably told the girl he loved her so she'd be more than willing."

I shifted my gaze to Mr. Millford. He nodded. "No one else but us has the story as far as we know, Emma, and we'll be the first to run it. That's why I called you in. I want you to sit down with Ed and tell him everything you remember from the murder scene, including what Clara said during the preliminary questioning. You *were* there, weren't you?"

"Yes, I was, but . . ." My temples throbbed. "My article, Mr. Millford. All the details are there. Why didn't you run it?"

With one woman dead and my cousin still missing, my concerns were petty. I *knew* that. Yet I couldn't help myself. Once again my employer had delivered a pat to my head before attempting to shove me aside.

He got to his feet and circled the desk to stand in front of me, where he smiled with grandfatherly kindness. "Now, now, Emma, don't be upset. Ed has managed to sniff out the whole story. The other papers, they all ran stories that included only half the facts. By waiting and running this as our headline, we'll outshine every other paper not only in Newport, but the whole of Rhode Island."

"Only because I've filled in the details." My heart thumped painfully in my throat. I tugged the bow at my neckline. "Why should I write three quarters of Ed's article for him when my own account of the murder was ignored?"

"Because nobody cared, Emma," my nemesis declared. "The locals couldn't give a fig about this Madame Duvreau—"

"Devereaux," I all but shouted. "It's a detail, Ed. Get it right."

This was met with an eye roll and a tug at the corner of his mouth. "Whatever her name is," he replied with infuriating calm, "she wasn't going to have Newport's full attention until now, when a local became involved. Now it's piqued everyone's curiosity. Now it's big news."

"I cannot believe you," I murmured. Faintly I heard Mr. Millford's gentle admonishment that I remain calm, see reason, but I couldn't calm

189

down. I was tired of being reasonable, dignified, *ladylike*. I'd had it up to the neat little bow on my collar with graciously stepping aside and letting Ed Billings steal my headlines. "A woman was killed—*killed,* Ed. Do you understand what that means? Do you have a thimble's worth of empathy in you? Do you even care that a life was snuffed out or that a young girl like Clara might hang for the crime? No," I continued when he opened his mouth to reply, "I don't believe you do. All you care about is seeing your byline beneath the front page headlines, and it doesn't matter to you how it gets there. Not even if you have to steal your facts from me."

"From you?" Ed chuckled, a sound that nearly drove me to commit murder myself.

Luckily for Ed, Mr. Millford intervened. "That's enough, both of you. Ed, come to think of it, it won't be necessary after all for you to consult with Emma."

I experienced a moment's elation that perhaps at long last I'd be shown some fairness, that I'd finally find validation as a reporter. And then Mr. Millford went on. "I'd quite forgotten I have Emma's article right here." He went back behind the desk and stooped to open the top drawer. He pulled out a sheaf of paper filled with familiar handwritten lines. "Here you go, Ed."

Open-mouthed and incredulous, I watched Ed take my article from our employer's outstretched hand. "Thanks," was all he said before he about-faced and strode from the room.

"Get the completed article to me within the hour," Mr. Millford called after him. "We'll run the presses this afternoon and have a special edition on the newsstands by tonight."

"I . . . but . . ." Turning back to him, I struck my fists on the desktop, making Mr. Millford flinch. "How could you? That is my article—my headline. How can you just hand it to Ed like that, as if feeding him with a silver spoon?"

His brown eyes regarded me coolly. "I've told you before, Emma. You do fine work. You'd make a fine investigative reporter . . . *if* you were a man. But you are not a man, Emma. And people don't want to read stories of violence and mayhem written by a woman. Not unless we're talking about fiction, and even then . . ." Trailing off, he turned his attention to an open ledger book in front of him. He picked up a pen and made a quick notation while I stood on the other side of his desk, thunderstruck and doing my utmost to prevent my stinging tears from falling.

He glanced up at me briefly before returning his gaze to the figures in his book. "That will be all for now, Emma. Sorry to have brought you all the way into town for nothing."

Even then, I didn't leave. I couldn't move. Surely that couldn't be all. Surely I couldn't be dismissed as easily as that. In my heart, I felt the spirit of my aunt Sadie give a nudge. I could all but hear her demanding justice, and prompting me to stand up—*speak up*—for myself.

But my throat constricted around the words, and my jaws ached from clenching my teeth. I knew if I attempted to push out so much as a whimper, those humiliating, bitter tears would spill over. Yet all the same, I couldn't bring myself to walk away.

Mr. Millford finally looked up again. This time he set down his pen and leaned back in his chair with a sigh. "Emma, this is the world we live in. Women simply don't report on heinous crimes like murder. I'm sorry. I'd change it if I could."

"Would you?" I managed, my voice rasping like pebbles over sand.

"I gave you a job, didn't I?" He attempted a placating smile.

I said nothing.

"And it's a job you're good at. Your Fancies and Fashions column is wildly popular."

Still, I remained silent. It had suddenly occurred to me that the less I spoke, the more conciliatory Mr. Millford seemed to become. I wondered where it might lead. . . .

He tapped his fingertips against his leather blotter. "How about if I start sending your society write-ups to the Providence papers? I bet they'd love to run them. Surely Rhode Island readers would eat up your accounts of Newport's social season. You know, the insider's view and all that. I'll bet none of the Providence papers has someone like you working for them."

Did he really think to placate me by expanding the circulation of my society page? I folded my arms and compressed my lips.

Mr. Millford snapped his ledger book shut. "All right, Emma. Ed gets this headline. But if you can crack this case—either prove or disprove Anthony Dobbs's and Clara Parker's guilt—that headline will be yours."

Bracing my hands on the desk, I leaned over and across, bringing my face close to his. "Do you swear?"

His eyebrow went up; I'd clearly taken him by surprise. "I . . . I suppose so."

"No, don't suppose. If I can do the job—get the information and write you one spectacular story—you will run the headline with my name beneath it?"

"How would you feel about a pseudonym?"

"*My* name, Mr. Millford." My hand closed around the nearest object, a heavy, brass-framed magnifying glass. I gripped the long handle as if the piece were a hammer and tapped it twice against the desktop. "My headline, my name. It's no more than I deserve."

Considering I'd been close to tears only moments ago, where on earth had this gumption come from? Silently I thanked Aunt Sadie while I continued to hold Mr. Millford's baffled, startled gaze with my own.

"All right, Emma. Yes. Your headline, your name. But only if your story is truly front-page worthy."

"Promise me."

"Fine. I promise."

I straightened and very nearly let out a whoop of triumph. Then his hand went up, the flat of his palm like a policeman's warning to halt. "I want a promise, too, Emma. That you won't go doing anything foolhardy or dangerous in order to get the story."

That gave me pause, but only for an instant. "Fine. I promise I won't do anything foolhardy."

He didn't seem to notice that I left out the word *dangerous* from my promise, or that we hadn't settled on the meaning of *foolhardy*. Certainly I would proceed carefully and logically, just as I had when I had previously sought to clear my brother's name of murder. If my careful and logical plan put me in danger . . . well . . . as I said, I had omitted that word from my promise.

For now, I'd leave Ed Billings to write his wretched article. My next stop, meanwhile, would be the jailhouse.

Promises were complicated, and that promise to Mr. Millford wasn't the only one I'd made in recent days. I'd promised Aunt Alva I'd find

Consuelo without involving the police. But just that morning I'd promised Derrick and Nanny and even myself that Consuelo's welfare would take priority over Aunt Alva's wishes.

Upon arriving on Marlborough Street, I entered the columned building and headed straight for Jesse's desk in the large main room. My palms sweated and my mouth ran dry, but I had to do the right thing, for my cousin's sake.

Jesse stood when he saw me enter through the wide archway, and strode to meet me partway across the room. Around us, police officers were milling around, consulting with each other, tapping on typewriters, and stuffing fistfuls of papers into filing cabinets. Along the wall where a pair of telephones was located, two plainclothes officers barked orders into the transmitters while pressing the receivers tight to their ears. A loud hum of activity surrounded me, yet it was the throbbing of my own pulse in my ears that drowned out Jesse's greeting.

He shook my hand, then kept hold of it as he led me back to his desk. Briefly my gaze landed on the workspace directly behind his, the chair unoccupied and the blotter swept clean of papers, notebooks, and pens. That desk belonged to Anthony Dobbs.

"What brings you here, Emma?" Jesse asked as he beckoned me into the chair that faced his across the desk.

I leaned forward, my hands tight around my purse in my lap. "I need to tell you something, but I need you to promise me you'll be discreet."

His brows gathered above his nose and his gaze sharpened. Promises were about to become even more complicated.

"This doesn't bode well so far, Emma."

I stole a quick glance over my shoulder. Briefly I considered asking if we could go somewhere more private, but I realized that would only bring more attention to us, whereas in the busy room, no one paid us any heed. I craned my neck in Jesse's direction and spoke quietly. "I need your help, Jesse, but in asking for it I'll be breaking my own promise to someone and . . . well . . . that person could make life difficult for both of us."

"Hmm, let me guess." His teeth nipped at his bottom lip. "Could we be speaking of Alva Vanderbilt?"

"Jesse, please . . ."

Anger claimed his features, but a wave of his hand signaled compliance. "Whatever you tell me will be held in confidence." Before I could begin my tale, he added, "For as long as it can be, Emma. But if what you're about to ask of me puts anyone in danger—yourself included—then I'll have no choice but to call in reinforcements."

"Fair enough." I took another glance around and leaned closer still. "My cousin Consuelo is missing. Has been since the murder."

"What?" Jesse went ramrod straight, his complexion turning ruddy. "And her mother didn't see fit to report this?" Realization dawned in his features. "I asked her where her daughter was that day. She lied to me—" His mouth opened, then snapped shut, then opened again. "You lied, too, Emma. At least by omission."

"That's not true. When you asked about Consuelo, Aunt Alva and I believed her to be in her room. We had no idea she was missing until after you'd left. You asked me to speak with her and I went up to her room for exactly that purpose. Only, she wasn't there. She wasn't anywhere in the house."

"And you have no idea where she went?"

"None."

"You've had no word from her at all?"

I shook my head.

"Good heavens, Emma, what were you thinking?" His voice rose an octave and I quickly shushed him.

"Jesse, please. No one can know."

"Why in the world not? Doesn't her mother want her found? Don't you? We need to notify the state police. Get the federal agents involved—"

"No, that's exactly what we can't do. Please calm down and listen to me."

It took him some moments, but Jesse managed to rein in his irate disbelief and I began explaining. It wasn't until I revealed what I'd

197

read in her diary that he seemed to reach an understanding. "So you see," I said, "we have every reason to believe she left the house of her own accord. It's too much of a coincidence that she might have been kidnapped on the very day she wrote about wanting to find a life of her own. Nor is it quite possible that she left Newport. She is too recognizable to have gotten far without word of her whereabouts reaching Aunt Alva or her father."

"Yes, I see your point there. But even so, the police could help you find her. She might have been home by now if you'd come to me sooner."

"Her mother doesn't want word of this getting out. It would destroy Consuelo's reputation, and with the Duke of Marlborough on his way—"

"Society people," he murmured, his derision plain. "How do you do it, Emma?"

"Do what?"

"Move in their world. Put up with their ridiculous notions."

I shrugged. "Is a ruined reputation a liability only in their world? No, Jesse. Every woman must be vigilant every moment of her life."

He let that pass, his brow furrowing. "So, you've checked with Miss Vanderbilt's closest friends?"

"Everyone I could think of that she'd go to for help."

"But for all you know, someone may have lied.

She could have been in a room right above your head, and you wouldn't have been the wiser."

I conceded the possibility. "I suppose that's why I'm here. I'm about out of ideas. Nanny is helping, of course, but so far she hasn't heard anything."

He pushed paper and a pen across the desk to me, then set a pot of ink at my elbow. "Write down the names of her friends for me."

While I complied, he sat back with a pensive look. When I finished I slid the paper back to him. He stared down at my list, chewing the inside of his cheek.

"If I'm going to be any help to you at all," he said, "I'm going to have to bring a few men into this."

"Jesse, you can't."

"There's no other way to keep an eye on the people on your list. But see here. What I can do is have my men report back to me on visitors to their homes, whom they're seen with in town, that sort of thing."

"Won't your men wonder why they're shadowing some of society's most prominent figures?"

Jesse smiled. "They might. But that doesn't mean I have to tell them." Through his coat, he tapped the badge she knew was tucked in the inside breast pocket. "This means I get to give orders without having to explain myself. But I can only use so much manpower before my chief starts asking questions, so if we don't find your cousin soon, Emma . . ."

His thought went unfinished, but I understood. We were fast running out of time.

I came to my feet and Jesse did the same. "I'm glad you finally came to me with this," he said. "It's in Miss Vanderbilt's best interests."

"I know. Thank you, Jesse."

"I'll see you out," he offered, but I didn't move to go.

"I do have one more favor to ask. Or two, actually."

His eyes closed briefly as he shook his head. "Why am I not surprised?"

Jesse denied my first request. Or Anthony Dobbs did, I should say, by having stated upon his arrest that he would refuse all visitors except his lawyer. This unexpected roadblock frustrated me no end, but Jesse would not be persuaded otherwise. I supposed Dobbs wouldn't have answered my questions anyway. My second request was more easily granted, and within minutes I stood where Jesse instructed me to, some three feet in front of the bars that lined Clara Parker's cell. In deference to her being a woman, the police had housed her in a small, little-used section of the jail where she would not suffer the indignity of being seen by any male prisoners.

Upon seeing me approach she jumped up from her sagging cot and gripped the bars in front of her.

"Oh, Miss Cross, I wouldn't hurt anyone. I swear I wouldn't. You have to believe me."

In my gentlest tone I said, "I'm not here to accuse you, Clara."

The poor thing still wore the maid's uniform she had been arrested in, except that the snowy white pinafore and the straight pins that held it in place were gone. Had the officers thought she might use the pins as a weapon, or strangle herself with the apron ties?

"As God is my witness, miss, I didn't take the scarf from Lady Amelia's room. I'd never seen it before . . . before . . ." Her head sank between her shoulders and her moan seemed to shiver up the bars of the cell. Her hair hung in limp strands around her face, and dark smudges made her eyes appear huge in her wan face. "Oh, please, miss, someone has to help me."

My heart went out to her and I very nearly eased closer to grasp the fragile hand she stretched through the bars. But at the far end of the aisle between the four cells stood a door with a tiny window, and on the other side of the wavy glass a grim-faced guard stood watching. Jesse's last words to me had been a warning to stay back or I'd be ushered from the building.

"I'm here to help you, Clara."

She seemed not to hear me, but continued her pleading. "And I heard those footsteps . . . they could have been the murderer's, but no one believes me."

"I know you did, Clara. Detective Whyte knows it, too, and I promise he's investigating all possibilities."

Her face inched upward, those impossibly large, red-rimmed eyes locking with mine. "Why are you here, miss?"

I tried to choose my words carefully. "Clara, it's come to the attention of the police that someone, a man, might have had a hand in Madame Devereaux's murder."

"The police have already asked me if someone put me up to it." Clara's voice trembled, its timbre as weak as a kitten's. "I didn't understand. They wouldn't tell me who they meant. I just kept telling them I didn't do it."

So she didn't know about Anthony Dobbs's arrest. I decided to take another tack. "Clara, dear, when you weren't working at Marble House, was there anyone special you spent your time with? In town, perhaps?"

A wary gleam entered her eyes and she took a long moment before answering. "I worked most of the time, miss. Six days a week. On Sunday I went to church. You know that. We both attend at St. Paul's."

"Yes, but what about Saturday nights? You

went off duty by seven o'clock unless Mrs. Vanderbilt was holding a party, yes?"

"Yes, but . . . why are you asking me these questions, miss?"

The police might not have informed Clara of Dobbs's arrest, but it *was* on public record and no one had instructed me *not* to tell her. I shot a glance down the aisle at our dour audience before hurrying on. "There's been another arrest in connection to the murder. Anthony Dobbs."

Clara let out a yelp and lurched backward as if I'd struck her. "Tony? Oh, God in heaven, why Tony?"

"You know him, Clara, don't you? And I don't just mean you know *of* him."

"Tony," she wailed, as if she hadn't heard me. "Not Tony . . . He didn't. He wouldn't . . . He promised—" Her whisper broke off and her lips clamped suddenly shut. Her eyes gaped wide as she peered at me with a terror-struck expression.

"What did he promise you, Clara?"

"That he'd let me be the one to talk to her. That he wouldn't threaten or . . . or hurt her . . ."

Another sideways glance revealed the guard pressing his face close to the glass with renewed interest. I held up a hand to silence Clara. Very low, I said, "I believe you're innocent and I want to help you, but I can't do that unless I know what happened that day. Why were you in the gazebo, and don't tell me you came out to see if anyone needed anything, because that simply doesn't make sense. There are other servants at Marble House whose job it is to do that."

I held my breath while Clara clearly warred with her fears and uncertainties. To help her along, I said, "You know me, Clara, and you've heard what I've done for other women in trouble. You can trust me."

"She threatened to report him to his superiors," the maid said in a rush.

"She . . . Madame Devereaux?"

Clara nodded in tight, frantic motions.

"The *he* you refer to is Anthony Dobbs?"

She nodded again, her eyes filling with fresh tears. "He wasn't doing anything wrong, not really. Those people, they're all criminals. Taking people's money in exchange for lies and false promises. He was keeping them under control, keeping them from running amok."

"Is that what he told you?" I couldn't quite keep the accusation from my voice, and Clara's response was to tilt her chin in defiance.

But her tears kept right on falling. I thought I'd have to prompt her again when she said, "I went out to the pavilion to talk to Madame Devereaux. To persuade her not to report Tony. To plead with her, threaten her if I had to. Oh, but I wouldn't have hurt her, not really." Her voice broke and she sobbed several times before continuing. "Besides, I never had the chance. I found her dead. I swear it, Miss Cross. The woman was dead when I arrived."

At that moment the main security door swung open. "Time's up."

I had come hoping to gain insight that might help clear Clara, even if it shifted the blame to Anthony Dobbs. Instead, I left the jailhouse with the heavy knowledge that, despite Clara's protestations, I now possessed the key piece that had been missing: her motive for having committed the murder.

Love was a compelling and often irresistible incentive. Every jury knew that.

CHAPTER 10

After leaving the jail, I started back toward home. Exhaustion tugged at every part of me, yet a nagging sensation told me I wouldn't likely find any rest again until late into the night. Today's developments had my mind running like an out-of-control racehorse.

On the other hand, Barney plodded along at his usual sedate pace, and long before the turn onto Ocean Avenue I'd made up my mind to put the remaining daylight hours to good use.

Clara's protestations about the scarf and the footsteps she'd heard claimed the greater part of my speculations. Unless Lady Amelia had been an accessory, how could someone have gained access to her possessions in the house and then make his or her way outside without being noticed? I thought again of Anthony Dobbs. A man of his height and bulk, who moved with all the grace of an ox, could hardly have tiptoed through the house unseen. Come to think of it, in all likelihood I'd have seen him during my pursuit of Consuelo's escaped cat, Muffy, which I'd chased into the library.

I'd probably have seen Clara or anyone else exiting the house before the murder as well. And that led me to suspect that the killer had entered the pavilion from somewhere on the grounds and not from inside the house. That meant the scarf had also already been outside somewhere, accessible to the murderer.

Poor Barney. I'm sure visions of fresh oats and cool water danced in his head, so I whispered a promise that he'd enjoy the very same treats during our stop at Marble House. In fact, when we arrived the groom's youngest assistant, a teenaged boy named Howard, seemed only too happy to unhitch Barney and take good care of him for me.

My conscience soothed for the time being, I circled the house and headed straight for the pavilion. Late-afternoon shadows cloaked the structure in an early dusk, but I bent low, searching for . . .

Anything that had been overlooked thus far. At the request of the police—much to Aunt Alva's dismay—the floor had not yet been scrubbed clean. The soiled tracks I'd seen that day, indistinct as they'd been then, had dried in the interim, been dragged around by the breezes, and now were nothing more than dusty traces of dirt and grass along the floor. Nothing that would suggest a shoe size or type. Still, I scoured the area beneath the tiled roof, looking for a scuff mark, a stain on the marble flooring, anything. Finding nothing new, I went to the railing where Jesse had deduced the murderer had jumped and then crashed through the foliage. I inspected the banister for scratches, dirt—anything. But again, I discovered nothing that hadn't already been noted by the police.

With a sigh I turned to face back into the pavilion, and something in the opposite corner caught my eye.

I strode to it and only just managed not to snatch it up in my haste. No, I wanted to study it right where it was, as well as consider the rest of the pavilion one more time. The table that had been set up for the purpose of reading fortunes still occupied the same space. The linen table-cloth still stretched across it, and on top of that stood the vase of sunflowers and daisies, now looking tired and faded.

I glanced around at the other vases set on small tables around the pavilion, each spilling sprays of sunflowers and daisies that had appeared a good deal happier two days ago. Then I directed my discerning eye back to the corner and the tiny petals that had attracted my notice.

They were neither yellow nor white, nor any other color associated with sunflowers or daisies. They were a deep, dusky pink—creased, browning at the edges and dulling to a rusty hue, but pink nonetheless. Frowning, I made another circuit of the pavilion, this time keeping tight to the rail, bent at the waist so nothing would escape my notice. It wasn't until I'd nearly returned to the first corner that another pair of similar petals met my scrutiny. They'd have been easily missed, wedged as they had obviously been by the breeze up against, and nearly under, the supporting strip that ran along the floor to hold the newel posts in place. In that very narrow gap, two more dusky petals clung. I wondered how many others there might have been that day. Would anyone have noticed them, or would they have disregarded them as merely part of the floral decorations?

A rational voice inside me suggested these petals might have simply blown in on the breeze. But a quick scan of the surrounding bushes and flowers revealed nothing of that specific color. The azalea bushes had long since lost their spring-time blossoms. Besides, my memory conjured them as alternating red and white, not pink.

My guess was these petals belonged to the rose bushes closer to the house, particularly the smaller English tea roses on either side of the terrace steps. If so, any one of Aunt Alma's guests might have tracked them in that day.

But then again, maybe not.

Quickly I opened my purse and rummaged through to find a handkerchief. Carefully, between thumb and forefinger, I plucked each petal from the pavilion floor and placed them between the folds of the linen. They stood out in detailed relief against the fabric, and I clearly saw now these were not rose petals. They were too small and altogether the wrong shape. Where rose petals were broad and tapered to points toward the tips, these were much rounder and smaller, more delicate. Pondering, I folded my handkerchief back up and hurried from the pavilion.

"Mr. Delgado! Mr. Delgado!" I picked up my skirts and, in a manner sure to receive censure from Aunt Alva were she to see me, ran along the garden path away from the house and toward the whitewashed toolsheds, designed to resemble quaint if ornate country cottages.

The man I'd hailed stopped with his hand on the latch of one of these sheds. He broke into a smile when he saw me. Eduardo Delgado, head gardener at Marble House, was a sturdy man, broad-chested, with a full head of silver hair, a leathery complexion, and long-fingered hands that reminded me of a musician's, except for the calluses. "Senhorita Cross, what a pleasure. Aren't you looking as lovely as a fresh summer day?" Even without the light Portuguese cadence, he spoke like a southern European, full of enthusiasm and a chivalrous flattery that always stopped short of being flirtatious. "Is there something I can do for you?"

I acknowledged his compliment with a modest smile of my own. Then I pulled the handkerchief from my purse. "Mr. Delgado, can you tell me what this flower is, and what part of the estate it grows on? I thought it might be a tea rose at first, but now I'm not so certain."

I unfolded the fabric and held it up for him. He squinted and pursed his lips. "No, not one of our tea roses. Even faded I can see the color is off. There is something roselike about it . . . but this is nothing I've cultivated for Mrs. Vanderbilt. It looks more like a wildflower to me."

"A wildflower? Are you sure?"

He shrugged. "There is nothing on the estate with these petals."

I almost questioned him about his certainty, but held my tongue. Aunt Alva wouldn't employ a head gardener who didn't know his cultivated flora like the back of his hand.

"Where did you come upon this?" he asked.

I met his gaze. "In the pavilion."

The word, once synonymous with carefree afternoon entertainments, had taken on sinister connotations for all of us, and I saw it in the creasing of his brow. Before he could reply, however, a whistled tune drifted from the gardens behind me. Jamie Reilly approached us gripping a sack overflowing with cuttings and twigs. "The east beds are all tidy now, sir," he said to Mr. Delgado. Then, "Good day to you, Miss Cross." He dropped his sack to the ground at his feet, removed his cap, wiped a sleeve across his perspiring brow, and set his cap back on his head. "Bit of a hot one, this."

"It's good you came along, Jamie." The note of affection in Mr. Delgado's voice was unmistakable, and I inwardly smiled at this evidence the two were getting on well. I'd helped Jamie secure the position as a favor to my maid, Katie, and looked forward to telling her of our success. "Senhorita Cross has discovered some curious flower petals. Perhaps you know what they are."

I held my handkerchief out to Jamie. "Do you have any idea where something like this would grow, and at this time of year?"

With a slight frown he peered at my find. "Looks like a sort of wildflower . . ."

"As I thought," Mr. Delgado said.

Jamie stroked a finger over one of the petals, imprinting a trail of familiarity across my palm even through the handkerchief. I didn't mind, in fact, quite the opposite. He'd never have dared touch something lying in Aunt Alva's or Consuelo's hand, and I was happily reminded that despite my grandiose connections, I was not someone to fear; I was simply Emma Cross, free to associate with whom I chose.

This passed through my mind in an instant, during which Jamie made his assessment. "For all these seem delicate wee mites, there's a hardiness to 'em and no mistake. I think it'd be a clinging sort of plant, probably along the cliffs."

"Along the cliffs . . . of course." I gazed out across the rear lawns to where they ended at the hedge bordering the Cliff Walk. I thought about the variety of ocean-hardy wildflowers that adorned the cliffs in a mosaic of color, even this late in the summer. "But how on earth could a flower clinging to the cliffs have crossed the border hedge and then traveled so far across the lawn?" Suddenly the petals' potential as a clue faded to nothing, for who would have been climbing cliffs before stealing into the pavilion to murder Madame Devereaux? I blew out a breath and spoke my final thought out loud. "It makes no sense at all."

"Terribly sorry not to be more help, Miss Cross." Jamie seemed to misread my look of dismay as disappointment in him. "Is it very important?"

"I'm sorry, too, senhorita, but perhaps you'll need someone smarter than this old man and that young Irishman"—Mr. Delgado cast Jamie a leathery grin—"to answer your questions." He tapped his forehead. "We know our gardens. But I'm afraid that is all."

"Thank you, Mr. Delgado, Jamie," I said a bit absently. I regarded the petals in my hand another moment before tucking them back away in my purse. We bid each other good day, and as I turned away to let them resume their work, I happened to glance up at the house. A willowy figure stood framed in an upper window, a high-coifed, slender silhouette I immediately identified as Lady Amelia's. She caught my gaze and very obviously flinched as if she had been caught observing us on the sly. She recovered quickly enough and waved, then turned back into the room. Had she merely been bored and looking for distraction, or had she been watching me for another reason?

I let myself into the house through one of the terrace doors. A maid dusting the painting frames in the main floor gallery greeted me cheerfully. A footman carrying silver polish and rags asked if he could do anything for me. Replying no, I asked him if his mistress was at home.

"I believe Mrs. Vanderbilt is resting in her room, Miss Cross."

As with Mr. Delgado, I acknowledged his answer absently and kept going. My feet took me, as if of their own accord, up the stairs, not to Alva's bedroom but to Consuelo's.

My gaze swept my cousin's bedroom—the shelves of costly European dolls, the heavily gilded furniture, the priceless art gracing the walls. A vase of fresh flowers caught my attention, but nothing in the mixed bouquet resembled my petals, nor appeared cultivated anywhere but in the estate's gardens.

I ventured farther in and sat on the bed, in almost the exact spot where Consuelo and I had shared our last confidences. Wave after wave of remorse washed through me. Why had I listened to Aunt Alva and gone against my better judgment? More importantly, if I hadn't, would Consuelo be here now, confiding in me, *trusting* me, as she had always done?

I glanced around again and suddenly realized what it was about this room Consuelo hated so vehemently. The dolls' vacant eyes watched me impassively, yet behind their dull expressions I sensed Aunt Alva's unyielding decrees. Her dictates were everywhere, from the paintings that reflected no young girl's fancies to the incomparable workmanship of the furnishings that made one afraid to touch or sit or even breathe in the wrong direction.

This room symbolized Consuelo's very existence in a way I'd never quite understood before, and now I realized part of my lack of comprehension had been due, quite honestly, to envy.

In my eyes she'd always had everything. Beauty. Intelligence. Privilege. Boundless resources. Had I believed those to be the ingredients of a happy, carefree life? On any ordinary day I'd have said no and meant it. But in my heart of hearts . . . I wasn't so sure. I couldn't but admit part of me had always been jealous of Consuelo in a way I hadn't envied my other Vanderbilt cousins. I thought briefly of Gertrude, Cornelius and Alice's elder daughter, just a year younger than I. She had been born to the same advantages as Consuelo, but possessed none of Consuelo's beauty, nor the inherent grace admired by everyone who knew her.

Consuelo had been blessed in every way a person could be, or so it had seemed from my skewed perspective.

I dropped my purse onto the bed beside me and lowered my face to my hands. But I just as quickly raised my chin and squared my shoulders. Had I wronged Consuelo? Advised her improperly out of my own petty jealousy? I swallowed painfully, knowing I deserved no bouts of self-pity. If I were guilty, then I had no choice but to own up to my fault and do everything I possibly could to make amends. I had to find Consuelo. And I had to support her as she wished to be supported, her mother's wishes be damned.

Even if I made a lifelong enemy in the process.

With that resolve urging me on, I left Consuelo's room. I needed to go back into town, and I hoped I might borrow one of Aunt Alva's smaller rigs to spare Barney the exertion. I didn't get as far as the staircase, however, when humming through an open bedroom door sent me to the threshold.

Hope Stanford sat at the dressing table with a leather-covered jewelry box open before her. Lifting a garnet brooch, she held it up against her summery white blouse with its wide, leg-of-mutton sleeves. After a moment's consideration she set the brooch beside the box and selected a pearl earring, which she held to her lobe in a gesture at odds with her no-nonsense manner and tight, unforgiving coif.

I knocked softly on the open door; her humming broke off and she looked up. "Oh, good afternoon, Miss Cross." She smiled self-consciously and returned the earring to the box. "I was just going through some of my jewelry. Most of it was my mother's, and I'm thinking of selling some, actually. A woman only needs so many baubles, after all."

I grinned and stepped into the room. "Aunt Alva wouldn't agree."

"No, I suppose she wouldn't. But she has had to endure some . . . let us say . . . wearisome influences in her life. Yet her heart is in the right place. She understands a woman needs independence, and that we should be taken seriously and have the same rights as our husbands."

"Does she believe that? I wonder." I perched on the chaise at the foot of the bed. "What about her own daughter?"

I shouldn't have said it, not to a virtual stranger, but I couldn't help myself. Maybe I'd simply grown tired of the Vanderbilt edict that family business never be discussed with outsiders. I wondered what Hope Stanford knew, if anything, about Consuelo's absence. Aunt Alva had probably told her guests Consuelo was visiting a friend in town.

Mrs. Stanford swiveled about on her tufted stool to face me. "That is a bit different, isn't it? Her daughter is very young. She needs a mother's guidance."

"She won't always be young, Mrs. Stanford. But she'll always have to live with the decisions her mother makes for her now."

"Yes, I suppose that's true." Mrs. Stanford tapped her chin. "But she'd also have to live with any disastrous decisions she might make if left to her own devices."

Her reply held a certain sense, I had to admit. I folded my hands in my lap and leaned toward her. "So at what point should a woman be allowed her autonomy?"

"Oh, my dear, that is different for every woman, depending on her circumstances. Take you, for example. Any fool can see you are entirely capable of taking care of yourself. Were I your mother, I would certainly grant you a good measure of independence. Why . . ."

"Yes?"

"Nothing. It's just that I've never had a daughter. Two sons, but no daughters. It's a shame, really, when I think of what I might have taught her. How she might have continued my efforts on behalf of women once I'm gone." Her eyes had taken on a dreamy quality, but now her gaze sharpened on me. "Because, mark my words, it's going to take many more years,

218

decades perhaps, for women's independence to be fully realized. Now, the temperance movement, on the other hand, will know success much sooner. We're quite close to . . ."

She rambled on about senators, congressmen, and potential bills waiting to be drafted, but I paid scant attention. Time was wasting, and the sooner I returned to town the sooner I could show Jesse the petals I'd found. I hoped he'd send them to a botanist to identify, and I hoped they would turn out to be more traceable than simply something blown in off the cliffs. It wasn't until Mrs. Stanford mentioned her husband's name that I snapped out of my reverie.

"Mr. Stanford," I repeated, blinking.

"Why, yes, dear. As I was saying, when we arrived in town—"

"Is he still in town?"

She flinched at my interruption. "Yes, he decided to stay with a bachelor friend while I visited with Mrs. Vanderbilt. We never expected my stay here to extend beyond a couple of nights, but, well, with all that's happened, the police prefer I don't leave Newport yet in case they have more questions, and I simply don't have the heart to leave your aunt all alone until things settle down."

"That's very kind of you," I murmured. Last night those men on Rose Island had said, "Hurry it up, dammit. Stanford's waiting." I'd discounted the possibility of there being any connection to Mrs. Stanford, but . . .

"Does your husband support the temperance movement?" I asked, once more interrupting whatever she'd been saying.

Her brows drew together. "Of course he does. That's why we originally came to Newport. He's been conferring with your town officials to shut down these ungodly taverns and usher in more wholesome means of entertainment. The imbibing of spirits only ever leads to . . ."

I blocked her out again. Why would a temperance supporter put in with molasses smugglers? Perhaps Derrick had been mistaken in his assumptions.

But what if he wasn't?

I came to my feet, once again making Mrs. Stanford flinch at my abruptness. "I have to go," I said. "Good day, Mrs. Stanford."

She didn't wish me a good day in turn. She only frowned at me as I hurried out of the room.

"I thought we agreed this was none of your business, Emma." Derrick's voice carried through the lobby of the Atlantic House Hotel; several guests, a porter, and the clerk at the check-in desk sent us inquiring looks.

Derrick seized my elbow and drew me into a corner half-hidden by an overgrown potted palm. "You promised, Emma."

"Did I?" I gazed up into his eyes—at this moment dark and fiery—and almost forgot why I'd come to see him. I'd made a quick stop at the police station to hand Jesse the evidence I'd found. He'd been skeptical but promised to have an expert examine the petals. Then I'd rushed here and found Derrick in, but not necessarily in the most receptive state once he heard my request. Or was he still fuming over my suggestion that morning that he might use Consuelo's disappearance to sell newspapers for his father?

"Derrick, don't you see that my cousin's disappearance and those smugglers might be connected after all? Those men mentioned someone called Stanford, and a woman by the name of Hope Stanford is staying with Aunt Alva. She was there when the medium died and Consuelo disappeared."

"And what? You think this woman is involved in smuggling?"

His mocking tone raised my hackles. "Don't be silly. But her husband is also staying in Newport. The pair are supposedly in support of the temperance movement, but what if her husband secretly isn't? What if—"

"There you go, jumping to conclusions and stretching the facts again." He crossed his arms in a defensive posture, yet his eyes never left mine as they narrowed pensively. I waited silently, letting him work through the same thoughts that had earlier occurred to me. "It would be a good cover, wouldn't it? The husband of a temperance leader flooding the market with illegal rum . . ."

I struggled to keep the triumph from my expression, though he quelled it quickly enough. "I still don't see how it could have anything to do with your cousin."

"Well, the man's wife *is* staying at Marble House. Maybe Consuelo heard something."

"That would mean Mrs. Stanford would have to be in on the crime. Could she be that accomplished an actress? I've heard of the woman's antics in town. Do you know she took a sledgehammer to a bar top?"

"I've heard the story," I said, remembering hearing the details from the woman herself only two days ago. "But it's not only the Stanfords who might be involved. There is also Winthrop Rutherfurd."

"Ah, yes. Winty."

"With his involvement we can't rule out a connection to Consuelo."

I could see from the softening of Derrick's jawline that I had him half-convinced of my suspicions. Please don't judge me harshly, but I used that moment to press my advantage.

"Derrick . . ." I laid my fingertips on his forearm, the summer-light weave of his coat sleeve softly nubby against my skin. "I'm sorry about this morning. I know you would never betray a confidence, mine or anyone else's. I wasn't thinking quite straight yet."

"I know." He covered my hand with his own, sending a warm shiver up my arm. "I'm sorry, too. I shouldn't have been angry after all you'd just been through. But it's true, Emma. I will never attempt to benefit from anything you might confide in me, except to ensure nothing bad happens to you."

His voice had become a balmy rumble; this, and the sudden warmth in his gaze, instantly became too much for me. Too revealing and too open, as if it were my turn now to respond, to reveal something of myself.

I wasn't ready. Not after adamantly turning down Derrick's proposal of marriage such a short time ago. Good grief, had it only been the morning of Madame Devereaux's murder? It seemed as though eons had passed since then.

Had I made the right choice? My head and everything I wanted for myself said yes; but that look in Derrick's eyes and the alarm building inside me suggested otherwise, and as the seconds passed I grew in greater and greater danger of falling prey to those suggestions.

Then Derrick removed his hand. I dropped mine from his forearm. We stepped apart. He coughed, I chuckled. A horribly awkward moment passed.

With a rueful quirk of his mouth, he said, "So, tell me about this latest plan you've cooked up."

CHAPTER 11

Derrick and I waited until the next day to implement my plan. I didn't relish the delay, but he insisted I go straight home after our brief encounter in the Atlantic House Hotel's lobby. He said I'd likely collapse if I pushed myself any further that day, and though I loathed admitting it, he was likely right.

That next morning I quickly donned the lime green walking outfit Gertrude had recently given me. With her usual lightning speed, Nanny had made the necessary alterations, along with adding creamy taffeta embroidered with green and pink flowers to the collar and cuffs, breathing new life into Gertrude's cast-off. I counted it among my most fashionable ensembles.

Why did I find it necessary to wear my best that day? Even as I stood before my mirror adjusting the matching flowered hat with its dyed-green feathers, I all but choked on the hypocrisy of wanting to look pretty for Derrick.

Downstairs, I practically inhaled a cup of strong coffee and the scrambled eggs Nanny insisted I eat. Then it was off to town. Rather than drive my rig, I hitched a ride with cousins Gertrude and Gladys, on their way to watch a tennis match at the Casino. They both approved Nanny's alterations on my outfit.

Derrick was waiting outside the Newport *Observer* when I arrived. "Are you sure you want to do this?" he asked in lieu of a proper greeting as he helped me down from my cousins' carriage.

"Of course I'm sure. Why wouldn't I be?"

He looked at me doubtfully. "I'd hoped a good night's rest might help you see reason."

"Derrick, if anything, the hours between our talk yesterday and today only strengthened my resolve. Those men on Rose Island tried to *kill* us. Don't you want to know who is ultimately responsible for that?"

"Emma, those men might have wanted to kill us, but I'm fairly certain they didn't get a good look at us. That means they don't know who we are any more than we know who they are. If you ask me, the safest course is to leave it be."

"And I say there is greater safety in knowledge." I raised my eyebrows in a silent dare to contest my assertion.

He only moved to open the door for me. "By the way, you look very pretty today," he murmured as I preceded him inside.

"Thank you." I broke into a grin, one I was glad he couldn't see.

After bidding Donald Larimer good morning we strode past his desk and continued down the corridor leading to the *Observer*'s workrooms.

We went into the office I shared with Ed Billings, one I rarely used as I preferred to write at home. Ed must have been out scouting news, for I saw no coat over the back of his chair, nor papers strewn across his desk, nor any other sign that he might be in the building. The typical drone of a workday filtered in from the newsroom and, farther back still, the presses. Derrick waited while I uncovered the typewriter. This was my reason for coming here: the use of the machine that would help conceal my identity. We conferred on wording, and then I tapped away at the keys. Some twenty minutes later we were back on the street, looking up and down the sidewalk for the opportunity we sought. Derrick spotted it, or should I say *him,* and let out a shrill whistle.

"Boy! Over here. Would you like a job?"

Instantly, the passing bicycle stopped, then turned about. Its rider wore navy blue trousers, a matching coat emblazoned with bright brass buttons that caught the sun, and the stiff, flat-topped cap of a Western Union messenger boy. "You got something you need delivered, sir?"

Officially, boys like this one delivered packages for Western Union for paltry weekly wages, and it wasn't unusual for them to earn extra cash by fitting a few private deliveries into their daily schedules. Derrick held out the two envelopes we'd addressed inside. "Can you deliver these for us by this afternoon?"

"Sooner than that, sir." The boy peered at the addresses. "Cost you a nickel each."

Derrick fished a coin out of his trouser pocket. We might have hired one of the *Observer*'s young newsies or office boys for the errand, but we had reasons for wanting to remain anonymous. "Here's fifty cents if you don't tell either addressee anything about who hired you."

The young man, a bit of dirt on his chin, grinned and made a gesture against his lips as if locking them. He pushed away from the sidewalk and rode off down busy Thames Street.

I found myself glad I'd worn Gertrude's lovely outfit later that evening when Derrick took me to dine at the White Horse Tavern, a quaint yet elegant eatery established long before the Revolution. While I'll admit nothing quite exceeds Nanny's plain but savory fare, I enjoyed my roast duck, rosemary potatoes, and glazed carrots immensely. Yet once again, the simple act of sharing a meal with Derrick brought to mind all the other things he'd invited me to share in his life, and if I laughed a bit too shrilly or talked rather too quickly, it was my feeble attempt to appear confident in the decision I'd made not to accept his offer of marriage.

From there we made our way to Bellevue Avenue and Mill Street, where dignified clapboard houses faced a grassy, tree-shaded square called Touro Park. At the park's center, the Old Mill Tower rose up against the evening sky, its unmortared stones forming several arches in a circular design nearly thirty feet in height. Some speculated Vikings had built it hundreds of years before Columbus set sail to this hemisphere; others held it to be nothing more exotic than the remains of a seventeenth-century windmill. For me, that night, the very sight of it made my breath hitch in anticipation.

We kept to the edges of the park and took up position under the shelter of some trees, pressed tight to the trunk of the largest among them. We didn't have long to wait. Other than the occasional muffled voice from one of the houses behind us, silence reigned in the neighborhood until footsteps alerted us to the arrival of the first of our quarry. Though the darkness as well as a broad-brimmed beaver hat concealed his features, the approaching man revealed himself as one of our target by striding to the tower and passing through the closest of its arches.

Soon carriage wheels echoed off the fronts of the houses directly across the park from us. The hansom cab stopped and a man alighted. Again we could not make out his face clearly, but after a quick look about and a word to the driver, this man, too, made his way inside the tower.

The carriage drove off, and Derrick and I used its rumble to conceal our steps as we moved closer, careful to stay close to trees and hedges and not daring to speak a word. Once again I applauded my choice in wearing my restored gown; being meant for walking, the petticoats were of the softest muslin that remained virtually silent when I moved.

We crept as close as we dared to the tower. Hushed voices drifted from inside.

"Have you lost your wits, summoning me here like this?"

"Me? You're the one gone daft. I told you the other morning when you intruded upon my breakfast that I didn't want anything more to do with you. I did what you asked. Now fulfill your side of the bargain and leave me alone."

The first voice was that of a stranger to me. The second voice—oh, that one I knew well enough. I caught Derrick's eye and silently moved my lips.

Winty.

A quivering realization went through me. This other man was the reason Winty hadn't allowed me to search his house for Consuelo the morning I'd visited him. Another visitor had gotten there before me, and Winty hadn't wanted me to discover him.

"I have no idea what you're talking about," that man said now, his voice deeper, gruffer than Winty's, suggesting he was older. "What do you want? Make it quick."

The individual I had already guessed to be

Hope Stanford's husband stepped into view through one of the arches. His rotund figure filled the space, though his head fell far short of the arch's zenith. With an impatient gesture he swept his beaver hat off his head, revealing a balding pate wreathed by tight, closely cropped curls that shimmered silver in the moonlight.

"What do *I* want?" It was Winty speaking this time. "You sent for me, remember?"

Pebbles crunched and suddenly both men were framed by the archway. Winty poked a finger at Stanford's frock coat. "I played your little game, but I swear, Stanford, if you drag me down any further I'll go to my father. We might not have quite the fortune we once did, but Father's still got his connections. He'll see you put out of business—any and all business."

"You wouldn't dare besmirch your own name, much less run confessing to your papa. Just think how disappointed he'd be to discover his dear Winthrop putting in with smugglers."

Derrick and I shot each other another glance.

"Damn you, Stanford. Look, let's just get this over with before someone spots us together. What do you want? If it's to help you again, you can forget it."

"Why do you insist on asking me what I want?" A rustle of paper disturbed the quiet. "You summoned *me*." Calvin Stanford thrust a piece of paper toward Winty. Winty stared at it dumbly before reaching inside his coat and pulling out a similar sheaf.

This time Derrick and I exchanged knowing— and yes, amused—looks; we knew good and well where those notes had originated.

"What the . . . ?" Mr. Stanford swiped the paper from Winty's hand and held it up beside his own. He squinted to make out the words. Then he snapped both pages to his side and began looking about, neck craning as he searched the shadowy park. "Damn it, we've been set up."

Derrick took my hand and together we stepped out from behind the concealing foliage. "Yes, you have."

Stanford drew himself up, his corpulent stomach a protruding mound beneath his coat. "What is the meaning of this? Who are you?"

Beside him, Winty stared like a frightened rabbit, his face gone as pale as the moon hanging above us. "M-Miss Cross . . ."

"You know these people?" A sneer grew on Stanford's face as he looked me up and down.

"I know *her*," was Winty's unsteady answer.

"And I know you, Mr. Rutherfurd, and all I can say is shame on you. Shame on you both." I shifted my attention to the other man. "What would your wife say, Mr. Stanford?"

"Who in the hell are you two?" the man demanded. "I won't ask what you want. The answer is obvious: blackmail."

I smiled. "There you are wrong, Mr. Stanford. Mr. Andrews and I have no interest in blackmailing either of you. We brought you both here tonight on a hunch that has proved correct. And now we have some questions we'd like answered."

"Well . . ." The man released a mirthless laugh that shook the loose skin bulging from his collar. "I've no intention of answering them. You, miss, should be home with your family, where a young lady belongs. And you, sir . . ." He trailed off, his gaze narrowing and his lips drooping at the corners. "I know you . . ."

"Do you indeed?" Derrick tilted his head as if in polite interest. "I'm sorry to say that if we've met I don't remember. However, I do seem to be learning quite a bit about you tonight. About both of you. Mr. Rutherfurd, I've heard a lot about you from Miss Cross."

Winty stuttered something unintelligible and I began to fear the shock of our little ruse might threaten his health.

"You're the Andrews heir," Stanford said slowly. "Of the Providence *Sun*. I've seen your picture. . . ."

Derrick gave a little bow. "At your service, sir."

At that moment Winty apparently found his tongue. "Miss Cross, what is this all about?"

"Don't be stupid, Rutherfurd. Despite what they say they're here to blackmail us." Stanford regarded Derrick and me with a resigned air. "How much?"

"Honestly, Mr. Stanford, that is not our intent. Not that I condone illegal activities, mind you, and Mr. Rutherfurd, I'm astonished at you." I paused to show them my best imitation of one of Nanny's chastising pouts. "But you can distill illegal rum until the cows come home for all I care."

It was Winty's and Stanford's turn to exchange surprised looks. I then garnered an admiring if begrudging one from Stanford.

"What we want to know . . . what we *demand* to know," I said, "is where you both were on the night before last. When the smugglers on Rose Island tried to kill us."

"What?" Winty's exclamation came out as a strangled gasp.

The type-written notes fluttered from Stanford's hand to land in the dirt at his feet. "I was nowhere near Rose Island the other night. I swear it."

"But men in your employ were," Derrick said.

Stanford scrambled to retrieve the missives before the wind took them, then straightened with an indignant snort. "What proof do you have—"

"They spoke your name, Mr. Stanford." I raised my chin at him, daring him to contradict what Derrick and I had heard with our own ears. "And just so you're aware, I've left a signed statement in my desk at the Newport *Observer* detailing everything that happened that night. If anything should happen to Derrick or me, rest assured that statement will be found."

I could feel Derrick frowning at me, though I didn't dare glance his way. I'd left no such statement and he knew it. But I resolved to do so at the very first opportunity.

"Now, then," I went on, "we'd very much like an answer. Or perhaps you'd care to take this to the police station. My very good friend Detective Whyte would be happy to take over the task of questioning you."

"She's telling the truth about that," Winty said to Stanford out of the side of his mouth. "She and that detective are friends." He turned his attention to me. "Miss Cross, as God is my witness, all I did was agree to drop a marker in the water at the edge of Rose Island, designating where a delivery was to be dropped off, and then retrieved by another vessel. That is the extent of my involvement."

"Yes, I saw you, Mr. Rutherfurd, and let me say that you are not cut out for a life of subterfuge."

"No, I don't suppose I am. But Stanford here agreed to pay off a couple of debts for me . . ." Winty stared at the ground.

Derrick cleared his throat. "So what's your story, Stanford?"

"I don't see why I have to tell you anything."

I raised an eyebrow and smiled. "Because if

you don't, I'll go to your wife with what I know. Your temperance-leader wife."

"See here, Hope has her diversions and I have mine. If you would refrain from sticking your nose in other people's business, you won't need to worry about men trying to kill you. Which I had nothing to do with, I might add." He mirrored my own yes-I've-got-you-trumped smile. "How did they try to do you in, if I might ask?"

"They rammed their steamer into our rowboat." The memory sent a shudder through me. "We jumped overboard at the last minute."

The man had the audacity to laugh—to wrap both arms around his stomach, lean over, and let go a belly laugh that resounded against the houses and made the rest of us cringe. "My dear Miss Cross, that was nothing more than a warning. If those vagabonds had wanted you dead, you'd not now be standing here speaking to me."

Derrick shot by me in a blur of overcoat and outstretched arms. Before anyone could react, his hands wrapped around Stanford's throat, and with the force of his stride he slammed the man up against the side of an arch and pinned him in place.

"No more games, Stanford. Did you or did you not give the order to have witnesses murdered?"

Winty let out a whimper.

His hands coming up to grip Derrick's wrists, Stanford rasped and sputtered. Derrick loosened his hold a fraction. The older man worked his head from side to side and dragged in a breath before speaking. "Of course . . . I didn't . . . you madman. I'm out to make money, and the quickest way to attract the police is to leave a trail of bodies in one's wake."

"He does have a point," I said. But then I strode to them and set my hands on my hips. "What about three days ago? Where were you the afternoon Madame Devereaux died?"

When Stanford didn't answer immediately, Derrick gave him a shove, his fists still knotted around the man's coat collar. "Answer the lady."

"I was at the Newport Casino . . . with several of your town councilmen." Stanford's thick lips pulled back in a self-satisfied sneer. "I'd be happy to give you their names if you require proof."

"I might at that, Mr. Stanford," I said.

Slowly Derrick's grip slackened and his hands fell to his sides. "I believe you. I'm not sure why, but I do." He stepped away from Stanford, his lips in a shrewd slant. "It occurs to me that if your wife gets *her* way, you'll make your money— plenty of it."

Stanford brushed at his lapels and smirked.

During the exchange Winty had stood as stiff as a pillar. Now his body sagged as he visibly relaxed. "Miss Cross, what were you doing on Rose Island?"

I shot a look at Stanford, then pulled Winty outside the tower. "Looking for Consuelo," I whispered once we'd moved several yards away. "When I saw you drop the marker into the water that afternoon, I thought perhaps it might have something to do with her. That maybe you were marking a rendezvous point to take her out of Newport."

"I told you I hadn't seen her. That still holds true."

"Yes, but it occurred to me you might be lying. You were behaving strangely the morning I came to see you." I flicked a glance at Stanford through the archway. "Now I know why. He was somewhere in your house, wasn't he?"

"Upstairs. And no, it would not have been a good idea for you to see him, not that it matters now." Winty frowned. "Do you mean to say you still haven't found Miss Vanderbilt?"

"No, I haven't. But I've got Detective Whyte involved in the search now." I briefly touched the back of Winty's hand. "We'll find her soon, I'm sure of it."

"Damn that mother of hers. . . ."

"Now, Mr. Rutherfurd—"

"No!" His eyes sparked fire, and his vehemence sent me back a step. I'd never seen him so impassioned. "If anything has happened . . . or happens . . . to Consuelo, it'll be Alva's fault. I wasn't good enough for her . . . Consuelo herself was never good enough for *her.* She drove her daughter away as surely as if she'd pushed her out the door."

I couldn't argue with him, but neither did I agree. I didn't feel it would be prudent to discuss family matters with him any more than I already had. That being the case, we had little more to say to each other.

We walked back into the tower. It seemed everything that could be said had been, and the four of us engaged in a kind of glaring standoff for several long moments.

It was Derrick who ended it. "Just remember that we know who you are and what you're doing. We'll be watching the two of you."

Winty opened his mouth as if to protest his innocence once more, but in the end he clamped his lips together and nodded. Stanford seethed through eyes gone narrow within pockets of sagging flesh. Obviously he was a man who didn't like being bested or not knowing exactly where he stood. Unfortunately for him neither Derrick nor I was about to offer any reassurances. Better to keep the man wondering what we might do with the information we had.

We parted ways with terse wishes for a good evening. Winty and Stanford walked together to the edge of the park, where they separated and went in opposite directions on Bellevue Avenue.

Beside me, Derrick let out a labored breath.

"Well, that was interesting. Not sure we learned much, though."

"We learned you were correct about the rum. And I believe those men on Rose Island acted on their own when they came after us."

"Maybe." Derrick stared pensively off into the distance. "Come, it's time I got you home."

"Oh, no, it isn't." When he shot me a puzzled frown I grinned. "It's time you took me to a tavern. Or several. I have a new theory that needs exploring."

Derrick groaned.

Against Derrick's protests, I managed to persuade him to accompany me to several dockside taverns. Quite simply, I told him if he didn't wish to come with me, I'd go alone. The first, a place frequented by ruffians off the scrod boats and crews from the various steam freighters putting into harbor, yielded us little information. Yes, Hope Stanford had been in several nights ago. She had raised a ruckus, banged her hammer on the bar top, but had left upon realizing her proselytizing was landing on deaf ears. Also, a large man had threatened to pick her up, carry her outside, and toss her over the nearby dock into the bay. But just as this rough-hewn crowd of mostly out-of-towners had no interest in being saved by Hope's radical views on the evils of alcohol, neither were they particularly eager to answer my questions. In fact, I believe they viewed my intrusion into their inner sanctum with the same mixture of suspicion and disdainful amusement with which they had viewed Hope's. And having the well-dressed Derrick beside me proved that a gentleman held no more sway here than a woman.

Our next stop brought us to The Red Mariner, a watering hole popular with local fishermen and dock workers. Here I spotted some familiar faces, young men I'd grown up with on the Point, others I knew from church, or from having attended school with their sisters. But one face in particular stood out, or, I should say, his bright red hair penetrated the gloom of pipe smoke and dim kerosene lighting. Grasping Derrick's coat sleeve I directed us toward a table in a corner near the bar.

"Good evening, Angus."

The boatman hunched on his elbows over the little square table, a mug of muddy-looking beer bracketed between his hands. "Emma? What the he—er—what are you doing here?"

"Is it all right if we sit with you?" Without waiting for permission I pulled out the seat opposite him and slid into it. Derrick reached for an unoccupied chair at a neighboring table, dragged it over, and straddled it backward. "Angus, this is Derrick Andrews. He's a friend of mine."

Unlike Hope Stanford's husband, Angus MacPhearson showed no hint of recognition at either Derrick's name or his countenance. He merely nodded in greeting.

"I was hoping to ask you a couple of questions, if you don't mind, Angus." I leaned a bit over the table to be heard over the low roar of voices and the occasional burst of masculine laughter behind me. A hush had fallen over the pub when Derrick and I walked in and a good twenty or so astonished faces had turned in our direction. Our novelty had worn off quickly enough, however, and the patrons had resumed their boasting, arguing, dicing, and dart throwing.

Angus leaned back in his chair, bringing his beer with him. He took a measured draft while studying me with his weather-crinkled eyes. Then he used his sleeve to wipe the suds from his mustache. "Are you hiring me to answer these couple of questions, Emma?"

I flicked a glance at Derrick, who dug into a pocket and produced another fifty-cent piece. He flipped it in the air; Angus reached out and snatched it.

"Ask away," he said.

Without further ado I said, "Were you here several nights ago when an older woman came barging in with a sledgehammer?"

The question clearly delighted Angus. He raised his mug as if in a toast. "Sure enough. I hadn't had that much fun in years. Crazy bi—ah—hellion, that one."

"Can you tell me what went on?"

"Sure. She shouted up a storm and swung that hammer of hers around like a castaway who's been sucking down seawater. Put at least half a dozen dents in the bar before Spence Arnold came up behind her and wrenched the hammer right out of her hands."

Derrick, who'd been scanning the establishment like an on-duty sentry, suddenly returned his attention to the conversation. "Spence Arnold?"

Angus gestured with his chin. Derrick and I both turned and craned our necks. I impatiently waved away curls of smoke drifting from the next table. Through the crowd I spotted a man a good head taller than anyone near him, his silvery hair thinning and his profile reminiscent of a primitive stone carving.

I pointed. "There he is. That's Spence. He's a carpenter. Does a lot of work on the houses on the Point." I turned back to Angus. "Any idea why Spence and no one else decided to disarm Mrs. Stanford?" At Angus's puzzled look, I clarified. "The crazy hellion with the sledgehammer."

"Oh. Well, most of us were too shocked at first to do anything but stare like a bunch of simpletons. I mean, what the he—er—what on earth? But Spence, he'd just gotten here. He took one look at her and said, 'Lady, I had enough of you over at the Oyster Club.' Then he stepped right in the way of that swinging sledge-hammer—right where I wouldn't have stepped for all the free grog in Christendom—grabbed the thing and yanked it right out of her hands. You should have seen her face. Ooh wee, if Spence weren't the giant he is, I think she might have swung a punch at 'im. As it was, she turned on her heel and stomped her way out the door. Old Spence, he followed her—I thought to make good and sure she left. But out on the sidewalk—I could see 'em through the window—he just give her back her sledgehammer and told her don't come back. Ever." Angus slapped his knee and let go a laugh.

"So it wasn't the first time Spence encountered the woman?" I asked.

At yet another questioning look, I clarified once again. "It wasn't the first time he'd run into this woman."

"No, but I hope for her sake it's the last."

"And no one else spoke to her at all?"

"Only Ted, the barkeep, and I can't repeat what *he* said to her . . . not to you at any rate." Angus scratched his chin through his abundant growth of beard. "Brady would have my hide if I talked to his baby sister like that."

I sat back. "I wonder if Spence will talk with us."

"Do you think he might have more to add about what happened at this other establishment . . . the . . ." Derrick groped for the name.

"The Oyster Club," Angus said.

I came to my feet. "Thank you, Angus. You've earned your fifty cents."

"Am I going to have to pay this Spence, too?" Derrick asked as he followed me through the crowd.

I merely shrugged and wound a circuitous path to avoid spilled beer and wobbly men. Spence Arnold, along with several others clad in plaid shirts and worn denims, had taken up position in front of one of the dartboards; money was exchanging hands at the surrounding tables.

"Mr. Arnold?" I called. "Yes, good evening . . . over here . . . oh, excuse me, sir, if I could just get by . . . ex*cuse* me!" I tugged my skirts out from between the back of one man's chair and the right hip of another who sidestepped too close, then nudged aside another fellow blocking my way. "Mr. Arnold!"

Spence finally turned, one hand raised to propel the dart clutched in his fingers. He squinted a moment before recognition dawned. "Arthur Cross's girl?"

"Yes, Mr. Arnold, it's me, Emma Cross. Might I have a word with you? It'll just take a moment."

A rumble of protest erupted around me. "I've got money on him!" one man shouted.

"And I've got money *against* him," another yelled.

I looked over my shoulder at Derrick. "Can you throw?"

"I've been known to hit the target upon occasion."

"Well, then, gentlemen, how about if my friend takes Mr. Arnold's place for just a few moments?"

My suggestion met with vigorous and deafening debate. Someone demanded that Derrick throw a dart to give them a preview of his talents. He smoothly stepped forward and without even removing his coat sent a dart hissing almost invisibly through the air. My next sight of the red and white feathered object was as it came to a trembling stop a fraction to the right of the target's dead center.

The onlookers fell into a hush that lasted all of five seconds before shouts rose, quoting odds and probabilities; fistfuls of money once again exchanged hands.

I could barely suppress my proud smile as I led Spence Arnold between tables to the other side of the room. When I turned to regard him he didn't look at all pleased at having been upstaged. I made a mental note to have Derrick compensate him for his time.

"Sorry to interrupt your fun, Mr. Arnold. I would never have done so if it weren't vitally important."

He crossed his arms over his chest and leaned against the wall. "Miss Cross, what would your father say if he saw you here?" His eyes remained kindly despite the admonishment. "This is no fit place for a nice young lady like yourself."

I didn't tell him that if my father cared so much about my safety, he wouldn't have gone to live in Paris, now would he? I still hadn't gotten over how neither of my parents had indicated any intention of returning home upon learning Brady had been accused of murder, but with an effort I hid my frown.

"Mr. Arnold, I understand you're familiar with a woman named Hope Stanford. Is that correct?"

"Mrs. Sledgehammer?"

I nodded. "Angus told me what happened here, but I wondered if you would tell me what occurred earlier that night at the Oyster Club."

A chorus of cheers went up from the vicinity of the dartboards. I couldn't see what had occurred, but Spence glanced over heads with a look of impatience, prompting me to add, "Please, it's very important."

"How important can it be? She came in hollering just like she did here. Slammed that hammer of hers against the bar. Said the demon spirits was destroying the moral fiber of the whole country. As if us islanders could give a hoot what happens beyond our shores."

I let that pass. "And were you the one who stopped her, like you did here?"

"Me? Nah, didn't have to—" Another roar went up, once again claiming Spence's attention.

"Why not?" I pressed, attempting to force him to focus.

"What? Oh . . . right. Because Ellie shoved her aside and took the hammer away."

"Ellie?"

"Yeah, the fortune-teller."

"Fortune-teller . . ." My heart began to pound. "Do you mean Madame Devereaux? Eleanora Devereaux?"

"Yeah, that's her name. Nice gal. Pity what happened to her."

"So, you knew her?" My fingertips trembled with each beat of my pulse. "How well?"

"She was a regular at the Oyster Club. Sometimes came here, too, but she preferred the taverns where the crowd changed from night to night."

"And why was that?"

"Business, Miss Cross. See, she'd wait till the customers had a few drinks in 'em, then go round offering to read fortunes. Made a tidy living that way. Can't say I blamed her."

"No . . . So what happened after she took Mrs. Stanford's sledgehammer?"

"Oh, she told that teetotaler off good and well. Said she had no stomach for hoity-toity upstarts imposing their prudish ways on a city like Newport. And then . . . this is where things got a little strange."

"How so?"

"The fortune-teller went into some kind of weird trance. At first I thought the apoplexy got her and she'd keel over. But she just stood there, staring at the other woman like she could see straight through her. And real quiet, she said something. Something that made Mrs. Sledgehammer turn all kinds of red. I've never seen that shade of red on a person before."

"What did the medium say?" I could scarcely curb my excitement or my impatience.

But Spence disappointed me with a shake of his head. "Couldn't hear the words. Just her voice, all low and strained, like she was trying to whisper while someone had their hands around her throat. The next thing I knew, the other woman grabbed her sledgehammer back and fled out the door. 'Bout an hour later I came over here, and there she was, ranting and carrying on like nothing ever happened at the Oyster."

Minutes later Spence rejoined his friends and resumed his dart game, and I strode out to the sidewalk with Derrick in tow.

"I'll have you know I was making tidy sums for a number of those fellows inside," he said. "I may have missed my calling."

We reached a dusty pool of light beneath a

street lantern. I stopped and gripped his sleeve. "Madame Devereaux was at the Oyster Club the night Hope Stanford walked in with her sledgehammer."

Derrick's features remained impassive. "I would imagine a lot of others were there as well."

"True. But not many others have the ability to seal Hope Stanford's mouth with a mere whisper."

CHAPTER 12

"What secret did Madame Devereaux know about Hope Stanford?" I pondered aloud as Derrick drove his carriage toward Gull Manor, my seaside home.

"One might wager the same secret we discovered." He adjusted his grip on the reins and steered the horse around a deep gouge in the dirt road. The carriage lanterns swung and sputtered, then burned steadily on. "Her husband is chin-deep in illegal activities. Whether Hope Stanford was privy to his little endeavor or not, she wouldn't have been happy to learn that an outsider knew. Especially if that someone threatened to go public with the information."

"Precisely." I turned to glance at him beside me on the curricle seat. The fog-tinged moonlight smoothed his features, making him appear younger, almost boyish. My heart gave a little skip before I shifted my gaze back to the road I knew so much better than he. "They knew each other in Providence," I said. "And Mrs. Stanford knew that the medium's name was actually Ellen Deere. I wonder what else Mrs. Stanford might have known about the woman."

"You think they each knew secrets about the other, and were using them against each other?"

"It's a very good possibility, given they have a common history to some extent. If only I could determine what that history is." Memory served me and I pointed straight ahead. "There's a sharp bend just after those trees, and then the turn onto Ocean Avenue. The road dips there, so be careful."

"Would you care to drive?" he asked with a note of sarcasm. But he slowed the horse's pace nonetheless.

"If only we could learn what the medium said to Hope Stanford that night at the Oyster Club." I tapped my fingers against the span of leather seat between us. "But if, in an attempt to make Hope stop her temperance efforts in Newport, Madame Devereaux threatened to expose her husband, it's not much of a stretch to believe Hope would want to silence her. After all, such exposure would discredit Hope forever. She'd lose all of her political influence."

"Maybe her husband did the medium in."

"It's altogether possible. Though how he would have gotten onto the estate without anyone seeing him . . . His wife might have helped, but I'd seen her in the garden with the other ladies just minutes before the murder. If they acted together, they acted with lightning speed."

"The same would hold true for Clara Parker and Anthony Dobbs," Derrick reminded me.

Calvin and Hope . . . Anthony and Clara. I

sighed. "But what of Consuelo? It can't be mere coincidence that she disappeared immediately after the murder. I know there must be a connection. Somewhere, there's a link and if I could only find it, I'd find both Consuelo and the murderer."

"Then perhaps you need to refocus your efforts." He shot me a pointed glance.

I pursed my lips. "Another attempt to persuade me to leave the investigation to the police?"

"Not exactly. But you've been focusing on people, and all that's done is lead you—us—round and round in circles. Why not focus on the clues instead, and see where *they* lead?"

We reached the turn onto Ocean Avenue, where the sudden hollow in the road bounced the carriage and knocked our shoulders together. Derrick's arm shot out in front of me—an attempt to hold me in the seat, I suppose—but in another yard or two the road smoothed and the carriage righted itself. The horse had slowed as well, and some ungovernable impulse sent me reaching out to grasp the sides of Derrick's face and pull him toward me for a kiss—quick, yes, but fully on the lips. My better sense looked on, horrified yet ineffectually mute, as I pulled away with a grin.

"You, sir, are a genius. That's exactly what I should do."

Wry bewilderment played on his features, but he nodded. For the next several minutes I ran through the list of clues while Derrick seemed to be concentrating uncommonly hard on the road. Occasionally he spared me a nod or a syllable that sounded like agreement with whatever I said.

"There is the murder weapon itself, the scarf belonging to Lady Amelia. Then there was the murder scene, which suggested to me that Madame Devereaux had been in the middle of reading someone's fortune right before she was murdered. The broken azalea bushes were probably where the murderer made his or her escape, and also suggested the murderer wore durable clothing, something not easily torn, because there were no scraps or threads found among the branches. The obvious conclusion is that the murderer was a man, yet a woman like Hope Stanford doesn't dress in silks or fine muslin. She wears thick cottons and sturdy serge. Nothing too frilly or feminine."

My deductions once again met with nods from Derrick.

"And then there are those flower petals I found inside the pavilion. The gardeners weren't able to identify them, so I handed them over to the police, who'll have a botanist examine them. But maybe I need to take another walk around the estate. Surely those flowers had to come from some-where nearby. Yes, so first thing tomorrow . . ."

We came to my driveway and the carriage bumped over the rocky, pitted surface. This time,

I noticed how Derrick held himself stiffly and kept firmly to his side of the seat. All at once, thoughts of evidence and clues slid away and the memory of what I'd done slammed into me, sending wave after wave of fire to my cheeks.

Had I actually kissed him? His suggestion had been so . . . well . . . ingenious . . . and it had quite taken me by surprise. I'd been going about this investigation all wrong, hoping someone might slip up and inadvertently admit the truth. But evidence doesn't lie. Clues don't make excuses. They lay out a trail from crime to culprit, if one is clever enough to follow them.

Was I?

Apparently not, if I couldn't decide on a proper course now. Should I apologize for my brash action? Say nothing? Make pleasant small talk? The heavy silence that fell over us seemed to make my decision for me.

Derrick turned the horse in a wide arc and brought the curricle to a stop in front of the house. Before I could make a move, he leaped to the ground and came around to help me down. My hand in his, we stood facing each other in the light spilling from my front parlor. Muffled from the other side of the house, ocean waves broke against the foot of the property.

I cleared my throat. "I . . . ah . . . well . . . thank you for all your help today."

"You're welcome, Emma."

"Would you . . . um . . . like to come inside?"

"No, thank you. It's late and I should be getting back."

But he didn't release my hand, or make any other move to leave. I stared into his face, into his eyes, which suddenly seemed darker than the sky overhead—dark with whatever thoughts he didn't see fit to share with me. The moment stretched, became uncomfortable, nearly unbearable, yet just as he didn't move, neither did I try to slide my hand free and step away. I wished he would say something. Was he waiting for me to do the same? To tell him, perhaps, why I'd kissed him when I'd made it clear we had no future together?

"I . . . it was such a good idea you had . . . about the clues . . . and . . . well . . . I didn't mean to—"

"You didn't," he said firmly. "And you don't have to explain."

"Oh, but—"

"It's much more fun if we keep each other guessing." The lamplight from inside caught the gleam of his teeth as he smiled.

"Is it now?" I slapped a hand on my hip. "Is that why we're standing here as though we're waiting for . . . for I don't know what?"

"Don't you?" Was it my imagination, or did he lean in, crowding me and depriving me of oxygen?

My instinct was to retreat a step, but my legs no

longer seemed adequate to support me. It was my turn to be mute. I shook my head.

He grasped my chin and raised it, then brushed his lips against mine. "Good night, Emma."

With that he swung up into the curricle and drove away. I watched him go until he turned onto Ocean Avenue and disappeared into the darkness. My fingertips quivered; my heart fluttered. My mind conjured a single word that summed up Derrick Andrews.

Fiend.

I was up with the sun next morning. When Nanny found me in the front parlor, I was sitting cross-legged on the braided oval rug in my dressing gown, with a tablet and pencil beside me and several items ranged in front of me.

Nanny hovered in the doorway, eyeing me with obvious puzzlement.

"Don't worry," I said, without looking up, "there is a method to my madness."

"To undo the work Katie did cleaning in here yesterday?"

I sat back, propped on my hands behind me, and contemplated my array of improvised evidence: a silk scarf, a deck of playing cards in lieu of actual tarot cards, several unlit candles, a small pile of coins, one of the men's flannel work shirts Aunt Sadie used to wear with her trousers when she did the gardening, and a handful of dusky pink blossoms I'd gathered from the lawn beyond our kitchen garden. These were merely tea roses, not the same as those I'd found in the pavilion, but today they would serve my purposes.

Nanny's worn, embroidered slippers entered my view. "What on earth are you doing?"

"Deducing, Nanny dear." I turned my face up to her. "These all represent the clues in Madame Devereaux's murder." I gestured at my little collection. "Up until now I've considered each one separately. But if they are to lead to the guilty party, they must be taken as a whole, all linked together. The same person has to have a link to each and every item."

She moved across the rug to perch on the edge of the wingback chair. "How is a candle connected to a flower?"

"My theory is this: Whoever murdered Madame Devereaux wore some sort of heavy fabric that didn't tear when he or she broke through the azalea hedges to make their escape. This may suggest a man and does tend to rule out most of Aunt Alva's guests that day. All but one of the ladies present wore silks, ruffles, and delicate pleats.

"Now," I went on, "the person also brought coins, which were found strewn across the table and spilled onto the floor." The coins in front of me clinked as I ran my fingers over them. "This, and the lighted candles, suggest the person had asked the medium to read his or her fortune, and had to have time to do so before the ladies and I went out to the pavilion." Next, I fingered the playing cards. "This theory is supported by the fact that we found tarot cards spread out on the table."

I paused and once again contemplated the scenario I'd devised. "So, either a man or someone dressed as, say, Mrs. Stanford went to the pavilion and asked for their fortune to be read. This person carried money, either in a purse or in a pocket, along with Amelia Beaumont's silk scarf. At the same time, he or she had been somewhere where pink wildflowers grow and managed to track them in, most likely on their shoes."

"Or in the cuffs of his trousers," Nanny said, "or the train of her dress."

"Yes!" I hadn't actually thought of that and rewarded Nanny with a grateful smile.

"Have you checked the Cliff Walk?" she asked. "For the flowers, I mean."

"Not yet, but I'm going back to Marble House later today. I'm hoping these flowers were *not* from the cliffs."

"Why not?"

I sighed. "Because if they are, they no longer stand up as a clue." Her frown prompted me to continue. "You see, anyone entering the estate from the Cliff Walk could easily have been seen walking across the lawns to the pavilion. The murderer would have been taking quite a risk of discovery. Plus, if the flower grows on the cliffs, how likely is it our murderer was scaling the precipices directly before killing Madame Devereaux? It doesn't make sense and yet . . ." I sat back again. "And yet I believe the flowers to be a key bit of evidence. Link these flowers to a person, and I truly believe I'll find both the murderer and Consuelo."

"You think the murderer has Consuelo?" Nanny's voice was grave, echoing my own inner sentiments.

"I didn't at first, and as much as I wish it were otherwise, yes, I do. And that terrifies me." I dropped my head into my hands. "And the thing is, the police won't believe it, not if they think Anthony Dobbs and Clara Parker are guilty. Oh, Nanny, why can't I figure this out?"

"I can tell you something that might possibly be of some help."

My head shot up. "Yes?"

"It's about that Lady Amelia. She's not what she pretends to be, that one."

I remembered Lady Amelia staring down at me from her window as I discussed the petals with Mr. Delgado and Jamie Reilly. For the most part, I'd believed her to be filling an idle moment. Could she, from that distance, have seen the petals in my palm and have cause to be concerned?

I returned my attention to Nanny. "What *is* she, then?"

Approaching footsteps sounded in the foyer and a moment later Brady stood in the doorway. He wore his blue and silver damask dressing gown, his flaxen hair tousled. "Em, you're awake. Good. I need you."

I'd barely seen my brother in the past several days. Since his exoneration and release from jail, he'd caught up on a lot of missed sleep while I'd kept busy tracking down Consuelo and a murderer.

Who could blame him? He still looked tired, yet the heavy shadows that had haunted his features were slowly fading beneath restored color and the sparkle that typically resided in his gaze, as though he expected a delightful surprise at any given moment. Yet now I detected something in his expression that convinced me he was about to toss a barricade between me and my plans today.

"What are you doing up so early?" I asked, not completely sure I wanted to know.

"I have been summoned," he said in an ominous tone. "To the big house."

Both Nanny's and my eyebrows shot up in astonishment. "Uncle Cornelius wants to see you?"

"Mm-hmm." He released a long breath. "What do you think he could want, Em? You don't think he's decided to press charges, do you?"

I almost said it would serve Brady right if Uncle Cornelius did press charges. Brady might not have murdered Uncle Cornelius's financial secretary, but he *did* attempt to steal business secrets with the intention of using them against the Vanderbilt family's New York Central Railroad.

Actually, Brady *had* stolen those secret plans right out of Uncle Cornelius's safe, only to have a change of heart at the very last minute. But as far as I knew, his bout of conscience had done little to endear him to Uncle Cornelius, who fired Brady from his position of clerk and ordered him never to show his face at the offices in New York, or at The Breakers, ever again.

I wanted to remind Brady of all that, and goodness knew he deserved his banishment. A quick glance at Nanny's pursed lips told me she agreed. But he'd been through so much already and looked so vulnerable standing there in his dishabille and worrying his bottom lip, that I took pity on him.

"Maybe this is a good sign," I said gently. "But why do you need me? I really don't think Uncle Cornelius would appreciate me tagging along."

He fisted his satin lapels as if hanging on for dear life. "I'm certainly not going alone."

"Oh, really, Brady, you've nothing to fear," I said with more confidence than I felt. "Besides, I have important things to do today."

He swept farther into the room and sank onto a footstool, his dressing gown billowing dramatically around him. "More important than your brother?"

My resolve weakened a fraction. "It has to do with Consuelo."

"Tell you what, then. You come with me, and then I'll help you with whatever else you have to do today." He leaned in closer, reaching for my hand. I reluctantly returned his grasp. "Deal?"

I thought a moment. Having Brady along at Marble House could come in handy, especially when it came to examining the Cliff Walk for my mystery flower. "All right. I'll come with you, although I highly doubt Uncle Cornelius will allow me to stay and hear whatever he has to say to you."

As I spoke those last words, the telephone bell jingled, and I reclaimed my hand. "I'll get it," I said, coming to my feet.

On the other end of the line, Jesse greeted me quickly. "Good morning, Emma. I have some news I thought you'd be interested to hear. That wildflower of yours? It's something we Islanders are all familiar with, so common we hardly notice it. Rugosa rose."

I wrinkled my nose at the unfamiliar term. "I've never heard of it."

"Well, no, most people wouldn't know it by name. As I said, it's so common as to be considered a weed. It grows along the cliffs, especially along Bellevue Avenue, and is one of the few wildflowers that blossom throughout the summer."

Images of the cliffs appeared in my mind. Not being a boater, it was a rare occasion for me to view the cliff faces. The beaches and my own rocky shoreline were far more familiar. "Can you tell me what the whole flower would look like?"

"Much brighter pink than the petals you brought us, of course, and with golden centers," he said. "I'm afraid this might not be much use after all. We'll look into it, but if rugosa roses are growing beyond the Marble House property, it's likely your petals merely blew in with the wind."

"Yes, I had the same thought." I sighed. "Thank you, Jesse. I appreciate your letting me know." After hanging up, I returned to the parlor to be practically accosted by Brady.

"Was that Cornelius? What did he want? You will come with me, won't you, Em? Just to be somewhere in the house in case I need you."

"You are such a child." I picked up one of the tea roses and flung it at him. Nanny chuckled. "No, that wasn't Uncle Cornelius, and yes, I'll come with you."

Apparently satisfied, Brady finally seemed to notice the candles, roses, cards, and other items strewn on the floor. He propped his elbows on his knees and his chin in his hands. "What have we here? Are we playing a game?"

"You're so right, Emma." Nanny huffed as she tugged her bulk out of the chair. "Such a child."

"Em, we have to go—now! The old badger said nine-thirty sharp and I don't dare be late!"

Despite Brady's shouts from his perch on my rig, I lingered inside the house. "Nanny," I said as she gave my hat a minor adjustment, "what were you going to tell me earlier about Amelia Beaumont?"

"Oh, yes, I'd forgotten with all of Brady's hubbub." She drew me farther away from the open front door as if to ensure our privacy from prying ears, not that Brady could have heard us or it would have mattered if he had. "Lady Amelia Beaumont hasn't got two cents to rub together."

"What? No!"

Nanny nodded sagely. "I've had it from Bonnie Preston, Mrs. Goelet's housekeeper over at Ochre Court, who heard it from the family's house-keeper in New York, who not only surmised it firsthand but conferred with Carrie Astor's lady's maid and Mrs. Frances Delafield's personal secretary."

Nanny's list of illustrious servants had me shaking my head in confusion until she said, "Don't you see, Emma? Lady Amelia stayed first with the Goelets last winter, then with the Astors in the spring, and finally with the Delafields before coming here to stay with your Aunt Alva." She compressed her lips and peered at me over her spectacles like a schoolmarm waiting for the figures to add up in my head.

"You mean she doesn't have a home of her own?"

"Nor maids nor carriages nor any prospects at all save for a trunkful of extravagant gowns."

"And the kindness of friends." I pressed my knuckles against my lips. "Good heavens. When all this happened and the police questioned Lady Amelia on the whereabouts of her scarf, it came out that Clara Parker had been serving as her lady's maid because Amelia's own had taken ill."

"Ill, my eye. The gentry are always quick with a story to cover their tracks. Lady Amelia's a fake, pure and simple. Oh, I've no doubt she was raised with a silver spoon between her lips, but the money's gone and unless she finds a rich husband quick, she'll be out of options."

"And in a way it makes perfect sense that she'd ingratiate herself to Aunt Alva," I said. "With Consuelo engaged, Amelia was probably hoping to be introduced to some of the castoff suitors."

"Emmaline Cross, what the devil are you doing in there?"

Brady's urgent interruption set my feet in motion. "Thanks, Nanny, this certainly sheds some new light on matters."

We'd no sooner arrived at The Breakers than a waiting footman whisked Brady upstairs. I was also led upstairs but at a much more sedate pace, and delivered to Aunt Alice, who was enjoying breakfast out on the upper loggia. Sunlight glittered on the ocean beyond the gardens, but the covered loggia was cool and shady.

"Ah, Emmaline," she crooned when she saw me. "Do join me for some kippers and eggs. Gertrude won't be up for hours yet. Parker," she said to the footman still hovering behind me, "please bring an extra place setting for my niece."

She said this last with an affection that drew my notice. Not that I ever doubted Aunt Alice's sentiments toward me. She might not approve of everything I did, but her fondness for me had always been evident. Still, she wasn't one to express emotion save the hearty self-satisfaction of having full control over her world. So then . . .

"I hear you've been to Marble House recently."

Ah. I sat in a cushioned chair beside her chaise lounge. "Yes, I was there when—"

"Oh, Emmaline, nothing good can come of associating with *that* woman. And now you're embroiled in a most unsavory matter."

By *that woman,* I knew she referred to Aunt Alva. I fought the temptation to remind her that associating with *her own* branch of the Vanderbilt family had brought nearly identical results not all that long ago. "I went to see Consuelo, Aunt Alice."

She blew out a breath, popped a morsel into her mouth, and took her time in answering. "That poor child . . . a lovely girl, and she's been made to endure so much because of that mother of hers."

I couldn't argue there.

"Tell me, how is the poor dear holding up?"

Here I needed to be careful. I appreciated Aunt Alice, I respected Aunt Alice, but I didn't trust Aunt Alice not to find a way to use the current situation to her advantage. She and Aunt Alva had long been rivals—their two monstrous houses stood testament to that. Would Alice use Consuelo's disappearance to fuel a scandal? My heart said no. Family history, however, warned otherwise.

"Consuelo is distraught," I said without lying. "This is not a happy time for her."

"Is it true—" Aunt Alice broke off as Parker reappeared carrying a tray. He set it down on the little garden table between Aunt Alice and myself, and lifted the cover off a plate heaped with golden scrambled eggs framed by two long, silvery brown kippers. Beside the plate sat a small bowl of sliced melon and strawberries.

"Did I mention I ate at home?" I said. Yet my stomach rumbled in appreciation of the aromas spiraling from the tray.

"You'll eat again," my aunt said with a dismissive wave, though an unnecessary one as I'd already set the plate on my knees and unwrapped my fork from the napkin. "You're too thin, at any rate."

Once again, not a point to argue over. Parker's receding footsteps prompted Aunt Alice to swallow a bite of kipper and lean toward me. "I had started to ask you. Is it true about Consuelo's engagement?"

"Surely Uncle William discussed it with Uncle Cornelius," I began, but she cut me off with another one of her waves, as if swatting at a fly.

"I mean that Consuelo is unhappy about the match."

"Oh." I set my fork on my plate. "Well . . . yes, it's true."

"What's wrong with the girl? My goodness, if I could arrange a duke for Gertrude, she'd be in raptures. If only we'd gone abroad last spring, instead of going back and forth between here and New York. Well, I suppose it couldn't be helped, not with this house in its final stages of reconstruction. Oh, but still, if *we'd* met the young duke first . . ."

I let her go on, all the while knowing that shy, awkward Gertrude could never have landed a man so high on the social register; nor did I believe my cousin would have wished for so public a life. But if Aunt Alice enjoyed reveling in her disappointed hopes, who was I to disillusion her?

We spoke of other things as well, all the while skirting another concern of my aunt's regarding one of her children, namely, Neily, and his association with a young heiress named Grace Wilson. As Uncle Cornelius's primary heir, Neily was expected to make a brilliant marriage; yet despite the Wilson family's wealth and Grace's celebrated beauty, his parents didn't deem her good enough. I couldn't help attributing their dislike to the fact that Grace's brother, Orme, had wed Carrie Astor—the Astors and Vanderbilts had been carrying on a thinly veiled social feud for years now. An upstart and a gold digger, Aunt Alice called Grace. That seemed harsh considering the Vanderbilts had built their fortune in trade only two generations previously. That hardly qualified them as *old money,* but once again I knew better than to argue with her.

Throughout our conversation, the greater portion of my thoughts dwelled on Marble House and Nanny's revelation about Amelia Beaumont. I had detected something not wholly genuine about the woman; her mannerisms seemed too practiced, as if she were moving through the acts of a play. Granted, all women of the upper classes cultivated a poised exterior, like a kind of genteel armor, but somehow Lady Amelia's armor didn't quite fit. Thanks to Nanny, I now knew why.

I also now had three reasons to return to Marble House: search for my wildflower, the rugosa rose; question Hope Stanford about her temperance efforts and deduce how much she knew of her husband's illegal activities; and learn more about Amelia Beaumont. I was impatient to be off.

Yet nearly an hour passed before Brady stepped out onto the loggia looking pale and a bit wild about the eyes. He circled me and went to Aunt Alice's side, and leaned down to kiss her cheek.

"It went well?" she asked.

Judging by his pallor I wouldn't have thought so, but Brady nodded somewhat shakily. "He gave me my job back." He sounded baffled, as though he couldn't quite believe it.

A jolt of surprise nearly sent my plate tumbling from my knees. I set it aside. "Brady, that's wonderful!"

He shrugged and sat down on Aunt Alice's other side. "I have you to thank for this, don't I?" he said more than asked her.

"Nonsense. I merely suggested he speak with you."

I tossed up my hands in a bid for details. "What did he say to you?"

"Awful things at first." Brady shuddered. "What a scoundrel I am, a traitor to the family, don't deserve the slightest regard, some things I won't repeat . . . and then . . . it was the da—" He darted a gaze at Aunt Alice. "It was the oddest thing. He admitted part of him admired my gumption. Can you believe it? Said if I ever betrayed him or the family again he'd see me behind bars for the rest of my life, but as long as I've learned my lesson, he could use a man with 'my cunning,' as he put it, on the staff of the New York Central."

I was dumbfounded—and not altogether pleased with Uncle Cornelius's reasoning, I must confess. It saddened me to think of my exuberant, slightly naïve older brother being absorbed into the high jinks of the railroad business. Being Uncle Cornelius's clerk was one thing, but contributing to the subterfuge that plagued the industry was quite another, and I despaired of the effect it would have on Brady's erratic but essentially goodhearted nature.

For now I let it go. Brady had a job again, and in the short term that meant fewer nights spent carousing and fewer days nursing the resulting hangovers.

Brady and I said our good-byes to Aunt Alice, but as we approached the staircase Uncle Cornelius's office door sprang open. "Emmaline, a word."

The aroma of cigars enveloped me as I followed the old gentleman into the inner sanctum so rarely open to visitors. Cornelius Vanderbilt was a man of middling stature, sagging about the shoulders and middle, so ordinary looking few would ever guess he controlled a fortune, a dynasty, and countless individuals. Yet, when he wished, he projected an authority that sped one's step in an eager effort to please. His "Emmaline, a word" had prompted me to obey without hesitation. It surprised me, then, that once the office door closed he fidgeted and avoided my gaze.

To fill the awkward silence, I said, "Uncle Cornelius, thank you so much for giving Brady a second chance. I know it means so much to him, and to m—"

Here he cut me off with a piercing gaze. "It was for you, Emmaline. I forgave him for your sake. And only for your sake."

"Oh . . . I . . . Uncle Cornelius . . . I don't know what to say . . ."

"You don't have to say anything. If you were a man, I'd have you work for me, Emmaline. I've never said that to a woman before, but it's the truth. Dang shame you weren't born a man. As it is, you're a good, sensible girl saddled with a dunderhead of a half brother." When I opened my mouth to protest, he held up his hand. "I'm sorry, but it's true. Oh, he's not stupid—far from it—but common sense? Not a speck! Just like his father. Thank heaven you're Arthur Cross's daughter and not the offspring of Stuart Braden Gale the Third. Even if he hadn't been lost at sea, that man never would have amounted to anything but the wastrel he was. A fortunate day for your mother when his yacht went down."

I gasped. "Uncle Cornelius!"

"Sorry." He had the good grace to look contrite. "I won't keep you any longer. I just . . . just wanted you to know . . . Well, dang it, you're like a daughter to me, Emmaline."

The poor man blushed to the tips of his ears. Like his wife, he wasn't one to express his emotions—not the tender ones, at any rate. I believe they both held demonstrations of affection as detrimental to their children, as if too much praise and kindness might produce slackers and weaklings.

His clumsy confession made him all the more dear to me in that moment, so much so I went to him, held his shoulders as I rose up on tiptoe, and kissed his cheek. "Thank you, Uncle Cornelius," I whispered, and hurried out the door.

Brady met me downstairs in the Great Hall. I seized his hand and tugged. "Come. Next stop, Marble House."

CHAPTER 13

Some ten minutes later Brady and I stood braced against a battering summer wind that plastered our clothes to our bodies. I held my hat in place; he held his at his side and squinted against the salty, sandy gusts. My stomach sank in disappointment.

"Well, that's it, then. I was wrong."

Below us, bright pink rugosa roses dotted the cliff face, pouring from between the rocks in cheerful bursts of color. I'd found my wild-flowers.

"Are you sure?" Brady leaned a bit over the edge, prompting me to grab on to his forearm. "The nearest ones are still a good distance away. They might merely resemble the petals you found."

That inspired a moment's hope, but then I shook my head. "As Jesse said on the telephone, there aren't many flowers that continue to bloom this late in the summer. And considering their size and color . . . No, it's the same. And this proves to me the wind carried them into the pavilion, and not the murderer."

"Don't despair, you've still got all the other clues."

"You don't understand. I'd thought this one would result in a breakthrough." Why had I believed that? Why had I put so much stock in a tiny, wind-borne flower that happened to wedge itself beneath the pavilion railings? The ocean breeze slapped my cheeks as though to slap sense into my head.

Brady had continued leaning over, scanning the promontory that fell away in dizzying heights to the ocean beneath us. I tapped his arm. "Let's go to the house. You can still be of help to me there."

We found Aunt Alva in her morning room, and the fact that she wasn't alone restored my spirits a fraction. Lady Amelia sat with her, enjoying a breakfast of pancakes, sausages, and fruit. Today she wore an ivory morning dress topped with an impossibly expensive, flowing caftan gown of beige silk stamped with a burgundy velvet design, and her beautiful golden curls were pinned at the crown of her head, encircled by a velvet ribbon that matched the gown. Amelia Beaumont looked the epitome of an aristocratic lady relaxing at home. She appeared so at home, in fact, that for a moment I wondered if Aunt Alva had had any inkling of what might be in store for her when she invited the younger woman here.

A permanent guest?

"Emmaline! And Brady . . ." Aunt Alva seemed genuinely pleased to see us. "Lady Amelia, may I present Miss Cross's half brother, Mr. Gale . . . Stuart Braden Gale the Fourth."

Brady, having removed his straw boater upon entering the house, waved it with a little flourish as he bowed to the ladies. At mention of his full name and numeral, Lady Amelia had sat up a little straighter, lifted her chin a little higher, and fully inspected Brady from head to toe. Yes, his was an impressive-sounding name, one that indicated an old Newport pedigree along with old Newport money. Unfortunately for Brady, as Lady Amelia would eventually learn, he possessed little of the former and none of the latter. While Gale *was* an old Newport name, and although Brady's father had styled himself Stuart Braden Gale III, no one could ever find evidence of either Stuart Braden Junior or Senior.

Still, on that particular morning, Amelia didn't need to know any of that. At her invitation Brady took the seat beside her at the round cherry-wood table and helped himself to an array of breakfast items. Aunt Alma seemed pleased enough with the arrangement and came to her feet.

"Yes, good, Brady, make yourself quite at home. I need to speak with Emmaline."

Brady and Amelia's murmured conversation followed us out of the room and down the sunny hall. Turning into the main portion of the house, she led me into the library. I'd wished to avoid this kind of detour to my plans, for all I'd wanted was to install Brady in the morning room to keep Aunt Alva occupied while I hurried upstairs to inspect Amelia's room and, if my luck held, ask Hope Stanford a few pointed questions.

Aunt Alva closed the library door, effectively sealing us in. "Why haven't you found her yet, Emmaline?"

The terse question took me aback and left me momentarily speechless.

"You promised you'd find her before anyone found out. That silly, foolish girl, running off, worrying me so. Vexing me beyond endurance. And so you are, too, Emmaline."

"I certainly don't mean to," I said. "I've been trying." Dared I tell her I'd enlisted Jesse Whyte's assistance? The thunderheads simmering in her expression warned me not to. I scrambled for the right words to placate her. "It hasn't been all that long, Aunt Alva. I realize every day she isn't here seems like an eternity, but she'll be back soon."

"How can you know that?"

I wandered to the camelback sofa near the window but didn't sit. Instead, I clasped my hands at my waist—an effort to appear calm—and faced Aunt Alva. "Consuelo has been terribly upset. You know that. She hated the thought of marrying the Duke, and sending me to persuade her backfired horribly. I believe she had been planning her escape, as it were, for days or perhaps weeks. The murder and the chaos that followed provided her with just the opportunity she needed to steal away . . . probably to a friend's home as we originally thought."

Did I believe that? The first part, yes. But my theory about Consuelo's disappearance? No. Not anymore. But I knew of no other way to prevent Aunt Alva from panicking.

"Then, why . . ." Her voice trembled and caught. She coughed, swallowed, began again. "Then why didn't you find her? You said you inquired with her friends."

"That's true, but either someone lied, or she has a friend we don't know about. Is that possible?"

"Of course it's not possible," she snapped. But then she compressed her lips and clearly considered the question. "I suppose . . . she hasn't always been with me. Before her little rebellion began I allowed her to mix with friends. Who knows whom she might have met last spring, someone who is here in Newport now."

"You see, then. All is not lost."

"How is it not lost?" Her voice rose to a wail. "Oh, Emmaline! She could be held somewhere against her will. Or she might believe she's safe while being led unspeakably astray."

She stumbled her way to the sofa and, as she sank to the cushions, grabbed my hand and pulled me down beside her. The sheer curtains in the morning room had been drawn, as Aunt Alva always insisted, so as not to reveal too harsh a reality before one was fully awake and ready for the day. But here, the daylight from the open window lighted her features to disclose the strain I hadn't detected before. Redness rimmed her eyes and she seemed somehow diminished—smaller, less robust, almost downright frail.

For the first time in my life, I saw not the formidable society matron who'd stop at nothing to reign supreme among the Four Hundred, but merely a mother who loved her child, who wanted only to hold her and know she was safe.

I set my hand on her shoulder. "I'll find her, Aunt Alva, I promise."

"No, Emmaline. I was wrong to insist." She broke off and a small sob escaped her. "I was wicked to burden you, but I'd thought . . ." She squeezed my hand, then released it and squared her shoulders. "I think it's time we went to the police."

"Yes!" My enthusiastic reply jolted her, and I hastened to temper my meaning before she guessed I'd already acted on the matter without her permission. "This is very wise of you. If you wish, I'll speak with my friend Detective Whyte—"

"Oh, would you, Emmaline?"

"Certainly."

"And can you guarantee that he'll be discreet?"

So much for the softer, more genuine Aunt Alva. "I'll do my best," I said, keeping the cynicism from my voice. And then, in a strategy she herself wouldn't have balked at, I twisted the situation to my advantage. "The reason I came today was to take another look at Consuelo's room. It would help if I could provide Detective Whyte with any further insight into her frame of mind when she left."

She nodded. "I'll come with you."

"Oh, but if you wouldn't mind, I'd rather go up alone. The fewer distractions the better as I look around."

"All right, then. If you need anything, just pull the bell and have someone come get me."

Need I say I had no intention of poking through Consuelo's room? Instead, I ran upstairs and quickly detoured into Lady Amelia's vacant suite. Wasting no time—for who knew how quickly she might tire of Brady's company?—I closed the door behind me and hurried to the armoire. The contents confirmed what Nanny had told me. The dresses were exquisite, but there were precious few of them, and with a little shuffling through the clothespress I discovered clever means of stretching a sparse wardrobe: lace collars and cuffs, silk blouses, embroidered and beaded overskirts—items meant to refresh and disguise previously worn gowns. I knew all about this; my own wardrobe consisted more of such add-ons than actual substance.

The caftan. I suddenly realized Amelia's outfit

today was another means of being able to wear the same undergown more than once.

I closed the drawer in which I'd been rummaging and stood, arms folded, a finger tapping my chin. What, if anything, did this mean? So what if circumstances had forced Lady Amelia to play a charade? If her childhood fortune had been lost, what other measures could she have resorted to? If I knew anything about the wealthy, it was that they didn't know how to be poor. If Lady Amelia wished to live in the style to which she had become accustomed, she'd need a rich husband and she'd need him fast. But that didn't make her a criminal; it simply made her determined to survive. And who was I to judge? I'd been lucky enough to inherit a house and a modest annuity from my aunt Sadie. Most women had no such benefactor.

A wash of shame heated my face and I very determinedly turned to the door . . . upon which a knock sounded. In the next instant the door opened and Hope Stanford scowled at me.

"What are you doing in here?"

I could have lied. I could simply have told the truth. I did neither.

"That's none of your business," I said coldly. "As a matter of fact, however, I'm glad you're here. I've been wanting to speak with you."

Her lips thinned at my sharpness. Obviously she was used to far more deference than I was inclined to show her. "Why, you impertinent girl. What can you possibly have to say to me in that tone of voice?"

"Impertinent? Mrs. Stanford, impertinent is running molasses into the area for the express purpose of manufacturing black-market rum."

"What *are* you talking about?"

"Impertinent," I continued, ignoring her question but noting the tic that suddenly tightened her left cheek, "is being chased by brigands who object to anyone witnessing their crimes."

"What has this got to do with me?"

"The question, Mrs. Stanford, is what has this got to do with your husband? And whether Madame Devereaux knew about his little secret."

"Oh dear . . ." One hand clutched her throat as her color drained away in a big whoosh. On unsteady legs she made her way to a tufted chair in the corner and fell into it with a thud.

I moved closer to her, standing practically toe-to-toe, forcing her to look up at me. "Well, Mrs. Stanford, what do you have to say? And no use denying your husband's involvement. He's already admitted it to me."

Her mouth opened, formed a trembling O. "He . . . he did? Oh, that stupid, sinful man."

Leaning low, I grasped the arms of the chair and brought my face close to hers, so close I saw the fear flickering in her eyes, smelled it emanating from her skin. "So the real question here, Mrs.

Stanford, is how much do you know about your husband's activities, and to what extent do you approve of them?"

"Approve? You're talking nonsense."

"Am I? What better way to make tremendous profits selling black-market rum than if all alcoholic beverages are illegal?"

She pushed forward so suddenly I was forced to straighten and step back. A moment later she was on her feet. Her eyes swam with tears, but also with a fierceness that sent me another stride backward. "I swear to you my temperance efforts are completely sincere and wholly aimed at what is best for this nation."

"Your husband apparently doesn't agree," I said, somewhat cruelly I must admit.

"No, he doesn't, much to his shame, if he had any. What am I to do? Stop working for sobriety? Abandon my life's work? No, Miss Cross, that I will not do, not as long as I have a breath in me. And if Calvin wishes to twist my work for his own selfish purposes, it's his sin, isn't it?"

"Why don't you turn him in?"

She raised her chin. "Because I firmly believe I don't have to. God will see to my husband. Eventually Calvin will be caught, if he doesn't mend his ways."

"And Madame Devereaux?" I whispered.

Hope turned away from me, showing me her straight, inflexible back. "She knew. Of course she knew, the busybody." She spun back around. Her color had returned, showing an angry, mottled red. "She was a *medium,* in touch with the spirits. Ha! She was a gossip and the worst kind of meddler. She knew just how many drinks to ply her victims with before she wheedled them with questions. She found out what she needed to know about Calvin up in Providence, and then she came to *me* with her demands."

"Money for silence," I said.

She nodded.

Very low, I asked her, "And did you decide to silence her in another way?"

Her chuckles took me by surprise. "In addition to being impertinent, Miss Cross, you are also highly amusing. Murder Madame Devereaux . . . for Calvin's sake?"

"For your own sake."

"Didn't I just say I'll leave Calvin's fate to God? I'll neither turn him in nor protect him."

"You'll profit if he profits," I pointed out, "but if he falls, you'll fall with him. Who would put any stock in a temperance leader whose own husband is in the illegal liquor trade?"

Once again, she laughed. "You underestimate me, Miss Cross. As for profits, I have what I need in this life. Greed is not one of my vices."

Her sensible, sturdy clothing and few adornments lent credence to the claim.

"And should Calvin be arrested for his crimes,

I shall be among the first to condemn his activities—not *him,* mind you, but the turpitude brought on by the demon spirits soaking his mind and his soul." She took several strides toward me, rousing the fearsome image of an avenging, hammer-wielding Hope Stanford. "Why on earth would I commit murder, Miss Cross, when I have the power of righteousness on my side?"

She didn't linger long enough for me to answer, but circled me and disappeared into the hallway. My senses were left buzzing, my thoughts in disarray. Yet, as when I questioned her husband and Winty, I found myself believing her.

I, too, turned toward the door; after all, it wouldn't do to be caught here by Lady Amelia, and I could rely on Brady's charms for only so long. As I passed the dressing table, however, I stopped, my attention caught by a gilt and ivory box sitting beneath the mirror. What kind of jewels would Lady Amelia have tucked inside? Were they real or paste? I was no longer sure why it mattered, yet, with a quick glance into the hallway, I opened the box and glanced inside.

And gasped at what I saw nestled among necklaces and brooches, bracelets and earrings.

I arrived back in the morning room breathless, my heart threatening to pound its way out of my chest. But the sight of one empty chair stopped me cold. "Where is Lady Amelia?"

Brady and Aunt Alva looked up from their breakfast plates without concern.

"Out walking," Aunt Alva said.

"Where?"

Brady pointed in the general direction of outdoors. "The gardens, she said. I offered to go with her, but . . ." A corner of his mouth pulled.

"Amelia enjoys a solitary walk in the morning," Aunt Alva supplied. "She's done so every day since she's been here. There's no harm in it." Her gaze narrowed on me. "Did you find anything interesting upstairs?"

She referred to my fictional errand in Consuelo's room. With some measure of truth I shook my head. "Nothing new, but don't worry. I'll talk to Jesse today." I turned to Brady. "We need to be going."

"Oh, but Brady and I were just becoming reacquainted. He's told me all about that wretched business with your Uncle Cornelius, and I told Brady he can very well come and work for me instead. I could use a good administrator for my estates here and in New York."

"That's very nice, Aunt Alva, but we really have to be going. And . . . and I'd like to say good-bye to Lady Amelia before we do. Wouldn't you like that, Brady? To bid Lady Amelia a good day?" I shot him a pointed glare.

Shrugging and tossing down his napkin, Brady came to his feet. "I suppose. Aunt Alva, thank you for breakfast." He leaned down to give her a kiss.

"Well, if you do see Amelia, tell her I'll be in my office until noon," Aunt Alva called after us.

"What was that all about?" Brady demanded as soon as we'd stepped onto the veranda and the French doors closed behind us.

With trembling fingers I opened my purse to show him. "I just found this in Lady Amelia's jewelry box."

What had been nestled among jewelry now lay atop my comb, extra hair pins, the key to my house, and a fresh linen handkerchief: a sprig of dried pink wildflowers with golden centers, the petals gone dusky from having been deprived of water and sunlight.

Rugosa roses.

CHAPTER 14

Brady stared down into my purse. "She might have found this the same way you did—blown into the gardens from the cliffs."

"Maybe . . . maybe not."

"What are you suggesting? That she went scrambling down the cliff face and picked these flowers herself?"

"No, I'm suggesting there is another, much more convenient source of these roses, and that whoever tracked them into the pavilion also presented Lady Amelia with this little spray. A woman doesn't keep flowers she picked herself in her jewelry box."

Brady frowned. "Where does she keep them?"

"Oh, Brady, don't be obtuse." I resisted the urge to shake him. "Don't you see, she secreted these roses away like a clandestine memento. I'd say this represents the affections of a man."

"Aah."

"Come on, we need to find her." I craned my neck and scanned the gardens directly behind the house, but no golden curls caught the sunlight. I took Brady's arm and randomly headed to the south side of the house. It didn't take long to comb the tree-shaded area. The estates along Bellevue sat on relatively little land, most of which stretched in front of and behind the houses. It took only moments to conclude that Lady Amelia wasn't strolling on the south side of the house.

We circled the rear veranda and this time set out to the north garden. As we neared the sheds, I saw Mr. Delgado, the head gardener, and hurried over to him.

He removed his cap and showed me a smile. "Good morning, Senhorita Cross, Senhor Gale."

We bid him good morning and then I said, "My brother and I are on our way home, but I'd hoped to say good-bye to Lady Amelia first. Have you seen her?" At his puzzled look, I clarified, "Mrs. Vanderbilt's guest, the very attractive lady with the blond hair. Apparently she enjoys a morning walk each day."

His puzzlement didn't appear to abate, and he shrugged. "I have seen no one this morning, Senhorita. Sorry."

"This is very odd," I murmured to Brady once the older man had left us to continue his morning tasks.

"Not necessarily. She's probably walking along Bellevue. And can you blame her if she needed time away from Alva the Anaconda?"

"Brady, really!" I landed a blow to his shoulder, which he took in stride.

"Sorry, but I find the analogy rather apt. Anacondas are known for suffocating their prey before they eat them."

"Come on, then. Maybe we can catch up with Lady Amelia."

Once back in my rig, we saw no trace of her along Bellevue Avenue, not as far as the eye could see in either direction. We headed north and rode a little ways, peering down side streets as we went.

"She's a fast walker, unless she hailed a cab or met an acquaintance with a carriage. We could try turning down the side streets," Brady suggested, but I shook my head.

"She might have taken any of them, or none of them. She could be in town by now. Or for all we know, while we searched the gardens she returned to the house." I thought a moment, then brightened. "It's all right. Lady Amelia isn't going anywhere any time soon. I'll simply wait until my next trip to Marble House, either later today or tomorrow. I'll have my answers from the woman, make no mistake."

"Say, isn't that Jamie Reilly? Where's he going in the middle of a workday?" Brady raised his arm to point toward Bath Road, which intersected Bellevue as it ran from town down the big hill to Easton's Beach.

Sure enough, the familiar golden red hair shone clearly from beneath a tweed cap. I did my best to hurry Barney along, and within a couple of minutes we caught up with the young Irishman. He greeted us with a friendly grin when we hailed.

"Miss Cross, what a lovely pleasure." He removed his cap and made a little bow. "Mr. . . . ah . . . Gale, I believe 'tis?"

Brady gave a cordial nod.

I switched Barney's reins into one hand and leaned the other on the side panel. "Whatever are you doing here, Jamie?"

"Ah, Mr. Delgado let me go early today, and I thought I'd ride the trolley into town."

"Early? Why is that?"

"Well, with summer waning, miss, there's less work to be done. I gather Mrs. Vanderbilt doesn't wish to pay out wages if it isn't necessary. Can hardly blame her, now can I?"

Maybe not, but I experienced a pang of guilt for those lost wages considering I'd helped Jamie procure his employment at Marble House. Surely this young man needed full-time pay for full-time work. He very likely sent part of those wages home to family in Ireland, as Katie did when she was able. I should have inquired with Aunt Alva, and perhaps Mr. Delgado, before recommending Jamie for the position of gardener's assistant.

"We could give you a lift into town," I offered, wanting to spare him the trolley fare. Brady shot me a glance, which I ignored.

"Thank you kindly, Miss Cross, but I always look forward to riding the trolley, and the walk to the stop will do me good."

"All right, then. Oh, and by the way. My

mysterious wildflower? It's called the rugosa rose. And it grows everywhere along the cliffs."

"Does it now? I suppose I ought to have recognized it then, oughtn't I, miss?"

"No more than I should have, but then all we had to go by were some wilting petals."

He tilted his chin. "You don't look happy to have solved your mystery, miss."

"No, I'm not, particularly. I thought it might be a clue to whoever murdered the medium. Well, I shouldn't keep you any longer. Enjoy your day, Jamie."

"And you, too, miss. Mr. Gale. A good day to you both."

As I swung my rig around to head home, Brady grumbled beneath his breath.

"What?" I demanded.

"You're altogether too familiar with people sometimes, Em. Offering the man a ride. You hardly know him and he's certainly not your social equal."

"Social equal? Why, Brady Gale, what a snob you are. He's a friend of Katie's and that's good enough for me."

"Friend of Katie's—Katie, your housemaid. That only further proves my point. It doesn't do for someone like you to overextend courtesies to such people, little sister. Don't think they don't know who you are. And they'll only take advantage of you in the end."

The flap I gave the reins was more due to my growing annoyance than any desire to travel faster. At any rate, Barney ignored the command and continued at his usual sedate walk. "Stuff and nonsense," I said. "Katie has been nothing but grateful and hardworking since I took her in, and Mr. Delgado seems genuinely pleased with having Jamie as his new assistant. No harm done as far as I can see nor any advantage taken."

"I'm not talking about helping people find work. I'm talking about trusting where you should show caution."

"Bah." I could have reminded him I'd placed my trust in him not very long ago, and he'd betrayed my trust by involving me in his scheme to hoodwink Uncle Cornelius. It didn't matter that my role was to help him return the stolen railroad plans. Had Uncle Cornelius chosen not to be generous, I might have been ostracized from the family. And as much as I sometimes complained about my Vanderbilt family . . . they were still my family.

A clip-clopping and the accompanying rumble of wheels alerted me to another vehicle approaching from a side street, yet I remained unprepared for the speed at which a curricle came bounding around the corner of Lakeview Avenue onto Bellevue. With only feet between us, I drew Barney up short, an action that elicited a startled snort from the animal and a hissed oath from

Brady. The curricle swerved around us, creaking and tilting sharply; it continued north at the same madcap speed.

But not before I registered the identity of the driver: Winthrop Rutherfurd.

I twisted round to watch the receding rig. "What was that all about?"

Brady shrugged. "He's in one devil of a hurry."

"Indeed he is." I was tempted to turn around and follow him, but he was already a number of streets away and hadn't slowed one bit; Barney would never be able to match that pace, much less catch up. I sighed, resigned to not being able to satisfy my curiosity, at least not at present.

"Maybe Winty'll give Mr. Reilly a ride to town." Sarcasm sharpened Brady's words. "He'd certainly get him there eons sooner than the trolley. But then, I can't see old Rutherfurd sharing his rig with a gardener. Might soil the Spanish leather."

"Oh, Brady, leave it, won't you?" I snapped as we continued to Ocean Avenue. My mind returned to other, more immediate mysteries. "What I'd very much like to know is who gave Lady Amelia that rugosa rose; or in other words, whom she might be dallying with. It can't be someone acceptable or she wouldn't have hidden the fact from Aunt Alva."

"Maybe it was Jamie Reilly," Brady murmured. He hunched deeper into the seat, arms crossed over his chest.

"Don't be boorish."

He scowled at me, but then his expression lightened. "Maybe it was me. Huh, Em? You think maybe I've been dallying with Lady Amelia? Maybe she and I were only pretending not to have met previously. A ruse to fool Aunt Alva. And you."

Alarm rippled through me for several long seconds before the tension drained away and I shook my head at him. "You are incorrigible. I have no idea why I put up with you."

"Because I'm your older brother and you adore me. Now, how about hurrying this old hack so we can get home and see what treats Nanny's cooking up for us today."

There was no time for treats when we arrived home. We found Nanny in the alcove beneath the stairs shouting into the mouthpiece of the telephone because she believed that to be the only way the person on the other end could hear her. The moment Brady and I stepped into the foyer, she broke off and gaped at us for an instant before speaking more quietly into the mouthpiece. "Never mind, she's here." She ended the call.

"I was just calling over to the Marble House to find you, Emma." Still in her house slippers, she shuffled over to us. "Oh, you'll never guess. Mable Hanson called me some twenty minutes ago. You remember Mrs. Hanson, don't you,

Emma? She lived over on Chestnut Street on the Point. That is, until her husband closed his butcher shop and they retired to a little cottage in Middletown, near Second Beach. They're on Paradise Avenue and can see the beach from their front windows."

"Yes, I remember the Hansons, Nanny." I tried to hide my impatience. "What did she want?"

"She thinks she might have seen Consuelo this morning."

"What?" Brady and I exclaimed together. My pulse spiked and I found myself gasping for breath. Once more in unison we asked, "Where?"

"On the beach. Strolling."

I whirled about and reached to open the front door. "I've got to go."

"Wait, Emma." Nanny caught me by the shoulder. "It's not likely she's still there. Mable knew we were looking for Consuelo because I'd spread the word among my friends, the most trusted ones, of course. But she doesn't have a telephone, you see, and her neighbor who does have one wasn't home at the time. She couldn't call me until she went into town over an hour later. She'd have gone sooner, but her husband was out with their carriage. And then I couldn't reach you right away because you'd already left The Breakers, and I just missed you at Marble House. So it's been a little while."

"A *little* while?" My eagerness deflated and I

wanted to stomp my foot and swear. I did neither, but instead gritted my teeth in frustration. "You're right. She wouldn't be on the beach for so long. Oh, what dreadful luck to practically have her in hand, only to have her slip away again."

Brady patted my back. "It's still a good lead, Em, your first real one. There aren't all that many houses in the immediate area, and if she was walking on the beach it's highly likely she's staying nearby."

"He's right," Nanny agreed. "It may be worth the ride down. You could ask around, maybe find someone else who's seen her. And let Jesse Whyte know."

"Do you know anyone who lives in the area? Other than the Hansons, I mean?"

Nanny was already shaking her head before I'd finished the question. Brady took a moment to consider before mirroring the gesture.

"Who on earth could Consuelo know who lives down there? Why, that's not even Newport anymore. It makes no sense." And then I remembered something Nanny had said. "Mrs. Hanson believes she *might* have seen Consuelo? What does that mean, exactly?"

"Well, she said one of the women walking along the shore wore a wide hat with a sheer but dark veil that hung down to her shoulders all around."

"*One* of the women?" Brady shot me a surprised look. "Did Mrs. Hanson know the identity of her companion?"

Nanny shook her head. "She said it was no one she recognized."

If I'd begun to be skeptical about this *sighting,* my doubts came on with storm force now. "One woman she didn't recognize, the other obscured by a large hat and veil. That isn't much to go on. In fact, it's next to nothing. Nanny, is it possible Mrs. Hanson was simply in the mood for a little excitement and dreamed up the rest?"

"Mable would *never.* The very idea, really." Nanny drew herself up with a shake of her jowls. "Mable was always a sensible, practical woman, never given to flights of fancy. What led her to conclude the woman on the beach was Consuelo was the way she held herself. Her figure, her posture, the dignity of her stride."

"Her stride? Oh, Nanny, that's rich." Brady laughed, earning him a slap on the arm, which seemed not to bother him in the least. He started to say more, but I cut him off.

"It's not all that far-fetched, actually. I believe I understand what Mrs. Hanson means. Come on, Brady, this deserves further investigation and you're coming with me."

"You didn't think I'd let you go alone, did you," he said as he followed me out the door.

⚫ ⚫ ⚫

With shaky legs I descended from my rig where the dusty road edged the sand of Sachuest, or as locals called it, Second Beach. Unlike the wide expanses of Bailey's or Easton's beaches, this was a lonely, narrow coastline between Sachuest Bay, an inlet of the Atlantic Ocean, and the salt marshlands that began on the north side of the road.

We had stopped at the western end of the sprawling, crescent moon strand. Just beyond, the land heaved upward to hilly, rocky terrain choked with cattails and dune grass. From there the ground continued to rise to the cliffs that formed Purgatory Chasm with its dramatic plunge and dizzying view of the ocean. Today, a small crowd, formed into a semicircle facing away from the road, obscured the view of both the chasm and the water.

A sense of foreboding made the eggs and kippers I'd eaten at The Breakers begin to churn. Newport's posh summer set descended daily on the superior facilities of Bailey's Beach; locals and those less well heeled enjoyed the boardwalk and entertainments to be found at Easton's, or First Beach, closer to town. To see more than a few people strolling Second Beach's sands was a rarity.

My boots sinking into the granular turf, I pushed my way through the nearest clutch of neck-craners, hoping against hope they were examining some fascinating object washed up with the tide.

Between milling shoulders, bonnets, and wide-brimmed hats, I could just make out a man in a dark serge suit bending low over what appeared to be a heap of sand littered with "red tide," the ribbons of crimson seaweed that periodically washed up on Newport's beaches and spoiled the enjoyment of summer bathers. Oh, I thought, perhaps everything was all right after all. Just a pile of seaweed, perhaps entwined with the nasty tentacles of some slimy jellyfish.

"My God." Brady stood at my shoulder, his voice a breath against my ear. "Is it . . . please say it isn't . . . Consuelo."

Being a head taller, he could see over the small throng and make out what I could not until we prodded our way closer. Then the ordinary beach debris these people were inspecting transformed before my eyes to elegant beige silk stamped with burgundy velvet.

"No, Brady," I whispered, my throat pinched tight—with shock and, I'm sorry to admit, with tremendous relief. "It's not Consuelo. Look at her clothes."

"Oh, my God. Lady Amelia."

The next minutes passed in a blur. Apparently someone who lived close by and owned a telephone—Mable Hanson's neighbor, perhaps—

had run home to alert the police. Soon the onlookers were pushed back to make way for a swarm of blue-coated police officers. A couple of them tried to herd me away along with the rest, shouting admonishments I ignored. I was going nowhere until I found out what had happened.

Although truth to tell, part of me didn't wish to know.

"Miss, you'll have to step aside. Oh, it's you, Miss Cross . . . and your brother, I see." I met the dark gaze of a policeman I knew, Scotty Binsford, who had not only attended school with Brady, but had been one of the investigating policemen when Brady had been accused of murder. I spared him a weak smile, for he'd whispered to me, upon Brady's release from jail, that he'd never doubted my brother's innocence.

Scotty turned to his associates. "They're all right." Then to me he said, lower, "Just don't get too close to the . . . er . . . body, Miss Cross. We're hoping our audience didn't already disturb important evidence, though for certain they've churned away any incriminating footprints with their own."

"Emma." Another police rig had just pulled up onto the sand beside the rescue wagon waiting to carry Lady Amelia away. Jesse stepped down and came striding over, kicking up whirls of sand in his wake. Just before he reached me he snapped out an order, crisp, terse words that didn't register with me but sent the others into a fresh flurry of activity. He gave me a quick embrace and set me at arm's length. "Emma, why is it you're always . . ." With a shake of his head he changed tack in mid-sentence. "How did you hear about this so quickly?"

"I didn't. I . . ." My gaze strayed to the beautiful blond curls spilling over the sand and partly across Lady Amelia's face and shoulders, the pins having scattered and whatever hat she had worn lost to the wind.

"Then why are you here?" He glanced over my shoulder. "Brady? What brought the two of you down here? And don't tell me you thought you'd fancy a stroll on the beach."

"One of Nanny's friends thought she might have seen Consuelo walking here," I said a bit shakily. "Brady and I came to see if we could find her." I pressed my hand to my mouth. "Oh, but it couldn't have been Consuelo. It must have been . . ."

Lady Amelia. Lovely, elegant, but not wholly genuine Lady Amelia. Even as I uttered my next question, I knew the answer. "D-did she drown?"

"I'll find out," he said, and moved off to confer with his men. He returned within moments. "She didn't drown," he said gently. "It doesn't appear as if she'd been any closer to the water than she is now."

Brady stepped up beside us and slipped an

anchoring arm around my waist. "What you just said, Em. It can't be right. It couldn't have been Lady Amelia Mrs. Hanson saw. According to Nanny, the sighting would have been more than two hours ago by now. We saw Lady Amelia at Marble House an hour ago at the most."

As he spoke, my gaze was drawn to the nearby cattails and rocky, weedy hillocks. Yes, a murder could easily take place here with little chance of anyone seeing. But what could have brought Lady Amelia to this nearly deserted part of the island? There could be only one connection between Lady Amelia and this place: Consuelo.

"You say you saw the victim recently?" Jesse reached into his coat pocket for a pencil and small tablet.

"Y-yes." I shook my thoughts away. "She was breakfasting with Aunt Alva. But she left quite suddenly, didn't she, Brady?"

"That's right. Said she was going for a walk." Brady glanced out over the calm swell of Sachuest Bay and then down at the lifeless woman. "Some walk. I wonder how she got all the way down here."

I stepped out of Brady's embrace. "Jesse . . . if she didn't drown, how did she die?"

He chewed his lip. "Do you want to see?"

I sucked in a breath and nodded. Still holding my hand, he led me across the sand, skirting the officers still examining the scene. Brady followed close behind us. At Lady Amelia's side—I couldn't yet bring myself to think of her as *the body*—Jesse pointed.

The tangles of her hair had been swept to one side. He spoke a single word. "Strangled."

I followed the angle of his outstretched finger; the same silk and velvet ribbon that had held her hair up earlier was now wrapped tight around her neck, its two ends dancing gaily in the breeze.

So like Madame Devereaux. Eerily, appallingly similar.

Brady swore.

"The same," I said, the words stinging like salt in my throat. "Dear heavens, Jesse, don't you realize what this means? Whoever killed Madame Devereaux also killed Lady Amelia. Clara Parker, and even Detective Dobbs, can be exonerated."

Brady gave a snort at that second suggestion, but Jesse was already shaking his head. "Hold up there, now. We need more evidence than this. For all we know at this point, this murder was random, or carried out by an imitator or an accomplice."

"But you already arrested Clara's so-called accomplice—Anthony Dobbs." I struggled to keep the anger from my voice. "Neither one of them could have murdered Lady Amelia."

"As I said, I need more evidence. Clues, a motive—"

At that I cut him off. "I can tell you the motive.

It's because she knew him, Jesse. I believe Lady Amelia was having an affair with the man who murdered Madame Devereaux." At his skeptical frown, I said, "The rugosa roses . . . she had a sprig in her room—in her jewelry box. Oh, blast, Jesse, you can't ignore this. You've got to—" My grip on my emotions was slipping. Brady set a hand on my arm.

"It's all right, Em. I'm sure Jesse has no intention of ignoring anything."

"Then there's this, too," I said, suddenly remembering a detail I'd forgotten in the shock of Lady Amelia's fate. "I'm sure this is merely a coincidence, and I wouldn't even mention it if . . . I probably shouldn't mention it, really . . ."

"Emma, as Brady said, I want to know about anything that could possibly have any bearing on this crime." Jesse held his pencil aloft and waited.

"It's just that as Brady and I were driving home from Marble House, Winthrop Rutherfurd passed us in his curricle at a runaway pace. He nearly hit us. He was heading north on Bellevue."

"That's it?" Jesse looked from me to Brady and back. "A man out driving in his rig?"

"Barreling along at a dangerous speed. It was highly suspicious. Isn't that right, Brady?"

Before Brady could answer, Jesse said, "I've seen Brady barreling along a time or two. I'm sorry, but I think you may be grasping at straws now." He wrote something in his tablet. "But what was it you said about Miss Vanderbilt?"

"Yes, Nanny's friend saw someone resembling Consuelo walking on the beach. She was with someone, another woman," I added. "That's why we came—to see if we could find any trace of her, either here or at one of the neighboring cottages."

"You thought you'd go door-to-door, did you?" Jesse looked at me askance.

"Well . . ."

"Emma," he said, "if Consuelo is hiding or if someone is holding her against her will, how do you think they'll react to you knocking on their door?"

"But we couldn't simply not come, could we?"

"What you could do is tell me everything you know and leave the rest to me."

I regarded the smattering of freckles across his cheeks and nose; the auburn hair, in need of a trim; and the easy confidence of his stance, something not always evident in the man but never missing from the officer. In his early thirties, Jesse Whyte wasn't young, not nearly as young as Brady, but his were the sort of features that would remain youthful until suddenly one day wrinkles bracketed his mouth and crinkled the corners of his eyes. Someday a bit of a stoop might bend his shoulders, and perhaps he'd walk with a hesitant gait. But his ready smile would always be there, and I couldn't imagine him ever being anything but amiable, dependable, responsible, and honest.

Honest.

An uninvited image formed in my mind— someone taller, more handsome, more exciting . . . but honest? When it suited him, yes. And when it didn't . . .

"Emma, will you please trust me to find your cousin? That *is* why you confided in me about her disappearance, isn't it?"

"Will you find her quickly?" I held my breath waiting for his answer, knowing I could put my faith in whatever reply he gave.

Yet honest Jesse gave no reply other than to give my hand a squeeze and offer me a small smile.

What else had I expected? He would never make a false promise.

The officers carried a gurney from the rescue wagon and placed it beside Lady Amelia. No, Lady Amelia's body. Their simple act rammed the truth home, straight through my heart. She was dead. Murdered. Whatever she might have been able to tell me, whatever connection there might have been between her, the rugosa roses, Madame Devereaux's death, and my cousin's disappearance, would never now reach my ears.

Tears burned in my eyes, and the next thing I knew a pair of arms went gently around me. Overwhelmed, I turned my face into Jesse's coat front and gave in to surging waves of futility, countered by the familiar comfort of my old friend's arms steadying me. Suddenly those arms felt all too right; all too easy to cling to and not let go.

But I did let go and with a shaky smile of gratitude, stepped back. Never a believer in coincidences, I no longer entertained the slightest doubt that today's events, and those at Marble House, were intricately connected to my cousin. But could I—or Jesse—find her in time to prevent yet another disaster?

Those doubts threatened to drown me.

CHAPTER 15

That night I tossed fitfully, tormented by dreams of Consuelo walking toward me on the beach, her delicate hand outstretched to me. A veil hid her face, but somehow I knew she was smiling, and the confidence of her stride told me she'd reconciled herself to her future, that she was no longer afraid, that she embraced the challenge. She was only some dozen yards away when suddenly she collapsed, a heap of silk and velvet ruffled by the breeze. I ran to her, calling her name, shouting, but when I reached her I found only twisted clumps of sand and seaweed . . . and a single rugosa rose wilting in the afternoon sunlight.

A sense of disorientation haunted me through-out the early-morning hours. I dressed having little sense of what I donned—something sensible in a dark blue muslin, I think. I breakfasted but tasted nothing. I stared out at the ocean beyond the morning-room windows and saw nothing . . . nothing but Lady Amelia's beautiful, lifeless face interchanging with that of my cousin. For the first time I wondered if Consuelo was even alive, and my heart clenched painfully.

Somehow I resisted calling Jesse, though every instinct willed me to crank the telephone and ask to be connected to the police department. Very well did I know that if Jesse had discovered anything new since yesterday, he'd have already informed me.

I had to ask myself, then, whether it was a yearning for information that continually turned my feet toward the alcove beneath the stairs, or a simple need for comfort, to hear that reliable, reassuring voice in my ear and know I was safe; know things would be all right.

I had felt that way yesterday, however briefly, and the essence, the warmth of that sensation lingered, sorely tempting me to reach for it again. I had only to say a word, give a sign, and the love of a good man could be mine for the rest of my life.

Light, speedy footsteps pulled me from my musing. I turned from the window as Katie entered from the hall.

"Miss, a visitor for you." Her smile held a hint of mischief that raised my guard, so I shouldn't have been surprised when she added, "It's that nice Mr. Andrews."

The tension inside me tightened another notch. If not for Derrick Andrews, my choices, my life, would be a raked and gently graded path laid out before me. But the mere mention of his name tossed up insurmountable barricades and made me realize there could be no easy way for me. No satisfaction in a practical, logical decision. I was not to be so lucky.

"Tell him I'm not receiving . . . no, tell him I'm not at home."

"Are you sure, miss?"

I hesitated. "Yes. No. I . . . um . . ."

Katie had turned to go, and now turned back, my words acting on her like puppet strings. A realization hit me a sobering blow: I would make no proper wife for either of the men currently haunting my dreams and waking hours. I was no sophisticated, poised lady, and in the elegant drawing rooms of the Andrews family, I would always yearn for my true self, and for the freedom that had become so precious to me. But with Jesse, I would just as surely pine for the excitement—and the passion—he could never give me.

Katie fidgeted with her apron. "Miss?"

"Oh . . . blast and dang it," I said, quoting two of Uncle Cornelius's favorite expletives. I hurried past her and found Derrick, hat in hands, waiting in the foyer.

"I know all about yesterday," he said without preamble. "You went down to the beach and stumbled on another murder. Emma, this reckless behavior—"

"I was looking for Consuelo, not a murder scene. What happened is not my fault, and believe me, I'd have much preferred yesterday's events never to have occurred. Poor Lady Amelia."

"Yes." He perused me in a manner that raised

goose bumps at my nape and renewed the nervous fluttering inside me.

Without warning he stepped closer and took me in his arms—not like Jesse's brief, comforting embrace, but a claim that made no pretense of politely asking but instead adamantly taking . . . while at the same time, somehow, giving. Almost suffocating, and yet spirit renewing.

"What if you had arrived at the beach earlier than you did?" His voice was as rough as sandpaper. "What if you had stumbled upon the killer?"

"I had Brady with me."

"Hang Brady."

"Don't underestimate my brother," I said defensively into his shirt collar. He held me tighter, then slowly released me and stepped back.

He raised a hand to cup my chin. "No one can stop you from walking into danger, can they?"

I stared back at him. I could have said I never purposely walked into danger, but simply embarked on any task that needed doing. My cousin needed finding. I couldn't abandon the search, not for anything. But he and I would continue to see it differently.

"All right, then." He dropped his hand to his side. "Come with me."

"Where?" I trotted to keep up as he exited through the front door and circled to the back of the property. He didn't slow his lengthy strides until we passed the kitchen garden and stable yard, and stood on the grassy verge overlooking the water.

With one hand he snapped open the buttons of his coat and shrugged the garment off. He tossed it to the grass a few feet away. "It's about time someone taught you how to defend yourself." He unknotted his tie and dropped it onto his crumpled coat.

"What do you have in mind?" I didn't at all care for the predatory gleam in his eye. I began backing away.

"Flight," he said, "is certainly a natural and legitimate response to a threat, and in all honesty the one I prefer you to choose. However, since you've proved stubborn time and time again, not to mention that sometimes flight isn't an option, we need to explore other avenues. Now stop backing away."

"Then stop frightening me. I don't like that look on your face."

"Are you a victim, Emma Cross? Is that how you see yourself?"

I halted my retreat and drew myself up. "Certainly not."

"Then come at me."

"That won't be fair. You're much bigger than I am. Besides, I've no doubt your expensive, private school education included the sport of boxing. You'll be far more experienced than I."

"You're right on all counts. But you do have advantages over me."

"Such as?" I managed to stand my ground as he came closer.

"When someone bigger than you poses a threat, you want to attack him from below. Your size will make that easier. Like this." Grasping my shoulder, he crouched a bit and jabbed four fingers straight at my throat. I braced for the blow, but he stopped an inch or two before contact. "Thrust up and straight into that little hollow below the Adam's apple. You try."

I mimicked his actions with some degree of finesse, I thought, until he scowled.

"Don't be afraid to hit me. You need to swing upward while spearing your hand like a bayonet. Put your strength into it."

"I don't want to hurt you."

A glint of fondness entered his eye, then was gone. "Don't worry, I'll live. The important thing is for you to learn how."

This time when he made a grab for my shoulders, I swung my right hand upward, fingers extended, straight into his throat. He grunted, released me, and stepped sharply back.

"Well done." He coughed and a rusty groan escaped his lips.

I felt a surge of triumph, tempered by a twinge of guilt. "I'm sorry."

"Don't be. Next . . ."

By the time Nanny summoned us for luncheon I'd mastered that and several other techniques. I'd learned how, whether attacked from up front or behind, to lift my foot and shove my heel directly into my assailant's kneecap. Not an ineffectual kick with my toes, as Derrick termed it, but a blow forceful enough to break the bone and topple a man several times my size.

Rather than slap or punch with my small hands, I learned how to stab my fingers into the soft skin underneath the jaw as well as into a person's eye, but lest I be accused of blinding Derrick, let it be noted we sacrificed a tomato from the garden for this lesson. I learned a man's most vulnerable points: the Adam's apple—any blunt blow should do; the soft dimples behind the ears—I should dig inward with my thumbs; beneath the rib cage—a jab of the elbow there; the nose—an upward thrust with the heel of my hand; and . . . oh, most shocking of all, the juncture of a man's legs.

I balked at practicing this, insisting the knowledge would be sufficient should I need to utilize the technique. It wasn't until a laughing Derrick revealed that all along he'd planned to substitute his open palm for his more . . . ah . . . susceptible area . . . that I agreed to slam my knee in an upward assault. He declared my efforts sound as I collapsed in an exhausted heap on the ground, and he beside me.

"Of course, the best plan is simply to stay safe, Emma."

"No one is ever completely safe," I reminded him.

In reply he stretched out on his back beside me and stared up at fleecy clouds racing the ocean breeze. I couldn't resist stretching out on the warm grass beside him. The sun felt heavenly on my cheeks, which heated further when Derrick caught hold of my hand. We remained silent until my thoughts returned to the reason for today's lessons.

"My cousin isn't safe," I said. "But I did promise Jesse I'd let him and his men scour the area around Second Beach for any trace of her."

Had I mentioned Jesse as a kind of defensive tactic, much like those Derrick had just taught me, in an effort to ward off feelings I simply wasn't inclined to acknowledge?

His hand stiffened around mine. "If there is anything I can do to help, just let me know."

I shot up to a sitting position. "Actually, there is. Why didn't I think of it sooner?" I tugged his hand to pull him up beside me. I reached out to flick bits of grass from his tousled dark hair, until the familiarity of the act had me snatching my hand back to my lap. "Remember how you dis-covered that Jack Parsons owned that house on the Point? Can you find out who owns the cottages around Second Beach? It might give us a hint as to where Consuelo would be staying."

"I can try. It's a lot more to research than a single house, and many of those cottages are probably leased for the summer, so it'll take that much longer to determine the current residents' names. But, yes, I'll do my best."

It was no small task I'd assigned him. Yet the readiness with which he'd accepted took my breath away and sent me awkwardly to my feet. "It's all right if you're too busy. I shouldn't encroach on your time this way. After all, none of this is your concern."

"I'm not too busy and I've made it my concern."

At that moment the kitchen door opened and Nanny stuck her head out. "If you two have finished waging your battles, I've got a hearty stew and fresh bread on the table."

In strained silence we made our way to the house. The conviction filled me that before we were through, there would be many more battles waged between Derrick and me.

The cell block door shut with a clang of finality I'd never grow accustomed to, no matter how often fate sent me back to this place. The very notion of being lawfully trapped behind that door, where sunlight became no more than weak, dust-ridden shafts of illumination sifting through the high-set bars, devoid of warmth, unable to penetrate the shadows . . .

I shivered and traversed the aisle until I reached Clara Parker's cell, walking lightly to muffle the echo of my footsteps against the walls.

"Who's there?" Clara's voice trembled like airy notes on a flute. I could just make out the angle of her cheek pressed against the bars of her cell as she attempted to peer down the aisle.

"It's me, Clara. Emma Cross."

She gave me no greeting, but waited silently for me to reach her. As always, I stood about a yard away from the cell door, conscious of the guard watching through the other side of a small square window. My only consolation was that it wasn't Jesse who escorted me back to the cells today. He hadn't been in the main station when I arrived, and I couldn't deny my relief. With the memory of his arms around me yesterday, seeing him today would have been uncomfortable at best, downright awkward at worst.

"How are you, Clara?" I asked when I reached the girl.

She frowned, obviously puzzled by the question. Looking at her surroundings, I could hardly blame her. The bleak contents and clammy stone walls of her tiny cell told me she was often cold, especially at night, and that her lungs no doubt felt the claw of the dampness; that she slept little on the lumpy mattress; that she ached from inactivity; that . . . I glanced down at a hardly touched plate of some unidentifiable porridge that occupied a wooden shelf beside her cot. She was hungry. And frightened. And feeling a miserable lack of hope.

The place reeked of mold and hopelessness, and I took shallow breaths in a selfish effort to avoid allowing that sense of despair to lodge inside me.

How I longed to see Clara free of this place, and to give her the hope she no longer believed in. I wanted to tell her how the circumstances of Amelia Beaumont's death would surely prove her innocence. But Jesse's admonishments yesterday stilled my tongue. Instead, I said, "Is it all right if I ask you a couple of questions, Clara?"

"Excuse me, miss, but what would be the use? No one but you believes I'm innocent." She hiccupped a sob, but then swallowed and recovered with a brave and stubborn tilt of her chin. "Not even Tony. A guard told me, just yesterday, that Tony claimed I killed the medium to keep him out of trouble."

I gasped. "He did not!"

"Yes, miss. He admits to the charges of ex . . . extor . . ."

"Extortion," I supplied.

She nodded. "Of making people pay him to overlook their little crimes, but he's telling any- one who'll listen I must have taken it upon myself to kill Madame Devereaux out of love for him."

"Oh, that fiend." My hands curled into fists. I suppose it shouldn't have surprised me that a bully like Anthony Dobbs would willingly sacrifice another to save his own cowardly skin. More than ever I wanted to reassure Clara, but once again caution made me hold my tongue. "Clara," I said as evenly as I could, "how much did you know about Lady Amelia? You served as her lady's maid at Marble House, yes?"

"I did, miss. She's a beautiful lady, very genteel. And, oh, her clothes . . ."

Clara had referred to Lady Amelia in the present tense . . . so no one had yet told her the news. "Her clothes are the finest," I agreed, "but not of great quantity, would you say?"

"I suppose not, but she could mix her attire and make it out she had more than she really did. Clever, that."

"And did she have many visitors come to see her at Marble House?"

"None that I knew of, miss."

"Did she go out often?"

"Never, miss. Except for her walks. Lady Amelia enjoys a nice long walk, mostly in the mornings, but sometimes later in the day, too, especially while Mrs. Vanderbilt is napping or working in her office."

"Do you know where she went? Did you ever accompany her?"

"Never, miss, but I assumed she walked in the gardens, and maybe along the Cliff Walk. I always had other work to do when I wasn't tending her." Clara moved back a few steps and sank onto the end of her cot. With her hands folded in her lap, she raised her thin face to me. "Why all these questions about Lady Amelia, miss? Is it anything to do with the murder?"

She asked that question with surprising calmness. I made sure to answer her in kind. "There may be a connection, Clara. I'm not yet certain." I opened my purse and removed the folded handkerchief I'd placed there before I left the house. Unfolding the linen, I held it out to her. She came to her feet and moved closer to the bars separating us. "Have you ever seen this flower before?"

Nestled in the fabric were, not the wilted petals I'd found in the pavilion, but the dried—and much more identifiable—sprig from Amelia Beaumont's jewelry box. Clara squinted to examine it.

"Doesn't that grow along the cliffs, miss?"

"It does. Do you have any idea how Lady Amelia might have come by this?"

"Well, no . . . She wouldn't have been able to reach any from the Cliff Walk, I don't think. She'd have to have climbed down." She almost smiled at that unlikely scenario.

"Can you think of anyone who might have given her such a flower?"

"Like . . . like a man, miss?"

322

I nodded.

"Goodness, no. Lady Amelia isn't the sort of woman a man would give wildflowers to, is she, miss? Any proper suitor would present her with roses or violets or . . . I don't know . . . properly cultivated flowers. Don't you think?"

And yet I had found this sprig of rugosa roses tucked intimately away among Amelia's jewelry. Why?

"Is there anything else you can tell me about her, Clara? Anything at all?"

She scrunched up her features. "Well . . . she cried sometimes. I never actually saw it, but more than once I could tell that her eyes were red and her nose runny. When I inquired she said the ocean air bothered her, but I doubted that, miss."

Surely with her fading prospects Lady Amelia had reason enough to cry; that didn't tell me anything new. I waited another minute, but when Clara had nothing more to add, I smiled sadly. "I'll have to be going now, Clara." Her features became pinched with what I could only call desperation. "Don't think you're forgotten in here. I'm working to find the real murderer and I promise, Clara, I won't stop until I do."

How hollow those words must have sounded from the other side of those bars. It was a promise I'd made her previously, yet here she still was. She bowed her head and stared dejectedly at the floor. "Thank you, miss."

"Oh, and when I leave the guard will bring in a basket of things I brought from home. There are some sweet rolls and blackberry preserves from Nanny, a shawl from Katie, and a blanket and . . . do you read, Clara? I included a couple of books."

"I can a little, miss. Thank you. Thank Mrs. O'Neal, and tell Katie I said . . ." She hiccupped again. "Hello."

That evening, a crash followed by a shrill cry sent Brady, Nanny, and me instantly to our feet. I don't doubt recent events had our nerves in a jumble, or we might not have had such startled reactions. As it was, we tossed down our napkins beside our half-eaten supper plates and hastened to the service hallway with no small amount of jostling once we arrived; there simply wasn't room for all three of us to fit through the narrow doorway.

I pushed my way through first to find Katie on her hands and knees, frantically reaching to gather up an array of forks, spoons, and dessert bowls—thankfully the little silver ones Aunt Sadie had left me—scattered across the floor. The fruit that had occupied the bowls now decorated the floorboards, slices of apples, pears, dates, and sprigs of fresh mint creating a colorful pattern among the fallen utensils.

"Oh, miss, it's all gone to ruin!" Sitting back on

her heels, Katie pulled her apron up over her face. "You'll turn me out for certain now!"

Behind me Brady blew out a breath. "Good heavens, girl, it's just spilled fruit. We thought you were being attacked."

He remained standing, leaning against a bank of cabinets, while Nanny and I both crouched to clean up the mess. First I pried Katie's hands away from her face. "Brady's right, Katie. It's nothing."

"All this wasted food, miss!"

"Never mind, girl. It happens. I've certainly dumped a tray or two in my lifetime." The gentle reassurance came from Nanny, who had shown the girl great patience in the months since she had come to work for me.

Earlier that spring Katie had been a frightened, silent shadow intent on hiding from the people and events that had caused her infinite pain: a forced liaison, an unwanted pregnancy, the loss of her previous employment. That her employers had been my Vanderbilt cousins at The Breakers was only half the reason I'd taken her in, nursed her when she lost the child, and given her a position and a place to live. When my aunt Sadie had been alive, this house, Gull Manor, had been a refuge for any woman in need, with few to no questions asked. This, much more than the house, had become her legacy to me. Because of her and what she taught me about the need for women to

325

help each other in any way possible, I could turn my back on neither Katie nor poor Clara.

Katie's wrists trembled in my grasp, and suddenly I guessed her distress hadn't necessarily been a result of spilling the tray, but rather the cause of it. My anxiety for her rose as I considered what possible mischief she might have gotten into. "Something is terribly wrong, Katie, isn't it? You know you can tell me anything. You can trust me."

To further coax her confidence I shot Brady a glance over my shoulder. He read me correctly and, pushing away from the cabinets, sauntered back to the dining room.

I tugged Katie to her feet. "There now . . . tell Nanny and me what the matter is."

"Oh, I'm just . . . just . . . Well, he's coming later to call—that's what!"

"Who's coming?" Nanny and I said together.

Katie drew in a deep breath and let it out. "Jamie Reilly," she whispered. "Oh, but if you don't want him here, miss, I'll tell him—"

After everything I'd witnessed earlier in the day, this simple return to normalcy brought a grin to my face. "Why, Katie, that's lovely. When is he coming? You'll need to be ready, won't you? Come, let's finish cleaning up our unfortunate dessert. Then we'll go pick out a proper frock for you and dress your hair."

Some forty minutes later a very different Katie

than the one I'd come to know stood before me. We'd chosen a gown with three-quarter sleeves, a simple scooped neckline, and a pintucked bodice. The pastel blue muslin brightened the clear blue of her eyes; her pink cheeks stood out prettily against her translucent skin. Always quick with her needle, Nanny tacked on a bit of pale yellow chiffon at the ends of the sleeves and used another length to make a sash. We had pinned Katie's russet curls, usually subdued in a tight bun, into a loose twist at the back of her head that allowed spiraling tendrils to cascade between her shoulder blades.

I stood back to admire her and judged our efforts enchanting. Her fidgeting made me frown. "Stop plucking at the chiffon or you'll tear it loose."

"Oh, miss, thank you ever so much. But . . . I don't think I'm ready for this."

"Nonsense. Of course you are. You and Jamie are friends after all."

"Y-yes . . . I suppose."

"Then think of this as merely associating with someone whose company you already enjoy." When that failed to lighten her mood, I smoothed my hands across her shoulders. "And if anything more comes of it . . . well . . . we'll just have to see, won't we?"

Excitement spun in the pit of my stomach. I couldn't help hoping, *wanting,* for Katie what I might never have myself. She'd been through so much in her young life, she deserved some measure of happiness. And she already possessed something I didn't—a much more ingenuous outlook on life. My perceptions had become infinitely more complicated because of the independence Aunt Sadie had allowed—no, insisted—I taste. And once tasted, self-sufficiency is not something easily relinquished.

How perfect, I thought. Katie Dillon and Jamie Reilly. Hailing from the same country, they were sure to have lots in common. Surely they were social equals, as Brady would put it, and held similar expectations about life. And Jamie's cheerful nature was just the thing to continue drawing Katie out, to help her find her confidence. Yes, this was something I would encourage.

At the clank of the front door knocker, I practically had to pry her fingers from the footboard of her bed and physically carry her down the stairs. Even as she trod each step, I continually whispered encouragements from the top of the stairs.

"Good evening, Miss Dillon," Jamie said when she worked up the courage to open the door, abruptly cutting off his knocking. Had he begun to think no one was home? I watched from the top landing, hidden by shadow; eavesdropping, perhaps, but with such a buoyant heart I could hardly be blamed. It was about time we had some happy news for a change.

Like Katie, Jamie had taken pains with his appearance. He wore crisp white linen beneath a plain serge coat and a blue waistcoat with shiny brass buttons. How fortuitous, I noted, that they'd both worn blue. Did that signify as a positive sign?

My hopes flourished yet more when Jamie whisked a bouquet out from behind his back, and with his free hand raised one of hers and kissed the back of her knuckles. "You're a vision tonight, Katie Dillon, and I'm a lucky fellow to be standing where I am, that's to be sure."

"Oh . . . I . . ." Katie took the flowers—from where I stood they looked like some kind of wild daisies—and buried her face in the blossoms. "Thank you."

When she didn't immediately raise her head, a bit of panic took hold of me. The two simply stood there, unmoving, saying nothing until the silence thundered in my ears. Jamie, at least, was grinning, his enjoyment of the occasion apparently not to be dimmed. With her back to me I couldn't see Katie's expression, and with all my might I willed her to invite him into the front parlor or the little conservatory at the back of the house—anywhere—but no words came out of her mouth that I could hear.

What an odd sort of friendship. I thought back

on what Katie had told me. She'd first met Jamie over the flour bins at the Brick Market. He'd bought barely enough for two loaves of bread, but they'd gotten to talking. Jamie had asked if she knew of anyone hiring a groundskeeper. Later, she would sometimes pass him on the street while going about her business in town, and once they'd met at Forty Steps, a wooden staircase leading down from the Cliff Walk to a platform just above the water's edge. A bit north of Marble House, it was where Bellevue Avenue's servants occasionally gathered for evenings of music and socializing.

To look at them now, one would never imagine them socializing anywhere, at any time. Though I suppose the commonality of shopping for food-stuffs did provide a sound topic of conversation, and an evening of frivolity surrounded by one's peers invited a camaraderie that might not otherwise arise. If only a similar camaraderie would present itself tonight, I thought almost desperately. *Katie, speak to the man!*

Finally, Jamie gestured over his shoulder, pointing his thumb at the door behind him. "There's a grand bonny moon out tonight, Miss Dillon. Would you care to walk with me?"

Her breathy response drifted up the stairs to me. "It's dark out."

"You can trust me not to let you step astray." He took the flowers from her and laid them on the side table beside the coat rack. His gaze strayed upward to my shadowy hiding place and I could have sworn he winked. Then he extended an elbow to Katie. "Shall we?"

Once the door had closed behind them I let out a rather long sigh of relief. I ran downstairs to find a vase for the daisies, but just as I reached for them the telephone clamored.

CHAPTER 16

"I need to speak to Miss Cross this instant!" The voice coming through the telephone line pierced like a darning needle against my eardrum. I whisked the ear trumpet away, yet I could still hear my aunt demanding my immediate attention.

"Speaking, Aunt Alva," I said calmly and, hoping she would take the hint, quietly. Rarely did she call me on the telephone, so the event of her doing so immediately raised an alarm. Still, nothing would be accomplished through hysterics.

"Emmaline?" Her voice became shriller. "Is that you?"

"Yes, Aunt Alva. What's wrong?" A sudden procession of fears marched through my mind. "Is it Consuelo?"

"Yes . . . or . . . no, she hasn't been found, if that is what you're thinking. But it's an emergency. Oh, Emmaline, I do believe this dreadful situation has made me ill . . . quite ill. I so need your help. There is no one, positively no one else I can turn to anymore. . . ."

"Aunt Alva, you're frightening me. Should I send for Dr. Kennison?"

"He's been and gone. And he said exactly what I already knew. My heart can't take much more of this strain."

"Aunt Alva," I said gently, "is it Lady Amelia?"

"Amelia? Good heavens, no. A shame, that—although why she strayed so far from Marble House I'll never understand—but no."

I wondered if it had occurred to Aunt Alva that perhaps Amelia Beaumont hadn't strayed anywhere, but had been dragged away by force.

"Emmaline, I'm coming right over."

The call clicked off and I was left to ponder her cryptic words for the next ten minutes.

Dressed like a widow in black bombazine, but with a white fox stole draped round her shoulders, Aunt Alva barreled in the moment I answered her footman's knock. She pushed past him and nearly shoved me over, but I managed to step out of the way just in time. Both she and the fox, its head still attached to the pelt and dangling against Aunt Alva's bosom, fixed mournful gazes on me for the span of an indrawn breath.

Then Aunt Alva did something I never could have imagined: She threw herself into my arms. The fox fur tickled my nose and I stifled an emerging sneeze. But my shock could not have been greater. Not only had the woman never set foot in my house before—I don't believe the notion had ever crossed her mind to socialize with me anywhere but in the luxury of her own home—but I had never seen this indomitable lady in so vulnerable a state.

We eased apart, and even by the light of the hall sconces her appearance shocked me. Her eyes were sunken, the shadows I'd noticed hours earlier darker and heavier, and her features had somehow thinned, giving her a haggard look that spoke of relentless strain.

"Please, come into the parlor and tell me what's wrong. Are you sure I shouldn't call for the doctor?"

"A doctor can't help me, Emmaline. My world is crashing down around my ears."

I led her into the parlor and we settled together on the settee. "I'm afraid Katie—my maid—has the evening off." I thought better of revealing Jamie Reilly's presence in my home, for some employers disapproved of their servants fraternizing with others even during their leisure time. "But I can ask Nanny to make us some tea."

"No—no tea. Nothing." She dabbed a handkerchief at the corners of her eyes. "Emmaline, he's coming."

I didn't need to ask. "The Duke? Surely that's no surprise. We've known that—"

"He's arrived in New York ahead of schedule. He could head north at any moment."

I gaped at her, a bud of anger unfurling at my core. "Is that what this is all about?"

"Don't you understand?" She fluttered her handkerchief at me. "We're running out of time! What will I do if he arrives in Newport—on my very doorstep—and his reason for coming is nowhere to be found? How will I explain?"

"I'm sure you'll think of something." I folded my arms and leaned back, trying and not wholly succeeding in keeping the disdain from tugging at my lips.

"Oh, that awful girl, how could she do this to me?"

Before my anger exploded into a barrage of harsh words, Aunt Alva turned to me full on, her tearful eyes giving her a lost and frightened look. "Oh, Emmaline, my poor girl! What if she's hurt? What if she's come to no good? I couldn't bear it. . . ."

I sighed and reached an arm around her shoulders. "Will it help you to know I might be close to finding her?"

"What?" The tears immediately stopped, making me marvel at how easily she could turn them on and off. "Where is she?"

"I can't tell you anything yet."

"Emmaline—"

"No, you'll simply have to trust me. When I approach Consuelo, I'll do so alone. No one else can be present or . . ." I drew in a breath as I prepared to speak, for the first time, of the conviction that had slowly been forming inside me. "We'll lose her again. I believe this, Aunt Alva, and you must believe it, too, and trust me, or risk losing your daughter forever."

She stared back at me, her gaze penetrating, searching, as if she could see the very workings of my mind. But as I regarded her in turn, I witnessed her own inner debate, the war between her fiercely independent and determined spirit, and a part of her she herself may not have known existed until this very moment: the mother's heart, which wanted nothing beyond having her child once more safe in her arms.

I didn't doubt the sincerity of the single tear that escaped the corner of her eye.

"Very well." She dabbed the tear away and came to her feet. "I'll trust you, Emmaline, because I don't see that I have any other choice short of shaking you until you tell me what you know."

The words startled me; I could almost envision her doing it.

"But should the Duke arrive before Consuelo is found—"

"We'll cross that bridge when we come to it," I said. "*If* we come to it."

"You'll keep me informed?" She adjusted the fox head dangling from her shoulder.

"No, but you'll be the first to know once I've found Consuelo, reassured her, and convinced her to come home."

"And if you don't? Good gracious, Emmaline, what if she insists on—"

I gently slipped my hand into the crook of her

elbow and started guiding her into the front hall. "Have faith. Consuelo is a smart girl. In the end, she'll do the right thing."

I thought Aunt Alva would protest again. She surprised me. "Yes, yes, she will. I raised her to do the right thing. She'll come around." At the front door she turned to face me. "Thank you, Emmaline, I feel infinitely better. Good night."

She hadn't been gone two minutes—in fact, I could still hear her carriage receding down the drive—when the service door opened and Katie came striding into the hall, Jamie following some several steps behind.

"Ah, you two. I suppose you saw Mrs. Vanderbilt's carriage in the drive. Wise of you to postpone returning to the house until she'd left. Not that you're doing anything wrong, mind you—"

I broke off as, without a word, Katie swung round to the base of the stairs and proceeded to stomp her way up. My gaze flicked to Jamie, hovering uncertainly beside the telephone alcove. He crumpled his cap between his hands.

"What happened?" I asked.

He shook his head. "I'm not quite sure . . . I . . ." He looked away. "I fear I might have become just a wee bit too familiar, miss. I tried sayin' I was sorry, but 'twas too late, the damage was done."

By this time Katie had disappeared at the top of the staircase, and presently I heard the thwacks of her shoes against the wooden steps leading to her attic bedroom. Jamie heard it, too; his gaze drifted to the stairs, then back to me.

"I'm sorry, miss." He looked crestfallen, almost devastated. "We were gettin' along swimmingly . . . I thought."

My first impulse was to berate him for pushing his advantage with Katie. But then I thought of Derrick, and of Jesse, how both men had made their feelings clear to me and how overwhelmed they made me feel. Yet . . . neither had taken advantage of me. They had simply been honest about their intentions.

And then I thought of Katie and all she'd been through the previous spring. If two men could overwhelm me, only think what even the most innocent kiss or caress might do to her, and the frightening, unwelcome memories that would come flooding back.

I drew in a breath. "Jamie, if you want my advice when it comes to Katie, if you are truly interested in her—"

"That I am, miss."

"Then proceed very, very slowly and allow her to let you know when she is ready to be more than . . . friends."

He stared intently at me, seeming to hang on every word. "I will, miss. If she'll see me again, that is. I believe she misunderstood my meaning about a certain matter."

I took "a certain matter" to be a polite euphemism for physical intimacy and smiled gently. "Well, you'll simply have to show her your honorable intentions. If nothing else, you'll see each other in town. Or perhaps at the next soirée at Forty Steps?"

"I do hope so, miss." He swung his cap back and forth a couple of times across his leg. "Well, I should be going now." He came toward me and I stepped aside to open the door for him.

"Come to think of it," I said, "how did you get here? Do you live close by?"

"An acquaintance does, miss. I hitched a ride with him. He's sure to give me a ride back to town."

"Oh, all right, then. Good night, Jamie. And don't worry too much. Katie will come around."

The next morning, I found Katie in the laundry yard, hanging up sheets and towels. The day was warm, but the ocean breezes brought an edge that hinted of the coming autumn. I pulled my shawl a little higher around my shoulders and sat on the wooden bench where Katie had set her basket, piled high with damp heaps of linen.

"Would you like to talk about last night?"

She shooed a fly away from her face and reached into the box beside the laundry basket for another clothespin. "Not particularly, miss."

"Jamie seemed terribly sorry for . . . whatever it was that happened."

"Men always are." She snapped a sheet over the clothesline and proceeded to secure it against the wind.

"Don't you believe he might be sincere?" When she shrugged, I studied her face, a task made difficult by her obvious attempt to shield herself behind a fluttering pillowcase. A shadow of doubt crept into my heart. "Was he being honest with me, or did something more serious happen than he let on?"

"Depends on what he said, miss." She had no choice now but to approach me. She reached into the basket for the next damp item to be hung, and I wrapped my fingers around her wrist.

"Sit."

She darted her gaze about as if seeking rescue. Finding none, she sighed and sat stiffly beside me.

"Now, what happened between the two of you?"

A flash of teeth caught at her bottom lip. She studied her hands in her lap. "Begging your pardon, miss, but it's a private matter and I'd like it to stay that way."

"Oh." That certainly put me in my place as a busybody and an overly intrusive employer. That fly returned to bother first Katie and then me, buzzing around my hair. The breeze kicked up, threatening to tug the aforementioned pillowcase from the line. Katie grabbed two clothespins and jumped up.

"Well, at least tell me this," I said to her back. "Are you all right?"

She finished securing the clothespins and returned to gather another sheet from the basket. Her arms full, she paused, looking down at me. "I am, miss, and thank you. I appreciate your lookin' after me and all. I assure you last night was nothin' like what happened to me . . . well . . . you know. It was nothin' I couldn't handle. Mr. Reilly just made me feel . . . uncomfortable, I guess you could say."

"I can certainly understand that," I replied truthfully. I stood and reached for a dangling corner of the sheet she held, then found the other. Together we stretched out the sheet and draped it over the line. As Katie moved to place a pin on the end nearest me, I placed a hand on her shoulder. "I am your employer, Katie, but I hope you'll also think of me as your friend. And I do hope you know you can come to me if anything is ever troubling you."

"I do know that, miss. Thank you." But all too quickly she turned away to resume her task. With a sigh I left her to it, saddened but not surprised that she wouldn't confide in me. It wasn't the first time she'd kept her secrets to herself.

And yet, as I walked to the end of the property and stood braced against the salty breeze, I felt a sense of gratitude. For a short time at least, I'd been given the gift of ordinary matters, one might even say mundane, a brief reprieve from danger and death and the mysterious disappearance of my cousin.

I myself ended that relatively peaceful interval, this time by seeking to satisfy my curiosity. Once more enlisting Brady to accompany me, I set out to the home of Winthrop Rutherfurd.

"Let me do the talking," I said as I steered us toward tree-lined Lakeview Avenue.

He angled a look at me from under the brim of his straw boater. "Have I ever been able to stop you?"

"No, nor I you. So please, let me ask the questions."

"There's no reason he should answer them, you know."

I smiled. "Oh, trust me, there is."

Brady studied me for several clop-clops of Barney's slow-moving hooves. "Blackmail, little sister? You *have* been busy, haven't you?"

It suddenly occurred to me I'd never fully explained to Brady about Winty's involvement in smuggling. But I wasn't about to embark on the details now. We'd reached Winty's rented house.

"So how are we going to ease into this?" Brady whispered in my ear as we approached the front door. "Pretend it's a social call?"

"Brady, do be quiet, please!" I raised the knocker and struck two resounding clanks. The door opened almost immediately, the face greeting us sending me back a step in surprise. "Mr. Rutherfurd."

He pulled a face and said rather less enthusiastically, "Miss Cross." His gaze shifted briefly to Brady. "Mr. Gale."

"Winty," my brother replied with a haughty grin that made me want to poke his ribs.

"May we come in?" I asked.

"Look, if this is about the other day . . . I'm sorry. I was in a bit of a hurry. Besides, the police have already been here asking questions, and they seemed more than satisfied with my answers."

"Were they? And did you tell them any semblance of the truth? Mr. Rutherfurd, I suggest you let us in or we'll be forced to discuss this matter here, and I cannot guarantee my voice will stay to a discreet level." I wasn't sure if it was that, or my pointed glare, that convinced him to step aside and open the door wider. Once inside he ushered us into the nearest room, a fussy, overdecorated little parlor that appeared little used. He didn't invite us to sit, but that suited me fine.

"Now, then." Having preceded him in, I whirled to face him. "Where *were* you going in such a hurry, Mr. Rutherfurd?"

"Town. Not that it's any of your business."

"Where in town?" This came from Brady and I shot him a scowl. Yet I repeated the question.

It was Winty's turn to glower at both of us. I simply raised my eyebrows at him and waited. "Long Wharf, if you must know."

"Why? What sent you there in such a hurry you nearly sent my rig off the road? You might have lamed my horse."

Winty shoved his hands in his coat pockets and strode past me. He went to the window and looked out over his neat front lawn, shaded by an old oak and a Japanese maple. His shoulders bunched. "I received a message from a dock-worker—"

"Are you personally acquainted with many of those?" I interrupted.

He spun about. "No, Miss Cross, I am not. But I paid this particular individual to relay any important information concerning . . ." He paused, blew out a breath, and gave a shake of his head. "Concerning certain investments of mine."

His look suggested I should know what he meant, which indeed I did.

"And . . ." I prodded. I sensed Brady's interest growing as, beside me, he craned his neck slightly.

"And I arrived too late. My associate"—I knew he meant Calvin Stanford—"had arranged for a pre-crated shipment to be loaded onto a steamer the night before. That steamer put out before I reached the wharf." He turned away again, this time to finger a lace runner spanning the top of a lovely little walnut spinet. His hand stiffened and I thought he might send the runner, and the delicate porcelain figurines ranged along it, hurtling to the floor. Then I distinctly heard "damn his eyes" whispered under Winty's breath. That, more than anything else, clarified matters for me.

"So I gather you're telling me Mr. Stan—" I glanced at Brady. "Your associate stole your half of your mutual investment. Is that correct?"

"Yes, that's correct," he said, mocking my tone. "And if you and a good dozen other lollygaggers hadn't been clogging the roads, I might have been able to intercept that damned boat."

"Rutherfurd . . ." Brady's voice took on a growling edge. "I'll thank you to watch your language in front of my sister."

Winty tossed up his arms. "Your sister, sir, has single-handedly become the bane of my existence."

"I beg your pardon!" My hands went to my hips. "It certainly wasn't I who led you astray, was it, Mr. Rutherfurd? No, that was your own doing. You made your bed, and now you must—"

"Miss Cross, my bed promised to be quite tidy until you decided to poke your nose into other people's business."

"I was only interested in the whereabouts of my cousin. Had you not conducted yourself so suspiciously, I would be none the wiser today.

345

Now, regardless of whatever excuses you gave the police for your reckless driving, can you prove you were at the wharf that day?"

"I can," he said with enough confidence that I felt half-inclined to believe him.

I folded my arms. "As well-known around town as you are, I suppose it should be easy enough to prove one way or another."

"Then go ahead and prove it, one way or another." His eyes narrowed, and a little shiver traveled across my shoulders.

Still, I asked, "At any point did you head in the opposite direction, to the beaches?"

He wrinkled his nose. "You mean to Easton's?"

"Or beyond." He must not have been reading his newspapers lately if he didn't automatically associate my questions with Amelia Beaumont's death.

"Good heavens, Miss Cross. If I want to stroll along a beach, I'll head over to Bailey's to mingle with my own kind. Our kind," he amended after an instant's pause. Was that an attempt to placate me? He blinked. "As it is, I don't much care for sand."

Neither do I . . . not anymore, I thought, remembering the sight of Lady Amelia's dress, like a heap of sand and seaweed.

I had one more question for him. "Have you heard anything from Consuelo?"

"No." He narrowed his eyes again and studied

me. "But why do I sense that you might have? Do you know anything about where she is? If you do, Miss Cross, please tell me. I have a right to know. I might . . . be able to help her."

Had he had a change of heart when it came to fighting for her hand in marriage?

"No, Mr. Rutherfurd, I don't know where she is, although I have every hope of finding her soon."

He stepped closer. "When you do, will you bring her here? To me?"

"That I will not, Mr. Rutherfurd." His expression fell, but I kept on. "You gave up any rights to Consuelo's confidence, first when you backed away so entirely at the news of her engagement, and second when you decided to put in with . . ." I smiled grimly. "Your associate."

A vein in his temple throbbed. "Miss Cross, I would thank you to leave. Now."

"We were just going. Come, Brady, I believe we're finished here. But, Mr. Rutherfurd, you might want to drive more carefully in the future."

The rest of that day, and the next, passed in a frustrating tedium of inactivity, at least when it came to discovering Consuelo's whereabouts. Derrick telephoned to tell me only that his "sources" were still working on digging up the property records on the cottages near Second Beach. He offered to come to Gull Manor to review what we already knew, and when I listlessly declined that idea, he proposed another lesson in self-defense.

Self-defense . . . against whom? Against him and the temptation he aroused in me despite my every resolve to the contrary. No, I told him, I was still sore from our last session. I didn't mention that the ache was inward rather than outward, of the sort that left no visible bruises.

Early the next morning he called again. This time, he had news.

CHAPTER 17

"Emma, I've dug up some names of people living near Second Beach, but from what I've been able to gather, it wouldn't make sense for your cousin to stay with any of them."

"What do you mean?" Clutching my robe tighter around me with one hand, I used the other to press the ear trumpet tighter to my ear.

The line crackled a moment, and then his voice came clearly over the line. ". . . Elderly couples, young families, a few immigrants . . ."

"No, none of those makes sense," I agreed without asking him to repeat whatever I had missed. "Consuelo certainly wouldn't know any immigrants—"

The word stopped me; I went silent, thinking.

"Emma, are you there?"

Rather stupidly, I nodded, and Derrick spoke my name again, more insistently this time.

"Yes," I said absently, and then with more force, "Derrick, what are the names of those immigrants?"

"Hold on." There came a muffled clunk as Derrick must have set down the ear trumpet, followed by the rustle of paper. "Some are owners, others are leasing the properties." I heard more rustling. "Here we are . . . Medeira, Quinn, Souza, Dwyer, Dietzman, Delgado—"

One name stood out in that hodgepodge of Portuguese, Irish, and German names. "Delgado!"

"Ouch. You needn't shout in my ear, Emma. How is Delgado significant?"

"Is the first name Eduardo?"

"It is. Do you know him?"

"Derrick, Eduardo Delgado is the head gardener at Marble House. My goodness . . . I need to think about this. . . ." The hand holding the ear trumpet drifted downward. My body thrummed with nervous excitement, but with bafflement, too. Everything I knew about Mr. Delgado contrasted sharply with the notion of his holding Consuelo against her will. Or, for that matter, hiding her from her mother.

Could Consuelo have sought his help and persuaded him to help her "disappear," at least until she came to terms with her future? When I considered it that way, it didn't seem impossible that the kindly man might help her—yet it would be at the risk of losing his job. There was no doubt he'd be sacked the moment Aunt Alva learned of a connection between him and Consuelo's disappearance.

"Emma? Emma! Are you still there?"

His query drifted up from my hand and quickly I raised the ear trumpet and leaned closer to the transmitter. "Oh, Derrick, I was so wrong about everything. I went off on wild goose chases because I let my imagination run away with me."

"What do you mean?"

I shook my head sadly, another gesture he couldn't see. "I convinced myself of a connection between the murder and Consuelo's disappearance. But there couldn't be. Mr. Delgado couldn't possibly have—"

"How can you be sure he didn't kill Madame Devereaux?"

"I *know* him. He's a decent man. So kind and—"

"Murderers don't go around snarling and openly threatening people, not as a matter of course."

"Yes, I know that." His condescension tempted me to knock the ear trumpet against the wall in lieu of swatting his arm, but I knew I'd likely end up breaking it. I paused to think back on the day of Madame Devereaux's murder and all the evidence I'd heard during the police questioning. "If I remember correctly, Mr. Delgado said he was conferring with Grafton, Aunt Alva's butler, about redoing a portion of the tea garden for the Duke of Marlborough's welcoming party. So he has an alibi."

"Would your cousin have confided in a servant? Especially an outdoor workman? An upstairs maid is one thing, but a gardener . . ."

"I have no way of knowing," I said truthfully, for I'd learned the hard way that I knew my cousin far less than I'd thought I did. "Except, of course, to go to his house and find Consuelo. Then we'll have our answers. Tell me the address."

"Oh, no, Emma. I'm not telling you anything. I'll go. Or better yet, Jesse Whyte and I will go together."

"You can't." I gripped the edge of the call box as if gripping Derrick himself. "If you go knocking on Mr. Delgado's front door, Consuelo will go running out the back door."

"Then we'll each cover a door," came his infuriatingly calm response.

"No, Derrick. It has to be me. She won't trust anyone else. I won't have my cousin traumatized."

But even as I spoke the words, I heard the lie in them. What reason did Consuelo have to trust me after our last talk? I had let her down and cruelly proved she had no one to turn to. No one but a soft-spoken servant who was too generous to turn his back on her.

Here was my chance to make amends. Whatever the future brought, surely I could make Consuelo see that she couldn't hide out in Mr. Delgado's cottage indefinitely. In that way perhaps I could help them both, for I didn't wish to see Mr. Delgado sacked. As for Consuelo, whatever she wanted, I would do my best to make happen. I would take her side no matter the consequences.

"Derrick, it has to be me and no one else. At least,

no one else in sight. The Duke of Marlborough may already be on his way to Newport and could arrive any day. Consuelo has a right to know this before she makes any decisions, and I owe it to her to explain matters calmly, without any pressure or interruptions. I have a plan. A compromise."

A groan filled my ear. "Please, Emma, not another one of your plans."

"Five minutes, Emma."

"That's not nearly enough time. A half hour."

Derrick and I stood on Second Beach, not far from where Lady Amelia's body had been found. He had parked his rented carriage a little farther along the sand, to blend in with a half dozen or so others ranged there. A little more than twice that number of people strolled the shoreline, tourists, from the looks of them, perhaps tired of the crowds and noise of Easton's Beach. For the moment, we were alone in our remote corner near the upswell of land that began the rocky approach to Purgatory Chasm.

A light wind blew off the water; the skies were clear but for some scuttling fair-weather clouds. No, the only storm brewing was the one in the pit of my stomach.

But I showed Derrick my bravest face. "I'll need at least a half hour to talk her into coming home."

He stared down at me, lifting a hand to raise my

chin to better view my face beneath my hat brim. "Ten minutes."

"Twenty-five."

"I don't like it, Emma. I don't know why I let you convince me of this much."

"Because you know my plan makes sense. You wait here with the carriage until I've had a chance to reason with Consuelo alone. There may be tears, recriminations—" I broke off, not wishing to delve into the reason for those possible recriminations. "Anyway, such matters can't be rushed."

"I can't see the cottage from here. I should at least be within viewing range, if not hearing."

I shook my head. "If she hears us approach in the carriage, she might run off. And if she sees me arriving with a stranger, we could have the same result. Besides, this is Mr. Delgado's house we're talking about. Despite your suspicions, I know he had nothing to do with Madame Devereaux's murder. I'll be safe as can be."

His mouth remained a stern line, his chin arrow-like in its severity. I smiled, hoping to melt a bit of his icy resolve, but his expression softened not in the least as he pulled me to him and pressed his lips to mine.

The breath went out of me and in the heat of that kiss, I'd have accepted any terms, any demands he might make. No wonder, then, that when he set his cheek against mine and whispered fiercely,

"Twenty minutes, Emma, and not a second more," I merely nodded in agreement.

With a last, shaky look back at him, I made my way up the road toward the dusty little lane that branched off of Paradise Avenue. It was true, Derrick wouldn't be able to see the cottage from the beach. I couldn't see it either until I was almost upon it, nestled within a stand of trees and surrounded by thickets of beach plum, the fruit long gone and the leaves that dark, tired green of late summer. To anyone traveling along Paradise Avenue, the place would be invisible.

The cottage itself consisted of a single, squat story, the shingled walls weathered and silvery, topped by a low-pitched slate roof. Open mullioned windows flanked either side of the front door, once painted blue perhaps, but now wind-battered to a dull gray so thin the wood grain showed through. A small shed stood to the rear of the property, a stack of wood piled along the wall I could see. The air was heavy with the scent of brackish water and warm, rotting foliage. Nelson Pond lay only a few dozen yards away, surrounded by a weedy marsh. With a deep breath I turned up the rock-strewn path to the house and knocked.

The door didn't immediately open, but hushed voices and the distinct thud of another door closing sounded inside. Another few moments passed. I raised my hand to knock again when the lock clicked from inside and the door creaked open a few inches.

"Yes?" A woman peered out at me, her face cast in shade. I could not have guessed if she was old or young, but one thing was certain: She was not well. Her skin stretched tight over sharp cheekbones, sinking her eyes deep into an emaciated face. Her lips were bloodless, her hands clawlike. I noticed this last when she raised a wadded handkerchief to her lips and coughed several times, the sound echoed by a rattle deep in her chest. She pulled a knitted shawl tighter around her.

My heart twisted for this woman, and my own doubts mounted. Had Derrick read the records wrong? "I'm sorry to disturb you, madam. Perhaps I have the wrong address."

She retreated a step and started to close the door. Impulse sent my foot out to fill the gap and stop her. Derrick wrong about a public record? The very notion screamed of impossibility. "Is this the home of Eduardo Delgado? Are you his . . . ?" Once again I tried to judge her age, but the ravages of her infirmity made it impossible. I also tried to remember if the head gardener had ever mentioned family members. "Wife? Daughter?"

"I am neither of those."

It was then I realized she spoke with what my American mind interpreted as not quite a brogue, but some regional dialect from one of England's more remote corners. That accent, along with her fair complexion and light, lifeless brown hair almost certainly ruled out her being Portuguese.

I had a sudden insight. "Are you renting this house from Mr. Delgado?"

"I . . ." Her gaze darted past me, then slithered warily back. "Yes. What of it?"

"How do you know him?"

"I don't know that that's any of your business, miss." Again she whisked the handkerchief to her mouth and coughed, the sound like shaken gravel. I winced but tried not to show it. "Is there anything else?" she demanded.

"There's someone else here, isn't there?" Seeing her bracing for a second attempt at closing the door, I came to the point. "I'm looking for Consuelo Vanderbilt. I'm told she's been seen walking on the beach. Is she here?"

Her eyes flashed with alarm, and though she recovered quickly, a shadow of fear continued to hover over her expression. "I've never heard of such a person."

"Now that, madam, is a lie. Of course you've heard of her. I don't care how new you are to this country, because she is as famous in Europe as she is in America. Everyone has heard of Consuelo Vanderbilt. Now"—I stepped up closer, nearly wedging myself into the few inches between the door and the jamb—"is . . . she . . . here?"

"Please—" She got no further before another coughing fit overcame her. Remorse at having overtaxed her rose up inside me and nearly had me turning about and leaving, but then the door opened wider.

"Stop badgering Marianne, Emma. She hasn't done anything wrong. She's been my friend. My only friend."

"Consuelo." The word slid from my lips, no more than a breath. There she was, standing right in front of me, her Angora cat, Muffy, cradled in her arms. The shock of finally seeing her, of having her within reach, rendered me otherwise speechless and immobile, as if she might flitter away at the slightest ripple of motion.

She let out a sigh and stepped back from the threshold. "You might as well come in. I doubt you're simply going to go away."

I followed her and the other woman, Marianne, into a tiny parlor. The room held a faded green sofa, a ragged easy chair, an equally shabby armchair, and a couple of side tables, all arranged around a central hearth of whitewashed brick. To the right of the fireplace an open doorway afforded glimpses of a stove and a bit of counter: the kitchen. A closed door stood off to my left, presumably a bedroom.

As if she presided over the tiny cottage, Consuelo gestured me to sit on the sofa. She took the easy chair and settled a purring Muffy in her lap. Marianne lowered herself slowly into the armchair, her effort obvious in how tightly she gripped the arms.

Consuelo wore a simple morning gown of coral muslin and no adornments save a single pearl that hung from a gold chain around her neck, a gift I knew to be from her father. Her hair had been braided and coiled at her nape. She sat with her back straight, her lovely neck leaning slightly forward as she regarded me with raised eyebrows, her expression halfway between resignation and amusement. Even in plain muslin, she looked regal, serene—and impossibly at odds with her surroundings. The dress was vaguely familiar to me, and I realized that when I had checked her dressing room for missing clothing I had only considered the more sumptuous items of her wardrobe, the gowns I'd grown used to seeing her in.

Simple attire, this shabby cottage . . . My confused mind grasped on to a single question. "What are you doing here?"

She smiled—almost. "*Not* marrying the Duke of Marlborough."

Did I hear blame in her words? "But what will you do? Where will you go?"

"The world is a big place, Emma."

That sent me to my feet. "No, it isn't. Not for you. Where can you go where no one will recognize you?"

"After a time, that won't matter anymore."

"What do you mean?" Her gaze shifted briefly to the other woman and I, too, looked at Marianne. My next words were addressed to the ailing Englishwoman. "What part are you playing in this? Have you convinced my cousin you can help her? For what price?"

She shrank deeper into her chair. It was Consuelo who spoke. "Leave Marianne alone, Emma. She has nothing to do with any of this."

"Then who is she?" I shot back.

Consuelo smiled. "My soon-to-be sister-in-law."

My heart ricocheted inside me. "Whom are you marrying?"

"That's none of your business, for I know you'll only run home to tell Mama. Suffice it to say I am in love and I am going to be married, and no one, not even you, can stop me."

"Oh, Consuelo . . . surely you haven't . . . please say he hasn't . . ."

She raised her chin. "Defiled me?"

Those words coming out of her mouth shocked me nearly as much as the thought of such a thing happening to my beautiful, sheltered cousin. I nodded, my blood freezing in my veins as I awaited her answer.

"No."

The breath and nearly all the energy I possessed rushed out of me. My limbs felt weak, yet I didn't seek the support of the sofa. No, I remained standing, gazing down at my cousin's defiant face. My instinct was to grab her by the scruff of the neck and drag her home, to end this unsettling chapter in the lives of everyone concerned.

And yet . . .

What if she really *had* found love with an honorable man? What if happiness awaited her, and all she need do was leave this island—and yes, everything she had known until now—and live a simple, honest life with a straightforward, unpretentious man, a life wherein they answered to no one but each other.

Did I or anyone have the right to deny her this? Did being born a Vanderbilt *have* to mean her destiny was predetermined?

Didn't that contradict everything I believed in?

Still, I needed to be sure she fully comprehended what was at stake: everything she'd leave behind, as well as the struggles she'd likely face.

"This man . . . it's not Winty, is it?"

"Oh, for heaven's sake, Emma! Winty? Really. As if I would ever give him a second chance."

"Then won't you please tell me who this man is?"

She combed her fingers through Muffy's wispy fur. "No, Emma. Not yet, anyway. You won't approve—no one will—but once we're married you'll see he is the right man for me."

At that moment a little brass mantel clock chimed the half hour. I'd been here more than the agreed-upon twenty minutes. Where was Derrick? I couldn't help a quick glance out the front windows—would I see him lurking among the trees? Perhaps he was watching the cottage but allowing me the time I needed to talk to my cousin.

I was beginning to doubt my ability to persuade her to do *anything,* much less return home.

With a cough, Marianne struggled to her feet and spoke for the first time since we'd entered the cottage. "Where are my manners? Shall I make tea?"

Consuelo quickly stood, bending to allow Muffy to leap with a gentle thud to the floor. "No, you sit, Marianne. I'll make the tea." Placing a hand on the woman's shoulder, she coaxed her back into the chair. I followed Consuelo into the kitchen, hoping appropriate words would magically pop into my head.

As I stepped through the doorway I stopped short, caught by the sight of what sat in the middle of the battered oaken table.

A bowl of bright pink flowers with golden centers . . .

Rugosa roses.

Consuelo had been talking to me, her words gone unheard by my ears. Now she fell silent, holding the tea kettle in midair between the stove and the water pump.

"Emma? What's wrong? You look as if you've seen a ghost."

I pointed a shaking finger. "Where . . . where did you get those?"

"Oh, those are nothing special . . . yet so much more special than anything Mama has cultivated in her gardens or the hothouse. Don't you think they're lovely?"

"Damn it, Consuelo!" My swearing seized her attention and she flinched. "Where did those come from?"

"The cliffs." She looked at me askance, as if I'd suddenly grown horns. "From Forty Steps. Why?"

I drew up with a gasp. *Of course.* Forty Steps, the wooden staircase that spanned the cliff face a bit north of Marble House . . . the very place where servants often gathered to sing songs, trade gossip, and enjoy their occasional time off. All anyone would have to do was lean over the railing and those flowers would be within reach.

I'd been right. Good heavens—the flower was the key, always present, a seemingly innocent, yet insidious connection between the victims, connecting everything and everyone. Rugosa roses . . . in the pavilion, in Lady Amelia's jewelry box . . . and at Forty Steps, where the servants went. Where Katie sometimes went.

Where the murderer had gone as well.

Understanding flooded me, turning my knees to

water. I gripped the back of a kitchen chair as a whistled song drifted from somewhere beyond the open windows.

"Who is that?" I demanded. But I knew. *I knew.* "Consuelo, quickly! We must—"

"Oh, he's home early again," she interrupted before setting the kettle back on the stove and breezing past me into the parlor.

CHAPTER 18

With a sense of horror I watched my cousin throw herself into a pair of outstretched arms . . . arms covered in rough-woven cotton.

"No work again this afternoon," I heard a male voice say through the blood roaring in my ears.

"Yes, but in a way I'm glad," my cousin replied. "You won't work for Mama much longer anyway."

Oh, God . . . this can't be happening. "Consuelo," I shouted, yet the sound of it seemed muffled and far away, as if I watched from some great distance as another Emma Cross attempted to stave off disaster. "Get away from him. He's dangerous. Don't you see? It's him. The man who murdered Madame Devereaux."

Jamie Reilly's arms fell slowly from around Consuelo and she turned to face me. Not the slightest alarm marred her calm expression. "Emma, don't be silly. Jamie had nothing to do with that. When I saw my opportunity to escape Mama's plans for me, he came to my aid."

"No, Consuelo. Oh, please, no. You must see. He's used you." Dizziness washed over me, making the room spin slowly and my thoughts swirl inside my head. I struggled to make sense of them, to push them past my lips. "You're not safe . . . none of us are safe."

A coughing fit behind me reminded me of Marianne's presence. What had Consuelo called her? I struggled to remember. Soon-to-be sister-in-law. Wobbly, I cast a glance over my shoulder at her. "You're his sister."

The woman gave a half nod. I turned back to the man standing far too close to my cousin. "You . . . you're not Irish at all. If she is your sister, then you've been faking an Irish accent all along. Who are you? *What* are you?"

He'd already removed his cap. Now he tossed it onto one of the side tables and made a mocking little bow. "James Reid, at your service, miss."

The brogue was gone, replaced by a provincial but quite English inflection—like his sister's.

"He needed to pretend," Consuelo said defensively, "in order to find work."

"In order to trick Katie into helping him," I amended. "First Katie and then me. Consuelo, he came to call on her just the other night. They—"

"Oh, stop it, Emma. Don't make up lies to persuade me to go home. You're wasting your breath."

"It's no lie, Consuelo." I shifted my gaze to James Reid. "Tell her."

"Tell her what?" He stuffed his hands into his trouser pockets and shrugged.

"Tell her you've been using her," I said. "That you've been courting Katie and dallying with Lady Amelia. And that you murdered her, too," I whispered. "On Second Beach."

"Emma! How can you say such a thing?" But even as Consuelo spoke, Marianne cried out, then fell to coughing so violently the other three of us instinctively surrounded her chair. Consuelo knelt before her. I hovered to one side. James gripped one arm of the chair and bent down low to speak words I couldn't hear. Then Consuelo ordered, "Get her some water."

James Reid straightened and disappeared into the kitchen.

"Consuelo, quickly," I said, "let's go."

"I'm not going anywhere." Gently she took the handkerchief from Marianne's trembling hand and dabbed specks of blood away from the corners of the woman's mouth.

"Consuelo, he's a murderer!" I said in an urgent whisper.

"No, Emma . . ."

"Yes!" Marianne rasped. "Go."

Consuelo went still. "What?"

"Go." Marianne's chest heaved, and with a mighty cough she seemed to clear some of the congestion away, enough to speak more than one word at a time. "I don't know if what this woman says is true, but—oh, Consuelo, forgive me! I thought perhaps he'd changed. That perhaps you'd helped him alter his ways. But trouble follows him—no, no, that isn't true." She broke off and twisted round to dart a glance into the kitchen, then turned back. "He makes trouble. He *is* trouble."

"Shut up, Marianne." James appeared in the doorway, holding a glass of water. Slowly he crossed the room, looked down at his sister, and raised the glass to his own lips to drink.

"Jamie!" Consuelo snapped to her feet. "Don't be cruel. I don't know what Marianne means, but you mustn't be unkind." Her hands went to her hips. "Now, what is this about Lady Amelia and Emma's maid?"

I stepped between them and gripped Consuelo's hands. "I found petals of rugosa roses in the pavilion the day after Madame Devereaux was murdered."

"So—"

"Listen to me! The day Lady Amelia died, I discovered a sprig of the very same flower tucked away in her jewelry box—her *jewelry box,* Consuelo. You know that means something significant. And now, today, here is the same flower in a bowl in this very cottage."

Consuelo was shaking her head, but more and more slowly, and I could see my words—and Marianne's—were having their effect on her.

"When he called on Katie," I continued, "he upset her terribly. She wouldn't even talk about it afterward."

"Money," Marianne said, the word sounding like a moan.

"Katie has no money," I retorted, incredulous.

"No, not Katie's money," the woman replied.

"Yours. He wanted her to try to get some from you."

"Get some from me how?"

"Any way she could," Marianne said. "Either by stealing it from wherever you kept it in your house or by persuading you to extend her . . . a loan, he called it. But in my heart I knew he'd no intention of ever paying it back."

Consuelo pulled her hands free of mine and glared down at the woman. "You knew about this?"

Marianne looked away and nodded once.

"And the rest?" Consuelo's voice rose, cracking slightly. "Is my cousin correct? Did Jamie . . ."

Marianne shook her head. "I don't know. . . ."

The horror running through me now filled my cousin's eyes. She spun about to confront James. "Is it true?"

He held out a hand. "Darlin', you can't believe any of this. Surely—"

"Drop that Irish brogue," I told him in disgust.

"Is it true?" Consuelo's shout filled the little room.

He shoved me out of the way and in a stride was before her. He seized her wrist and tugged her closer. "Darlin', I'll take care of her. She won't go telling anyone her lies. I'll help you get away and then we'll be together, as we planned. Think of it, Consuelo. We'll find a little house some-where far away from here. Down south, or out west where we can be free. Where your mother will never find you."

"Let me go." Consuelo tugged free and stumbled backward, nearly falling before catching her balance on the back of the sofa. Hatred robbed her face of a portion of its beauty as she regarded him. "Why?"

A world of accusation filled her single-worded question, and his expression changed from one of supplication to shaking fury. "Damn your meddling soul, Emma Cross." Then, to Consuelo, "We might have been happy. Remember, this is *her* doing, not mine."

Did he truly believe that? Had he hoped that by marrying Consuelo he would one day acquire a piece of the Vanderbilt fortune, perhaps when one or both of her parents had relented—or died? Those questions stuck in my throat as once again I wondered what was keeping Derrick. Fear for him crept up my spine, for I knew, as surely as I knew my own name, that nothing but foul play could have delayed him. Had James come upon him as he'd made his way toward the cottage?

Again, the questions stuck in my throat. If Derrick had a plan, I could foil it by bringing attention to his proximity to the cottage.

James's assertion had rendered the rest of us mute. No one spoke, no one moved, until he suddenly strode to the closed door on the far end of the room—the one I'd assumed led to a bedroom—and swung it so wide it hit the wall. As soon as he disappeared inside I moved to Consuelo and took her hand.

"Come. Now is our chance to get away." I cast a glance at Marianne; would she betray us? Then I glanced around for Muffy. Consuelo would never leave her pet behind, but I didn't see the animal anywhere.

In the next instant James stepped back in the parlor, holding an object that turned my blood to ice. A wooden barrel rested in the crook of his right elbow, his fingers curled around a trigger, his left hand aiming the long end of the weapon directly at me. At first my mind conjured a rifle, but soon the barbed, steel shaft protruding from the wood identified the piece as a harpoon. A single shot, but deadly.

Perhaps he recognized my realization that he'd have only one chance to kill me, for he shifted his aim to Consuelo.

"No!" I bounded toward him but stopped short. My sudden movements might cause his fingers to twitch against the trigger. I held out my hands. "All right. What do you want?"

His sister spoke up first. "Tell them, James. They at least have the right to know the truth."

He shrugged. "Perhaps you're right, Marianne. Surely Consuelo will understand once she learns what happened to us." To my dismay his hold on the harpoon didn't slacken. But then, neither

371

would my scrutiny. I vowed not to take my eyes off him, to seize any advantage should one arise. "Our story begins in England, in Oxfordshire, at Blenheim Palace."

Consuelo gasped.

"What does that mean?" I demanded.

"Blenheim is the home of the Duke of Marlborough," she whispered hoarsely.

James nodded. "Indeed. My father was first assistant to the house steward. My mother, the housekeeper's assistant. Marianne was an upstairs maid." He shot his sister a fond look. "She was about to be promoted to lady's maid to the Duke's sister, weren't you, Marianne?"

She nodded slightly, her face sickly white.

"As a boy I had worked with the grounds-keeper, but a few years ago I became a footman." James's expression darkened. "We were working hard, but going about our lives well enough until one day last autumn my father was accused of stealing and doctoring the house account books to cover his guilt. The Duke threatened my father with prison if he didn't confess to the crime. My father was innocent, but—devil be damned—his word would never hold up against the Duke of Marlborough's. Innocent or no, he'd rot in prison and the rest of us would be turned out to starve on the streets.

"So he confessed, and we were sacked anyway. All of us. Tossed out without references and nowhere to go. And do you know what happened then?"

I shook my head. Beside me, Consuelo trembled. Marianne sat with her head bowed, hands clenched around the arms of her chair.

"Winter set in," he said matter-of-factly, almost amiably. "We'd gone to Oxford to search for work and found none. None that'd take us without references, that is. The four of us were living in a one-room attic with the sky showing through the gaps in the thatch. The rain came through as well, and then the snow. We fell behind on the rent, so the landlord threatened to send us packing. That was when our mother became ill. Pneumonia. She was dead within the fortnight."

Marianne moaned, then bit down on her bottom lip and tightened her grip on the chair until her knuckles threatened to burst through the skin. She was so frail and forlorn, so defeated that, despite everything, I pitied her. I wanted to go to the woman and comfort her. I think Consuelo did, too. She looked down at Marianne but seemed to be holding herself back, perhaps debating if the Englishwoman deserved her sympathy, perhaps merely too afraid to move.

"Not long after, my father lay in the pauper's grave alongside her." James spoke more quietly now, as if the memories proved too much and the fight had gone out of him. "Hanged himself from the rafters one day when Marianne and I had gone begging for food."

"Oh, good Lord," Consuelo whispered through the hand she pressed to her mouth.

"Ah, but it doesn't end there." A smile dawned on James's face—demonic and chilling. "With Marianne showing signs of consumption, I knew we wouldn't last much longer where we were. England had become a hell for us. So I did anything I could—and yes, that included begging, cheating, and stealing—to scrape together enough money to book our passages to America. We arrived in New York early last spring."

"Your story is a terrible one," Consuelo said when he paused, "and surely you didn't deserve what happened to you. I'm sorry for it. But why all of this? Why all of your lies?"

"Isn't it obvious, Consuelo?" At the risk of tearing my gaze away from James and his speargun, I turned to her. "The Duke of Marlborough. Even in America, they found they couldn't escape the man."

She shook her head at me. "I still don't understand."

"Revenge." I turned back to James. "Isn't that right?"

James smiled shrewdly. "It was all too perfect. When I learned the bloody bastard was coming here to become engaged to Consuelo, I knew fate had arranged retribution in my family's name. He needs your dowry to pay his debts and save his blasted estate. I intended to make sure he never got it—not one bloody cent. I moved us to Newport and soon enough learned that fate was even kinder than I had imagined. Pubs are a wondrous source of servants' gossip, and I learned Consuelo wanted no part of this marriage. And then I met Miss Katie Dillon." His brogue returned, dripping with mockery. "A bonnie lass, she is, and most accommodatin'."

"You used her . . . and Emma . . ." Consuelo trailed off in a clear attempt to gather her thoughts. When she spoke again, her voice was clearer, stronger, her back straighter. "And me, apparently. But why murder Madame Devereaux?"

"Ah, an unplanned complication, that. Seemed the old boot was genuinely clairvoyant after all. Somehow she knew what I was planning. Knew I was going to spirit you away from Marble House, and she threatened to expose me if I didn't pay her. So pay her I did." His sister coughed, and James regarded her briefly. Then his gaze shifted to me. "I believe you found my coins scattered about the pavilion, Miss Cross. Aye, I didn't have time to collect them, what with Mrs. Vanderbilt and her gaggle of quacking cronies waddling down the garden path. I'm afraid I had no choice but to leave a bit of a mess."

"And Amelia Beaumont—what of her?" I demanded.

"A lovely diversion, and a willing accomplice." At Consuelo's and my shocked looks, he laughed. "Oh, not to murder, but in helping me arrange to get Consuelo out of the house. It was Amelia who called for the carriage that whisked Consuelo away from the property that day."

"Why would Lady Amelia agree to help you run off with another woman?" But the answer was obvious before I'd even completed the question. "Money. She needed it as much as you do. You promised her a share of whatever you eventually got from Alva and William."

Consuelo groaned. "What a fool I've been."

"Amelia guessed you committed the murder, didn't she?" I said. "After all, you used her scarf. My guess is she had given it to you as a lover's memento and was afraid to admit that to the police for fear she'd be incriminated."

James gave a casual shrug. "I took no pleasure in silencing the lovely Lady Amelia."

"Oh, God." Holding her stomach, Consuelo sank down onto the sofa. I thought she might become ill and went to sit beside her.

Reaching an arm around her, I gazed up at James. "So what happens now?"

"What happens now, Miss Cross, I'll take no pleasure in either."

With startling fierceness, Marianne pushed to her feet. "Enough, James. You can't go on trying to right past wrongs with more wrongs." She stopped and coughed into her hand. When she recovered she went on, "What happened to us had nothing to do with either of these young women—"

"Marianne . . ."

"No, James! Let them go and you and I will leave here. We'll go far away. To Canada, perhaps. Anywhere. It doesn't matter as long as no one else is hurt. As long as *you* don't hurt anyone else."

"I wish it were so simple, Marianne."

"It is." She moved slowly toward him, taking such tiny steps they were almost imperceptible. She didn't stop until she was in front of him, the distance between them marked by the two-foot length of the harpoon. If he shot now, he would hit her point-blank. She held out her arms to him and used his pet name, a sister appealing, perhaps, to the boy he had been. "Give it to me, Jamie. Please, dear little brother, if you have any love for me at all, hand me that weapon."

I froze. Would she make a grab for the harpoon, perhaps wrench it out of her brother's hands? I shifted forward on the sofa, at the same time grasping Consuelo's hand, ready to spring up and bolt with her the moment the weapon was out of his control.

With a near roar he used the barrel of the harpoon to shove Marianne aside. She stumbled and landed hard on the floor on her backside.

Consuelo and I came to our feet, but in the same instant James pinned us in place by swinging the harpoon's spear in our direction.

"Let's go." He gestured to the door with a jerk of his head. Then he ordered Consuelo to open the door, and for the two of us to step out together in front of him. Marianne's sobs followed us across the threshold, her broken pleas soon muffled as James kicked the door closed behind him. "That way—toward the pond."

Where was Derrick? Wildly I glanced around me, hoping—desperately praying—I'd see some telltale sign of him crouching in the bushes, perhaps waiting for us to pass so he could jump out and overpower James. But only the breeze rustled the foliage, and only birdsong and our crunching footsteps disturbed the silence of the day. Farther off, the ocean waves sighed against the shore.

James prodded us past the cottage in the opposite direction of Paradise Avenue. Literally prodded, for every so often I felt the sting of the spear's arrow against my back. The farther we walked the spongier the ground became, until the turf squelched beneath our feet. Water soaked into my low-heeled boots, and Consuelo attempted to raise her skirts clear of the clinging weeds.

It was a losing battle. We'd entered the marsh, a thick, briny soup surrounding Nelson Pond.

Consuelo and I had to shove the thickening growth of cattails out of our way, and I was all too aware of them falling back into place behind us, closing us in, cutting us off from any hope of rescue.

Derrick. In my deepest core I knew some harm had come to him—or he'd have been here. That was as far as I allowed the thought to develop; I refused to let it roam any further. I might not survive the day, but in the end, Derrick had to be all right.

He had to.

But what of my cousin? Suddenly, those lessons in self-defense filled my mind. Derrick had revealed a man's most vulnerable places, along with how best to attack each one. Somehow, I had to find a way to reverse course and face James— I needed to be facing him to launch my assault— but without provoking him to pull the trigger. Here in this lonely, quiet place, he could easily kill one of us with the harpoon and then strangle or beat the other to death.

I made a quick assessment of my surroundings, searching for any possible weapons. There was nothing . . . nothing but weeds and water and all those cattails, too flexible to be of any use. Besides, we were nearing the pond now, and the cattails thinned out.

"If you're looking for your gentleman friend, I'm afraid he won't be joining us."

"What did you—" My throat closed around the rest. I stopped walking, started to turn around to confront him, but a thrust of sharp metal between my shoulder blades stopped me cold.

"He bled a lot, that one. But then a shovel to the head will do that. Surprising you didn't hear it from inside the house. I'm fairly certain he's dead, or will be shortly. At any rate, he's not going anywhere. I locked him in our shed. Now walk."

Oh, Derrick. I'm so, so very sorry. . . .

"You're the worst kind of monster and I hate you." As Consuelo spat the words over her shoulder at James, she reached over and pressed a hand to my back.

Her attempt to comfort me proved short-lived when James used the harpoon to smack her arm back down to her side. "Now, I'm sorry you said that, darlin', because you and I might have walked away from this together. The choice would have been yours. But it seems you've made it."

"I'd never go anywhere with you."

"James," I cried out as despair threatened to engulf me, "let Consuelo go. She—"

"I'm not leaving without you, Emma. Oh!" A loud squelch sounded as the marsh sucked her foot in deep. Her ankle turned and she went down with a yelp and splash.

I turned as if to reach for her, but instead I threw myself to the ground directly in James's path. His boot struck my side, not a kick but merely a stride. He clearly hadn't expected my move, and now I wrapped both hands around his ankle and tugged with all my strength. He toppled over me, landing facedown in the muck. Thankfully his torso landed clear of me, and I scrambled out from under his legs. He'd dropped the harpoon. I started to lunge for it, but he was already moving, already turning over and attempting to right himself, a thunderous look twisting his features.

Remembering what Derrick had taught me about a woman's strength being primarily in her legs, I raised my heel and shoved it into his face. There came a crack and blood spurted everywhere—from his nose I thought, but I didn't take the time to be sure. I raised the same foot again and brought it down on his kneecap. A shriek tore from his throat and he instinctively reached one hand to his leg while the other continued to cradle his face, the blood pouring through his fingers.

"Consuelo," I shouted. "Run!"

To my dismay she didn't, but instead half-crawled, half-slithered in her wet skirts to retrieve the speargun. James was too fast for her. Reaching out, he managed to grip the butt, and in another motion would have had the weapon in his arms. Rising onto my knees, I threw myself down on him, knocking him over onto his back and me prone on top of him. His muscles tensed beneath me, and I knew I hadn't much time before he'd overpower me, flip me over, and probably wrap his free hand around my throat.

I had no intentions of dying. The harpoon slipped from his tenuous grasp, and this time, from the corner of my eye, I saw Consuelo swoop it off the ground and push to standing.

"Emma, move!"

But I couldn't. James's arms went around me, squeezing the breath out of me. His arms were powerful, those of a workman, and he might as well have gripped my throat. Black spots danced in my vision and the surrounding weeds went dark. But I could still move my limbs and now I forced my knee between his thighs and blindly rammed it, high, until it met with a barrier of flesh.

James let out a roar. His arms fell away and I crawled off of him. He rolled to his side, knees drawn up, both hands cupped at the juncture of his legs. I thought I had him, oh, I truly did. But before I could reach Consuelo and take the harpoon from her, she pulled the trigger.

CHAPTER 19

The steel shaft hissed past me in a blur of reflected light . . . and pierced the wet ground about a foot from James's head. As the arrow trembled back and forth and settled into stillness, my heart dropped to my feet.

One shot only—taken and missed. James's eyes went wide and he darted an astonished look in Consuelo's direction. Then he was scrambling to his feet and blocking our path to the arrow. Blood smeared most of his face and his legs shook beneath him, but I knew he was only marginally less dangerous than before.

"Consuelo, go!" This time I shoved her hard to force her to move. "Find help!"

It might have been those last words that forestalled her protests and sent her running in a wide arc around James. With a twinge of relief I saw that she still held the harpoon. She might not have even realized it, but now James couldn't reload and use it on me. The same thought must have crossed our minds at the same time, for he spun around to yank the arrow out of the marsh.

He gripped it like the spear it was and came at me. I waited until he was almost within striking reach before ducking out of the way and side-stepping to my right. He was swift to follow, but

I kept moving, away from the pond and deeper into the cattails again. He was having trouble moving—I'd done some damage. I racked my brains to decide how to do more.

And then, through the reeds, I glimpsed hope. Frail and faltering, but hope all the same. I knew what I had to do.

Circling James, I moved toward the pond again, forcing him to turn his back to the figure approaching through the cattails. Meanwhile I prayed he'd think panic had me moving blindly, and that he wouldn't recognize my attempt to manipulate him.

One other quick prayer ran through my mind, and to help facilitate its being answered I made as much noise as possible. I stomped my feet to raise loud splashes. I cried out as James came closer. I pleaded with him not to hurt me.

Only a few feet separated us now. With the pond at my heels I'd run out of room to retreat, for my skirts would only ensnare me in the water and make James's task easier. He came on slowly, in no particular hurry. With a swipe of his sleeve he cleared the blood off his face. He believed he had me and quite possibly he would have, if his sister didn't just then emerge from the cattails, creep up behind him, and bring the shovel in her hands crashing down on the top of his head. Just as when Consuelo had shot at him, his eyes opened wide—but now they held no surprise, no conjecture, merely a blank stare. Then his knees buckled and he hit the ground.

The fight seeped out of me and I sank to the ground as well, but I wasted no time in crawling to him and sliding the arrow he still held out from between his fingers. Instinct sent me scrambling to put distance between us again. Then I sat up and glanced up at Marianne. She stood over her brother like an avenging angel, the shovel gripped in both her hands.

"Thank you," I managed between heaving breaths.

She let out a loud cough, one that must have taken great effort to suppress as she'd sneaked up behind her brother. "I couldn't let him hurt anyone else."

"No."

"Please believe I didn't know until today about the others—those two women. I—" She coughed again, long and hard, the force of it doubling her over.

"I believe you," I said when the fit subsided. From where I sat, with the wet ground soaking the back of my skirts, I studied James's inert body. "Is he . . . ?"

Still holding the shovel, Marianne crouched beside him and held her hand close to his nose. "He's breathing."

I crawled back to them. "Let's get his suspenders off. We can use them to tie his hands and feet." I hesitated. "Did you see Consuelo?"

Marianne nodded as she began unhooking the suspenders from her brother's trousers. "I sent her on to the nearest cottage for help. Someone in the area might have a telephone—"

"Someone does," I said, remembering one of the local residents had called the police after Lady Amelia's body was found on the beach. "As long as Consuelo manages to find someone home and explains what happened, help will arrive." I knew that to be true because I knew these islanders. They would waste no time in taking care of their own. "Let's hurry. There's someone else who might be gravely hurt. James said he's locked in your shed. He needs me. . . ."

Within minutes we had James secured. Not that he'd be waking up anytime soon, from the looks of him, but we were taking no chances. When I finally stood, the results of our tussle asserted themselves in the form of aches and sharp pains in every part of me. I gazed down at the man, feeling a fool for having been so easily taken in by him, and so furious with him I could feel nothing even approaching pity for his current state. But all of that passed in a second or two. I gathered my sodden skirts and hurried as fast as I could through the weeds and back toward the cottage. After a minute or two Marianne followed; I heard her soggy footfalls and her occasional coughs, but I never once glanced back. I only looked ahead.

· · ·

A half-rusted padlock greeted me with its unyielding presence when I reached the shed. A sense of denial filled me and I seized the door handles, tugging for all I was worth. While they banged in and out the inch or two allowed by the lock, I shouted Derrick's name. I pounded. I kicked. I leaned my forehead against the splintered wooden panels and wept.

Finally, after what seemed like an agony of forever, a hand came down on my shoulder. As I turned to peer through my tear-blurred eyes, Marianne reached for my hand and pressed a small iron key into it.

"He had it in his pocket," she said. "When you said he'd locked someone in the shed, I thought I'd better search him for it."

The metal was cold against my palm, a small but solid reassurance that helped restore a modicum of sanity. Had I really fallen apart so easily? I'd ponder the reason for that later, but now I fumbled a few times but managed to slide the key into the lock and turn it.

"Derrick?"

At first . . . nothing.

Panic nudged once again. Making out his outline in the windowless gloom, I fell to my knees beside him. "Derrick . . . I'm here. Can you hear me?"

A shadow fell across the doorway and without

looking up I ordered, "Marianne, get water . . . and a rag or washcloth . . . quickly!"

She hurried off. A groan sent my heart against my ribs. "Derrick?"

His fingers flexed, and then his hand inched toward his head to finally press against a spot at the back, just below the crown. A louder groan met my ears.

"Don't try to move yet," I said when he attempted to press upward. I shifted around him and drew his head into my lap. His eyelids fluttered and opened, his gaze instantly finding me in the darkness.

The smile that followed reached inside me and wrenched away my last reserves of strength. I simply curled, no longer able to hold myself upright, until my forehead touched his. Tears overflowed and sobs wracked my body.

"Emma? What did he do to you?" His voice resonated with dread and once again a speck of reason returned, enough to set my needs aside in favor of his. When his arms reached for me I embraced him in return and spoke into his ear.

"He didn't hurt me, Derrick." Not significantly, but I didn't say that. "I'm fine. It's over. All over now."

A laugh broke from deep inside him. "You mean you . . . dear God, Emma. You brought him down, didn't you?"

"I had help. If not for his sister, I might not have . . ."

"Sister?" With a sharp breath he turned on his side, rested there a moment, and struggled up onto an elbow. His other hand went beneath my chin, raising it slightly. "I have a lot to catch up on, don't I?" The question ended with another groan, his hand pressing the back of his head once again. "From the beach I saw him riding in the back of a wagon along Paradise Avenue. He could have been anyone heading home for the day, but something . . . I don't know what . . . made me follow. He turned onto this side lane"—with a jerk of his chin Derrick indicated the scene visible through the shed doors—"but when I followed, he'd vanished. I thought he'd gone inside the cottage."

"He ambushed you," I finished for him.

"Hit me—hard." Again his hand drifted to the spot on his head. I reached up and examined his skull gently with my fingertips. The swelling was pronounced, and exceedingly tender, judging from Derrick's wince.

"He told me he'd left you bleeding badly."

"Am I?"

I searched his hair with my fingertips, and was relieved when they came away dry. "I don't see any blood, and I'm not surprised that he lied. If it's any consolation, I believe we bested him with the same weapon he used on you. A shovel. But come, let's get you inside. Jesse should be here soon."

Slinging an arm around him, I helped him stand, and together we made our way into the house.

"Just start at the beginning, Miss Reid."

We sat around the kitchen table—Jesse, Derrick, Marianne, Consuelo, with Muffy once more ensconced on her lap, and I. A group of officers had trudged into the swamp to collect James, and he was even now being transported to the jailhouse in town. From the cottage's other rooms came the sounds of another team of policemen opening drawers and cabinets, pulling cushions from the furniture, and collecting any evidence they could find. They wouldn't discover much, at least not in the way of tangible clues. James Reid had left his murder weapons behind at each crime scene, and his motives were even now being revealed by his sister's trembling, halting narrative.

As she spoke, Jesse took careful notes in the tablet that had become so familiar to me in recent weeks. He paused in his writing to ask, "So you say your father did doctor the Duke of Marlborough's house accounts, as he was accused of doing?"

Marianne nodded. "He did, but not for the reasons the steward believed. You see, he did it to protect my brother. It was James who had been stealing from the Duke. Stealing provisions and selling them in the nearby villages. He was undercutting the local merchants and lining his own pockets nicely."

"Did you know of this at the time?" Jesse asked.

"I had begun to suspect. Then when Father confessed to the crime, I knew. Oh, Jamie had always been a difficult boy. Always in trouble, getting into fights. Always blaming his misdeeds on others."

"Was he often violent? Was he ever brutal with you?"

Marianne bristled as if offended by the notion, then settled back in her chair. "No, sir. Never. Not with my parents either. He was always fiercely loyal to the family. Loving, really."

Consuelo leaned forward a little. "Then why did he allow your father to take the blame for his theft?"

Marianne looked down at her lap. "He simply . . . did. I can't explain it. It's as if he cannot connect his wrongdoing with the consequences. I believe he even manages to convince himself he's done no wrong."

Jesse was nodding before she completed the thought. "I've seen other criminals like him. Somehow they believe they're in the right, as if society has forced them to do the only thing they could to survive." He sighed. "Doesn't exonerate them, though. So, he blamed the Duke for everything that happened to your family."

"Yes, sir." Her voice was like a fluttering breeze and her eyes misted. I admit mine did, too, as I recalled the details of the elder Reids' fate.

"And after you were turned out . . ." Jesse trailed off, seeming as affected as the rest of us by what we had learned about those weeks after the family had been sacked. After a moment he continued more firmly, "Eventually you came to America, where James learned of the Duke's impending engagement to Miss Vanderbilt. You came to Newport and—" He glanced up, frowning. "How did Madame Devereaux become involved?"

"I remember James saying she truly was clairvoyant," I said, "that she knew about his plans to run away with Consuelo."

"She wasn't clairvoyant." Marianne clutched her hands together on the tabletop. "It was I. I told her. I hadn't meant to, but I was frightened of what the future held, and when I heard there were several fortune-tellers in town, I sought one out. Madame Devereaux took me to her flat, to her little parlor draped in tapestries and overflowing with pillows. The air was thick with cloying incense—my mind was already whirling, but then she plied me with glasses of sherry. Little ones, so I hardly realized how much I had." She paused and sent each of us a beseeching look. "I only meant to ask if things would turn out well. I didn't mean to divulge all those details."

"That's how fortune-tellers work, Miss Reid," Derrick said.

Marianne's gaze shifted to Consuelo. "I swear I never mentioned your name. I only said he was plotting to woo one of Newport's wealthiest heiresses."

"It wouldn't have taken much for her to figure out the rest," I said, and reached to give her hand a pat. "You have nothing to blame yourself for. You were as much your brother's victim as the rest of us."

"No." Her protest made everyone at the table jump. "I was his accomplice. Always, all my life, ever since he was born. He had a charm, you see. A darling, endearing way about him, and I loved him very much. There were many times I tried not to, but I couldn't help myself."

"I understand," Consuelo said simply.

"Do you?" Marianne shook her head. "I don't think I do, not really. If only I'd done something, told someone." She drew a sharp breath. "Detective Whyte, I am guilty and I shall bear the consequences."

"I won't lie to you, Miss Reid," he said, but not without kindness. "There will be an inquest and your actions will be scrutinized. There may be charges. Accessory to kidnapping, for one—"

"I won't be pressing charges, not against Marianne," Consuelo blurted. "Nor will I allow Mama to press charges. That must be her side of the bargain. Besides, there was no kidnapping. I went willingly enough. Foolishly," she added in a more uncertain voice, "but willingly."

"Bargain?" I repeated. "Does that mean . . ."

"Yes." Consuelo met my gaze steadily. "I'm going home."

The next hours passed in a blur. Under police escort Consuelo and I accompanied Derrick and Marianne to Newport's tiny hospital, with Muffy brought along in a blanket-lined basket. Derrick was diagnosed with a mild concussion and released two hours later with instructions to rest and apply ice periodically to the lump left by James's shovel. While no one advised him as to where to find ice in August, I didn't worry. Despite doctor's orders he had already insisted on returning to Marble House with Consuelo and me, and Aunt Alva always had plenty of ice stored deep in her cellars.

Marianne, however, was admitted and tucked into one of the hospital's two dozen beds. With great relief she learned she was not consumptive. The doctor diagnosed chronic bronchitis, though had she waited much longer to seek treatment her condition might have become irreversible.

I promised to help her once she was discharged,

and she gripped my hand as tears rolled over her cheeks to darken the pillow beneath her head.

"I don't deserve it, Miss Cross."

"Nonsense, Marianne. You deserve a chance to start over. I'll help you through the police questioning and then we'll see about finding you employment. This might sound boastful, but I do have some rather lofty connections in this town. In the meantime, you'll stay with me."

"Oh, I couldn't impose—I can't pay you."

"No talk of that. I live in a drafty old house by the sea, with more room than I know what to do with." I leaned in closer to her and whispered, "Besides, Aunt Sadie demands you stay with me."

"Aunt Sadie?"

I smiled. "You'll soon learn all about Aunt Sadie. Suffice it to say you won't be the first lost soul to find her way to Gull Manor. Myself included."

With Marianne finally calmed and drifting off to sleep—poor thing was exhausted, both physically and emotionally—I rejoined Derrick and Consuelo in the small lobby that had once served merely as the central hall of a private home. Hefting Muffy's basket, Consuelo came to her feet.

"Are you ready?" I asked her.

"I think so," she said. "Will you come with me?"

"Of course I will." I shot a glance at Derrick. "We both will."

Consuelo frowned. "Do you think that's a good idea? Mama might object to an outsider hearing about family matters."

"I think it's a perfect idea. After what Derrick endured on our behalf he's hardly an outsider. And besides, bringing him will set your mother off-kilter just enough for you and me to be able to get a word in edgewise. But . . ." I hesitated, my sweeping glance encompassing her from head to foot and back. "What are you going to do?"

I meant about the Duke. Consuelo let a long moment pass before replying, "I'm not entirely sure. I'm hoping the answer comes to me on the ride home. But I've learned something, Emma, about both the world and myself. There are realities that cannot be ignored and rules that cannot be broken, or chaos results. I was raised in a certain way and I can't hide from that. I can't pretend I'm something I'm not any more than you can."

With her head held high she swept away and pushed through the street door. She hadn't answered my question, but neither had she avoided it. Something in those final words bored through me, especially when Derrick offered me his arm. I took it and we joined Consuelo outside, but her voice echoed inside me. I broke rules and too often found myself swimming in chaos.

Repeatedly I told Derrick I wouldn't marry him, yet here I was, on his arm. Like Consuelo, I had a decision to make. Wholly accept the person I was—and send Derrick away once and for all—or continue pretending I could have my independence . . . and him, too.

When we arrived at Marble House some twenty minutes later, Aunt Alva astonished us all. Instead of launching into the expected tirade about where Consuelo had been and how she could have been so inconsiderate as to have caused so much worry, she silently, tearfully wrapped Consuelo in her arms and held her tight.

This happened right inside the front door, amid the cold, formal surroundings of marble floor and walls and soaring ceiling. Hardly what one envisions for a joyous reunion. Grafton, quick to act, had shooed any servants in the vicinity below stairs, relieved Consuelo of Muffy's basket, and now skillfully ushered mother and daughter through the house and into the relative privacy of the morning room, where, at this time of day, no one would likely happen by. Derrick and I followed at a distance, respectful of this intensely personal moment while at the same time cognizant of my promise to remain at hand for Consuelo.

He and I lingered in the corridor just outside the doorway. While Derrick turned to gaze out the French doors at the rear of the property, I couldn't help watching as Consuelo and Alva parted just enough to look at each other.

Shock filled Consuelo's expression. "Mother! You're ill!"

"No, dearest, not ill. Only worried about you. Are you well? Did you . . . come to any harm?"

"No, Mama. I am quite well. And I'm sorry I ran off."

"Are you? I'm sorry I forced you into an engagement you didn't want."

Just as my mouth dropped open, Aunt Alva made a telling gesture that suggested her remorse might not be as sincere as she'd have Consuelo believe. With a hand pressed to her heart she made a clearly visible struggle to catch her breath; she even added a raspy little cough. For effect?

Hmm . . . Yes, the strain of Consuelo's disappearance had taken its toll on Aunt Alva; I'd seen that for myself in recent days. But I'd still maintain the woman was as healthy as any of the costly horses in her stables.

"Come, Mama, sit down." Quickly Consuelo pulled out a chair from around the table and pressed her mother into it. She took the chair beside it and sat with her knees nearly touching Alva's. "You *are* ill," she said, reaching for her mother's hands. "Please don't lie to me. You're ill and it's my fault, isn't it?"

"It's nothing, really. I'm sure to recover

completely now that you're home. The doctor said . . . oh, never mind. Consuelo, where were you? I worried so!"

Consuelo caught my eye through the doorway. Before parting with Jesse, the five of us—Derrick and Marianne included—had agreed upon the story that would enter the record books as well as the newspapers. It would be a sordid tale involving James Reid, Amelia Beaumont, and Madame Devereaux, wherein James would be accused of double homicide. To explain Consuelo's presence at the crime scene and her seeking help at a neighboring cottage, we would put out that she had gone for a carriage ride with her family's "good friend" Derrick Andrews—quite properly, of course, in an open carriage no one needed to know was mine—and, upon hearing shouts and screams from the Reids' cottage, they stopped to investigate. There would be no mention of Consuelo running away, and especially no hint that she had ever so much as spoken to James Reid. If the accused decided to bring her name into his testimony, the rest of us would deny all knowledge of his claims.

Yes, we would be perpetrating a fraud. Yes, Jesse in particular would be compromising his scruples. But at the same time we were saving a young woman's future. Consuelo's reputation would never recover should the truth ever get out. Whatever her future held, we would see to it there would be no shadow cast by recent events.

"I was with a friend," she said now in reply to her mother's question. "No one you know, Mama, and I'm not going to reveal her identity to you. Suffice it to say she stepped in when I most needed someone and if not for her, I wouldn't be here right now. I mean I wouldn't be *home,*" she added hastily when her mother's eyes widened with alarm.

Then Alva turned a suspicious look on me.

"No, Mama, I wasn't with Emma. It was Emma who found me today and persuaded me to come home."

"Who's *that?*" Alva thrust a finger at Derrick's back.

I placed a hand on his arm. Wincing slightly, he turned around and we walked into the morning room. "Aunt Alva, I'd like you to meet Derrick Andrews, of the Providence Andrews family. He was of great assistance to us today. Derrick, Mrs. Alva Vanderbilt." I knew better than to introduce her as Mrs. William Vanderbilt, what with the recent divorce.

Her eyes narrowed. "Andrews, as in the Providence *Sun,* I presume?"

"A pleasure to meet you, Mrs. Vanderbilt, and yes, my family owns the *Sun.* But, no," he said in response to her unspoken question, "I'm not here in any official capacity. You'll see no articles about any of this in our paper."

Her light scowl persisted for several more seconds. Then she apparently dismissed him. "Consuelo," she whispered with a tremor, "the Duke is on his way to Newport. What shall I tell him when he arrives?"

Once again her hand strayed to her heart—one would swear unconsciously. Yet I knew her. Alva Vanderbilt never made a move that wasn't both planned and determined.

Consuelo straightened in her chair, squaring her shoulders and raising her chin—the posture of a confident, independent woman capable of guiding her own life. A fierce light I'd never seen before entered her eyes. To me, she became suddenly older, worldlier, more her mother than ever before, yet, somehow, more beautiful than I'd ever seen her.

"You'll tell him he's most welcome. And that I accept his proposal of marriage. I shall be his wife. I shall be the Duchess of Marlborough."

CHAPTER 20

That night I wrote my article for the Newport *Observer.* Was it the article I truly wished to write—would have written, under normal circumstances? No, because for my cousin's sake it contained inaccuracies my reporter's heart found difficult to live with. Still, it was with pride and no small sense of elation that I delivered my account of the Murder at Marble House into Mr. Millford's hands the following morning.

I stood at his desk, bouncing a little on the balls of my feet as I handed the sheaf of paper across to him.

He didn't glance up from the figures scrawled beneath his nose. "Hmm . . . morning, Emma. A little busy right now. What's this?"

"My article, Mr. Millford."

He still didn't glance my way. "Was there a function last night?"

"No, Mr. Millford. I cracked the case, found Madame Devereaux's murderer, and here—" I shook the paper to rattle it. "Here is my account of the whole affair."

He peered up at me from over the rims of his spectacles. Furrows formed above his nose. "You did, eh?"

"I did, sir."

"Hmmm . . ." He reached up and took the article between his middle and index fingers, as if afraid to grasp it fully. Several tense moments crawled by as he scanned my handwritten words. "Hmmm . . ."

"Well?" My voice rose a notch.

"Well, what?"

"Mr. Millford, you promised if I got the story you'd give me the headline. In my name," I added, enunciating each word.

"I did, did I?"

"Mr. Millford, you know you did." Despite the conviction of my claim, I wondered. The man often said things he later forgot, whether genuinely or conveniently. I held my breath as I waited.

Finally, he nodded. "All right, Emma. You'll have your headline."

"Oh, Mr. Millford, really?" Quickly realizing the stupidity of that question, I gathered what I could of my professional dignity, thanked him, and headed back home. The next morning, Sunday, I ran to greet the delivery boy halfway down my driveway.

"Good morning, Miss Cross." He brought his bicycle to a halt and reached into the basket stuffed full of the day's edition. As he handed it to me, he eyed my dressing gown and hastily pinned-up hair. "Something special in the paper today?"

"You bet there is, Peter. My first real headline."

"Do tell."

I shook the paper to unroll it, then stretched it open to unfurl my headline in all its bold-print glory.

BAILEY'S BEACH TO HOLD
SWIMMING RELAY FOR CHARITY

"What?" I stared at the front page, but no matter how hard or how long I searched, my story simply wasn't there. "I don't understand. He promised . . ."

"Miss Cross?"

I lowered my hands, the paper crushed between them. "Nothing. Have . . . have a nice day, Peter."

With that I turned and dragged my feet back up the drive. Inside, I shoved the paper into Nanny's hands. "He broke his promise. Oh, damn that man!"

"Emma! A lady doesn't speak that way. But which damn man broke his promise?"

I waved a hand in the air and walked mutely past her into the morning room. There, at the table, I sat absently stirring my spoon around in the porridge Katie set in front of me; I neither saw nor ate any of the sweet concoction of oats, honey, and raisins. My stomach pitched and rolled. My pulse points hammered away and my temples throbbed. How could Mr. Millford do this to me?

"Oh, Emma, look." Nanny spread the newspaper open in the middle of the table. "Here's your story. Your first real news article. How nice is that?"

I dropped my spoon into my bowl, raising a little splash, and jumped to my feet. Bending over the table, I frantically scanned the articles on the two open pages. Then I plunked back down into my chair, heartsick and furious.

"The middle of page four? He stuck it on page *four?* And judging by the size of it he must have edited out half of what I wrote. And the byline— E. Cross? Not Emma, but *E?* Oh, Nanny, this is so unfair. This is a travesty."

Wallowing as deeply as I was in my misery, I didn't at first notice that Nanny didn't move to comfort me as she normally would have done. Instead, she stood silent and unmoving, her plump arms folded across her chest as she used to do when Brady or I had been naughty. When I finally glanced up at her, she caught my gaze with an uncommonly stern one and raised an eyebrow above the rim of her glasses.

"It is a start, Emma. A small triumph, but a triumph all the same. Now pick yourself up and start planning your next article, which, with any luck, will be on page three."

Dear old Nanny.

As abruptly as I had entered my cousin's world, I just as quickly made my exit. The Duke of

Marlborough arrived in Newport in early September, along with a crisp wave of autumn air. I was not at Marble House to help welcome him. I wasn't invited, nor had I expected or wished to be. I was, after all, merely a poor relation, as far beneath a duke's notice as the servant who shined his shoes. Besides, I could not have smiled and pretended to be delighted for Consuelo's good fortune. I could not have raised my glass to toast her impending nuptials.

However, I did have occasion to glimpse the Duke, for I covered a host of other social events held in his honor: a lawn tennis tournament at the Casino, a cotillion at the country club, and several receptions, dinner parties, and balls.

I did hear, or rather Nanny heard through her unerring grapevine, that Consuelo made her mother proud through it all. She impressed the Duke with both her beauty and bearing, and the date for the wedding was set for November 6.

I wished her well and vowed to keep her in my prayers.

Within a week of James Reid's arrest, Clara Parker had been released and cleared of all charges. In a generous mood—getting her way did that—Aunt Alva offered her her job back, but for now Clara was visiting her parents off island in New Bedford. Anthony Dobbs was a free man as well—for now. He still faced extortion charges, yet the smirk he sent my way in town just yesterday spoke of an abundance of confidence. It wouldn't surprise me if he never spent another moment inside a cell.

In the meantime, life at Gull Manor continued as always, as steady and predictable as the daily tides, except that our number had grown by one. Marianne and Katie took to each other immediately, in their quiet way becoming fast friends. Marianne's health improved daily, partly due to the care she'd received at the hospital and partly, I was certain, due to the healing effects of Nanny's hearty cooking and our fresh ocean air.

Her lot was to improve even more one sunny, blustery morning, when the bang of the front door springing open echoed through the house.

"Employment," Brady cried out upon stumbling with loud footsteps into my front hall. "For Marianne!"

His none-too-steady pronouncement prompted me to abandon my breakfast and stick my head out the morning-room doorway. "What are you yammering about, and where were you all night long?" I studied his rumpled suit, disheveled hair, and crooked smile. "Stuart Braden Gale, are you drunk?"

From behind me came Marianne's breathless question. "Did he say employment? For me?"

Brady managed to steady his stride as he continued down the hall. Just before he reached me he straightened his coat with a tug and ran a hand over his mussed hair. Where he had lost his hat, only the wind knew. "Good morning, sister."

I turned my face away and fanned my hand at the air in front of my nose. "Phew! Goodness, Brady, it isn't even eight yet. Shame on you!"

"Not to worry, Em, this isn't from this morning. It's left over from last night." With that he leaned in to kiss my cheek. I pulled away, but only a little, and his dry lips grazed my temple. I shook my head in admonishment.

"Do you honestly think that makes it any better?"

With a hand on my shoulder for leverage, he circled me and strolled into the morning room. There he accepted a quickly poured cup of coffee from Katie, who lingered as if ready to catch the mug should it slip from his hands. He managed to hold on to it and straddled the chair I'd vacated moments ago. With his chin resting on the carved oak back, he grinned up at me where I stood framed in the doorway. "You can blame Neily. He did the pouring. He's decided to forgive me, you know, and it would've been rude of me to deny his hospitality. But—" He broke off for a gulp of coffee, then made a face when the hot liquid apparently scalded his mouth.

I walked into the room and reached for my own cup, all the while making sure not to let the disapproval slip from my features. Not that

Brady's carousing surprised me or particularly exasperated me, as long as it didn't happen too often—and lately, it hadn't. In fact, this was the first time I'd seen my brother tipsy since before that awful night he was accused of murder at The Breakers. Yet, someone had to be the voice of his conscience, and in recent years the task had fallen to me.

"But what?" I demanded, one hand around my cup and the other perched at my hip.

"Grace Wilson was with us for a little while last night—oh, don't scowl, Em, it was all quite proper. Grace and her brother came by the country club for supper while Neily and I were there. Anyway . . ." He trailed off and this time nearly did spill his coffee as he attempted to turn around to face the table. His feet caught in the chair's legs, which immediately became in danger of toppling. I steadied him with a hand on his shoulder at the same time Marianne leaped up and snatched his cup before it fell.

He let go a bark of laughter before finally managing to untangle himself and swivel to face the table. "Thanks, Marianne. That would have been an awful hot mess."

"Mr. Gale, you mentioned my name just before," Marianne said, setting his coffee cup on the table. "May I ask why?"

"Indeed you may, for it's the whole reason I had Neily's driver bring me here this morning rather than sleep it off at The Breakers. I knew you'd want to hear right away. Grace Wilson—she's a lovely young society girl—needs a lady's maid. Are you interested?"

He might as well have told Marianne an English duke had just arrived in town and wished to marry her. Her face lit up with such joy I felt the echo of it in my own heart, and for a moment I thought she was going to hug Brady. She didn't, but turned and caught Katie in her arms and the two cried out happily. It was at that moment Nanny shuffled into the room.

"What's all this fuss about?"

"Oh, Mrs. O'Neal, I've got employment!" Marianne's face turned somber as she regarded Brady. "It's true, isn't it, Mr. Gale? What if this young woman meets me and doesn't care for me? She might not offer me the job. I've never actually been a lady's maid before, although before we . . . we left the Duke's employment I'd been training to—"

Brady held up a hand. "The job is yours if you want it." He glanced a bit sheepishly at me. "Once I said it was a favor for you, Em, Neily and Grace didn't hesitate. Miss Wilson would like to see you later this morning, Marianne. She said around ten."

"Thank you, Mr. Gale. Thank you." She said it several more times before Katie whisked her away to prepare her for her interview.

I pulled up a chair beside Brady. "Thank you. That was well done."

"Proud of me?"

I leaned closer as if to kiss him, and instead delivered a playful slap to his cheek. "Don't be haughty. But, yes, dear brother, I'm proud of you."

"I suppose you'll be moving back to town soon, Brady." After filling a bowl with porridge, Nanny sat down across from us. "Now that you've got your job back and all."

"It is about time I returned to the old digs. I'm horribly outnumbered here, what with all you ladies. Rather like a buck trampling the flowers. What do you think, Em? Sick of me yet?"

"No one feels trampled, Brady. Stay here as long as you like. But if you're longing for your privacy, that's fine, too. Just do try to stay out of trouble."

He seemed about to retort when the telephone rang. I jumped up and made my way to the alcove beneath the stairs.

"Hello, Emma?"

The voice at the other end sent a little jolt through me. "Yes, Derrick. Good morning. How are you feeling?"

We hadn't spoken in a couple of weeks—not since escorting Consuelo home. I'd driven Derrick back to his hotel, saw him into the lobby, and thanked him fervently. He'd waved off my gratitude with a gallant nod, shook my hand, and

411

wished me well. He told me he'd remain in Newport a few more days until his doctor thought it safe for him to travel, and then he'd return to Providence. Then we'd lingered, silent and awkward, until he'd said, "Well, then," and I'd responded with, "Yes," and watched as he climbed the stairs to his room. Our parting bore the stamp of finality, and I hadn't expected to hear from him again, at least not so soon.

It was better that way; it was time for both of us to move on.

"The head's still a bit tender," his voice said now into my ear, "but the dizziness is gone."

"I'm glad to hear it. So, I suppose you must be home now?"

"Ah, you could say that, yes."

In spite of all my convictions, that "yes" made my heart sink just a little, and I struggled to keep the disappointment from my voice. "That's good. I hope you had an enjoyable trip. Your family must be very pleased to have you back."

"Emma, I'm not in Providence. I'm still in Newport. Can you meet me in town in a little while? At my hotel? There's something I need to show you . . . and discuss with you."

Oh, dear. Was he going to propose again? He was, wasn't he? Why else would he still be in town? And after all we'd been through, after he'd nearly lost his life because of me, how could I bear to hurt him?

I had no wish to. Yet, however much affection I felt for him, I couldn't but admit that part of me had been relieved to see life return to normal, to be able to carry on with my days in a calm, rational manner. To feel in control and wholly myself again, which simply wasn't the case when Derrick was near. Consuelo's words echoed inside me.

There are realities that cannot be ignored and rules that cannot be broken, or chaos results. . . . I can't pretend I'm something I'm not any more than you can.

I was what I was: simple, often headstrong Emma Cross, who never could and never would be comfortable putting on airs. And Derrick couldn't change what he was: the scion of a wealthy, powerful family for whom propriety and appearances were too vital to be ignored. If Brady was a buck trampling the flowers here at Gull Manor, in Derrick's world I'd be the goose ruffling the feathers of all the swans.

"Derrick, I don't think that's a very good idea," I said into the telephone.

He was not to be deterred. "It's important. Please."

I squeezed my fingers around the ear trumpet. If Consuelo could find the courage to face a future she didn't want, surely I could find the courage to tell Derrick Andrews once and for all that, while I would always care for him, I would never be his wife. Surely I could find the fortitude to finally set him free.

But that, I knew, could not be accomplished over the phone. "I'll meet you outside your hotel in an hour."

After asking me to drive us to the Point, Derrick was oddly silent during the ride. Despite my reporter's nature I didn't question him. My answers would come soon enough.

He directed me down Third Street, and when we came to Walnut Street, he instructed me to turn right. We halted in front of my family's three-story clapboard home.

"What are we doing?" I asked with a little chuckle when he didn't immediately say anything. "You're being terribly mysterious."

His indrawn breath somehow raised butterflies in my stomach. When I thought I could stand it no longer, he said, "I've purchased a house here on the Point."

"Oh, is that all?" Another, lighter chuckle released some of my tension, although not all. So he wouldn't return once and for all to Providence and disappear from my life. I admit to a host of mixed emotions, some of which I didn't care to examine too closely. Yet I couldn't deny a surge of relief that when we did say good-bye, it wouldn't be forever. "You were afraid I'd disapprove, were you?" I looked around at the houses lining the street, most of which had been occupied by the same families for decades, some for generations. "I wasn't aware any homes were for sale. Which is it?"

"That one." He raised his hand to point.

My jaw dropped open. He pointed to the house I'd grown up in.

A frantic parade of explanations ran through my mind: it was a joke; he actually meant the house next door; he'd only rented one of the apartments . . .

But there was no mistaking the line of his forefinger, or the apologetic frown tightening his brow.

"But you can't have." My voice shook slightly. "It's not for sale. I'd have known if it had been for sale."

"They didn't want you to know, Emma. Your parents needed the funds, and they assumed you'd try to stop the sale. One of the tenants is moving out in two weeks. I'll take over that flat."

The trembling that began in my heart spread to encompass all of me. "Oh, God. Please tell me this is a joke."

When he said nothing I dropped the reins and climbed down from the rig. Blindly I scrambled over the curbstone and headed for the front door. I don't know what I would have done when I reached it—barged inside, startling poor Mrs.

Carter and her sister as they sat hunched over their knitting?

I never made it that far, for Derrick came up behind me and seized my wrist. He turned me about, and I very nearly swung my free hand, palm flat, against his cheek. Oh, I wanted to slap him—every fiber in my being demanded it. Yet my hand stopped in midair as the two of us stood frozen, there on the narrow brick walkway, me panting and Derrick beseeching me with his eyes.

"How could you? How could you betray me like this?"

"Would you rather it had gone to strangers?"

"I'd have bought it myself!"

"With what?"

I tugged to free my wrist, but he held on relentlessly. "Uncle Cornelius . . . or Aunt Alva. They'd have bought the house for me." Yet even as I made the claim, I knew—I *knew*—I couldn't have accepted their money. Castoff clothing and telephones were one thing, but a house? Damn my pride, but yes, I would have allowed my family's home to go to strangers rather than accept my relatives' charity on so large a scale.

Another realization hit me. It wasn't Derrick who had betrayed me. It was my parents. Yet again. Always so caught up in their own artistic world, so oblivious to the realities of anyone else's. But, after all, this was their house—or was—to do with as they pleased. Another blow struck me. I'd wanted them home not long ago, when Brady had been accused of murder. I'd wanted my parents here to help, to offer comfort, to lean on. . . .

They were not coming home. Ever. Perhaps that is what this house had come to mean to me—a promise that they would be back someday. But this drove home the fact that they'd chosen Paris, and all that city had to offer, over their children. I shouldn't have been surprised. But the wound cut deep all the same, so deep that for a moment I couldn't breathe.

"You could have said something," I said weakly. "Instead, you sneaked around, buying my home out from under me." Why was I continuing to blame him? Somehow, I couldn't stop myself from lashing out at him. Perhaps only because he was here, while my parents were not. "What about Brady? Shall he have his things removed immediately?"

Derrick released my wrist. "Brady can continue to occupy the top floor."

"How accommodating of you."

"Free of charge."

I shook my head. "We won't accept your charity, Derrick."

"Emma, please." He reached for me again, not to seize me, but to lay a placating hand on my shoulder. The weight of it infused me with warmth. I wanted to step away, but I couldn't . . .

simply couldn't make my feet move. "I'm sorry," he said. "Father's financial agent heard about the house going up for sale and contacted me immediately. He knew I was thinking about investing here in Newport. It all happened very fast—"

"Have you not heard of the telephone, Derrick? It's a wonderful invention, and a very fast means of communication. I have one in my home, in case you'd forgotten. I'm sure the Atlantic House Hotel has at least one at their guests' disposal."

His hand left my shoulder. His cheek gave a telltale twitch. "I thought it was the best solution—better, as I said, than letting your house go to strangers."

"I intend to buy it back," I announced, surprising myself, and him, judging by his expression. When he started to speak, I cut him off. "No, I don't have the money—yet. But in time I will. Somehow. I'll work harder, write more articles. Promise me, Derrick. Promise me that when I have the money, you will sell me my house back."

He studied me a long time. Gradually the pain of guilt smoothed away and the familiar Derrick reappeared: patrician, confident, and just a little bit cocky. "You know, Emma, there's a way for this house to be yours without your having to buy it."

He smiled his dashing, heart-melting, infinitely

infuriating grin, and everything inside me froze. I braced for his next words, certain I knew what they would be. A war of uncertainty waged inside of me, along with a wisp of anger. Would he actually dangle my childhood home in front of me as an enticement to marry him? Could he be so manipulative?

The words never came. He merely stood there, smiling, allowing his implied meaning to stew inside me. Villain.

I raised my chin. "I'm going home. Would you like a ride into town?"

"No, thank you. I need to speak with the tenant who's moving. I'll make my way back into town later."

"Well, then, good day to you, sir, and enjoy your house. For now." With that I strode past him, climbed back into my carriage, turned Barney about, and drove away, leaving Derrick standing in front of his new property, thinking whatever he would.

It was only once I'd turned the corner that my eyes began to burn and my surroundings blurred. Good gracious, I'd lost my house, my childhood home. . . .

No, that wasn't it, not entirely. I couldn't have said exactly *what* it was. Mere emotional exhaustion, perhaps. Yet, by the time I reached the other end of Third Street, the breeze had dried my tears to sticky tracks against my cheeks and, in spite of everything, a little smile forced its way to my lips. I might have lost my house to a sneaky rogue who believed he could manipulate me . . .

But I hadn't lost *him*—I hadn't lost Derrick, however much I kept telling myself I needed to set him free.

No, he would be here, an on-and-off Newporter, and—

I put from my mind any further thoughts of what that would mean. I simply refused to consider it.

Derrick would be here, and for now . . .

That was enough.

AFTERWORD

Consuelo Vanderbilt did indeed rebel against her impending engagement to the ninth Duke of Marlborough in the summer of 1895. In her mind, she was already engaged, however unofficially, to the much older Winthrop Rutherfurd, whom she fondly referred to as "Winty," and with whom she had come to an understanding of a romantic nature some weeks earlier, while riding bicycles together with friends and family in New York. Her ambitious mother had other ideas. Upon arriving in Newport that summer and discovering that Consuelo had found means of seeing Winty, Alva resorted to holding her daughter a virtual prisoner at Marble House, refusing entry to any of her friends and possibly even faking a heart condition to play on the naïve eighteen-year-old's sympathies. Alva's ploys worked; overwhelmed by her mother's domineering personality, unable to call upon the support of friends or family, and defeated by a complete sense of isolation, an unhappy Consuelo relented and married the Duke that November.

According to the history books, Alva Vanderbilt's temper was legendary, and in fact few people possessed the fortitude to stand up to her. Perhaps her temperament was the result of living in the "gilded cage," of feeling dissatisfied with society's approved means of channeling a woman's ambitions. Her dedication to women's suffrage was very real, although I have set her involvement years earlier than it actually occurred. It was by the second decade of the twentieth century that she would become a politically active participant in the cause, and Marble House became a gathering place for the growing movement. By then, a newly divorced Consuelo supported her mother in these endeavors. Finding common ground and coming together, finally, as equals, the two forged a stronger and far more sympathetic relationship than they had ever enjoyed previously. Alva spent her later years in France to be near her daughter, who, in 1921, happily married a man of her own choosing, Frenchman Jacques Balsan.

Readers who are familiar with Marble House might wonder why I set the murder in a generic "garden pavilion" rather than the iconic Chinese Tea House that graces the rear lawns to this day. The answer is simple: The Tea House didn't exist in 1895, and wouldn't until 1914. After marrying her second husband, Oliver H. P. Belmont, in 1896, Alva closed Marble House until after his death in 1908. The house had stood empty for more than a decade, but then she moved back in, commissioned the Chinese Tea House to be built, and used both structures to host rallies and fundraisers to support the right to vote for women.

Center Point Large Print
600 Brooks Road / PO Box 1
Thorndike, ME 04986-0001 USA

(207) 568-3717

US & Canada:
1 800 929-9108
www.centerpointlargeprint.com